RIVER
OAK
PUBLISHING

This is a work of fiction. The names, characters, places, and incidents are either from the author's imagination or are used in a fictitious manner. Any resemblance to actual persons, living or dead, events, or establishments is purely coincidental.

Avenged
ISBN 1-58919-964-2
46-611-00000
Copyright © 2002 by A. Russell Chandler

Published by RiverOak Publishing
P.O. Box 700143
Tulsa, Oklahoma 74170-0143

PROLOGUE
Northern Pacific Ocean
September 1, 1983

Just minutes after 5:00 P.M. local time on Wednesday, August 31, 1983, a Korean Air Lines flight took off from the airport in Anchorage, Alaska, carrying 269 people—240 passengers and 29 crew members. In a few hours, they would cross the International Date Line and leave August 31 behind forever. The flight, destined for Kimpo Airport in Seoul, Korea, bore the designation *KAL 007*.

Lengthened considerably by flying through multiple time zones, August 31 had been a tiring day of travel for the passengers of Flight 007. Most had begun their journey in New York City seven hours earlier, departing JFK Airport just after 2:00 P.M. After crossing the continent, the passengers had arrived in Anchorage for a brief layover before continuing on to Seoul. With an hour to burn before takeoff, several passengers disembarked to stretch their legs and explore the airport shopping center. Some, like Congressman Larry McDonald, stayed on the plane and slept.

A Georgia Democrat, McDonald chaired the John Birch Society and was well to the right of almost any Republican in either house of Congress—with the possible exception of Senator Jesse Helms from North Carolina. That same evening, both Helms and his colleague, Steve Symms of Idaho, were aboard another Seoul-bound flight originating from Los Angeles. Flight KAL 015 also stopped in Anchorage during the afternoon hours of August 31 and shared a parallel transpacific flight plan with KAL 007. McDonald had not managed to get on the same plane with his fellow congressmen, but the three men had planned to meet early the next morning in Seoul, where they would attend a celebration with officials of the South Korean government.

Thankful for a respite from the cramped airplane cabin, a tall, elegant woman with black hair and dark eyes chose to wait quietly near the gate assigned to Flight 007. Her five-year-old son slept with his head nestled against her shoulder. Anyone who sat nearby could hear the boy's heavy, labored breathing. Instead of producing the light snores of a peacefully sleeping child, he sounded more like an old man, gasping for breath at every intake and reluctant to exhale. At the disturbing rattle, several waiting passengers glanced over at the woman and child, but they saw no look of alarm on her face. If their eyes stayed on the pair just a second too long, it was undoubtedly because of the mother's striking beauty.

Meanwhile, the 007 flight crew completed their preparations. A computer had drawn up the flight plan. The crew had received notice from the control tower that the radio beacon normally used for navigation between Anchorage and the coast was out of service for maintenance. Unable to rely on the inertial navigation system (otherwise known as the INS), which controlled the autopilot, the crew needed to use an alternative procedure for the first leg of the flight. The pilots chose the less familiar heading-mode method and programmed a setting of 246, taken from the standard navigation charts. The magnetic code would be sufficient to keep the flight on-track until the INS could take over.

The flight plan followed a well-known route, designated by a series of waypoints beginning with Cairn Mountain, 175 miles southwest of Anchorage. Next came the tiny fishing village of Bethel, perched on a Bering Sea inlet. Soon after, the plane would leave the North American continent and, from there on, the waypoints would be purely arbitrary—mere geographic points spaced approximately 300 miles apart across the northern Pacific. In keeping with their imaginary quality, these points had arbitrary-sounding names: NABIE, NUKKS, NEEVA, and so on to NOKKA, which lay about thirty minutes before the first dry land—the coast of Japan. As long as the INS worked properly, all the crew had to do was manage to stay awake during the eight-hour flight across the dark northern Pacific. As dull as this flight plan was, that would be no simple task.

Because of light headwinds, the pilots had delayed takeoff for forty minutes to keep from arriving at Seoul's Kimpo airport at 5:30 A.M.—half an hour before it would open. But finally, at just after 5:00 P.M., Flight 007 took off facing 320 degrees to the northwest.

Shortly after takeoff, the mood onboard was relaxed as the crew settled in. The flight progressed normally as the plane continued to gain altitude and passed over the first waypoint. Before beginning her standard routine in the main cabin, the head flight attendant poked her head around the cockpit door and asked the pilots if they would like some coffee. Faced with what was sure to be a long and monotonous trip, both pilots requested an extra large cup—caffeinated.

After almost an hour in the air, Flight 007 passed safely over Bethel. But just minutes later, as they crossed the Alaskan coast, the pilots were unaware that the plane was beginning to drift off of its established route on a steadily northward vector. The magnetic heading was still in place; the INS was not engaged.

The plane's computers soon announced the crossings of NABIE and NUKKS, which the unsuspecting crew reported to the tower. As long as the plane stayed longitudinally aligned with the waypoints, the computers would continue to read them at the appropriate times. Only a careful review of the latitude coordinates against the flight plan would have signaled trouble. Lulled into a false sense of security by the routine nature of the flight, the pilots didn't review the coordinate information.

Just two and a half hours into the flight and flying far north of the designated flight plan, Flight 007 lost radio contact with Anchorage. From that point on, they had to communicate by relaying through KAL 015. The latter flight, which was a few minutes behind 007 and now well to the south of them, had no trouble picking up Anchorage. Still the crew of KAL 007 didn't notice anything abnormal.

The flight attendants changed from their ordinary clothes into *hanbok,* the traditional Korean skirts and blouses. They served food and drinks, then started the in-flight movie, *Man, Woman, and Child.* At the approximate halfway point of the scheduled flight plan, the plane crossed the International Date Line. August 31 was now history for the passengers of KAL 007.

Soon after, the aircraft, now more than 100 miles off-course and flying at an altitude of 26,250 feet, drifted into Soviet airspace.

It was 5:30 A.M. local time at Dolinsk-Sokol Air Defense Base on Sakhalin Island and Colonel Gennadiy Nikolayevich Osipovich sat waiting in a ready room, dressed in a pressurized suit. Thirty feet away, his plane, an Su-15, stood ready to go. If an urgent message came in from the national Command Center, he could be inside the cockpit within seconds and in the air soon after that. Nothing ever happened, and Colonel Osipovich and his comrades just kept waiting, night after night.

But on the morning of September 1, all of that was about to change.

Flying directly toward Sakhalin Island and now 200 miles off course, KAL 007 crossed the Kamchatka Peninsula. It re-entered international waters over the Sea of Okhotsk, and kept on flying for another hour in the direction of Sakhalin. Beyond Sakhalin lay a huge Soviet military installation near the Siberian city of Vladivostok on the mainland, over which the Korean Airlines jet would pass if it kept flying on its current vector.

But as far as the Flight 007 crew was concerned, they were crossing the NIPPI waypoint, with about ninety minutes left to Tokyo. Having left Anchorage behind completely, Captain Chun Byung-in radioed the control tower at Narita Airport to let them know he was raising altitude, a routine activity to save fuel. The Narita tower gave him the go-ahead. "Roger Korean Air zero zero seven," said the voice in English. "Climb. Maintain three five zero. Leaving three three zero this time."

At 3:23 A.M. Japanese time, exactly two-and-a-half hours before their scheduled arrival in Seoul, Captain Chun informed Narita he had climbed to 35,000 feet.

Colonel Osipovich was now in the air over Sakhalin, piloting his Su-15 designated as No. 805. There were several other planes in the squadron, mostly MiG-23s, all of them hunting for the unidentified intruder.

All around him the skies were inky black. Finally, at five seconds after 3:15 A.M., Tokyo time, the dim lights of the intruders' plane came within view. "I see it!" the colonel shouted into his radio.

"I am closing on target," he announced, and a minute later he locked on his missile warheads. His radar wasn't working too well, but he was used to things malfunctioning. All he cared about was what would happen to him if he failed in his mission.

Colonel Osipovich flashed his onboard lights for a warning, but the enemy didn't respond. He fired some tracer shells right past the intruder's nose and, again, there was no response.

As he watched, the target climbed 3,000 feet and kept on flying in the same direction.

Jennifer Stuart sat with her face pressed against the window. At her side her little son slept on, still rasping like a lung patient with advanced emphysema. The window was cold to her touch, but was much warmer than outside the plane, where the temperature was -50°C. Out there she couldn't see anything but a satiny darkness. No stars. No moon. Only a flat black—

A flash shot past her window.

There it went again, a quick burst of light. *What was that?* Had she been without sleep too long? Was she starting to see things? But, no. There went another flash, and another, and another, until she saw a dozen bright bands arcing past the wing.

Although beautiful, something about the sight made her shiver. Instinctively, she reached down and pulled her son close.

The colonel stared into the darkness above the instrument panel of his Su-15, wondering what command would order him to do now.

"What are instructions?" he demanded over the radio to Deputat Ground Station.

"805, awaiting instructions."

"Affirmative," he said. He clinched his teeth in frustration, but he didn't let his voice show his irritation. *Awaiting instructions,* he thought bitterly. That meant nobody on the ground had the guts to make a decision. They had to have somebody from Moscow do it for them.

"805, patching you through."

So I was right, he said to himself. *Waiting on the word from some general—or better yet, a political officer.*

The enemy's plane slowed down, and the colonel slammed on his air flaps to brake, but just as he matched the enemy's decreased speed, the plane sped up again. His cursing was interrupted by a voice on his radio.

"Colonel. This is *Glozá*. Report." The voice faded out, then back in, as though it were coming from a long way away. " . . . Do you read me, Colonel?"

Osipovich shot an angry glare at the radio. *Who did they think they were, these political officers in Moscow,* he fumed. *We should have already done something by now. Instead—*

Then, as though *Glozá*—"The Eyes"—could actually see him there in the cockpit, the voice through the radio said, "I know what you're thinking, Colonel. Don't try to second-guess us. You will be allowed to act when we tell you to act. Just report the situation."

"The target has not responded to warning shots," Osipovich reported. "Cannot chase it much longer. I am already abeam of the target."

From the radio came a few seconds' worth of static, and then the voice of *Glozá* returned. *"Presch',"* the voice said. "Stop the intruder. Shoot it down!"

He had wished for a decisive order from the ground, and now Colonel Osipovich had it. Ahead of him he could see the intruders' taillights, and with the push of a button he knew he could obliterate the enemy's craft. But the swiftness of *Glozá's* command made him hesitate for a moment. Did the disembodied voice really know what it was ordering?

Osipovich gritted his teeth and said over the radio, "I'm dropping back already. Now I will try the rockets." He had no choice. At least that was what he kept reminding himself. He had no choice.

"Affirmative, 805," Deputat Ground Station replied. "Prepare to lock on missiles."

But before he could send back an "Affirmative," *Glozá* came back on. "Pilot 805, what are you waiting for? *Shoot . . . down . . . the intruder . . . NOW!*"

The Russian colonel muttered an expletive under his breath as he shot a darting glance at his radio again. *You think it's so easy, YOU come up here and do it.* But his only verbal response to the command was, "Affirmative. I am in lock-on . . . "

They must have given the same order to his comrade in the MiG-23 designated No. 121, because he heard 121 say, "Executing."

"I am closing on the target," Osipovich announced, "am in lock-on. Distance to the target is eight kilometers."

He armed his missiles, and then, with a sharp intake of breath, he pushed the *FIRE* button. Beneath the hum of the aircraft he could hear the supersonic sigh of the missiles leaving their berth under the wings and hurtling toward their target.

Away they went, into the darkness, and ahead of him he saw a quick flash of light through the clouds. Then nothing. It was twenty seconds after 3:26 A.M., Tokyo time.

Captain Chun and the other two crew members in the cockpit lurched forward at the sudden jolt. The plane shook for a moment, as though a hurricane-force wind had hit it. The lights overhead flickered as the windows began to rattle.

As a result of the missiles' impact, the aircraft only dropped altitude slightly. But when the captain pulled back on his stick, nothing happened. Instead, the plane started on a slow arc downward. Now the rattling became a steady, dull rumble, gathering volume as they drifted ever so slowly toward the icy Sea of Okhotsk far below. Soon the whole aircraft shook.

Back in the cabin, the flight attendants frantically called out for the passengers to stay quiet and sit down. A service cart filled with half-empty drinks broke loose from its mooring in the galley and careened down the aisle, spraying ice and liquid as it went. One flight attendant pushed her way past it and waved her arms, trying to get someone—anyone—to listen to her instructions. Yet no one was listening to anything now but the weird groaning coming from outside the aircraft.

The blast—whatever it was—had ripped open a thin gash on one side of the plane. The passengers riveted their attention to the hole as it split wider and wider like a tight pair of pants tearing at the seam. Nobody screamed at first, and even if they had, no one would have heard. From the opening came a loud roar and a deep sigh as the pressurized air rushed out.

A man in a business suit sat near the hole. With his tie whipping about his face, he was pulled straight out of his seat, his mouth gaping wide with terror. His glasses flew off his nose toward the hole and through it, and his body lurched after them as though he were just stepping outside to retrieve them. He frantically tried to grab hold of an armrest, but the vacuum proved too strong and hurled him into the void.

Into the cabin blew a cold deeper than anyone onboard had ever felt, and the passengers were all gasping for breath as though their lungs had collapsed. Within a matter of seconds, everything liquid—even the moisture in people's nostrils—began to turn to ice.

Meanwhile, oxygen masks popped out of the ceiling and people scrambled to put the masks on themselves and their children. A sudden blast of hot air began to blow out of the air ducts as the heaters came on in automatic response to the severe temperature drop.

On the loudspeaker, muffled voices shouted back and forth in Korean. Then Captain Chun tried to make an announcement in English, to tell the passengers to stay calm and remain seated. But it was no use and, after a few garbled sentences, the captain gave up.

People screamed. Some cried. A few of them climbed out of their seats—arms and legs flailing—intent on fleeing the doomed plane. But they had nowhere to go.

Little Jon Stuart was wide awake now and crying uncontrollably, his breaths coming in deep, desperate gasps from inside his oxygen mask. "What's wrong, Mommy?" he screamed. "What's happening to the plane?"

"It's okay sweetheart," his mother moaned. She pulled a blanket tightly around him in a futile attempt to protect him from the bone-chilling cold and held him even closer. With her mouth against his ear, Jennifer yelled against the deafening noise of rushing air and screaming engines, "Don't be scared, Jon." She rocked him back and forth, attempting to quell the fears of her child in the face of impending doom. "Everything's going to be okay. No matter what happens, Jesus is with us. Jesus will take care of us!"

Colonel Osipovich desperately scanned the skies for any sign of the enemy plane. There was no visual contact, but the target had been hit by two air-to-air AA-3 missiles. There was no hope for the intruder.

Deputat Ground Station called him. "805, report status of target, over."

"Target is destroyed. Repeat, target is destroyed."

"Affirmative, 805," Deputat replied.

And then came that other voice, the voice of *Glozá*—The Eyes in Moscow, watching it all from afar, safe in some comfortable Kremlin ministry office. "Well done, 805," it said. "The people of the Soviet Union thank you. You have just made history, and history will judge you a hero."

"I am breaking off the attack," Osipovich answered. As for what he had just achieved, he didn't even want to think about it. He had no idea who the intruder was. And he didn't care. His superiors didn't ask him to know or care, and he didn't want the responsibility. The plane he had just downed was nothing more than a blip flashing on a radar screen, and his career had depended on his ability to erase that blip.

"DEP, 805," he said into his radio, weariness etching his voice. "Request permission to return to ground. Over."

Surely I'll have the rest of the day off, he thought. He would retire to his bunk with a liter of vodka and, hopefully, by the time he awoke again this whole thing would seem like a bad dream.

As the seconds passed and Flight 007 dropped lower and lower, the air grew less and less thin. The plane made huge, ever-widening spirals in an effort to try and hold its head up and hit the water horizontally.

The control tower at Narita Airport, completely unaware of the attack taking place in the skies over the Soviet Union, received one last garbled transmission:

"Tokyo, Korean Air zero zero seven . . ."

"Korean Air zero zero seven, Toyko," the tower responded.

" . . . Fifteen thousand . . . holding with rapid decompressions. Descending to ten thousand . . ."

A group of Japanese fisherman would later report that at about 3:38 A.M., they saw a flash of light, then heard a loud boom. After that, all was silent except for the sound of the waves as the ocean swallowed Korean Air Lines Flight 007.

CHAPTER ONE

Rose Hill Mausoleum

Sunday, September 18, 1983

At this moment, Jonathan Stuart would have given everything, all he had accumulated in more than forty years of striving, just to have his wife and child back. And if he couldn't have them back, he would still give anything just to be able to shed some tears and relieve his grief. But the tears wouldn't come. So he stood there dry-eyed, his shoulders heaving with sobs that never quite reached his throat.

Gray skies matched the somber mood, and puddles from an early afternoon rain shower dotted the cemetery. But the two coffins, one the size of an adult, the other painfully small, remained safe and dry inside the crypt. Even though they didn't hold Jennifer and Jon, they symbolized all that remained of them—a memory only—since their bodies lay somewhere deep beneath the waters somewhere off Sakhalin Island.

Jonathan stood sandwiched between the minister on his right and Sonny Odom on his left. Rows and rows of people assembled around them, all dressed in black with heads bowed and faces ashen. Jennifer's involvement with charitable causes—everything from a fine arts foundation to a soup kitchen—had placed her in close contact with a wide spectrum of New Orleans society, and hundreds of mourners had gathered to attend the memorial service for Jonathan's wife and son.

"As we contemplate this tragedy, we look for answers . . ." The minister inhaled deeply. ". . . And there are none." His voice trembled slightly as he spoke.

"We look for justice. And there is none. At least, not here on earth."

Jonathan couldn't bring himself to raise his head. Instead, he studied his black wing-tip shoes.

"We look for meaning," the minister continued, "and there seems to be none." Again, he paused. Whether for dramatic effect or to regain his composure, Jonathan couldn't tell.

"I know many of you must be asking God, 'Why?' I, myself, am overwhelmed with that question."

Only the mournful sounds of muffled sobbing punctuated the heavy silence.

"But if there is some meaning to be found . . ." the minister's faltering emotions could no longer be restrained, and he coughed to clear his throat.

" . . . If there is some way to keep their tragic deaths from being in vain, then it will come through those who knew these two best, and who loved them most."

Jonathan's in-laws clustered on the clergyman's right side, and the minister shifted away from Jonathan to face Jennifer's father and mother, her brother and sisters and their spouses, as well as her nieces and nephews—little Jon's cousins.

"At this time, of course," the minister went on, "our sympathies go out first and foremost to those closest to the deceased—to Jennifer's parents and the rest of the Revier family. And especially to Jonathan, young Jon's father and Jennifer's husband of eleven years." The minister turned back to him and laid a light hand on his shoulder. "Many of us remember the challenges Jonathan and Jennifer faced at the birth of this, their only child, and the subsequent difficulties they endured with their boy's respiratory ailments and his weak heart." The minister offered a somber smile as he shoved the notes of his pre-written sermon into his Bible.

"The doctors didn't expect Jon to see the age of two, but they didn't know what kind of people his parents were—or how powerful their determination, how unfaltering their love for each other and for their boy . . ."

As the minister droned on with his extemporaneous remarks, Jonathan raised his head just high enough to glance at the tiny casket inside the crypt.

Since the moment Jonathan first learned the news of the deaths of his wife and son, the world around him had become hollow. Void. Only he remained. He'd had no family other than Jennifer and Jon. His father, long dead and buried in a grave Jonathan had never even visited, and his mother, were both gone. An only child, the sole family member he could claim was the man standing at his left, and he wasn't even a blood relation. Sonny had married Jonathan's mother after Jonathan left home, and though he had always respected Sonny, they had never been particularly close.

As for Jennifer's family, the preacher might want to make everything sound neat and proper by implying he and they would stick together in this time of sorrow. But Jonathan doubted they would ever have much more to say to one another now that they'd lost the two people they shared in common. Nearly twelve years had passed since Jennifer first brought him home to meet her family. Yet he could still recall with vivid clarity how he felt when he realized they—her mother especially—considered him beneath her. Jennifer had always pretended not to notice, even when her parents tried to talk her out of marrying him, but Jonathan never forgot. It was easy to remember. Their opinions hadn't changed much after all this time.

At least he agreed with her family about one thing. They all considered Jonathan responsible for the death of his wife and child. If he hadn't been always working, always building his company, always striving to achieve more, Jennifer and Jon would never have been on that plane.

He had convinced himself that he did what he did for them. But he knew it wasn't so. He worked hard because he didn't know how to do anything else—and he had worked much harder before he ever met Jennifer. Back then, he had thought nothing of pulling sixteen-hour days, seven days a week. Only when she came along did he slow the pace down—to six days a week.

Jennifer had always been open with him, keeping nothing secret. But in those early days, she would plead with him, to no avail, to tell her about his past. Then, she would accuse him of hiding something. He tried hard to convince her that if he'd hidden anything from her, he'd hidden it from himself as well.

When he thought of his childhood, he had to reach far back to find any good memory of his father. He could remember the day his dad brought home his first baseball and bat and glove. And he could remember tossing the ball with him. Lots of men lamented the fact that their fathers had never played catch with them, but Jonathan's father had. He could remember his dad pitching to him and teaching him to hit the ball. Jonathan hit the ball again and again and again. He could also remember his father yelling at him every time he missed, finally yanking the bat out of Jonathan's hands and making his son pitch to him. He deliberately hit the ball straight at Jonathan so hard that if he hadn't jumped out of the way it could have given him a concussion.

Folks had said something happened to Jonathan's father in the war over in the Pacific. And once, when he was nearly too drunk to talk, he had let loose with a story about a Japanese prison camp where they had tortured him for days and days. As for Jonathan, he didn't much care why his father behaved the way he did. He only cared about the effects. Even as a grown man, Jonathan shuddered at the vivid memory of his father beating his mother. But he never let himself think of all the times the man had beaten *him*—until the day he was finally big enough to confront his father.

It happened when he was fifteen, the one time he raised his hand against his father, not in defense of himself but to protect his mother. Jonathan left childhood behind forever that day, and he realized it even then. His father took off a few months later and never came back, but the angry man had left a significant imprint on his son that would affect him for the rest of his life.

Baseball itself was one reminder. Jonathan had paid for college partly on an athletic scholarship. After graduating from college, he had gone straight to the war in Vietnam. Later on, when he looked back on it, he knew even that choice was in response to his father. He had to go fight his own war in East Asia and prove he could come away unscathed. Sometimes, though, he would remind himself his father had been an infantryman, a *real* soldier, whereas he was "just" a pilot, fighting the war from up in the clouds. At other times, he would wake up sweating from nightmares about the villages he had napalmed.

His career in business, especially, was intended to distance himself from his father. The man had failed at every enterprise he had attempted, whether it be sales, running a repair shop, or driving a truck. The only success he had really known was that of being a drunk, a terror, and a disgrace to his family. Jonathan, on the other hand, had come home from Vietnam and entered into a partnership with two other entrepreneurs to purchase an ailing hospital. None of them had much money, and they were leveraged to the hilt. But through hard work, a few fortunate breaks, and more hard work, they had built a multimillion-dollar health-care network.

In 1976, Jonathan bought out his two partners and soon took the company in a new direction, working to build joint ventures overseas. They had interests in Europe and, more remarkably, the Soviet Union. Jonathan even learned to speak Russian. And his business had spread to the Far East as well, starting in Japan. The Japanese may have tortured his father, but Jonathan did business with their sons and daughters and, through his connections in Japan, had begun to explore the Korean market.

Yet long before that ever happened, something much more important had come into his life.

There had been a few other women before Jennifer, but he had never known her kind of love before. He doubted he would ever know it again. He had said as much, even when she was alive. No one had ever accepted him the way she did—just as he was—with all his imperfections as well as his strengths. With everyone else, he always felt the pressure to perform. Only with Jennifer did he begin to allow himself to relax a little, to let down his guard. And he had loved her just as much as she had loved him.

To others, she might have seemed as cool and contained as Jackie Kennedy. One only had to mention her *Revier* family name for people to behave differently. As a member of one of the leading families in the city, she had a lot to live up to. But she had entrusted Jonathan with her vulnerabilities, the anxieties instilled by her upbringing. And, even though Jonathan didn't know about such things from experience, he could sympathize, just because he loved her.

He used to joke and tell her, she came from "the New Orleans Reviers," whereas he belonged to "the South Alabama Stuarts." And though she had gladly given up her name for his, when they first talked about having a child, she had plainly told him if they had a boy she wouldn't name him Jonathan. It didn't matter that the name had belonged to his father and to his father's father, and that it constituted the only thing about his parent Jonathan had wanted to preserve and pass on. Jennifer had said, "I'm not letting your great-grandmother name my son."

The time she first made her pronouncement, ten years before, the issue had been a purely academic one. They weren't expecting a boy—or a girl. They wanted to get pregnant, but couldn't, and for several years they went to doctor after doctor and tried all kinds of methods without success. Then came the day when he was out of town on business and she called to tell him the news that she was expecting. She was so full of joy that she even gave in to him on the name. Jennifer decided that if they had a boy, the child would be Jonathan Stuart IV—Jon, to distinguish him from his father.

Jonathan and Jennifer had a few months of unbroken happiness. Jonathan had never felt closer to the Revier family. For once, every piece of his life seemed to be in place. Then, in the fifth month of the pregnancy, several tests were done. They were delighted to learn they were indeed having a boy—but other test results told them things they didn't want to know. The baby's heart and lungs weren't developing the way they should and, as the time approached for Jennifer to give birth, Jonathan became increasingly worried. On the day when little Jon finally came, Jonathan barely got to see him. The nurses whisked the baby off to an intensive care unit, where he spent the next six weeks—six long weeks—fighting for his life.

Day and night, Jonathan stayed at his son's side. He talked to him through the protective mask he had to wear in the special unit. During those long days, Jonathan only went to the office when he had to, and later when he looked back on it all, he realized his company really could survive without him there to make every decision. At the time, he cared only about his boy.

For days and weeks and months after their son left the hospital, Jonathan and Jennifer worried that he would never have a chance to grow up and do the things other children did. Perhaps when he got older, they were told, he would grow stronger, but all they could do for him until then was to love him and encourage him.

During that trying first year of Jon's life, Jonathan sensed he and Jennifer were moving in different directions for the first time in their marriage. Jennifer had been raised with all of the resources available to the upper class, but no amount of money or medicine or influence was able to transform her child from weak to strong, from threatened to safe. For the first time in her life, she started asking *why*.

Jonathan, on the other hand, came late to the party of wealth and power. His hardscrabble, dusty, Alabama rearing had undergone a total renovation with his entrance to the halls of business success. So far, hard work and bootstrapping had been enough to overcome every challenge—and his efforts had been amply rewarded. He possessed enough self-confidence to believe he could find a way over, under, around, or if need be, straight through, every obstacle in any road. He, too, asked *why* regarding Jon's health, but he really wasn't asking the same question.

Jonathan blamed two of Jennifer's high school classmates for this new wrinkle in his relationship with his wife. When word about Baby Jon's health problems made the rounds through New Orleans' gilded grapevine, these women called and asked if they could drop in to see Jennifer. Jonathan was grateful for the frozen casseroles they brought for them to heat up between hospital visits. And he appreciated the cheery "Welcome Home, Jon" signs and teddy bears they placed around the nursery in anticipation of the baby's homecoming. But he resented the spiritual advice and counsel they proffered to his hurting and worried wife. He figured, in her current state, his wife didn't need religious mumbo-jumbo added to the mix.

However, Jonathan began to see a distinct change in Jennifer after she'd had several visits from her old school chums. When Jennifer's language about Jon began changing from words of doubt and fear to words of hope and security, Jonathan noticed. He was pleased to see her smiling again. But, when Jennifer tried to explain to him that she had "become a Christian," he didn't understand. He had too much respect for his wife to let his cynicism show, but he couldn't believe she had bought into religion—hook, line, and sinker. To him religion was useful only to those weak enough to feel a need for it. What he couldn't figure out was why Jennifer felt such a need and he didn't. He had always assumed she was too smart for such nonsense. Smart and logical. Never given to impulse or emotional gambits. She was the only woman he had ever known who could hold her own with him.

He couldn't argue with the results, though. He had never seen his wife so peaceful, and in the midst of such a devastating situation no less. While he got angry with God and the doctors for allowing his son to suffer, Jennifer grew more accepting and trusting. After a rather lengthy and uncomfortable discussion about religion, Jonathan and Jennifer finally agreed to disagree. As long as she didn't try to convert him, he would put up with her newfound faith if it made her happy.

In the summer of 1983, on Jon's fifth birthday, Jonathan presented him with a special gift of a baseball, bat, and glove—all made for little hands. The boy wouldn't be able to use the bat for a while. Hitting a ball pitched to him would be a triumph of hand-eye coordination beyond the capacity of most five-year-olds. Still, father and son stood out back of their home, tossing the ball back and forth. Even though Jonathan threw it as gently as he could, Jon only managed to catch it on every fourth or fifth throw. Yet no matter how many times his boy failed, Jonathan remained patient.

On their last afternoon together, Jon caught the ball three times in a row, and his father was effusive with praise. "Everybody's going to want you on their team when you get to school," Jonathan told his son.

"I wish I were going to a *real* school," Jon replied. "You know, first grade and not just kindergarten."

"But think," Jonathan ruffled the boy's hair and smiled down on him. "If you were starting first grade next week, then you and Mommy couldn't come to Asia with me." Even though she stood out of earshot from their conversation, Jennifer waved to them from the deck and smiled.

"Where's Asia?"

"Asia is a place a long ways away," Jonathan said, crouching down beside his boy. "It's on the other side of the world, and people look and talk different from us, and they eat different foods. You'll see. You and Mommy are gonna meet me in Korea, then we're going to Hong Kong, and Singapore, and Thailand . . . " They had gone over all this before, of course, and Jonathan knew the names of those places were just abstract ideas to his son. Jonathan also knew, as long as the three of them were together, where they went didn't really matter to the child.

On Sunday afternoon, Jonathan waved goodbye to his family as he boarded a flight to Seoul. If things went as scheduled, Jennifer and Jon would follow him three days later, arriving in Seoul on KAL Flight 007. Before he left home for the airport, he held a package out to Jennifer.

"Just a little something for you to read on the flight," he said as he watched her unwrap the small box to reveal a thin, leather-bound Bible he'd had embossed with her name in gold on the front.

"Oh, Jonathan . . ." she whispered, as she opened the Bible and silently read the inscription he had written to her, *To the person who has the faith I lack. Study this book well so you can explain it to me when I get where you are. All my love, Jonathan. 8-28-83.*

The tears spilled down her cheeks by the time she finished reading. She leaned forward and buried her face in his neck, weeping quiet tears. Jonathan wrapped her in a tender embrace and waited for her words to catch up with her feelings.

"Thank you, Jonathan," she said, sniffling. "This means so much to me. You've been so understanding of my faith these last few years. I'm so thankful we have each other and we love each other in spite of not always seeing things the same way. I do love you."

"I love you, too," Jonathan answered. "And I will miss you and Jon terribly until Thursday in Seoul. I can't wait to have those days together. Given the potential for the company's business in Korea and Japan, this trip may change our lives forever."

After his arrival in Seoul, Jonathan called Jennifer from his hotel room the day before her own departure. "Don't work too hard," she said just before she hung up the phone. "Remember, we're going to be there on Thursday morning. Will we see you at the airport?"

"I'll be there," he answered. "You just get on out here, okay? I love you."

"I love you too, Jonathan." She blew him a kiss. Then, with a click, the phone connection broke.

"Jonathan." Sonny's low voice jarred him out of his reverie. He could tell from his tone that Sonny had been trying for some time to snap him out of his daze.

Jonathan looked around. Except for a few people at the far end of the cemetery getting into cars to leave, they were alone. "Where'd everybody go?" he mumbled, sounding and feeling as though he were a million miles away.

"It's time to go," Sonny said, taking him by the elbow. Jonathan resisted, and stood there still staring at the mausoleum door. "We don't need to stay around here and watch them . . . finish up," Sonny gave Jonathan's sleeve a gentle tug.

"Where'd everybody go?" Jonathan asked again.

"They were all tryin' to crowd around you," Sonny said, "and I just told them you needed a little breathin' room." Jonathan could feel him studying his face. "Jennifer's mother asked if you'd be all right, and I told her I'd take care of you."

The next thing Jonathan knew, he and Sonny were sitting side by side at a bar on Carrollton Avenue.

"I know it's a hard thing, Bubba," Sonny was saying, looking down at his drink. "Ain't nobody knows it better than me, losing two wives—first Peggy, then your mother." Jonathan shot a quick glance his way, but Sonny just kept staring at the rows and rows of bottles behind the bar. "You remember what Willa's last six months were like."

"Difficult for all of us," Jonathan agreed, taking a sip of the drink in front of him. His lips drew into a pucker. "What *is* that?"

"My drink of choice, Bubba," Sonny replied. "You weren't respondin', so I figured I'd order you what I was havin'. Crown Royale and Diet Coke."

"Have two." Jonathan slid his drink toward Sonny and held up a hand to get the bartender's attention. "Chivas and water," he said. When the bartender brought his drink, he took a cautious sip. "Mmm, that's more like it." He set it down in front of him and smoothed out his napkin, then he picked up the little red straw they brought with his drink and tapped it on the bar.

A retired Marine Corps Master Sergeant, Sonny maintained his military bearing even when he'd had one drink too many, a more frequent occurence since Jonathan's mother had died. But he still wore his clothes starched to perfection, and he had a broad, V-shaped chest, straight wide shoulders, and hands almost the size of footballs. At sixty, his auburn hair showed no trace of white.

Sonny had never told Jonathan a great deal about his past, and Jonathan hadn't pressed him. He knew Sonny had earned a distinguished record in several military conflicts, and though his fighting days were long over, he made a little money here and there as a "security consultant." Jonathan had never queried him as to what that meant exactly, but he was pretty sure he knew.

"What's today?" Jonathan asked. "Sunday?"

Sonny nodded.

"Back to work tomorrow." Jonathan sounded almost happy when he said it.

Sonny raised his eyebrows. "Really? You don't think you need a little time off?"

Jonathan shook his head. "Somebody's gotta run the show at Quality Health."

"Maybe so," said Sonny, "but it ain't gotta be *you* all the time. That's what vice presidents are for."

Jonathan snorted and took a sip of his scotch. "Nobody else knows what's going on but me, and that's the way I like it."

"Maybe so, Bubba. Maybe so." Sonny swirled his glass, so the mahogany brown drink tossed back and forth, the ice cubes riding the cold wave from one side of the glass to the other. He took a sip, catching an ice cube in his mouth and chewing on it before speaking again. "All I know is, back when Peggy died," he said, "I tried the same thing. For a while, seemed like I was workin' better than ever. But two, three months went by, and I started to realize, in spite of what I mighta thought, I wasn't so—"

"Listen," said Jonathan, pointing toward the television mounted above the bar.

"President Reagan today denounced the Soviet Union for what he called its 'horrifying act of violence,'" a news correspondent reported from in front of the White House. "And many here and abroad are wondering how the United States will retaliate for the downing of the jetliner."

Jonathan sat forward, trying to drown out the low hum of voices wafting from the tables behind him.

"But most sources," the reporter continued, "are of the opinion that the U.S. will do nothing because it *can* do nothing. If the Administration in Washington is looking for hopeful signs of support from its European allies, a source told us, they will be looking for a long time. Meanwhile in Europe as in the United States, there is mounting speculation that Flight 007 was indeed a spy plane under orders by the CIA, as the Soviets charged when the Kremlin announced—"

Jonathan sat back again, and turned toward Sonny. "Let's get out of here," he said. "I need to go home and get some rest before tomorrow."

"You sure you wanna be alone, Bubba?" Sonny motioned to the bartender for the check.

"I was *born* alone, Sonny," said Jonathan, taking one last drink and standing to his feet.

The officer stood at attention before his superior, who sat at a desk flanked by portraits of Lenin and General Secretary Andropov. "You understand why we have called you here?" the superior stated flatly, looking up at the man.

"Yes, Comrade General!" the officer replied.

"Stand at ease." The general, a beefy man in his sixties, had clearly enjoyed at least a decade of the easy life, warming a desk in a soft Moscow staff job by day and downing drinks with the Party brass by night.

The officer relaxed slightly, but not much, maintaining a modified position of attention.

The general gave him a curious look and shrugged his shoulders. "Very well," he went on. "Now, you and I both know, by giving the order to destroy that intruder, you protected all the peoples of the Soviet Union from aggression and possible war with a hostile regime. Not only do you and I know as much, but all those who are in a position of importance understand it as well." The general raised his bushy eyebrows. "Including General Secretary Andropov."

"Yes, Comrade General!" said the officer in front of him, seemingly unmoved by the words.

"As I say," the general continued, "the entire leadership is grateful for the service you have done by making the decision to destroy the spy plane. However . . ." He gazed out the window, where an aging set of plush velvet curtains framed the view of a gray Moscow street. The general looked back at the officer. "However, we are—how do I say this? We are concerned lest other military officers should get the idea that excessive zeal is the best method of approaching a situation."

The officer said nothing.

"By that, of course, I'm not saying you were excessive in your actions," the general qualified. "However, it should be no secret to you that this honorable act on your part puts us in a somewhat difficult situation with regard to the American regime."

"With all due respect, Comrade General," the officer said, "what about our duty to defend our borders?"

The general smiled. "Good point, good point. It is precisely your concern for our people's lawfully established borders, and your devotion to defending them, which I believe qualifies you for re-assignment to your new position."

"Yes, Comrade General?"

"I know you enjoy a challenge," the general went on, "and therefore we would like to give you an opportunity for the greatest possible growth."

"And where might this be, Comrade General?"

"At the frontiers of socialism," the general rose from his seat to look the officer in the eye. "In a place where the greatest, most decisive battles on behalf of our people are being fought." He paused. "Afghanistan."

"Afghanistan?" The officer echoed the general. His face showed no change of expression, even though he knew the re-assignment was like a sentence to a prison camp—perhaps worse.

"Effective in exactly thirty days," the general confirmed.

"Yes sir, Comrade General," said the officer. Nothing in his demeanor betrayed a single emotion.

CHAPTER TWO

The Pirelli tires on the shiny black Porsche Carrera screeched, and a bevy of startled Friday-night partygoers scattered from the path of the juggernaut as it rounded the corner and sped toward the Garden District of New Orleans. The convertible roared up St. Charles Avenue and whipped onto the I-10 west-bound entrance ramp. Once on the expressway, the driver sped the car up to seventy miles per hour.

With the top down, the deafening wind ripped through the open cockpit of the automobile as he accelerated past eighty, and then ninety. The speedometer passed the 100 mph mark as he wove in and out of the light traffic. The cars he passed looked as though they were standing still. But if Jonathan got any excitement out of the fact that he was now driving twice the legal speed limit—110 mph and climbing—his grim expression didn't show it.

Midnight. And August 31 had just become September 1, 1984—the first anniversary of the international incident that had taken his wife and child from him. In spite of his joyless countenance, Jonathan felt as alive now, flying down the road, as he had at any moment in the past year.

These days, people assumed he had a suicidal urge. He had recently received a six-month suspension of his corporate pilot's license for reckless endangerment. The reason didn't lie in his lack of skill as an aviator. He was the only executive he knew who flew his own jet. His abilities, honed by combat missions in Vietnam, made him a flyer to compare with those who did it for a living.

But, he could never be a professional pilot—and not merely because of the pay cut. He was careless. People on the ground had begun to realize that fact just as well as people in the skies.

Jonathan wasn't suicidal, he was only pressing himself to test every boundary and unexplored fear. Skiing and white-water kayaking weren't enough anymore. He had to be rock-climbing or skydiving—close to the edge of death in order to feel something besides the numbness.

It would be easy, he knew, to go flying off the road and over an embankment. At this speed—the Porsche had a top end of 155 mph, and he was pushing the limit—it would mean instant obliteration. Or he could ensure his death even further by smashing into the concrete column of an overpass. As long as he did it correctly and made sure there were no cars directly behind him, he might not harm anybody else. By taking himself out of the picture, he thought, he'd be doing the world a service.

Passing Moisant International Airport, he entered the less trafficked twelve-mile expanse of the Bonnet Carrie spillway. The other westbound vehicles no longer looked like they were standing still. They appeared to be traveling in reverse. He knew at this speed, his radar detector was virtually worthless because he was outdistancing its range. Yet the realization didn't faze him. So what if he got caught? So what if he went to jail? As long as someone bailed him out by Monday, he could be back at his office to "run the show," as he had once put it when talking to Sonny Odom.

Running the show—now that's a laugh. Even now, careening down the interstate on his rocket with wheels, he smiled as he thought about it. No one ran the show anymore. He knew that better than anyone. There were a few signs of trouble here and there. Signs a perceptive observer might pick up on. Yet the business hadn't begun to suffer so much that just anyone could tell. But it would happen. He knew it would. In the old days, people used to always say it was fitting that his company had the word *health* in its name, because it was one healthy enterprise. Now it had become like him. Unchanged on the outside, dying on the inside.

Once upon a time, he had lived in a world where he greeted every day with anticipation, jumping out of bed. First to arrive at the office, he would usually be the last to leave. If anyone asked him why he worked so hard, his only answer was a laugh. It was an adventure to him, not work. He was creating jobs, turning a profit by providing goods people needed, and it thrilled him.

Then he lost Jennifer and Jon. And with them had gone everything he loved—except work. Work was all he had before his family, and work was all he had left. At least that was what he told himself, and he felt sure he was right.

But Sonny's prediction on the day of the funeral had come true. For the first few months, he felt as though nothing had changed. He was as sharp as ever. He worked hard and played hard. The new Porsche—not the kind of car Jennifer would have wanted him to have—made him feel alive. Not just alive, but powerful. Powerful, because he could walk into a dealership and pay cash for it and because no one could pass him on the road when he was behind the wheel. At work, he had pushed harder still, and those who knew him best said he was making a good show of getting over his grief—but shouldn't he slow down? Still, he refused to listen.

Then, inexplicably, something had started to slip. By the fourth month, he'd begun to realize it. Now, instead of meeting each day with excitement, he struggled out of bed and trudged into work like someone punching a time clock. In his own eyes, he no longer served any function other than to sit behind his desk and watch the bureaucracy grow. Every so often, he had to be on hand to make a presentation or to negotiate a deal. On those occasions, he sometimes felt the old spark. But it disappeared as quickly as it came. Eventually, he knew he would sell the company, yet even that undertaking required energy and enthusiasm he found himself lacking.

As one month drifted into another, only one thing remained that gave Jonathan's life meaning. Rage.

He had undoubtedly been feeling this rage at a subconscious level for a year, but it had taken months to reach the surface. For a while, he focused his anger on Jennifer's God. It was totally beyond Jonathan's understanding how God could have allowed, or caused, Jennifer and Jon to die in such a horrible way. Wasn't Jennifer the one who had blindly trusted God? What kind of a god rewards faith with ten or twelve minutes of sheer terror ending in bone-crushing extinction? And what kind of god allows innocent five-year-old boys to die at the hands of madmen? *The kind who is either too weak or too callous to stop it,* Jonathan figured.

In either case, Jonathan found the idea of God too intangible now. When his wife had embraced a faith in God, he had opened his mind to the possibility himself. But look where it landed her. He was way beyond such thinking now. Jonathan was a pragmatist, a hands-on fixer of things. What he needed now was not a God to love, but a person to hate. Somebody to get even with for the death of his wife and son. It would do no good to be angry with God—though he was. It didn't even help to be angry with Russia for shooting down a jetliner, or with Washington for doing nothing about the deaths of innocent American passengers. He hated the people who had killed his wife and child, and he hated the government in Washington, which talked tough but did nothing. However, the lack of a real *person* to focus his rage on was nearly driving him mad.

The vast scope of the series of events that had taken Jennifer and Jon from him would boggle anyone's mind. Yet, he felt certain, at the center of it all a handful of people—maybe even just *one* person—had ordered the shootdown of KAL 007.

He couldn't bring Jennifer and Jon back to life. But if he could get revenge on the man responsible for their deaths then, at least, he would feel some kind of release. He would no longer feel as powerless as he did now. Then, maybe he wouldn't be so likely to do foolish things like he was doing tonight.

He slowed the Porsche and exited at La Place, more than thirty miles away from his point of origin, even though he'd left downtown just twelve minutes before. Getting back onto I-10 heading east, Jonathan pulled over to the side of the highway and sat there with the engine idling, looking into the dark Louisiana sky. Thunderclouds were gathering in the west, obliterating the stars, and the flares of two nearby oil refineries reflected off the low clouds and dimly illuminated the road ahead. Only the sounds of the frogs and the locusts, with the steady *whoosh,*

whoosh, whoosh of cars passing on the interstate, kept him company while he tried to sort things out.

Earlier that evening, he'd had his first date with a woman since Jennifer's death. He had escorted Kim Welch to a black-tie affair at the International Trade Mart.

Kim, an art dealer who had moved to New Orleans just six months ago, had strawberry-blonde hair, long legs, and an athletic frame. Dressed in a simple black backless evening gown, she had attracted admiring looks all night. Of course, her beauty constituted only part of the reason everyone turned to look at them when they got off the elevator together. The other part was the fact that Jonathan Stuart had officially come out of mourning.

Not that he lacked opportunities. New Orleans was full of women in their mid-thirties who would gladly have turned a wealthy widower into an ex-widower. But he had been a hermit for months now—longer than anyone expected.

As for Kim, either she was extremely patient and kind, or just willing to put up with him out of her own interests. Or both. Whatever the case, she had been a friend in recent months, and she had asked him to be her date at tonight's event. He had joked that surely a woman as stunning as she could find plenty of easier targets, but she had slipped her arm through his and told him she wanted him to be her date. So there he was, getting off the elevator with her.

They made the rounds, chatting with the mayor, with Senator Long and various U.S. and state representatives, and with other bigwig businessmen and dignitaries, including the governor. The notorious lecher gazed at Kim with drooping, lustful eyes while telling Jonathan it was good to see him at a social event again. Almost everyone there knew Jonathan, and they made a big to-do over him.

"Jonathan," said the governor, pointing him toward a burly, square-jawed figure with a hooked nose and swarthy skin, "I want to introduce you to Viktor Tchinkov, who's with the new Soviet trade delegation."

Jonathan just stood there, looking into Tchinkov's narrow black eyes, while the governor chuckled and said to the Russian, "Jonathan here is a big part of the reason why we have the delegation in New Orleans. Why, he was trading with your country back when most businessmen in this city were so cautious they—"

Jonathan shut out the rest of the governor's platitudes. The Soviet, seeming to glimpse something in Jonathan's eyes, put out a hand with a defiant smile, as though he knew Jonathan wouldn't take it.

Jonathan didn't often find himself speechless, but at this moment he felt his face flushed with heat as the blood rushed into his brain. He could not respond. He simply walked away, leaving Kim with the sneering diplomat and the puzzled governor.

He found a somewhat secluded spot on the balcony outside, looking out over the swollen Mississippi twenty-two stories below.

"Don't go off and leave me with the 'Gray Wolf' like that," said a soft voice behind him.

"Which one?" he asked, turning back toward Kim.

"Which one do you think?" She motioned with her upraised glass toward the silver-haired governor, who had already turned his full attention to a redhead.

"Sorry," he said. "I don't suppose I'm much fun . . . even now."

She laid a gentle hand on his shoulder, but he went on talking. "It just . . . sickens me to see *him* here."

"Who?" asked Kim, looking confused.

"The Russian," he said. "I don't even know the guy, but that doesn't matter. It's just who he is . . . what he represents. I look at him, and I see—" Suddenly he caught himself and glanced at her. "I'm sorry," he said. For the second time in thirty seconds, he apologized. He had gone a whole year without saying those words twice. "I must be an awful bore."

"No, you're not," she said, and she moved closer to him as though to prove her sincerity.

He could feel her warmth, smell the faint scent of her perfume as she raised an arm and touched one of her earrings.

"Listen, Kim, would you mind if we got out of here?"

"No problem," she said softly. "I understand. We could go have a drink somewhere, or . . ."

"Come on." He grabbed her hand, and they walked back through the main reception hall. As they re-entered, he noticed that the Russian seemed to have become the center of attention, surrounded by a group of charmed listeners, mostly middle-aged women.

"Yes," Tchinkov was saying in answer to someone's question, "we wish relations between our countries were better, too, but with the present climate in Washington . . ." In spite of his square head and stringy hair, he was a rather handsome man, six feet tall and probably five years older than Jonathan.

"But enough politics," said Tchinkov, interrupting himself, all the while matching Jonathan's stare as he steered Kim across the room. The Russian picked up a serving spoon from the table behind him and tapped his champagne glass so that everyone in the ballroom—eighty or ninety people—stopped and turned toward him. "To the wonderful city of New Orleans and its fabulous people," he announced, raising his glass. At these words, people nodded their heads and smiled. Tchinkov tossed his drink down in the Russian style, and the rest followed suit.

As he neared the exit, Jonathan froze and stared at the foreigner.

Tchinkov wasn't finished. "You have all been most gracious. You have welcomed me—and with me the whole Soviet people—into your hearts." Then, with a leer that would have suited the governor, he turned his gaze on Kim. "But most of all," he said, "I toast your beautiful women."

"I'll drink to that," said the governor, and everybody chuckled—except the First Lady of Louisiana.

Just as everyone raised their drinks to their lips, Jonathan grabbed a glass from a passing waiter's tray and, likewise, clicked the spoon for everyone's attention.

"I'm sure Mr. Tchinkov would also like to join me," he announced, "in drinking a toast to the 269 passengers who died onboard Korean Air Lines Flight 007." He looked around him at the stunned faces of the other guests. In the ensuing silence, he could hear faint whispers, and he saw people staring back at him with a mixture of annoyance and pity. He didn't know quite what he was doing, but he couldn't stop himself either. Tchinkov, meanwhile, simply stood by with his arms folded, nodding his head and smiling.

"May God rest their souls," said Jonathan, his voice as loud as a cannon in the deafening silence of the ballroom. With that he tossed down his drink, but no one—not even his date—followed suit.

After another agonizing spell of deathly quiet, there followed a quick rush of gasps, and then the room broke into a buzz of frenzied whispers.

Everyone else now looked at Tchinkov. He had stopped smiling and had pasted on an expression of sympathy, which infuriated Jonathan more than his bogus grin. "While you have my most sincere condolences," the Russian said, "perhaps you should not blame the law-abiding citizens of the Soviet Union. If you want to point the finger, point it at your CIA, who ordered Flight 007 to go on its illegal spy mission, and thereby caused the deaths of its passengers!"

Jonathan rushed toward Tchinkov, who was standing some twenty feet away. Several people moved aside as he barreled forward. But just as he reached out his hand to grab the Russian, Leonard Krygowski stepped between them. The former New Orleans Saints defensive tackle turned local FBI agent could always be found hovering in the shadows of any New Orleans soiree that involved international figures.

The bear-like Krygowski held Jonathan at bay while several other men stepped between him and Tchinkov. "I'd take it easy if I were you, Mr. Stuart," Krygowski growled into Jonathan's ear.

Jonathan shook his head as though trying to wake up. He looked at Krygowski's thick, heavy features, scarred from various football injuries. He might want to tangle with Tchinkov, but not with this big grizzly bear. "It's okay, Len," he said. "My date and I were just leaving."

"Good decision," said Krygowski, still standing his ground between the two men.

As he ushered Kim to the elevator, Jonathan managed to exchange a few angry glares with Tchinkov. While they waited for the elevator doors to open, the governor stepped into their path and graciously offered to escort Kim home. "I only want to be of assistance," he offered with a frown of seriousness wrinkling his face.

At that moment, the elevator doors opened, and Jonathan brushed past the governor, pulling Kim into the elevator with him.

On the ride down, he could feel her looking at him, and he heard the toe of her shoe clicking impatiently on the floor as the elevator carried them slowly to the parking garage. Although embarrassed he had made such a scene, he also felt a certain strange exhilaration.

As they crossed the parking deck, he noticed a black Mercedes limousine parked across three spaces. Inside sat an Asian-looking man smoking a cigarette and reading a paper. When Jonathan and Kim walked by, the man studied them with a cold, suspicious glint in his eyes. Jonathan knew it had to be Tchinkov's car and driver.

With one last surge of anger, Jonathan yearned to go over and—do *something*. He didn't know what. Maybe smash a window, or knock out a light. But of course all those things seemed too juvenile, too insignificant; so he did nothing. *This guy's a real Ivan the Terrible,* Jonathan thought. And the driver glared at him as though he knew what was on Jonathan's mind.

Neither Jonathan nor Kim said anything on the ride back to her place. But as they passed through the French Quarter, she placed a cool hand over his white knuckles resting on the gearshift.

"You want to come in?" she asked as he pulled to a stop.

He smiled at her, grateful for the gesture, but heard himself saying, "Thanks— but I think I need to be alone."

She shrugged her shoulders and pulled her hand away, unable to hide her hurt feelings. "I understand," she said. "It's tough when someone opens old wounds."

Sitting in his car with the motor idling, some of his rage soothed by the exertion of driving like a maniac, Jonathan could think straight again. He now knew what he wanted. From the moment he first saw him, Tchinkov had looked like he was spoiling for a fight. Well, if that was what the Russian wanted . . .

Jonathan pulled onto the highway and headed back into town.

Twenty-five minutes later, having returned to town at a more reasonable speed than he left it, he drove up Poydras Street toward the Trade Mart. While en route, rain had begun to fall, so he stopped to put the top up on his convertible. Now, he pulled over at an inconspicuous spot and shut off his engine. After sitting for a few minutes at the curb, Jonathan was about to turn into the parking garage to check on Tchinkov when the Russian's limo pulled up in front of the Trade Mart.

A few minutes later Tchinkov, not quite walking a straight line, emerged from the building with his date on his arm. Jonathan hadn't noticed her at the party, which was another indication of just how distraught he had been. Even from a distance, she looked like a high-class call girl. The driver whom Jonathan had dubbed "Ivan the Terrible" jumped from the car and shot swift glances first to his left, then to his right. Jonathan ducked down behind his steering wheel, raising his head cautiously just in time to see Ivan opening the limo door for his passengers.

The woman climbed into the car. But instead of joining her, Tchinkov blew her a kiss and pulled Ivan aside. They exchanged some words, and Ivan closed the passenger door, slid into the driver's seat, and drove into the night. Meanwhile Tchinkov raised his arm and hailed a taxi.

When the cab eased into the flow of traffic, Jonathan followed several car lengths behind. *What will it hurt for me to follow him?* Jonathan thought. *Just play a little cat-and-mouse?* Apparently, Ivan was taking the woman home while Tchinkov went somewhere by himself. Although Jonathan congratulated himself on finding Tchinkov this way, he wondered what the man was up to.

Much to Jonathan's surprise, the cab stopped at the corner of St. Charles and Napoleon, and Tchinkov got out. After paying off the taxi and watching it disappear down the street, the Russian got behind the wheel of a nondescript late-model gray Chevrolet parked by the curb. Clearly Tchinkov didn't want to be followed, which only served to heighten Jonathan's curiosity.

Tchinkov eased onto St. Charles, made a legal U-turn across the boulevard, and headed back toward town. Jonathan, not bothering to look around for police cars, made a quick illegal left from Napoleon onto St. Charles. *I'd better keep a wide gap,* he thought. *A car like mine is pretty noticeable.* But fortunately the light rain had picked up a bit, meaning that Tchinkov would have his wipers on, and he'd be looking ahead rather than studying his rearview mirror.

The Chevy turned right at Jackson Avenue, deserted at this time of night. Jonathan knew in a situation like this, rain or no rain, his pursuit would eventually be noticed. So, he took a sudden right onto Prytania Street, then an immediate left, and began to trail his quarry on a parallel route one block away.

In order to keep track of the Russian, he had to speed past the cross-streets and then creep through the major intersections—looking for some sign of the Chevy. He managed to catch up with the Russian and tracked him for several blocks before he found himself stuck behind a senior citizen for one long, slow block. By the time he reached the dead-end at the river on Tchoupitoulas, he'd lost the Chevy.

"Where did he go?" Jonathan asked aloud through gritted teeth. He wasn't about to give up so easily. Acting on a hunch, he turned left onto Tchoupitoulas and sped down river.

His hunch turned out to be wrong. He saw no signs of the gray Chevrolet. He made a quick U-turn, retraced his path, and continued upriver to Louisiana Avenue. Still no gray Chevy.

He was just about to give up when he caught a glimmer of light to his left. Slowing, he turned to look and saw a car in the dark shadows of the Louisiana Avenue wharf. Its headlights were off. But as the driver got out, in the brief flash of illumination from the interior light, the vehicle looked as though it might be the Chevy. The vehicle's door closed, and a dark figure disappeared into an open warehouse.

Maybe Tchinkov set this whole thing up. The thought crossed Jonathan's mind briefly. Maybe Tchinkov was following *him*, not the other way around, and now he intended to lure him into the shadows and finish what they'd begun earlier at the International Trade Mart.

"What now?" he whispered to himself. He made a series of left turns until he was on Annunciation Street, out of view from the wharf. Then, he parked his car and locked it, smiling at the futility of the gesture. Anyone who left a Porsche for fifteen minutes in this neighborhood would be lucky to find even the chassis and wheels remaining when he returned.

He crossed the street and walked into the darkness toward the wharf, alongside the warehouse, then into the building itself. The rain had stopped, and the air hung damp and heavy. There were no security lights, and he had to feel his way through the shadows. But from what he could tell, the vast warehouse appeared to be abandoned, empty, except for a few hulks of heavy machinery scattered about. The place smelled of diesel fuel, rust, and foul river water.

What could Tchinkov be up to? In the gloom, he could barely make out the yawning doors that led from the warehouse to the dock, beyond which he could see a few lights from Marrero, Louisiana, on the other side of the river.

As Jonathan edged farther along the wall of the warehouse, straining for any sign of the Russian, the sound of dripping water a few feet from him seemed to ricochet as loud as gunshots. He felt a trickle of sweat run down his brow. He inched along the inside of the wall that ran adjacent to the wharf itself, taking care where he stepped so he wouldn't make any noise. As he crept forward, he heard excited voices outside along the water, but the farther he went, the fainter they sounded.

Finally he came to a window and peeked out to see two men talking. Dust and cobwebs obscured his view, but in the moonlight he could make out the sturdy shape of Tchinkov and beside him a smaller figure whom Jonathan didn't recognize. They were talking in hoarse whispers while walking away from his end of the wharf.

Jonathan could not pick out the words Tchinkov was saying to the other fellow, but he recognized the tone. It sounded like the Russian was berating the smaller man, who cowered like a whipped puppy. Their voices grew still fainter as they moved farther down the wharf toward the river. To get within earshot, Jonathan would have to creep out of the warehouse and down onto the wharf itself.

Suddenly, both the absurdity and the danger of his position struck him. *What am I doing tiptoeing around in the dark, dressed in a tuxedo?* He was about to turn around and forget it all when another thought struck him. *What was Tchinkov doing tiptoeing around in the dark?*

Jonathan knew he had to find out. It didn't matter what consequences he might face. He had to know.

So as the men moved farther away, he sprinted through a nearby doorway to a shadowy area beside another warehouse door, which placed him much closer to Tchinkov and his friend. Just as he reached his objective, the two men stopped and looked out over the river.

"To reiterate," Tchinkov said, "you are never again to contact me directly. Is that clear?"

The other man didn't answer.

Tchinkov took an envelope from his pocket. "Here are your thirty pieces of silver." He stared at the younger man as he waited for him to take the money. "Now give it to me!"

The two exchanged envelopes, then turned and began walking briskly back in the direction from which they had come.

Jonathan realized they were about to pass directly in front of where he stood, so he pressed up against the doorframe. Unlike most of the other warehouse doors, this one was shut. Besides, even if he'd had time, he could never open it quietly enough to slip back in unnoticed. As the pair came within fifteen feet of him, Jonathan willed himself invisible and pushed more tightly against the door.

But as he did so, he knocked over a short two-by-four board that had been leaning against the doorjamb.

The two men looked directly at Jonathan. The smaller man wheeled about and ran quickly to Jonathan's left, into the warehouse, and away. But Tchinkov stood his ground. He looked directly at Jonathan and yelled in his native tongue, "You!"

Jonathan knew if he didn't act fast, they'd be fishing his waterlogged body out of the Gulf of Mexico a few days from now. Tchinkov put his hand into his pocket, and Jonathan surmised what he was reaching for. He didn't know whether to step farther away or closer. He couldn't outrun a bullet, but maybe he could somehow stop Tchinkov from firing. Just then, he stubbed his toe on the dislodged board. The momentary pain that shot up his leg brought with it a plan.

Jonathan could see Tchinkov pulling the short metal barrel of a pistol from his coat pocket. Without looking away from Tchinkov, he began cowering as though begging for mercy. The Russian stepped closer, and his mouth exploded into a terrifying grin. "It is not often," he announced in English, "that one makes a new enemy at a party and then has the pleasure of killing him later that night."

"I didn't mean what I said . . ." Jonathan hoped it sounded like a whimper. He raised his left arm slightly, holding it over his face to shield him from Tchinkov.

But with his other hand, he reached down in one fluid motion and grabbed hold of the two-by-four.

Tchinkov raised his weapon toward Jonathan's face. *"Teper' ty dolzhen oomeret."* He lingered over each syllable.

Under the circumstances, the meaning of his words—"Now you must die"— would have been clear to Jonathan even if he hadn't studied Russian for four years. But Tchinkov's face registered his surprise when Jonathan responded in the Soviet's native tongue.

"You first."

Jonathan held a firm grasp on the board and whirled it upward, straight toward Tchinkov's gun. All his years of baseball went into that motion, and the stationary pistol made a much easier target than a ninety-mile-an-hour fastball. Just as Tchinkov depressed the trigger, the board hit his hand with a resounding crack.

The blow knocked the pistol onto the wooden deck, and its report echoed across the river, the bullet flying harmlessly astray. Suppressing a cry of pain, Tchinkov doubled over and lunged at Jonathan.

Moving quickly to his right to avoid the punch, Jonathan came back with a right jab to Tchinkov's left jaw. Still Tchinkov rushed at him, but Jonathan hit him again and again in the face. Finally, after a kick in the kneecap, Tchinkov fell to his knees.

Jonathan knocked him onto his back, then pounced on his chest and began hitting Tchinkov's face over and over. He drew blood, and soon his fists were covered with it, but he kept on swinging. Crazed with pent-up rage, he pounded Tchinkov's face until the man's body went limp.

A strong smell filled the air—stronger than the diesel fumes, or the river, or even the sweat of two men struggling. The overpowering, metallic scent of blood permeated Jonathan's senses, and his flesh tingled from the red droplets that had splashed up on his face.

He heard the sound of a ship's horn off in the distance and, as though waking from a dream, he looked down and saw a man with his face beaten almost beyond recognition. He felt for Tchinkov's pulse, looking away from the blackened eyes, the broken nose, and the bloody mouth.

Thank God he still has a heartbeat. Jonathan stood up.

What should he do now? If he just left him this way, the police would start to ask questions, and the trail might lead back to him. They had publicly antagonized each other. There were witnesses who could attest to the fact. Len Krygowski would come forward if no one else did—and Len was an FBI agent. He had to do something to cover his tracks . . .

He pulled a Rolex Presidential off of Tchinkov's right wrist, along with two gold rings from the man's left hand. One of those looked like a wedding band, and Jonathan felt a moment's remorse, but the feeling passed as quickly as it came. He took the jewelry, along with the pistol and the two-by-four, and threw them into the river. Then he rolled Tchinkov over. From the back pocket he pulled out a wallet and flipped it open. There was a surprisingly large wad of bills, mostly hundreds. Jonathan removed the money, then wiped his fingerprints off the leather by rubbing it on Tchinkov's coat. He tossed the wallet to the side, the way a mugger would have left it.

He drove down Tchoupitoulas, maintaining the speed limit, even though he wanted to get out of there as quickly as he could. Two police cruisers passed by, headed toward the warehouse with lights flashing and sirens blaring. The night watchman at the wharf must have been awakened by the sounds of gunfire, found the body, and called them.

Jonathan looked at his eyes in the rearview mirror. *Am I cracking up?* he asked himself, startled by the crazed expression he saw on his face.

He hated to admit it, but at this moment he felt exhilarated.

Instead of heading toward home, Jonathan continued into town and stopped at a gas station, where he washed the blood off his hands. Looking at his face in the men's room mirror, he wiped off the traces of blood and checked for any damage. Only his right hand was cut. Otherwise, Tchinkov hadn't touched him.

But his tux was rumpled and soiled from the wharf and had a dark streak down one lapel. Not only that, but as he looked himself over, he saw something that stopped him cold. His right cuff link—his *monogrammed* cuff link—was missing.

He stared at his bare cuff for a moment, then shrugged it off. He was feeling too good to worry over it. He took off the jacket and the tie, which also had a dark spot or two, removed the remaining cuff link, rolled up his sleeves as best he could, then walked casually back to his car.

From the gas station he drove to the Seamen's Mission on Magazine. Just inside the vestibule of the mission stood a collection box. Tonight was going to be a fruitful night for the mission's coffers.

For good measure, after stuffing Tchinkov's wad of hundreds into the slot, Jonathan took a few more bills from his own wallet and added them. *Penance*. He looked up at the figure of Jesus on a crucifix and remembered Tchinkov's battered face and how much he had enjoyed bloodying it.

Behind the wheel again, he headed for home but had another thought and made a U-turn. All the liquor stores in the city were closed for the night, so he drove by a local tavern and bought a bottle of Dom Perignon. They weren't supposed to sell it for take-away, but when he offered $150 for a single bottle of champagne, it was suddenly possible to bend the rules. After giving a thrilled flower lady $75 for her remaining supply of roses, he was on his way.

Even without her makeup and dressed in a terry cloth bathrobe, Kim looked gorgeous to Jonathan, as though he were seeing her for the first time. She looked tired but didn't appear to have been sleeping.

"Jonathan," she said, looking at her watch. "Do you have any idea—"

"How sorry I am about tonight?" he interrupted, producing the flowers from behind his back. With the other hand he brought out the champagne.

Startled, she looked down at the flowers and the bottle, and then up at him, a mysterious smile forming on her fine lips. "Well, you weren't *that* bad of a date," she said, stepping aside to let him in. As he walked past her, the lingering scent of her perfume made him think about things he hadn't even considered since Jennifer's death.

He followed her into the kitchen. While she reached over the sink for a vase to put the flowers in, he set down the bottle. "Kim, listen." She turned around, holding the vase and now standing just eighteen inches away from him. "I really am sorry about tonight."

She lowered the vase to the countertop and returned his gaze.

"I—" he started to say, but she put a finger to his lips, then took his two hands in hers.

"It's okay, Jonathan." She glanced down at his scarred hand, then looked up at him. "What's this?"

"Oh, uh . . . I got locked out of my car, and I had to jimmy it open."

"Mm-hmm," she said, studying his face closely. She seemed to hesitate, then said, "Best not to ask, huh?"

"That's right," he whispered, and he pulled her to him, forgetting all about Tchinkov and the wharf and the cuff links and . . . everything. For the first time in a year, his thoughts weren't on Jennifer.

CHAPTER THREE

Jonathan didn't have much time over the following week to think about what had happened on the wharf Friday night. Every evening after work, he showed up at Kim's, and he never drifted off to sleep until just before dawn. But when he went in to the office after just a few hours of rest, he found himself completely refreshed, as though he'd had the best night's sleep of his life.

His new enthusiasm showed immediately in his work. For the first time in a year, there was a hum of excitement at Quality Health, and the rumor quickly spread— *The chief is back.* No one could get close enough to ask him about the source of his renewed vigor, but he was honest enough with himself to realize Kim was only part of the reason. He also had Tchinkov to thank.

No concrete evidence of his victory remained, except for the cut on his hand. And that was healing nicely. The business pages and local news didn't mention anything about the Russian trade delegate. And, although he was thankful not to find Tchinkov's picture in the obituaries, Jonathan was dying to know what had happened to him.

On Friday morning, a week after the black-tie event at the Trade Mart, he got his wish when an enormous figure appeared unannounced in the doorway of his office. It was Len Krygowski, the FBI agent. Krygowski's broad shoulders looked powerful on the football field but seemed a little absurd crammed into a business suit. His bulbous nose, broken countless times in his nine years with the Saints, seemed to guide his whole face as he looked from left to right around Jonathan's office.

"Come in, Len," Jonathan said without standing up. "I guess you just didn't have time to ask my secretary if I was busy or not."

"Nope," Krygowski said, looking around. "Official business. Couldn't wait." He studied the décor—pale gray walls, white built-in bookcases, burgundy leather chairs, thick oriental carpet. "Very tasteful, Jonathan," he said. "Nothing extravagant, just tasteful. I shoulda known you'd have good taste. Who's your decorator?"

Jonathan smiled as he stood up, extending his hand. "Now, Len, I'd hope my federal tax dollars aren't going to pay for a decorator as expensive as the one who did this office. So . . . what can I do for you?"

Krygowski held onto Jonathan's hand and squeezed it hard enough for Jonathan to feel the still-lingering pain from a week before. "Looks like you got some scars here," the agent said, looking down and examining the knuckles.

"Just a little accident," Jonathan answered, forcibly extracting his hand from Krygowski's grip. "You know how things happen. Just a tad too much to drink one night. No big deal."

Len sat down. "Humph. Were you drinking white Russians or black Russians?"

At those pointed words, Jonathan's eye twitched, but he hid it by pretending to notice something on the carpet. He sat back down in his chair.

Krygowski pulled a wrinkled photograph from his coat pocket. "Does this guy look familiar to you, Jonathan?"

Jonathan took the picture and looked at it. It was a grainy black-and-white photo of a male in his fifties. Balding on top, the man was slender, skinny even, with a beard, mustache, and glasses. After studying it for an appropriate amount of time, Jonathan handed it back. "No," he said. "Don't recognize him."

He was telling the truth, and it appeared from the look on Krygowski's face, the agent knew he was. Nodding his head, Krygowski put the photo back in his coat pocket and sat there with a patient smile. He crossed his legs and put one hand on top of the other on his left knee.

Jonathan stared at Krygowski, and Krygowski stared back at Jonathan. Even though he wanted to speak, just to break the uncomfortable silence, Jonathan sensed if he did, he would show some kind of weakness, and Krygowski would have an advantage over him. Someone had to make the first move, and it would have to be the FBI agent.

After what seemed an eternity—although it couldn't have been more than thirty seconds—Krygowski sighed and glanced over Jonathan's head at the view out his window. "You know, Jonathan, a strange thing happened last Friday night. Apparently there was a foreign national, highly placed diplomatic type, who wandered down to the Louisiana Avenue Wharf and got mugged. They took his watch, his ring, and all his money. And there was a lot of it." Krygowski paused and smiled, still looking out the window over Jonathan's shoulder, his gaze so intent Jonathan wanted to turn and look. "Strangest thing," Krygowski went on. "You'd a thought they would have left him alone after that, considering the stash of money they lifted off of him. But, boy, they beat him to a pulp. He looked *bad*. Real bad. Broken hand, broken nose, concussion, cuts all over his face. Yep, pretty bad shape, that fellow." His voice trailed off.

This time Jonathan did speak. Looking at his watch, he said, "Well, Len, that's an interesting story, but I've got a meeting at 10:30, so why don't you—"

"What do you think, Jonathan?" asked Krygowski, ignoring his interruption. "Why do you suppose a foreign guy would be down at the dock like that? Think maybe he was meeting a hooker?" Krygowski shook his head, as though he had examined that question himself already. "Nah, why would he? He already had an escort-type booked for the evening—*very* nice lady." Krygowski looked at Jonathan and smiled a conspirator's smile. "I mean, she was nice. Kinda lady you'd take to a black-tie type affair, and nobody'd guess in a million years she was on the clock. No, weren't no hooker."

The phone rang. Jonathan picked it up and barked to his secretary, "Hold my calls." He knew if his conscience were clear, he would have told his visitor to cut to the chase. But his conscience wasn't clear. And maybe that's what Krygowski was testing. Even so, if Krygowski suspected him, why was he putting on this big song and dance?

"So, Len," Jonathan said. "This foreign guy with the hooker—was he the guy in the photo?"

"No, this is him," said Krygowski, nonchalantly pulling out a picture from his coat pocket and laying it on the desk. Jonathan picked it up and gasped. It showed Tchinkov more or less the way he had left him on the wharf, or more likely the way he looked when they brought him into the emergency room. A man with his face literally rearranged.

"Oh, gosh, I'm sorry," Krygowski said now in a disingenuous tone. "I showed you the wrong photo." Hastily he pulled it back and in its place set out a studio-quality portrait photo of Tchinkov in a suit and tie, with every hair on his square head swept into place. "This is the guy." He looked up at Jonathan, as though a thought had only then occurred to him. "Oh, yeah—I forgot—you *know* this guy! Seems like I remember you two having some kind of little disagreement at the Trade Mart." He slapped his forehead. "That's right! Then maybe you *can* help me figure this thing out!"

Jonathan was growing tired of Krygowski's baiting, and he decided that if the agent wasn't going to get to the point, then he would. "So you want to question me about his assault, is that it, Len?"

Krygowski narrowed his eyes and stared at Jonathan, then burst out laughing. "Ah, come on!" he said. If he'd been sitting close enough to Jonathan, he probably would have punched him playfully in the arm with one of his beefy fists. "Why would a guy with as much money as you mug somebody? I mean, you corporate types, you might steal a couple million, but never a couple hundred, ha-ha!" He glanced at Jonathan, who wasn't smiling. "Oh, did I tell you about all the money? Yeah, this mugger, see, he was either a real Robin Hood type, or he had some kind of guilty conscience, I don't know. Saturday morning, Sixth District gets a call from the sisters at the mission hall on Magazine, and turns out that in one night they raked in $2,675. Can you believe it? That's a good *month* sometimes for the sisters. And a 100-ruble Russian note too."

There followed another long silence, during which Krygowski gave Jonathan another meaningful stare. "I have this very distinct recollection," he said, "As I recall, earlier on the same evening in question, you tried to tear the victim's face off. If I hadn't grabbed you, you would have succeeded." He laughed. "You shoulda been a running back!"

Jonathan sat quietly, staring back at Krygowski. Clearly the FBI agent had perfected his interrogation style over the years, and even though he was sure Krygowski had him, Jonathan wasn't going to admit anything he didn't have to.

"Now people used to tell me," Krygowski was saying, "they used to say, 'Lenny, you're too dumb to do anything besides tackle meatheads on the football field or cut up beef in your dad's butcher shop.' I figured maybe they were right, and I did get my head banged up on the field a couple times. But you know, Jonathan, I can still tell the difference between the smell of skunk and the smell of perfume. And every once in awhile there's something that happens that's so obvious that even this big, dumb jock can figure it out." He tossed something onto Jonathan's desk. "This is one of those times."

The object spun like a top on the hard glass surface, but before it had stopped spinning, Jonathan could see what it was. If he weren't careful, he might forget himself and snap at Krygowski for tossing his $500 cuff link so carelessly. As it was, he just stared at it as though he had never seen it in his life, even though his initials were clearly visible.

"*JWS*," said Krygowski, peering closely at the cuff link. "What's the W for— William?" He smiled. "Whitakker? Westmoreland? Wittenberg? I'd figure one of you rich guys had some kind of fancy middle name like that." He looked at Jonathan's face for signs of a response. "And by the way," he went on, "out of respect for you, I haven't spoken to your girlfriend—"

"My what?"

"Uh, Miss Welch. Kim Welch? Aren't you two seeing each other? Anyway, I haven't spoken to Miss Welch yet. But I imagine that while she could help establish your whereabouts at a certain point during the night of August 31, it's quite likely neither she nor anybody else can account for what you were doing at about 12:08, when a shot was fired at the wharf."

"I see," said Jonathan gravely. He felt a little sick. "I see where you're taking this. Maybe I should call my lawyer."

Krygowski calmly inspected his fingernails and then looked up at Jonathan. "Oh, I don't know if that will be necessary," he drawled. "Just wait till you hear the rest of the story. 'Cause you know what, Jonathan? You are one lucky son of a gun." He broke into a big smile. "Yes, indeed, you are the lucky one. You know why? Because we figured out why Tchinkov was down there, and it wasn't to meet some woman—not even so he could roll around on the dock with *you*." Krygowski shook his head. "Mm-mm. No, he was meeting that little putz in that first picture I showed you, and . . . let's just say he was buying some crib notes for the test."

"I don't follow you," said Jonathan.

"Well, I can't say exactly." Krygowski looked up at the ceiling. "But let's just imagine you were some scrawny little wing-nut who worked as an engineer at the Michoud Test Center over in Pearl River, Mississippi, and let's say you had access to highly sensitive test results for the space shuttle. And let's suppose you had zero principles, were greedy, and got in touch with a representative of a hostile foreign government. That's the story of our friend in the first picture, and let me tell you, that joker ain't gonna see daylight for a long, long time." He laughed. "'Course, I didn't figure none of this out myself. No, sir. This is comin' from the boys who know everything." He nodded. "This is comin' from over at the CIA—" He whispered the name as though it were holy. "Where they *really* know what's goin' on."

Jonathan didn't care about the CIA. "So what about Tchinkov?" he asked, feeling more bold with his growing awareness that he was off the hook.

"Tchinkov?" Krygowski laughed. "By the time we—I mean, the CIA—got done talking to him, he probably wished you'd killed him. He realized pretty soon that it would be smart to turn sides, especially considering what would happen to him if he ever set foot in Moscow again. He's got a new identity, which you helped him obtain by moving his face around a little bit, and he's gonna disappear somewhere. Therefore, he's a lot luckier than his friend from Michoud . . . but like I said, not nearly as lucky as you, Jonathan."

Krygowski crossed his legs. "Not only are you never gonna see Tchinkov again, but you managed to stumble across an important spy and, in the process, turned an asset to our side. Washington had been wondering where the leak in our shuttle system was, and now that we've found it, they would probably be glad to come down here and pin a medal on you if I could prove you were the perpetrator." Hands now in his pocket, Krygowski began to jiggle his keys. "But that's not how I see it. I think the best reward might be to leave out any names altogether. That way the provincials get to rub Washington's nose in it a bit by busting this spy, and a certain prominent citizen gets to keep his privacy and position."

He stood up, and Jonathan didn't know whether to thank Krygowski or say nothing at all.

Krygowski pointed a finger across the desk at Jonathan. "Let me give you a little unsolicited advice, my friend. You are one high-strung, tightly wound, radical non-conformist, and that was so even before . . . your misfortune." He said the last two words in a low, apologetic voice. "But if you stick around here, you are going to eventually get yourself in some kind of trouble. Odds are, the next fight you pick with a Russkie ain't gonna turn out so pleasant. Therefore, and this is my unsolicited advice, I recommend you take off on a trip or something." He smiled. "See the world, have a fling, I don't know. Maybe take that pretty lady with you." He shrugged. "Or—maybe not." Suddenly he became more serious. "But I do think you need a change of scenery, Jonathan. For your own good."

In his relief at how well things were turning out, Jonathan was speechless, but Krygowski didn't seem to mind doing all the talking. As the FBI agent stood in the doorway to leave, he said, "You know, Jonathan, in another lifetime you might have been a good FBI man or—God forbid—a criminal. You got nerves of steel, you know that? Nerves of steel. I gave you plenty of chances to break, but you just sat there as cool as you please."

"Thanks, Len," said Jonathan with a smile. "And just so you know, it's Wilson."

"Huh?" Krygowski put a hand up to his ear.

"Wilson—Jonathan Wilson Stuart. Old family name. But I didn't grow up any kind of rich boy, not by a long shot."

"Listen, neither you nor me," said Krygowski in a tone of camaraderie, stepping back into the office and motioning Jonathan to come closer. "Look," he said in a low voice, "you seem like an all-right kinda guy to me, Jonathan, so I'm gonna tell you somethin', and you can do whatever you want to with it."

Jonathan waited, wondering what possible further revelations there could be.

"This guy Tchinkov," Krygowski whispered, "he's not exactly what I would call major KGB material. He cracked like a glass bowl, first off, and started tellin' us all kinds of things we didn't even ask. Me and another Bureau guy were in the room, and CIA was tryin' to get rid of us so they could debrief him." He chuckled. "But he started the debriefing early. Why, he even asked if *you* were CIA."

"What?" asked Jonathan.

Krygowski nodded his head. "Kept asking them why you were so worked up about the KAL 007 flight, and of course they didn't tell him. Wanted to see why he had such a guilty conscience—or maybe what he knew about 007."

"And?" Jonathan stepped around Krygowski and walked to the door, which Krygowski had opened when he was in the process of leaving a moment before. Jonathan pushed it shut. He turned back towards Krygowski and drew in a breath. "What did he say?"

Krygowski shrugged. "Well, it was all kinda muddled. Asked if you somehow had him linked with this Drakoff guy—"

"With *who?*"

"Drakoff was the name he used." Krygowski ran his hand over what was left of his hair. "I mean, this is way over my head, lemme tell ya, Jonathan. But I heard him say he'd worked with this Drakoff guy at some ministry in Moscow, and Drakoff had to leave in sort of semi-disgrace because of . . . "

"Because of what?" Jonathan interrupted impatiently. "Just tell me what the guy said, Len."

"All right." Krygowski sighed. "The only reason I'm tellin' you this is, maybe, somehow, this'll help you let the whole thing go." He glanced back at the door and lowered his voice to just above a whisper. "Tchinkov said he'd heard a rumor that this other guy Drakoff was the one who gave the order to shoot down the airliner. He knew him for a while, but Drakoff got sent away because what he'd done was such an embarrassment."

"Sent away—where?" asked Jonathan, his heart pounding.

"Worst place you could go if you were a Russian," Krygowski answered. "Afghanistan."

After Krygowski left, Jonathan sat hunched over his desk for a few minutes, trying to jot down some notes for an upcoming business meeting. After five minutes, all he had written on the pad in front of him, aside from doodles, were two words. Looking down at his hands, he saw that they were shaking.

Drakoff. At first he had taken down the name in case he forgot it, yet he knew he would never forget. From that moment until the day he died, he told himself, he would always remember the name of Jennifer's and Jon's murderer.

Or at least, the name of the man reported to be their murderer, he kept reminding himself, trying to keep a cool head. After all, Krygowski had called it "hearsay evidence." But what reason would Tchinkov have to lie?

He swiveled in his chair to stare out at the river. *The fact that I stumbled across this name the way I did can only mean one thing,* he thought. *Fate, or Providence, or God—if he even exists—meant for me to learn it.*

For more than a year, hatred had grown steadily along with a sense of helplessness at the events that had taken his family from him. The anonymity of his enemy had only added to his frustration, but now he knew.

Knew what? A name. Nothing more. Just a name. What would he do with it now that he had it?

"Drakoff." He said the name out loud, then looked around. "Drakoff." He said it again, feeling foolish that he had somehow thought the mere speaking of the word would have some kind of power all its own.

He tried to picture what Drakoff might look like, and the only image he could call to mind was that of a Nazi commandant from an old World War II movie—maybe Erich von Stroheim in *Five Graves to Cairo*—jackboots and jodhpurs, a sharp nose and jaw, and icy blue eyes behind a monocle. A name—and an image straight out of Central Casting. What good did any of that do him?

I have to do something. Jonathan didn't know what step to take, but he finally had something to act on. There was a real target for his hatred and rage. It wasn't much information, but Jonathan had succeeded with less.

He turned away from the window and glanced at a phone message he had received earlier that morning. Absent-mindedly, he read the urgent message from his CFO, Frank Crosby, requesting a return call. Jonathan let his gaze roam aimlessly over his desk. Suddenly, he jerked to attention as his eye fell on the word he had written underneath Drakoff's name. *Afghanistan.*

"Afghanistan." Jonathan said it louder. "Afghanistan. I'm going to find you, Drakoff. Afghanistan isn't big enough for you to hide. I'm going to hunt you down like a dog. No matter what it takes, I'm going to make you pay for killing my wife and son."

His mind made up, Jonathan buzzed his secretary. "Tell Frank I'll catch up with him tomorrow," he said. "I've gotta get to an appointment."

"Appointment?" the secretary asked. "I didn't have you down for anything until—"

"This thing just came up," said Jonathan, impatience tingeing his words. "If anybody calls, just take a message and I'll get back with them later."

His so-called appointment was at the New Orleans Public Library's main branch downtown, where he located and checked out every book he could find about Afghanistan. There weren't many. He found plenty of books about Britain or even China, but those were major countries. And there were quite a few travel books on Switzerland or Jamaica, because people went to such places for vacation.

But nobody much cared about Afghanistan, himself included. Until now. The remote nation, landlocked in the mountains between Iran, Pakistan, and the Soviet Union, had no oil and no major exports to speak of. Until a few years before, he would have been hard-pressed to find the country on a map.

Actually, it wasn't true that no one cared about Afghanistan. The Soviets obviously did, as they had proven by sweeping into the country with their tanks at

Christmas of 1979. At the time, Jonathan had been concerned because he was planning to take his business into Russia, and he'd wondered how the incident would affect relations. It had posed a minor setback for him, but only a minor one, and the U.S. reaction to the invasion hadn't gone much beyond the boycott of the 1980 Olympics in Moscow.

The library had three books on Afghanistan. One was a U.S. government publication from the '50s. Another was even older, a British travelogue from the turn of the century. At least the third had come out since the war began. He checked out all three and spent the rest of the afternoon looking for any newspaper or magazine articles he could find.

When he returned home, he called Kim and said he thought he might stay in that night. "I've got some work to catch up on," he explained.

"Why don't you bring your work over here?" she asked in a coy tone.

"Sounds nice." He tried to sound lighthearted, but all he could think about was the evening of reading that lay ahead of him. "I just don't think you'd let me get any work *done.*"

"*Au contraire,*" she answered, sounding a little peeved. "You forget, I have a business of my own."

"Oh, I didn't forget," he rushed to say. "It's just that I . . . well, like I said, I just need to stay in tonight."

"Whatever you say, Jonathan," she announced dryly, and he could tell from her voice, she wasn't pleased.

He didn't even read his mail, scan the paper, or turn on the TV. As soon as he hung up the phone, he plunged into the stack of books and photocopies he'd brought home from the library.

He read all evening long, pausing only long enough to order a pizza. Within a few hours, he knew more about Afghanistan than 99 percent of all Americans.

Jonathan quickly absorbed as much information as he could find. Though the Soviets had fought in dozens of places by proxy, this was the first time they'd actually committed their own troops to an extended conflict since World War II, and it had become the longest war in their post-revolutionary history. So far, they had killed or wounded 300,000 Afghans and caused millions more to flee—but at a high price. Each year, they lost 5,000 of their men in battle, and another 5,000 to hepatitis, pneumonia, and typhoid.

They had 115,000 troops involved in the war, and after nearly five years of fighting, the Soviets, at present, controlled only 18 percent of the country. Of all major cities, they could claim only Kabul, the capital, and Jalalabad, former playground of the nation's aristocrats. Even there, Soviet rule remained shaky.

They should have studied their own history better, Jonathan thought as he reviewed what he'd learned. Conquerors had been invading Afghanistan since the time of Alexander the Great, not because they wanted the country itself, but because they wanted to pass through it. The landmass sat at the crossroads of Asia, on the way to powerful empires such as Greece, Persia, Arabia, and India. Throughout the centuries, army after army had fought to gain a foothold there, and sometimes they won—for a time. But Afghanistan always ended up back in the hands of the Afghans.

In the 1800s, Britain and Russia had competed for the country in a superpower struggle they called, "The Great Game." The British were certain they could break the pattern of history and subdue the Afghans as they had many others. In the 1830s, when they installed a puppet ruler in Kabul, an Englishman boasted to an Afghan that his army had marched into the country without firing a shot. The Afghan just looked into the sky and said, "Yes, I am thinking. You people have entered this country, but how will you get out?"

By the time they finally did, a century later, they had fought a hundred campaigns with the Pushtun tribesmen of Afghanistan. In one battle, 15,000 Brits fled from Kabul to Jalalabad, but only one of them survived the journey, a doctor who almost died of starvation before anyone found him. Historians usually refer to Japan as the first non-white country to defeat a European foe in war since the Middle Ages, as it did Russia in 1905, but the Afghans had chewed the British up and spit them out more than sixty years before.

After the attempts to conquer Afghanistan by the British and the Russian empires, no one bothered the country for a long time. Then came the Soviets, the slowest and most patient invaders the country had ever seen. In the 1950s, they supported democratic reforms in the Afghan government. In the 1960s, they offered economic assistance, building a road from the USSR into Afghanistan. In the 1970s, they gave aid to a Marxist faction that ultimately took power. And at the end of the decade, they brought in their army on the very road they had built years before.

But instead of gobbling up Afghanistan, they had gotten themselves bogged down in a war that became more miserable every day. *"Worst place you could go if you were a Russian,"* Jonathan thought, recalling Krygowski's words. He stared at a picture of a fierce-looking Afghan resistance fighter in one of the magazine articles. The man wore a loose-fitting shirt and pants with a headdress, his face dirtied from days in the field. But what caught Jonathan's attention was the fierce look in his eyes. *Those are some tough characters,* he thought. *Nobody rules them.*

He glanced up from his reading to the clock on the mantelpiece. After one in the morning.

He stretched, but he didn't feel sleepy. Picking through his mail, he saw nothing of interest, so he tossed the stack aside in favor of the newspaper. He thumbed through the pages, paying little attention. First he glanced at the sports scores, then the financial news. Finally, he picked up the front section to see what was happening in the world.

A story at the bottom of the third page caught his attention, and he did a double-take. For hours now, he had been seeing the word *Afghanistan* over and over, and it startled him to find it again—this time in a current news story. Of course, they regularly ran little blurbs about the war, but he'd never paid much attention. Now he leaned forward in his seat and read.

Afghan Leader to Reagan:
"How Long Must the Killing Go On?"

WASHINGTON (AP)—In a press conference on Thursday, Afghan Relief Commission director Amal Rashid called on President Reagan to support the resistance movement in his country "with more than mere words." Citing the President's frequent remarks condemning Soviet aggression, Rashid demanded that the President take measures to halt the war between the Afghan resistance, or *mujahideen,* and the invading Soviet army. "For five years the Russians have been killing our women and children," stated Rashid. "How long must the killing go on before you will take action?" Rashid, whose organization raises humanitarian aid for the mujahideen, said their greatest need is not food or medicine, but weapons. "We are not asking you to fight on our behalf," he explained. "We ask only that you arm us." According to Rashid, topping his list of needs is the Stinger surface-to-air missile, currently possessed only by the United States and its NATO allies. "With several hundred of these," he asserted, "we could drive back the Soviets." Short of such an extraordinary level of military assistance, Rashid indicated that "three or four" Stingers would make it possible for the mujahideen to prove their effectiveness. "The Soviets maintain domination by air superiority," Rashid said. "Imagine what would happen to their morale if we began shooting their warplanes from the sky." In conclusion to his address to the president, Rashid stated, "If you will not help us, we will have to go elsewhere for help." Asked if he was referring to the militant regime in Iran, Rashid refused to comment, adding only, "Anyone who could provide us with this assistance will be a hero to the Afghan people."

Jonathan folded the paper so that the story was on top and he sat, staring at it for a long time. Two phrases stood out at him. *"Imagine what would happen to their morale if we began shooting their warplanes from the sky"* and *"Anyone who could provide us with this assistance will be a hero to the Afghan people."* As he sat there in his chair, the house silent except for the ticking of the clock, he heard another voice. *"Worst place you could go if you were a Russian."*

At some point he must have dozed off. His dream began with a real memory—a happy afternoon he and Jennifer had spent soon after they learned she was pregnant with Jon. They were in London, her favorite city, walking along Piccadilly toward the Ritz to have afternoon tea. Jonathan had never much cared for the snooty ways of the hotel staff, but he liked to make Jennifer smile, and she loved her teas at the Ritz. They were walking along arm in arm, talking and laughing, and up ahead he saw the London offices of Aeroflot, the Soviet airline. In the front window stood a model of a passenger plane, huge, in true Russian style. Perhaps fifteen feet long. On that day, he had pointed it out to her. But she was impatient to get to the Ritz, and they had moved on.

Then the dream broke from true-life events. Before his eyes, the model began growing, expanding until it smashed the glass of the storefront window. He looked around for Jennifer, but she was gone. Frantically he turned back toward the jet, and it just kept growing, now covering the street, and extending toward the front of the Ritz.

Where was Jennifer? Around him he saw nothing but shattered glass and a sidewalk suddenly empty of everyone but him and the expanding aircraft. In the window of the jet he thought he saw a face. *Jennifer? Jon?* Then he looked again, and it was the face of the Nazi commandant—*Drakoff*—watching as Jonathan passed by; leering, laughing. By now the plane, which had assumed full size and crushed everything around it as though the buildings were mere papier-mâché, began to take off. The roar of it filled the silence of the empty street, and Jonathan felt helpless. *Can anyone stop it?* Desperate, he looked around for something, a weapon he could use against the intruder. Then, he heard a soft voice speaking to his right, and he saw a man dressed in clothes like the Afghan in the photograph. The man held something out to him, a long cylinder, like a telescope. He smiled and said something to Jonathan, but Jonathan couldn't hear over the roar of the plane. *What?* he screamed.

Then the man spoke again. *I said . . . shoot down the plane.* Still smiling, he released the cylinder into Jonathan's hands.

At that moment, Jonathan realized what he held. A missile.

Go on, the man said. *Go on. Now you will be avenged.* Jonathan took the missile, aimed it, and fired. In an instant, the plane shattered in a great blast of glass and metal that knocked him backward . . .

Jonathan bolted upright. The clock was still ticking as before, and if he could believe what he saw on its hands, he had been asleep for less than a minute.

Jonathan had other things on his mind when he got to the office, but he remembered he had promised to return the call from his CFO, Frank Crosby, so he dialed the number on his message slip.

Frank was in Philadelphia on some business and, before he left, he had joked to Jonathan that he was going into enemy territory—the home base of Allied Health, Jonathan's chief competitor. He picked up on the third ring.

"Hi, Jonathan. Thanks for calling me back. I met with Mueller at Allied yesterday." Frank lowered his voice as though the information he was about to share was top secret. "Let me tell you, I've said it before, but I know for sure now. That guy wants your company."

"Really?" asked Jonathan. "What'd he say?"

"Well," Frank chuckled, "he made me a tentative offer."

"Oh yeah?" Jonathan sat forward in his chair. "How much?" When Frank told him, he said, "Not bad. Not bad at all."

"Jonathan, you sound like you'd actually consider a deal." Frank sounded nervous.

"So what'd you tell him?" asked Jonathan.

"I told him you wouldn't be interested, of course!"

"Good, good." Jonathan thought for a second. "That way we can drive the price up."

By the time he got off the phone with Frank, Quality Health was up for sale.

Then he called Sonny Odom in Alabama. He had been wanting to talk to him since the middle of the night, but decided to wait until a decent hour.

"Sonny," he said. "How would it be if I jetted over for a visit this afternoon?"

"Well sure, Bubba," Sonny answered. "Is everything okay?"

"Everything's fine. I've just got an idea I need some help with. Say, about five o'clock?"

"Fine. I'll look forward to seein' you."

Up until he'd had his pilot's license suspended, he could have flown the corporate jet. As it was, he needed to make arrangements for someone else to fly him, so he buzzed his secretary. Then, it occurred to him that he should call Kim. She was no dummy. If he told her he couldn't make it again tonight, after a solid week of nonstop nights together, she would know something was up.

He knew she deserved better. But he had a new obsession now.

Sonny Odom grew up in Alexander City, Alabama, where he'd worked in the textile mills through his teen years. When the Korean War came, he'd seen it as his chance to escape a lifetime in the mills, and he signed up for the First Provisional Marine Brigade. He followed this up with three tours in Vietnam—a fact that he said demonstrated his lack of good judgment. During the '50s and '60s he also fought in a number of "limited engagements" here and there, undeclared actions that didn't get much mention in the history books—or, in the case of a certain failed invasion of Cuba in 1961, too much mention. He was nominated for the Congressional Medal of Honor and awarded the Navy Cross for his single-handed assault on a Vietcong machine gun nest, which saved the lives of his entire platoon.

Sonny had often intimated that he earned a little money here and there as a consultant for corporations concerned about protecting their executives overseas, and he periodically taught various security and quasi-military courses. Jonathan figured that was just part of it, and that Sonny's full resume would probably look a lot like a mercenary's. From listening closely to little things Sonny had said over the years, he discerned his stepfather was one-part Patton and one-part G. Gordon Liddy—in addition to his one-part Southern gentleman, which was how he carried himself around others. He seemed to know people all over the world. And if there was one business cliché Jonathan knew to be true, it was the old adage: "Connections are everything."

Sonny still lived in the house he had shared with Jonathan's mother, and her memories filled the place. Maybe that was why, upon Jonathan's arrival, he found his stepfather sitting in a shaft of sunlight at the kitchen table, drinking his Crown Royale and Diet Coke. In the background, Willie Nelson crooned, "City of New Orleans."

Sonny offered Jonathan a drink, but Jonathan wanted to keep a clear head and wished Sonny would do the same. "Don't worry, Bubba," said Sonny, as though reading Jonathan's thoughts. "I'm clear as a bell. Now, if there's one thing I know about you, it's that you don't just up and stop in for a visit unless you've got something on your mind. So tell me."

Jonathan drew a deep breath. "Well, the fact is, I need your help."

"You told me as much on the phone," Sonny replied. "Didn't have to fly all the way back here just for that."

So Jonathan began talking, and he told Sonny things he hadn't shared with anyone, not even Kim. His feelings since Jennifer had died. His uncontrollable rage. The Tchinkov incident, the revelations about Drakoff, the article he'd seen in the paper—and his plan.

When he finished, the two men sat there for a long time, neither one speaking.

"Now let me get this straight," said Sonny finally, taking another sip of his drink and sitting up in his chair. "You wanna go to Afghanistan and find this yahoo you think is responsible for killing Jennifer and Jon."

"I know it sounds insane," said Jonathan, "but I'm dead serious. And before you tell me all about how this won't bring them back, let me just say that I know all that, but—"

Sonny held up a hand. "I wouldn't insult your intelligence like that. Your mother could get as riled as anyone I ever knew," he said thoughtfully, "but she had her head on straight, and you inherited her good sense." He studied Jonathan's face for a moment and went on. "And that's what worries me. But even besides all that, Bubba, I got news for you. You don't just hop on a plane and check in at the Kabul Hilton. Getting into Afghanistan and back out, without getting yourself killed in the process, is only slightly easier than going to the moon and back."

"Believe me, I understand," said Jonathan. He pulled the newspaper clipping from the breast pocket of his sport coat and pointed to it. "That's where this guy Rashid comes in. I figure if I can give him what he wants, he'll give me what I want. Safe passage."

"What he wants," Sonny repeated. "You mean Stingers? Where you gonna get those?"

"That's what I'm asking *you.*"

Sonny lifted his eyes heavenward. "Lord, Willa," he said. "Did you hear what your boy just asked me?" He looked at Jonathan. "Do you realize you have just attempted to involve me in a crime punishable under international law?"

"What are you gonna do, arrest me?"

Sonny laughed. "All I'm saying is—"

"Well, now I'm going to commit another crime under U.S. law," said Jonathan, "as administered by the Securities and Exchange Commission."

"I can't wait to hear," said Sonny with an amused smile.

"Allied Health stock is about to go up," said Jonathan, "because they're going to acquire Quality Health—even though they don't know it."

"I think I'll hold off on any calls to my broker," Sonny responded. "So you're selling your company?"

Jonathan nodded his head. "It'll probably take three months to complete the deal, but let's just say I'm not exactly hunting for a job. I might have a couple of bucks to put into this mission—including money to hire you for your full-time assistance and expertise." He paused. "Say, ten thousand a month?"

Sonny whistled. "What would I do with all that money?"

Jonathan shrugged. "I don't know, retire maybe."

"I'm retired already. And enjoying it."

"Ah, I know you better than that, " Jonathan shot back. "You're just like me. Can't sit still for a minute. I'm offering you a project to focus your energies, and make a little tax-free income while you're at it."

"Tax-free?"

"Well, we aren't gonna tell the government about this, are we?"

"True, true." Sonny thought for a long time. "It's an interesting proposal, Jonathan. I'd like to be able to help you out, and I could use the money, not to mention the fact that it sounds like fun in some warped kinda way that no sane individual would understand."

"But?" Jonathan could hear a refusal coming.

"But," Sonny went on, "the risks are sky-high, and I'm not so sure I feel good about the basic idea behind it anyway. Revenge is a dangerous motivation, and it can lead to deadly consequences. A man who lets his emotions control him don't usually last too long in the line of fire, 'cause he lets his feelings impair his thinking."

Jonathan shrugged. "I'm going to do it whether you get involved or not."

Sonny smiled. "I know. I also know you're not exactly what I'd call a hothead—not most of the time, anyway. Besides, I feel like I'd be doing right by your mother if I stuck around to make sure you didn't get yourself into too much trouble."

"Is that a yes, then?" Jonathan asked, raising his eyebrows.

"It's a 'yes, but,'" Odom answered. "I'd be willing to let you use some of my contacts and give you advice and help along the way. Just don't expect me to actually go into any dangerous situations with you. A long time ago I promised God that if He'd only save my hide in the field, I'd quit getting myself into those situations. I figure I ought not to tempt Him any more. I'll advise you, and I'll help you get what you need. But this is *your* fight."

"Fair enough," Jonathan said, thrilled, but also a little shocked that Sonny had actually gone for the idea.

Sonny sat in silence for a time. Then he looked up and extended his hand to Jonathan. "Looks like we got a deal, Bubba. Now, we need to get busy. I hope you don't plan on gettin' any sleep for the next six months."

Jonathan shrugged. "I haven't had a good night's sleep for the past year anyway." He thought for a moment. "Back when I was building my business, I used to say I'd sleep when I was dead." He pointed at Sonny. "Now I've got a new motto. I'll sleep when Drakoff's dead."

"I suppose I can drink to that," said Sonny, raising his glass in a mock toast. "To my re-enlistment in the Cold War. It's nice to be back in on the action."

CHAPTER FOUR

One afternoon six weeks later, Jonathan stood at a pay phone on a narrow side street along the wharves in New Orleans. Across the street, a squat building in desperate need of paint housed a seedy bar that catered to sailors. Hand-painted across a broken Pearl Beer sign were the letters, R 'n' R, presumably the name of the establishment. Iron bars covered the windows. From the outside, the place looked deserted, but it didn't sound that way. Country music pulsed from the interior, and Jonathan had to cover one ear just to hear the dial tone on the receiver in his hand.

Maybe he hadn't made the best choice of phones; but he was here now, and it was the date and time he had arranged for his discussion. Besides, calling from here was a lot smarter than placing the call from his house. He wouldn't be leaving a trail that could lead back to him. From his pocket, he withdrew a matchbook from Antoine's, a stylish restaurant in the French Quarter. He dialed the number he'd written on the inside of the cover.

A man answered on the second ring. "Yes?"

"I'm the friend," Jonathan said.

He heard the voice on the other end draw in a breath. "Yes, we were looking forward to your call."

I'll bet you were, Jonathan thought. During the past three weeks, he had sent them five envelopes with no return address, each containing fifty $100 bills. Anybody would be curious by now. "You saw the note with the last letter?"

"We have made all the arrangements as you have stated."

"Good. See you there." Jonathan hung up the phone, and only then did he realize how hard his heart was pounding.

He opened the door of the booth to let in some fresh air and paused to listen to the dull twang of country music emanating from the R 'n' R across the street. Several blocks away stood the warehouse where he had fought Tchinkov. The remembrance made his blood pressure rise.

He wore a jogging suit. Always a runner, he had picked up the pace of his workouts considerably since making his decision to go to Afghanistan. Attached to the waistband of his pants was a Walkman, but he wasn't listening to music. The tape bore the title, *Advanced Russian Conversation,* and it was every bit as boring as the name sounded. Yet, he needed all the language practice he could get now, and his runs, which stretched from three miles to seven—sometimes ten—gave him a perfect opportunity to study.

He started walking toward his car, which he'd parked next to the front door of the R 'n' R. Just as his hand grasped the door handle, something—no, someone—careened out of the bar.

Jonathan quickly sized up the sailor. A huge man, more than six feet tall and probably weighing 250 pounds, shot toward Jonathan like a mortar shell. At an obvious size disadvantage, Jonathan wisely got out of the way.

As he watched the sailor land in a heap on the sidewalk, the bartender stood scowling in the doorway. "Get your sorry hide outta here, boy," he snarled, ignoring Jonathan. "And don't come back till you pay your bill!"

The drunken sailor gingerly picked himself back up and stood between Jonathan and his car, but Jonathan wasn't about to be intimidated by the situation. "Excuse me," he said, brushing his way past the man.

The smelly, bald-headed sailor, with a three-day growth of beard, stood there wobbling, trying to fix an eye on Jonathan. He mumbled something, and Jonathan turned around.

"What did you say?" Jonathan asked in a clear voice, now putting his hands on his hips.

"Hey, bud," said the bartender, for the first time seeming to notice Jonathan. "I wouldn't pick a fight with old Vasko there. He might be drunk, but he's—"

Jonathan wasn't listening. "What did you say?" he asked, but this time in Russian.

The sailor looked surprised, then he broke into a big grin. "I said," he slurred in Russian, jerking a thumb toward the bartender, "that this scum isn't fit to lick out the toilet bowl on a Soviet vessel."

"I see," Jonathan answered. "What's the problem?"

"What's he saying?" the bartender asked, stepping closer.

"Is there a problem?" Jonathan now asked him.

"Yeah," snarled the bartender, jerking a thumb at the sailor. "That lying cheat owes me sixteen dollars, and now he claims he doesn't know what I'm talking about."

With the words *"Nye behspocoytyes, ya oostroyoo vashi dielah*—Don't worry, I will settle your affairs," Jonathan reached for his wallet. Then, he paused. "I need to practice my Russian for a business trip," he told the sailor. "If I pay your tab, how about we go grab a few beers and chat?"

"What's he saying?" the bartender demanded again.

"That would be good," answered the sailor.

Jonathan handed the bartender a twenty, and told him to keep the change.

"Thanks, bud," said the bartender, obviously surprised. He pointed at Jonathan's clothes. "This ain't exactly the kind of neighborhood to go jogging in."

"Thanks for the tip," Jonathan told the bartender. He turned back toward the sailor. "I'm Bill Miller," he said, sticking out his hand.

"Bill Miller," the Russian repeated. "What about that beer you promised me?"

"Not a problem." Jonathan said in English. He looked at his watch and grimaced. "How bout I give you some money to keep your tab going tonight, and I'll buy you a beer another time soon?"

"Hmm?" asked Vasko in Russian, looking confused. "I don't speak much English. Just *thanks, where's the bar,* and *draft please!*" He broke into a loud guffaw, and Jonathan laughed too.

"Listen, Vasko," said Jonathan, switching back to Russian. "I've got to get to another appointment but I want to keep in touch." He pulled out a $100 bill. Vasko's eyes got big. "You keep that for yourself," said Jonathan. "But tell me where I can reach you if I need you."

Jonathan flew to Washington D.C. the next morning and took a taxi straight from Dulles to the Crown Bookstore on Montana Avenue. Arriving early for the 2:00 meeting, he sat in the park across the street, along with a few workers taking late lunches. He walked up and down the block, observing the passing crowd and checking to make sure no one followed him.

He didn't look like Jonathan Stuart of New Orleans anymore. Though he would normally have taken the fastest flight, he had chosen one with a stopover in Atlanta. He didn't want to run the risk of leaving Moisant, where he was likely to run into someone he knew, wearing a disguise. So, when he got to Hartsfield International in Atlanta, with an hour layover between planes, he had gone into a large restroom and occupied one of the stalls nearest the back wall.

Packed in his carry-on bag, he had a mirror, a quick-drying kit for dying his hair dark brown, a fake mustache of matching color, and a pair of glasses with clear, non-prescription lenses. He felt a little foolish—not to mention a little nervous—putting on the disguise. But after he had completed the transformation and had walked around the airport to try it out, he realized it wasn't really a big deal. Nobody paid any attention to him. Besides, there wasn't anything illegal about putting on a disguise. If he were questioned, he had an elaborate story prepared, all about a practical joke and a friend he was meeting. But Jonathan was sure he wouldn't be stopped.

After strolling around in front of the bookstore for a moment, he checked his watch and entered. In the birthday card section, Jonathan observed a handsome man with a Mid-eastern appearance in a navy business suit. He was looking at a card with a rainbow-striped balloon and a big red 3 on the front. Jonathan looked at him for a second, then said, "I bought that same card for my nephew."

The man glanced up at Jonathan, his dark eyes flashing, and he intently studied Jonathan's face before he said, "Did you find that it was appreciated?"

"Very much." Jonathan nodded his head.

The man looked back at the shelf and put the card away. Then, he glanced sideways at Jonathan and nodded almost imperceptibly.

Jonathan followed him out of the bookstore and down the street at a safe distance. Two minutes later, they were seated in a booth at the Old Country Deli, a block away. He had selected the locale because he'd remembered from a previous visit that its long narrow dining room had only high-backed booths, which made eavesdropping difficult. He had carefully chosen the time too. At two o'clock, most of the lunch crowd would have left, giving them a good chance of getting the right table, but the place would not be emptied out either.

After they had ordered sandwiches, the Afghan leaned toward Jonathan. "I am Rashid," he said, putting out his hand.

Jonathan shook it. "William Masters." In cleaning out some old files, Jonathan had found a pile of business cards collected over the years. In some cases, he'd completely forgotten the face that went with the card, and he was about to throw these away when an idea occurred to him. Jonathan didn't feel confident of his own ability to come up with convincing pseudonyms, or to keep track of his current pseudonym if he had to use several. But if he didn't remember the men whose names appeared on the cards, they probably didn't remember him either, and therefore their names—which sounded real because they *were* real—could serve him well over the course of his mission.

"Of course," said Rashid with a sly smile. "You have been so generous with us, Mr.—Masters. I feel we already know one another. If more Americans would help us in the substantial way in which you have, our brave men could drive out the Communists by the spring of next year. But tell me." He leaned closer and said in a confidential voice, "Unless I am mistaken, you are not one of our faith—not a Muslim. And so I am curious as to your interest in our struggle."

"It's simple enough." Jonathan looked Rashid in the eye. "We have the same enemy."

"I see," said Rashid, nodding his head. "Communism."

"No, you don't see. The Soviets."

"Ah." Rashid smiled. "The *Shuravi*, we call them."

"All right, the *Shuravi*," Jonathan answered with a thin smile. "That has a good ring to it. I think, Mr. Rashid, when it comes to hating the *Shuravi*, I may excel above any of your countrymen."

"Quite an astonishing claim," said Rashid, his eyes betraying nothing of what he thought or felt. "Do you care to explain your reasons? I would not imagine you have known many of them here in the United States—"

"I am not here to discuss myself," said Jonathan abruptly. "As for what I wish from you, we will get to that presently, but first I will explain what I am willing to provide you."

"Yes?" Rashid leaned forward.

"I read about you in the newspaper," Jonathan said with a thin smile. "In your press conference the other day—did you mean what you said about your greatest need?"

Rashid stared at him intently. "Perhaps you should be more specific."

"I think you know what I'm talking about," said Jonathan. "There was something you mentioned, and you said anyone who could obtain these things for you would be a hero to your people. I took that to mean if someone were willing to help you meet your objective, you would help him meet his. Am I correct?"

Rashid put up his hands. "But unless you have extraordinary pull—say, a couple of dozen key committee members in your pocket—I don't see how you can sway the Congress. Your government is forbidden by international law from providing us with these weapons . . . and so the war goes on, and more of my people die." He watched Jonathan's face, and seemed to hesitate. Then he added, "But that is not the concern of my particular organization anyway. We exist in order to channel funds from contributors such as yourself to help the civilian population of our country, with medical supplies, food, clothing . . . "

"Yes, of course," Jonathan nodded, easily seeing through the man's thinly veiled attempt to cover his tracks. "But supposing a friend of your country were able to arrange a shipment of . . . those items you need—I recall you used a figure of 'three or four' . . . do you suppose your mujahideen would ensure him safe passage into the country to deliver them personally?"

Rashid's black eyes gleamed, cold and direct. "Assuming those items could be obtained without our breaking the law or insulting the hospitality of your country, we would be foolish to refuse them. Arrangements could be made for a safe passage."

"And for a meeting with Massoud?" Massoud and Hekmatyar, as Jonathan had learned from his Afghan research, were the two main resistance leaders. They were both Muslims, both fighting a *jihad*—a holy war. But that was about as far as the similarity went. Hekmatyar, an Ayatollah Khomeini figure, was just as apt to turn his guns against fellow mujahideen as on the Soviets. Massoud, on the other hand, had a romantic image, and commanded respect among Westerners for his heroism and his relatively democratic style.

"Certainly," said Rashid, after a moment's pause. "That is outside my area of operation, but I have connections with Massoud, yes. And he is used to meeting with guests. You—or whoever you send—would not be the first."

Jonathan had barely touched his sandwich, but Rashid was already finished. He pulled out a package of Turkish cigarettes and raised his eyebrows quizzically. Jonathan waved a hand to indicate that he didn't mind if Rashid smoked. After watching him search his pocket for a lighter and come up empty-handed, Jonathan said "Here." He handed him the matches from Antoine's, on which he had written Rashid's phone number.

"Thank you," said Rashid, lighting up in a big cloud of blue-gray smoke.

"Mr. Rashid," Jonathan said, "I cannot guarantee the success of my plan. However"—he reached into the inner pocket of his jacket and took out an envelope—"I'm offering this as a further token of my good will."

Rashid took the envelope. "You are indeed generous, Mr. Masters," he said, feeling the weight of it. He narrowed his eyes. "Very, very generous."

Jonathan knew what the last sentence meant, and he headed off Rashid's suspicions. "I would imagine you have already invested the gifts you received earlier, and you will move quickly to invest the money in that envelope too," he said. *Investment,* of course, could mean anything from turning it over to an arms dealer to placing it in a Swiss bank account. As long as the money ultimately went toward the mujahideen war effort, Jonathan hardly cared. "And a government informer would also make the same assumption. If I were one of those, believe me, I would not turn over so much money to you, knowing I would probably never be able to get it back."

Rashid nodded his head, and looked satisfied. "Very well, then." He leaned a little closer. "Perhaps I can give you some useful direction in this matter of obtaining these items we are discussing."

"Oh?"

"Yes." Rashid took a puff on his cigarette, and Jonathan could tell he was trying to look nonchalant. *Or was he trying to look like someone who was trying to look nonchalant?* "There is a man named Luis Rodriguez," he began, "who operates from the city of Miami, Florida. You know him?"

Jonathan didn't think it would be wise to lie about this. He shook his head.

"I suspected not. Yes, well, there was a rumor that this Rodriguez received some stolen merchandise that was reported missing from a General Dynamics plant a few months ago. The stolen goods were some of the very items we need." He paused. "Actually, the story was that they wound up in Medellin, Colombia."

Jonathan raised his eyebrows. "Really?"

"Yes," said Rashid. "Specifically, in the hands of this Mr. Rodriguez's cousin—Hector Valdez."

"Hector Valdez," said Jonathan. *"The* Hector Valdez? The big Cartel boss?" Like anyone else who followed the news, Jonathan had heard of Hector Valdez. He'd seen the film clips of him leaving in triumph from a courtroom in Bogotá after winning his fight against extradition to the United States, and had heard stories about the murders of law-enforcement officers and rival drug lords.

Rashid nodded his head. "Rodriguez is one of Valdez's key suppliers. So, perhaps that might be a good place to look."

Jonathan laughed. "Yeah, maybe. I'm not much one for sticking my bare hand in a rattlesnake's hole."

"As you wish." Rashid reached into his pocket for a pen. "I can give you his phone number if you would like."

"Oh, you've spoken with him?"

Rashid shook his head. "No . . . We've never had the kind of money available to even begin speaking with him."

But Jonathan suspected another reason. This Rashid didn't seem like a fool to him. He didn't want to deal with the Medellin Cartel any more than anybody else did.

Seeing Rashid was looking for something to write on, Jonathan said, "Why don't you just write it on that matchbook?"

"Hmm?" Rashid looked at him a little absentmindedly.

"The matchbook I just gave you."

"Oh, of course." So Rashid wrote down the number just below his own. When he was done, he glanced briefly at the front of the matches before handing them back to Jonathan. "He operates publicly as a manufacturer's representative for Colombian textiles."

"Thanks for the information." Jonathan shifted uncomfortably and glanced toward the door. It was time to wrap this little rendezvous up. "Now you know what I want, and I know what you want. My next move is to find out if I can get you the . . . supplies you need. We need some way to communicate, and I'm not too crazy about the phone lines."

"Yes, of course," said Rashid, thinking. "Can you receive the *Washington Post* in . . . whatever place it is you live?"

"I suppose so."

"The personal advertisements, then," said Rashid. "You take out an ad, then you call me. The number you have is a special line. No one answers but me, or else my machine. You call and say what day the ad will run—nothing more, mind you, just the day—and I look for the ad."

"Which should be written in code, I assume," said Jonathan.

"Mr. Masters," Rashid said with a coy smile, "we in the East are quite adept at speaking in riddles."

Across the street from the Old Country Deli, two men sat on a park bench. One of them read a paper. The other stared off into space as though taking in what little sun there was on the fall afternoon. The sunbather yawned and stretched—a signal to another pair of men on the rooftop of the building facing the deli.

"There he goes," said the one reading the paper.

"Yep," said the other man. "Him and 'the friend.'"

The one reading the paper glanced across the street at the two men exiting the deli. "I can't understand why they put *us* on this. We don't know nothin'."

"Beats me," said the sunbather, who had returned to staring into space, seemingly oblivious to everything around him. "I just hope they're getting lots of pictures."

"I'm sure they saw the tip-off, Rusty," said the first man. "*We're* the ones who don't know what we're doing."

"Don't say that," said the sunbather, whose name was Rusty Wharton. "First week on the case, and I'm getting up to speed. If we give them what they want on this one, prove ourselves, who knows?"

"Yeah, who knows," the other man said. "Maybe they'll demote us even further."

Wharton glanced sideways at his partner and smiled to himself. "We've got to work on your attitude, Frazier. Okay," he said. "They're splitting up." He watched as Rashid and the mysterious stranger parted ways without shaking hands or making any acknowledgment that they even knew each other. "We'll have lots of artwork on this other bozo. Assuming he's one of the known dealers, we should have an ID in a couple of days."

The war on the other side of the world dragged on. The mujahideen scored their victories, but the Soviets—the hated *Shuravi*—always struck back, killing and maiming the villagers.

The invaders wielded other forms of destruction as well. Inside Kabul, one of the few Communist strongholds, the government and its sponsors from Moscow continually worked to solidify their police-state apparatus, arresting those suspected of anti-government sympathies—questioning, torturing, imprisoning, killing.

Within the past year, rumors had spread of a particularly vicious Soviet officer whose tactics made him remarkable even among his cohorts—quite an astounding claim. They said he loved to watch soldiers rape men's wives in front of them, then kill the children and the wives while the men watched. He had a fondness for blinding his victims, it was said, and he loved to prolong their tortures.

But those were all just rumors. No mujahid had ever been brought before him and lived to tell about it. Some doubted his existence. No one, not even a *Shuravi*, they said, could be so evil. He had become a mythic creature, like a vampire. And still the legend spread of this devil in human form, a man the people knew only as "the Butcher of Kabul."

CHAPTER FIVE

The FIM-92A Stinger missile, developed by General Dynamics in the early 1970s, replaced the old "Redeye" as the surface-to-air missile, or SAM, of choice for the U.S. military. Its infrared guidance system made it effective for destroying helicopters or low-altitude planes at a range of up to three miles. Its size, at five feet long and thirty-four pounds, made it a handy little powerhouse. On a modern battlefield, Stingers could decide the fight.

Jonathan found it ironic that Congress wouldn't authorize the sale of Stingers to the mujahideen, because the weapon seemed almost designed especially for the war against the Soviets. Not only did Stingers operate best at high altitudes and in cool climates, but nothing else could do as much to close the gap between the low-tech guerrilla force on the ground and the high-tech invaders in the air.

But the fact was, Congress had *not* authorized their sale, and even if it had, the federal government would take a dim view of Jonathan, a private citizen, negotiating this deal. Therefore his every move had to be very discreet.

Besides the government, he had this Rodriguez fellow to contend with. And Rodriguez, if Rashid was even vaguely telling the truth, had some pretty formidable connections down south. At a press conference a year before, President Reagan had denounced Hector Valdez specifically as a man who murdered two ways—by executing dozens of enemies with hit squads and by killing thousands of young Americans with his cocaine. And this was the guy Jonathan was dealing with—or at least, his arms supplier and, more importantly, his cousin.

Assuming Rodriguez was in tight with Valdez—and there was no reason to assume otherwise—Jonathan would have to offer him something better than money. Something untraceable, the kind of gift you give the man who has everything. Diamonds. And not just any kind of diamonds either, but rocks of an extremely high grade, designated J-internally flawless by jewelers.

Jonathan did a little research with various diamond brokers around the country, ascertaining what they might have available on short notice. To do so took awhile, but he and Sonny needed time, anyway, to plot out his strategy for dealing with Rodriguez.

Sonny had taken over the guestroom of Jonathan's house and stayed for days on end while they continued to form their game plan regarding Jonathan's Afghan mission. Jonathan had known they would have to spend a lot of hours together if they were going to be partners in this enterprise, but he had dreaded having his house invaded. As it turned out, though, he found he enjoyed having someone around all day. Since Frank Crosby and Mueller's people were now busy negotiating the sale of the company to Allied Health, he had turned over all day-to-day operations to his COO, and only went in to the office once or twice a week. As for a social life, he had none. His relationship with Kim had ended as quickly as it began. At times, he felt a little guilty for dropping her. She had been nothing but kind to him. But now his attentions focused on other things, and he didn't think about her often.

He spent his time planning, or more specifically, training. Sonny had greatly increased the pace of Jonathan's workouts, and every morning at 5:00, he would get up and pound on Jonathan's bedroom door. "Rise and shine, Bubba," he'd shout. "There's another great day out there waitin' on you, but you gotta go out there and get it." A moment's silence. "Good seven-mile run'll make the whole world seem bright."

As soon as Jonathan emerged, dressed in workout clothes, Sonny would go read the paper. By the time Jonathan had stretched, run, and come home and showered, Sonny would be dressed and cooking breakfast.

"If there's a great day out there waiting for me," said Jonathan one morning as he walked into the kitchen, rubbing a towel over his head to dry off from the shower, "how come *you* don't have to go out there and get yours too?"

"'Cause . . . I get my day delivered to me at my door."

Jonathan walked over to the stove, where Sonny stood. "Smells great," he said. "What is that—ham and eggs?"

"Yes, sir," said Sonny cheerfully as he stirred the eggs with a spatula. "Sorry I don't have no biscuits this morning."

"Oh, just the ham and eggs will be fine." Jonathan lifted the cover of the skillet where Sonny had two slices of ham simmering.

Sonny looked up at him and laughed. "Oh, no you don't. *Your* breakfast is ready." He nodded toward a plate on the counter with a bowl of wheat germ, an orange, and two slices of unbuttered wheat toast.

"Gee, thanks, Mom," said Jonathan as he took the plate and headed for the table.

"You'll thank me when you're walkin' twelve, fifteen miles a day over them mountains and not fallin' out," Sonny said. "Them Afghans are like mountain goats, lemme tell you. They ain't gonna wait on anybody who can't keep up, and there's no way in but over the mountains."

Jonathan, now sitting at the breakfast room table, laughed. "Rashid looked kinda pudgy to me."

"Yeah," said Sonny, looking up as he scraped the eggs with the spatula out of the skillet and onto a plate. "I doubt he's been within a thousand miles of there in five years. Probably a city boy from Kabul at that."

"I'll bet you're right." Jonathan began eating. "Well," he said between bites of food, "I guess we're just about ready for me to place my call to Rodriguez, huh?"

"Just about," said Sonny as he brought his plate over and sat down. "This may be the first and last piece of advice I give you, but are you really sure you want to keep going down this road? Have you thought about the fact that you might not make it out of this plan of yours alive?"

"Sure . . . I know that's a real possibility. But getting vengeance on Jennifer's and Jon's killer is worth the risk."

"I don't know, Bubba," Sonny drawled. "Doesn't the Bible say something like, 'Vengeance is mine; saith the Lord'?"

"Yeah, Jennifer mentioned something about that a couple of times. But, I guess what I'm hoping is that He'll let me wreak some vengeance for Him," Jonathan answered. "We know a crime has been committed, and justice is due. Doesn't God care about justice?"

"Maybe so, but there ain't nothin' you can do that is going to make it right," Sonny responded, eye-to-eye with Jonathan. "But like I told you a few weeks ago, this is your fight. My job is to make sure you don't do something stupid enough to get yourself killed. I've got a lot of paying-back to do to God for me not getting my own self killed a dozen times or more. If I can find a way to do the same for you, then that's my mission."

Jonathan didn't respond, but he thought Sonny was a deeper man than his rough exterior suggested. The more he got to know Sonny, the greater his appreciation grew.

Sonny broke the silence by changing the subject. "Now, about Rodriguez, I say we're just about ready, but not quite. Getting the wherewithal to pay him is only half the matter. Much more important is figuring out how to keep you out of a situation where he can take advantage of you."

"Hardball is hardball," said Jonathan, peeling the skin off the orange. "I've dealt with some pretty rough customers in my time. If there's anything I know how to do, it's negotiate."

Sonny chuckled. "I don't think you understand me," he said, cutting into a slice of ham. "By 'take advantage of you,' I don't mean he'll make you pay 10 percent more. I mean he might get you surrounded, kill you, and keep your diamonds *and* his Stingers. Understand?"

Jonathan nodded his head.

"One thing you're gonna need when you go to see him," said Sonny between bites, "is a sidekick—somebody to watch your back."

"You?" asked Jonathan.

Sonny held up his hands. "Uh-uh, no way, not me. Like I said, I'm strictly your behind-the-scenes man. No, I'm talking about some professional assistance. I've been working on lining up a couple of boys for you, and I've got two picked out—both of 'em speak Spanish, by the way—but they're both . . . uh, busy for the next few weeks." He said it with a twinkle in his eye.

"Let me guess," answered Jonathan, laughing. He tried to think of some international hot spots where the services of an all-purpose fighting man might be required. "Nicaragua? Angola? Beirut?"

Sonny shook his head. "I don't know, but you need somebody who can go with you into this situation and watch your back—but won't go blabbin' to the FBI or whoever."

"Hmm," said Jonathan, then he smiled. "I think I've got someone who might fit the bill."

By the time Jonathan called Rodriguez, six weeks had passed since his meeting with Rashid. He found a new pay phone and dialed the number from a pay phone. Someone answered on the third ring.

"Hello, I am attempting to reach Mr. Rodriguez," Jonathan said.

"Mr. Rodriguez is not available at this time," the voice said, and offered no further details.

"Hmm," Jonathan replied. He had accented his voice slightly, and he was talking very properly, the way a foreigner would. "This is highly unfortunate. Please tell him I am calling on the recommendation of a Mr. Hernando Cruz."

That detail was thanks to Sonny, the master of research and contacts. Cruz, a small-time mercenary with whom Sonny had been acquainted, had worked for Rodriguez until his unfortunate demise in the crash of a twin-engine aircraft over the Everglades a few years earlier.

"Hold on," said the voice now. "I'll see if I can find out when he'll be back."

"Thank you." Jonathan waited for Rodriguez, hoping he'd respond quickly to the name of his deceased crony.

"Yeah?" another voice barked into the phone.

"Mr. Rodriguez, my name is Andres Boltar, and your friend Hernando Cruz recommended that I call you."

"Oh yeah?" Rodriguez asked. "You must have me mixed up with someone else, my friend—I never knew any Hernando Cruz."

"Then why do you say, 'never knew'?" Jonathan asked. "You speak of him as though he were deceased, which he is. He once told me how helpful you'd been to him at Little Green Bay, and said you were a man to count on."

"Who are you?" Rodriguez demanded. "And what do you want?"

"I'll get to that shortly," Jonathan said. "I called you because I'm looking for some equipment, and Hernando had indicated to me that you were the man to talk to."

"What equipment?" asked Rodriguez irritably. "All I got's textiles."

"Of course. However, Hernando said you have occasionally helped clients who want to purchase and export more advanced manufacturing equipment than is available in their home areas. I have a client who is looking for . . . some rather hard-to-find items. Perhaps if I could have an opportunity to bring my client to you and let him tell you what he has to offer in return for your services?"

Rodriguez was silent for a long time—so long Jonathan wondered if he had hung up the phone. Finally he said, "Now who are these friends of yours?"

"I should not like to say too much more at present," Jonathan answered. "But my client oversees a small cottage textile operation in northeastern Africa."

"Northeastern Africa? You mean like the Middle East?"

Jonathan chuckled coyly. "As I said, I do not wish to divulge many details. The only important thing now is that my client needs the proper equipment, and he realizes that it does not come cheaply."

The reference to money seemed to soften Rodriguez. "Tell me more."

"Well, Mr. Rodriguez, as we say in Arabic, '*Nye behspocoytyes, ya oostroyoo vashi dielah.*' Do you catch my meaning?"

"What is that?" asked Rodriguez, sounding irritable again. "Speak English or Spanish—I ain't got much time."

Good, Jonathan thought, but he tested his theory twice more, once with a bawdy saying, and each time the Colombian demanded that he quit speaking gibberish.

This satisfied him that Rodriguez didn't know anything about either Russian or Arabic, and that was exactly what he had hoped.

Jonathan had known the sailor named Vasko would come in handy at some point and, after calling Rodriguez, he drove out to the wharf to find him. He located the sailor in a dive identical to the R 'n' R, and after buying him the beer he had promised, he presented him with a proposition. "Vasko," he said, "how would you like to make $5,000?"

"Five thousand dollars!" the Russian bellowed, which was okay because no one in the bar except for Jonathan could understand what he was saying. "That will buy a lot of beer! Where you get all this money?"

"Oh, I just have a little extra cash stashed away for when I need it," Jonathan said, a little amused. "But you must work for the money this time. The work is easy—you just need to help me with a little practical joke. Here's what I'm prepared to offer you. $2,500 in cash up front, plus a trip to Miami, along with expenses while we're there. Hey—I'll even buy you a couple drinks once we get done with our business." Vasko raised his bushy eyebrows. "And in return, here's what I want you to do . . . "

Three days later, after going through a heavy search, Jonathan and Vasko sat across from Rodriguez in a back room at the Los Caballeros Café in Miami. Jonathan, under the alias of Andres Boltar, wore his get-up from the meeting with the Afghan in Washington. He dressed in a summer suit, which was out of season for early December, but helped him seem more like a foreigner—a little out of step with the current fashion.

Beside him sat "Colonel Fatah," a big burly Arab who didn't speak a word of English, or Spanish, for that matter.

Vasko, a.k.a. Colonel Fatah, looked terrific in his burnoose, and his years at sea had given him the swarthy appearance of a desert nomad, the image aided by a scruffy two-week-old beard. Every viable cell in his alcohol-damaged brain seemed to have been marshaled to the task of playing his part, and he gave what was probably the performance of his life.

Rodriguez was an oily-looking creature with jet-black hair and an unkempt mustache. He wore a well-tailored suit but looked skinny in it, and Jonathan figured his Colombian colleagues must be paying him partly in cocaine.

"Of course you will understand, Mr. Rodriguez," Jonathan said in his mildly accented English, "that we are not at liberty to divulge the name of Colonel Fatah's organization, but I don't imagine that is your concern in any case, yes?" He laughed.

Rodriguez wasn't smiling. "So where do you fit in?"

"I am only a broker," Jonathan said, trying to appear modest.

"Bull." Rodriguez glanced up at one of his thugs standing behind Jonathan.

Jonathan just smiled at Rodriguez. From the moment he first made contact with Rodriguez until now, he hadn't allowed himself to get scared, because he knew fear would be his undoing. He had to stay cool. And besides, this Rodriguez looked like a wimp. A pushover. When you could see a man's motivations—in this case, coke and money for flashy cars and suits and the other junk that went with the lifestyle— it was easy to know how to manipulate him. A dangerous man was one who didn't want anything. Or didn't want anything Jonathan could provide.

Rodriguez seemed to draw strength from his henchmen, and he sneered at Jonathan. "So what does the towel-head want?"

Vasko, seeing Rodriguez pointing at him, grunted in inquiry.

Jonathan looked blankly back at Rodriguez. "If you knew who this was, you would not show such disrespect."

Rodriguez glanced around with a snarl, like a kid who had been yelled at by the teacher and was trying to recover his self-respect. Then, he straightened in his seat. "Okay," he said, enunciating his every syllable. "Please tell me what I can do for you gentlemen—that is, assuming I can do anything at all."

Jonathan turned to Vasko and said, in Russian, "He wants to know how you like the weather in Miami." After Fatah replied that he found it unbearably hot, but he didn't mind going anywhere if he could make $5,000 just for wearing a silly costume, Jonathan said to Rodriguez, "The Colonel says he would like to acquire four Stinger missiles to further the people's war in his country."

Rodriguez cocked his head to one side and sniffed. "And what country is that?"

Jonathan turned to Vasko and in Russian said, "This guy doesn't have any manners. He says you look fat and lazy." Fatah clenched his fists and cursed at Rodriguez. Jonathan turned back to the Colombian. "Now you've made him angry. He says that's not important—do you want to make a lot of money or not?"

"Depends on what you're offering," Rodriguez answered.

"I misunderstood him," Jonathan explained to Vasko. "He apologizes and says now that Russians are the toughest turkeys there are." Now Colonel Fatah took a more reasonable tone, though with suspicion in his voice.

71

"He would be willing to pay you one million dollars in flawless diamonds," Jonathan translated for Rodriguez, "which could be assessed by an appraiser of your choosing."

A long moment of silence followed, and Jonathan could see Rodriguez running the math in his head. He guessed the other man was figuring his markup, then adding to it, trying to come up with a number that wouldn't be so high as to scare off Boltar and the colonel, but one that would leave a ton of money on the table.

Rodriguez leaned forward and opened his mouth to speak.

But it was Vasko who, caught up in his act like a child performing for adults, spoke first. "Hey, when do we get to have that drink you promised me?" he said to Jonathan in Russian.

Jonathan thought fast. "Oh, Señor Rodriguez," he added, smiling, "Colonel Fatah has just improved on his already generous offer. He has just said he will make an extra $100,000 in either cash or diamonds available to you as a finder's fee."

"Hmm." Rodriguez sat back in his chair. "Like I said, all I have access to is textile equipment." He shrugged. "What other people do, that's none of my business. But I'll tell you this—even if I do find somebody who deals in the kind of specialized materials you need, they may want another $100,000. For one thing, Stingers come three to a crate, so to get four, they'd have to take one out of a second crate, which would increase the cost per piece." He put up his hands and smiled. "At least that's what people who know about such things tell me."

"So you are saying 1.2 million dollars for four Stingers?"

Rodriguez nodded his head slowly.

Jonathan said to Vasko, "Listen. In about a minute we're going to get out of here, and then you won't have to wear that stupid costume anymore. We'll have a drink at the airport bar." The Russian nodded and said he was looking forward to that.

"What's he saying?" The Colombian sounded just a little eager.

"He says his organization is able to meet your price," Jonathan replied, careful to keep his face neutral.

Rodriguez, who had leaned forward again in excitement, seemed to catch himself again. He sat back and said coolly, "Yeah, well, this is all assuming the things are even available. You're talking about something way out of my line."

"I'm sure," said Jonathan. He glanced at Colonel Fatah, who looked a little restless, then turned back to Rodriguez. "I will call you a week from today and check with you. Is that satisfactory?"

Rodriguez shrugged. "Call me whenever you want."

"And the colonel has authorized me to act on his behalf from here on," Jonathan said, "so you probably won't be seeing him again. Is that satisfactory as well?"

"Long as I get my money," said Rodriguez, sniffing.

The federal government knew a great deal about Luis Rodriguez, and they regularly monitored his meetings. Two special agents, under the assumed identities of Cuban-American drifters, lived in a ratty apartment building across the street from the Los Caballeros. The two conducted round-the-clock surveillance of the café and coordinated with another team running wiretaps on Rodriguez's home.

This particular Saturday evening, the wiretap team recorded a very interesting conversation between Rodriguez and his cousin, the well-known Medellin kingpin Hector Valdez. After translating it first from the Spanish, and then from an elaborate code used for secure communication between the two, they gathered that Rodriguez had located an Arab who wanted to buy four Stingers—*lollipops* in their code—for one million dollars. Initially, Valdez scorned the idea of dealing with what he called a "camel driver," but when Rodriguez told him the Arab had offered to pay in diamonds, Valdez sounded more interested.

Still speaking in code, Rodriguez had laid out his plan. They would lure the Arab down to Colombia, take his diamonds, and kill him. Then, they'd put a key in the man's pocket for a locker in the Bogotá airport with a kilo or two of cocaine in it and leave the body for police to find. That way, according to Rodriguez, their friends in the police force could get credit from the Yankees for busting another drug kingpin, even if it was an Arab and not an American, while Valdez got to keep his missiles as well as the diamonds.

Valdez asked Rodriguez how *he* expected to profit from the deal, and Rodriguez replied that he just wanted to make up for some bad blood in the past, and he would be happy with whatever Valdez felt he deserved from the deal. Then, Valdez suggested that if the camel driver seemed so eager to buy the Stingers, he would probably go a lot higher. Therefore Rodriguez should send back word that the price had gone up to $2 million, of which Rodriguez would get to keep 10 percent.

A week later, the team monitoring the wiretap heard another conversation about the Stingers, this one between Rodriguez and "the Arab." They tried to get a trace, but the call was too brief. However, they learned Rodriguez was taking $200,000 from the Arab on top of the $200,000 he was getting from his cousin. Apparently they agreed to meet and have an appraiser of Rodriguez's choice assess the rocks. The meeting would take place in Bogotá at the beginning of January.

They relayed this information to different agencies, including the CIA, where a rookie field agent named Rusty Wharton and his sidekick, Frazier Hollis, had been following a certain Amal Rashid, a small-time agent of the Afghan resistance who had stated publicly that he was in the market for Stinger missiles.

When Wharton got the lead on Rodriguez, he was excited. From wiretaps made before he was assigned to the case, he had known Rashid had talked to Rodriguez about Stingers—a purchase that had never gone through. Wharton had faithfully monitored all of Rashid's meetings in the month since he took on the assignment, but so far his surveillance had yielded nothing. As for the character he and Hollis had observed leaving the deli with Rashid in Washington, they had never been able to place a positive ID on him. Apparently, he wasn't part of any known circuit of arms smugglers, and the lead had gone dormant. But then, Wharton saw the photos of the "Arab" in Miami. He didn't recognize the man in the burnoose. But the one with him. The one in the business suit . . .

"It's the same guy from the Old Country Deli," he announced to McGinnis, his section chief.

"Hmm." McGinnis sat back in his desk and studied the photos. McGinnis wasn't much older than Wharton, but his potbelly and balding head made him look older by ten years. "Yeah, I'd say you're right."

"So what's next?" asked Wharton. "What do we do now?"

McGinnis said he would review the information from the agents in Miami and get back to him.

The next day, Wharton met again with McGinnis, who told him, "I think the thing to do now is wait."

"What do you mean?" asked Wharton.

"Well, you heard what the boys in Miami said," the chief told him. "I don't think your Arab is going to be coming back alive from Colombia."

"Still," said Wharton. "Shouldn't we have somebody down in Bogotá to monitor the deal?"

"Oh, we will," said McGinnis. "Don't worry about that."

Rashid's system worked quite well. All Jonathan had to do was call Rashid's number and say "Twelve twenty-nine," meaning the ad would appear on December 29.

The advertisement itself would be meaningless to anyone else, but crystal-clear to Rashid.

Ray, I found a great sale. Going south to do some shopping. Will be in touch. Meanwhile, you work on the vacation plans.

—Bill

As for the trip down south, Jonathan and Sonny had known Rodriguez would want to lure him onto his turf to do the deal, but Sonny still didn't liked the idea. "I just hope you know what you're doin', Bubba," he said again and again. They had argued over the plan, with Sonny insisting Jonathan try to get Rodriguez to agree to a stateside exchange. But he had to admit that would never happen, if for no other reason, because the Stingers were in Colombia. So Jonathan would have to go into "the rattlesnake's den," as Sonny called it.

But at least he wouldn't go alone. Sonny's two contacts—the ones he had mentioned before—were available for the trip. Both Phil Neeley and his buddy Jose Gonzales were fluent in Spanish, and both were Force Recon veterans who'd each done two Vietnam tours. Both had been discharged from active duty for overzealous behavior. Gonzales had punched out an officer and Neeley, as an instructor at Force Recon school, had hazed a trainee whose father happened to be an attorney. Rather than go through a lengthy lawsuit, the Corps had sent him back to Lanett, Alabama. Both men had bummed around in recent years, mostly doing odd jobs and getting into trouble. Neeley had raced dirt-track cars, so Sonny designated him as their driver.

Jonathan asked Sonny to find an armor-plated Cadillac, and he located a three-year-old white Fleetwood—complete with armor plating and bulletproof glass—in Caracas. The vehicle wouldn't withstand heavy arms fire but, as Sonny said, the Colombians might get suspicious if he showed up in a tank. Hopefully the Cartel boys would only bring small arms to the meeting. Jonathan didn't even want to know what kind of subterfuge Sonny had gone through to locate such an object. All he did was write the check.

Neeley and Gonzales would fly into Caracas with Sonny a week before Jonathan arrived in Bogotá. They were to pick up the car and rent out a garage space, where they'd spend a couple of days installing additional goodies on the Cadillac. Then, they were to drive to Bogotá, a journey in itself. They were likely to run into bandits on the road, although their armored car offered some security.

Once they arrived in Bogotá, they would rent a villa on the city's fashionable north side, one with an enclosed garage in which to store the vehicle. Though they wouldn't be there for even a week, they would give three months' rent in cash to a landlord too pleased to ask any questions.

The actual mission itself would present all kinds of other obstacles, many of which could be fatal. Through Sonny, Jonathan had paid the men $50,000 each in advance, and would give them another $50,000 upon a successful conclusion of the mission.

This was a costly undertaking, no doubt about it. But with the sale of the company, Jonathan had made a number of large deposits in overseas bank accounts, far from the curious eyes of the federal government. When Rodriguez had upped the cost of the Stingers, it hadn't caught Jonathan by surprise. After all, this was the ultimate seller's market. And he had purposely waited for a final price tag before arranging to buy the gems. Even split among five different purchases from brokers all over the country, they still must have seemed like a lot of diamonds to the men who sold them. But for that kind of money, nobody asked questions.

The beautiful stones glittered together in a simple little bag, which Jonathan hid away in the lining of his carry-on. He wasn't too worried about them being discovered. Customs officials in Colombia wouldn't expect anyone to smuggle something like that *into* the country. Yet, it seemed a shame to turn them over to the likes of Rodriguez and his cousin.

Just before he left town, Jonathan found a response to his personal ad in the *Washington Post.*

> *Bill:*
> *Our friend: 1383 Mangrove, Kar. Call before you go; then I'll call him.*
>
> *—Ray*

It took Jonathan awhile, but he discerned that *Kar.* must be Karachi, Pakistan, a likely point of entry for anyone going into Afghanistan. He was able to obtain a Karachi street map on special order from a New York City map store. On it, he found Mangrove Road in the center of town.

Now he knew where to ship the Stingers when he got them. He had only to travel to one of the most hostile places on earth, right smack in the middle of drug dealers' turf, and come out alive—*with* the Stingers.

Andres Boltar reserved a flight to Bogotá on January 4. But if anyone happened to be waiting for him in the airport, they were in for a disappointment.

George Watt, on the other hand, arrived two days earlier. Watt, a Canadian citizen with light brown hair, sideburns, and brown eyes, was largely the creation of Jonathan, who made good use of his increasing practice with disguises, including the addition of brown contact lenses and a minor but noticeable accent. But Watt also owed a great deal of his existence to Sonny, who, with $5,000 of Jonathan's money, had arranged the phony passport.

For the flight to Colombia, Jonathan brought a briefcase filled with reading material on Colombia, culture, geography, politics, language, and the like. Before digging into his homework, he habitually pulled out another thin book he had carried with him wherever he had gone since Jennifer's death.

The leather binding was still new and uncreased, and the pages unmarred. The cover still carried the name of its original owner stamped in gold leaf—*Jennifer Revier Stuart*.

A few weeks after the shootdown of KAL 007, Jonathan received a letter from Korean Air Lines. Apparently, an item belonging to Jennifer Stuart had been recovered from the airport in Anchorage, Alaska. As next of kin, Jonathan was asked to confirm that the Bible they had found was, indeed, his wife's. For some unknown reason, Jennifer must have left the Bible behind at the gate before re-boarding the plane. Jonathan had been stunned to recover what was, by Jennifer's admission, the most important gift he had ever given her. By carrying it with him, he felt a strange, bittersweet connection with her.

Once his plane took off and settled into its cruising speed and altitude, Jonathan flipped on the overhead light and fanned through the pages of Jennifer's Bible.

For a fleeting moment, Jonathan considered praying and asking God to help him get out of Colombia alive. But was that right? Wouldn't it be like the no-atheists-in-foxholes routine where soldiers promise to stop cheating on their wives if God will save them from the artillery raining down upon them? Jonathan was going to Colombia for the express purpose of buying illegal military hardware, which would allow him to act out his vengeance. This trip was just the first necessary step to fulfill his plan to find—and kill—Drakoff. *There's no way I am going to ask God to keep me from getting killed so I can kill somebody else,* he thought.

For the first time in the weeks since putting his operation into motion, Jonathan's conscience pricked him. *Why do I feel guilty?* he wondered. *This hasn't bothered me before.* Then he realized he was allowing a new variable into his air-tight equation. God.

How dumb can I be? he wondered. *Bringing God into things only makes everyone start feeling guilty. I don't need the guilt—and I don't need a crutch.*

The pinging of the plane's intercom snapped him back to the here-and-now. The captain turned the seatbelt sign on and asked everyone to buckle up as the plane entered a stretch of turbulent air. Jonathan closed Jennifer's Bible, put his tray table up, and buckled his seatbelt. The increasing bumps and jolts of the plane mirrored the activity going on in his mind. He hadn't been this introspective for a long time. And he wasn't sure he was happy with the direction his thoughts had taken.

For lighter fare, he picked up the travel book on Colombia he had brought and buried himself in it while the plane rocked and rolled. It offered all sorts of useful advice. Such as:

While enjoying the country's physical beauty and its wonderful people, behave as though on a battlefield—alert, cautious, and ready to fend off any kind of attack. Bandit gangs terrorize the country and seem to have an affinity for vulnerable tourists. The local authorities often collaborate with the bandits and, when they do not, are either unable or unwilling to help luckless tourists. Before deciding to visit Colombia, take this state of affairs into account. Just the same, throngs of visitors have reached, seen, and enjoyed Colombia—and returned home unscathed.

He hardly found this information comforting. Maybe God really was trying to tell him something. Maybe he ought to ask for help.

As the plane smoothed out and the *Fasten Seat Belts* sign illuminated, Jonathan let the paperback drop to his lap, and he fell asleep. He didn't wake up until the announcement came on for the passengers to extinguish all smoking devices and return seat backs to an upright position.

The Bogotá airport seemed almost deserted. At first he wondered if something was wrong. He and the other passengers waited for a long time while the customs agents went through their things one by one. Though the wait seemed tedious, it had the advantage of making him less nervous when it came his time to undergo scrutiny.

"Name?" the customs official demanded, bending down and looking up at Jonathan as though inspecting his nostrils for contraband.

"George Watt."

The official, who wore a blue police-like uniform, laboriously wrote this down in longhand in a notebook by his side. He looked at the passport, decorated with a maple leaf. "Canada?" he asked.

"That's right."

Again the same scrutiny, as though he could read Jonathan's mind by somehow looking through him. "Why you here?" he asked.

"On business."

The customs official looked at him blankly.

"I sell large industrial equipment," Jonathan said, trying to sound as uninteresting as possible. He reached for his carry-on bag, where he had stowed away a manual from a manufacturer, but the official put up a hand.

Scrutinizing him one more time, the Colombian jerked his head to signal his permission for Jonathan to move on. As he picked up his things and headed toward the door—naturally, he hadn't checked a bag—Jonathan felt like the man's eyes were boring into his back.

The streets were still wet from a passing rain shower, and the temperature felt a touch on the cool side beyond the sliding door. Even so, Jonathan was sweating profusely when he left the airport. He kept his eyes on the pavement, dodging puddles.

Only a few people stood on the sidewalks, and fewer cabs waited out front. In fact, the outside appeared to be as deserted as the interior of the airport, and the whole area had an oppressive atmosphere. Evidently, this was a place where people feared to walk around in the open.

In light of the empty sidewalk, Jonathan saw no reason why anyone should bump into him, but a man did. Hard. And he mumbled an apology in English as he went on by.

Fortunately Jonathan had the presence of mind to grab the man by the elbow. The Colombian turned back, eyes flashing anger, almost hatred, at Jonathan. With his other hand, Jonathan felt the place where his wallet should have been. Of course it was gone. *Stupid,* he thought. *From now on, all valuables go in the front pocket.*

"My wallet," Jonathan said, feeling a little unnerved. The last thing he needed right now was a scene.

"Mm?" said the man, trying to look confused. *"No habla Englis."*

Just then a clean-looking bright yellow taxi pulled up, and the driver said, "You need some help, *Señor?*"

For a split second, Jonathan wondered if the two men had some kind of dual scam going. But the one who had taken his wallet—who he now realized was just a boy no older than seventeen—handed it back and walked away at a quick clip.

"Come," the cab driver said, reaching over and opening the door. "You get in. I take you to hotel."

Jonathan stood there for a second, contemplating the situation. Suppose Rodriguez had planned something like this as a trap? What if he got half a mile down the road and then the driver turned down some byway and pulled out a sawed-off shotgun? But he convinced himself he was just on edge. Rodriguez and company would be expecting Andres Boltar, not George Watt. And on January 4, not January 2. Besides, after the unnerving experiences of the last few minutes, the sight of the cab driver had been a relief. So he got in.

They drove for a few minutes in silence, then the man said in a grave tone, "When you in Bogotá, you watch out. Is dangerous city."

"Thanks," said Jonathan. "I've heard that before."

Just for the sake of caution, he got the driver to let him out a few blocks from his destination. The man demanded a fare that seemed to be about twice as much as it should be, but Jonathan didn't want to quibble, so he paid it. From there he walked on to the San Diego Hotel on Carrera 13, where he would find Jose Gonzales waiting in the lobby.

CHAPTER SIX

Jonathan quickly sized up Neeley and Gonzales and decided Sonny had chosen well. They were competent, no-nonsense ex-Marines with plenty of experience and, from what he could tell, plenty of enthusiasm about the opportunity he had given them. The two were also strangely likable—the sunny, slightly smart-alecky Gonzales and the brooding, intense Neeley, who reminded Jonathan a little bit of himself.

Promptly at 10:00 A.M. on the appointed morning, Jonathan—now once again assuming the role of Boltar—called the number Rodriguez had given him.

"So you arrived safely, Mr. Boltar?" Rodriguez asked.

Jonathan couldn't tell if he heard disappointment in the other man's voice or not.

"Certainly," he said. "Why shouldn't I? But let's not waste time making small talk, Mr. Rodriguez."

"Fine. You need to pick up the appraiser at—"

"No, *I'll* tell you where we will pick up the appraiser." Jonathan wasn't about to have Rodriguez choose the spot. "Have him waiting at the corner of Carrera 7 and Calle 11, just across the street from the Supreme Court—or Palacio de la Justicia as you call it—in twenty minutes."

"Fine. But I want to hear back from him by noon."

"You will." Jonathan hung up the phone, then said to Gonzales, "All set. Just keep your eyes open."

While Jonathan and Neeley waited at the villa, Gonzales picked up the appraiser. He checked the man's bag. Satisfied that it contained only ordinary gemologist's instruments, he then draped a hood over the jeweler's head and instructed him to lie down in the back seat until told otherwise. They drove around town for half an hour, cutting through back alleys and side streets. Finally confident that he wasn't being followed, Gonzales returned to the villa.

As soon as the jeweler had been led to a small basement room, the hood was removed. Jonathan brought out a briefcase, popped it open, extracted two small pouches, and set them before the man to determine their value. After less than an hour of analysis, the jeweler said something in Spanish to Gonzales, and Gonzales turned to Jonathan. "He says he's finished."

"Ask him what value he determined."

After an exchange of words, Gonzales said, "He says he reports only to Hector Valdez."

"Tell him," said Jonathan through gritted teeth, "if he doesn't cooperate, he's gonna wind up fertilizing Valdez's cocaine crop."

They exchanged a few more words in Spanish before Gonzales turned back to Jonathan. "It's worth $2.2 million, he says—worth every penny."

"Good." Jonathan smiled and nodded at the appraiser. *"Gracias."*

At exactly 12:00 noon, the appraiser called Rodriguez and reported that the gems looked fine to him. Rodriguez told him where they could meet at 12:30, but when the jeweler relayed this information to Gonzales, Jonathan shook his head. He called Rodriguez back.

"We meet in the same spot, Rodriguez," he said.

"Okay, man, okay," said the Colombian. "I didn't know you had such an attitude. Okay, we'll see you there."

Neeley handcuffed the briefcase containing the diamonds to the jeweler's wrist to make it more difficult for anyone to run off with the $2.2 million. Gonzales then replaced the hood on the jeweler and helped him into the back seat of the Caddy. Neeley slid into the driver's seat while Gonzales and Jonathan got into the back on either side of the appraiser.

As they drove back to the original rendezvous point, Neeley followed a zigzagging path of streets. They threaded back and forth over Carrera 7, which led them southward to the Palacio de la Justicia. Two blocks from the rendezvous, Gonzales removed the jeweler's hood. As they neared the intersection, the man pointed out a Mercedes 500 SEL. As they pulled up next to it, they saw Rodriguez in the back seat with one man driving and another riding shotgun. Rodriguez took one look at the four of them, then signaled stiffly for them to follow him.

The two cars careened along another crazy path through the streets of Bogotá, the white Cadillac on the heels of the red Mercedes. First they headed northwest, traveling eight blocks and then turned right on Avenida 15 past fashionable stores and shops.

Neeley looked at Jonathan in the rear view mirror. "We're being followed by cops."

Jonathan raised his eyebrows. "You sure?"

Neeley nodded his head. "They've been behind us for several blocks, and now they've turned onto this street."

"Okay," said Jonathan, trying to think fast. "Just keep driving. Let's see how this plays out." He looked back at Gonzales. "Ask that guy if he knows what's going on."

Gonzales turned to the jeweler. *"Que sabes de ese asunto?"*

The appraiser, obviously frightened, said something in a protesting tone.

"He claims he doesn't know what's going on," said Gonzales to Jonathan with a smirk.

After a couple more turns, they emerged onto Avenida Jimenez de Quesada and traveled west toward the industrial sector. They rode for several more blocks, passing out of the western part of town and into a region of deserted factories.

"Now there's another *federale*," said Neeley, "and the first one is speeding up." At those words, the first police car pulled around, passed the Caddy, and worked itself between the car and the Mercedes in front of it. The policeman in it turned on his siren and his lights, and then the one behind did the same. All of a sudden they were slowing down, and they came to a stop in front of an abandoned factory.

For a moment the only sound was that of their engines. Suddenly, Rodriguez's car peeled off, and the men in the Cadillac found themselves sandwiched between two police cars.

All four men sat motionless in the Cadillac as two police officers, one from each car, approached them. Both officers kept their right hands on their holstered revolvers.

Pulling open a panel in the door beside him, Jonathan said to his two assistants, "I think it's time we go for plan B."

The other two men nodded their heads.

Just as the cops were abreast of the car, Jonathan lowered the window, and almost in the same motion, lifted an Uzi out of the hollow door compartment and fired it into the air. Bullets sprayed everywhere. One round, ricocheting off the metal roof of the factory, careened into a traffic sign a few feet from the police car.

The two policemen hit the dirt, scrambling for the nearest cover. At the same moment, Gonzales, who had his own Uzi stashed in a compartment just like Jonathan's, opened the rear door, jumped out, and blasted the front tires of the rear vehicle and the rear tires of the front vehicle. Laughing and whooping, he jumped back into the car, continuing to fire into the air as he did. Now Neeley let out a whoop, too, and pulled away from the curb, tires squealing.

As a final farewell, Jonathan popped two smoke grenades out the window.

Down the road, Jonathan kept looking out the back window, waiting to see the dreaded police lights behind him. But he had a growing suspicion that the two officers had been acting on their own—or rather, on Rodriguez's behalf. There was still at least some kind of law around here, and if they had been on real police business, they would have requested backup immediately. Gonzales listened closely to the scanner he had installed on the Cadillac, but no one seemed to be saying anything about them. Jonathan felt certain he had guessed right.

Knowing they didn't need to speed, but wanting to avoid any possible sentries Rodriguez might have posted, Neeley took extra care as he drove them toward the villa. Meanwhile, Gonzales had blindfolded the frightened jeweler again. Once they had gotten safely inside the garage, Jonathan ordered him to take the man into the house, remove the briefcase, and handcuff him to a bed, then tape his ankles together with duct tape.

Jonathan got on the phone and dialed the number he had used earlier for Rodriguez. But when an unfamiliar voice answered, he hung up.

He cursed and checked his watch.

Fifteen minutes later, he tried again. Still no luck.

He tried again after another fifteen minutes, again with the same results. Meanwhile Neeley sat near a window of the villa, watching for any unwanted visitors.

After an hour of trying, Jonathan finally reached Rodriguez.

"Mr. Rodriguez," he demanded, even more irritated now because of his trouble in getting through, "what are you trying to pull—sending the police like that?"

"You're asking me?" Rodriguez demanded, sounding not at all surprised to hear Boltar's voice. He must have heard from his friends the *federales*. "Looks like to me *I* was the one who got set up, and I was just lucky my driver could get me out of there in time."

"We all know full well who had the police in on this," snapped Jonathan. "For that matter, I'm not even certain they *were* the police."

Rodriguez seemed to back down just a little bit. "Maybe it was just a mistake, man," he said. "Maybe a traffic check or something, I don't know. Look, we'll just set up the same exchange for tomorrow, same time, same place. That cool?"

Jonathan didn't say anything for a few seconds. "Rodriguez, you are pushing your luck," he said finally. "This time we will follow a different plan, because right now you have completely lost my trust, and it will take a lot for you to regain it."

"What different plan?"

Jonathan had come up with it while trying to reach Rodriguez. "We'll rendezvous at the same place. You wait for us on the street corner, but instead of following your vehicle, we will pick you up, and you will get into our car after we have made absolutely certain that you are not under surveillance."

Rodriguez was incredulous. "Into *your* car? You must be out of your mind, Man! What? Do I look like I want to commit suicide?"

"You and you alone," Jonathan went on. "It's your town. We're just guests here."

"No way!"

"Then forget about the diamonds."

"Okay, okay . . . "

Confident Rodriguez's greed had given him the upper hand, Jonathan went on. "You will then direct us to a rendezvous point away from the center of town—but not more than ten kilometers outside the city limits, understand?"

"Yeah, I can do that."

"And just in case I have to explain, Mr. Rodriguez . . . should we have another run-in with the police, we will know who's to blame, and we'll take appropriate action. Do I make myself clear?"

"What about the jeweler?"

"He stays with us."

"I don't like this plan, Boltar."

"Did I ask whether you liked it?" Jonathan asked. "I'm not interested in what you like. Just be there like I said."

Rodriguez hadn't done any cocaine all morning. He'd thought it would keep his head clear if he didn't. But this was turning out to have the opposite effect. He had begun drumming his fingers while on the phone with Boltar, and now he couldn't stop. Hesitating for a moment, he reached into his pocket, got out his spoon, and took two quick snorts. Instantly he felt better. Much better. It provided him the strength he needed to do what he had to do now.

Rodriguez dialed Valdez in Medellin. He had to go through three different people before he finally heard Valdez growl into the receiver, "Yeah?"

"Hector, it's me," said Rodriguez.

"Everything go smoothly?" Valdez demanded.

"Uh, yeah, well not exactly . . . It wasn't quite like we planned."

"Not exactly? You got my diamonds or not?"

His voice trembling, Rodriguez told Valdez what had happened. After he had finished, there was a long silence. "Hector?" Rodriguez said. "Are you there?"

"I'm paying you $200,000," said Valdez finally, "which is more than you're worth, and still you can't even run a simple operation. I've already overlooked your multiple blunders in the past—a lot more than I would have let you get away with if you weren't family. But you listen to me, Cousin. Family don't mean squat when there's this much money at stake—you got me?"

Rodriguez had expected Valdez to be upset, but the conversation was taking an even more unpleasant turn than he had anticipated. "But this camel driver," he insisted. "He's suspicious, Hector. Very suspicious. And smart too. You don't understand—"

"No, you're wrong. I do understand, Cousin. I understand that you're worse than worthless to me. I thought you told me the camel driver wouldn't be a problem."

"I've got a plan," said Rodriguez. "We meet tomorrow morning ten kilometers out of town to make the exchange. I get to choose the place, and I've already got something in mind. A valley with no back door, you know what I'm saying?" He broke into a nervous laugh.

Valdez said nothing.

"You don't get it?" Rodriguez asked. "See, I keep hold of our merchandise, then he shows me the diamonds." He chuckled again. "But then, here's what happens. I end up leaving with our stuff *and* the diamonds, and he leaves in a body bag with his two—"

"Wrong," said Valdez coolly.

"Wrong?" Rodriguez hesitated, and suddenly he was afraid his cousin had somehow learned he was double dipping, skimming an extra $200,000 out of Valdez's take. He had no doubt Valdez was telling the truth when he said family didn't mean much next to a sum of money that big—even if it was only about a day's pay from Hector's perspective. He had crossed the line with Hector one too many times, and even in his addled state, he knew it.

"Yes, wrong. Because you're not going to get your slimy hands on our merchandise—or his. You just go ahead with the plan like the man says, but come tomorrow, Cousin, I'm gonna be there."

"You?" Rodriguez's heart sank. "Hector, why go to all that trouble?"

"I didn't want to have to deal with this personally, but you've left me no choices. I'm never gonna forget how you "handled" this. With some people, if you want a job done right, you do it yourself."

"Uh-huh." Rodriguez swallowed hard.

"First thing I'm gonna do when I get there . . . No, on second thought, I'm gonna make a phone call now and get it done pronto. I'm gonna take back possession of all our merchandise from you. You can't be trusted with as much as a slingshot, let alone . . . that."

"Whatever you say," Rodriguez cautioned, "but I don't think Boltar will get out of the car unless he knows for sure we have our merchandise on hand. He'd start shooting, and the first person he'd kill would be me."

Valdez didn't say anything for a long time.

"Hector?"

"All right, fine. We bring the merchandise and show it to him. But he pays me personally."

"Okay, then."

"And listen to me carefully," said Valdez. "If I find out you have crossed me in any way—I mean *any* way, well . . . I won't be responsible for what happens to you."

Valdez hung up, leaving Rodriguez to listen to the loud buzz of the dial tone.

If Valdez thought he would surprise the "camel driver" by showing up personally, he was wrong. Jonathan figured all along a man like Hector Valdez wouldn't trust Rodriguez with a transaction this big.

That night, he and Neeley and Gonzales stayed very busy. Neeley had purchased a Black and Decker airless spray unit and, after protecting the car windows and the chrome with paper and masking tape, they painted the white Cadillac navy blue. He had also purchased a dozen high-intensity lamps, which he placed around the vehicle to heat the finish so it would cure somewhat overnight. In the meantime, Gonzales went out on the town and "borrowed" a new license plate.

They prepared a light meal, which they shared with the jeweler. They treated him with civility, but when it came time to discuss their plans for the next day, they put him well out of earshot. For one thing, he could just be bluffing about not understanding English.

The three of them worked long into the night, preparing things they would need for the next day. Neeley was the first one up in the morning, and he went out into the garage to inspect his paint job. Later, he showed Jonathan. Although rudimentary, it should be effective. Any lookouts they encountered on the road would have an eye out for a white car and might not even notice a blue one. Besides that, they had a new license plate.

At 9:00 A.M., Jonathan reconfirmed the pick-up with Rodriguez. "Oh, by the way," Rodriguez said, trying to sound nonchalant. "Just one thing, Mr. Boltar. The rocks. Instead of putting all of them in the briefcase, I want you to take out my commission and put them in a separate bag, which you can hand to me after we make the exchange. Would you do that?"

"Whatever you say, Rodriguez," Jonathan replied. "It's all your money as far as I'm concerned. I don't care what happens to it once it leaves my hands and I have my equipment."

Jonathan chuckled to himself after he got off the phone. So his guess had been right. Apparently Rodriguez had been forced to go back and report his screw-up to the big boss—presumably, Hector Valdez. And now there would be additional personnel to oversee today's transaction. Therefore Rodriguez had to go to just a little more effort to cheat his cousin.

Screened by the corner building, the four men in the newly blue Cadillac approached the rendezvous point in such a way that Rodriguez couldn't see them. Neeley was driving again, and Jonathan rode shotgun. In the back sat Gonzales with the jeweler, who again had the briefcase containing the diamonds handcuffed to his wrist.

After a quick glance around for anything unusual, Gonzales got out of the car and moved to a position half a block away from Rodriguez. He stopped a young boy and gave him a thousand pesos, about $3, to deliver a two-way radio to the man standing down the street. He pointed Rodriguez out for the boy. It was a risk in this corrupt town. The kid might just take the money and the radio and run. But miracle of miracles, he did exactly as he was told.

Gonzales watched the exchange from the cover of a doorway, then immediately signaled to Jonathan and Neeley, still a block away in the car. Jonathan brought his radio up close to his mouth. "Rodriguez, this is Boltar. Do you hear me?"

Looking around, Rodriguez edged his way to the shelter of a statue in the middle of the square, just in case any shooting started. "Yeah. Where are you?" He sounded nervous. "You're supposed to be here."

"I am aware of that, but there has been a change in plans. I want you to start walking south on Calle 11, toward the July 20th Museum, until you reach the far edge. We will be watching you, and I don't expect anyone to be following you. When you reach the corner of Carrera 6, tell me."

"Listen," Rodriguez said angrily, "what's this all about?"

"Just do it," Jonathan said, "if you ever want to see your money."

So Rodriguez started walking in the direction specified. When he reached the corner he mumbled into the radio, "I'm here."

"Okay, turn left on Carrera 6 and continue walking until I tell you otherwise." Gonzales had stepped out onto the sidewalk and begun walking about fifty feet behind Rodriguez while Neeley pulled the Cadillac into the street and trailed Gonzales at a discreet distance. Over a series of turns through narrow corridors, crossing several streets, Jonathan led Rodriguez to another location. There was definitely no one tailing him. At a spot not far from the Archeological Museum, they drove up behind him, and Jonathan opened the door.

"Get in, Rodriguez."

He got into the car, immediately followed by Gonzales, who pushed him down to the floorboards. Neeley pulled away from the curb, cautiously checking his rearview mirror.

They drove around for fifteen minutes or so before allowing Rodriguez to sit up. By then, Gonzales had frisked him and found a 9-mm Beretta, which he confiscated.

"Okay, Rodriguez," Jonathan growled, "take us to the rendezvous."

"Head south on Carrera 4," said Rodriguez, sounding a little shaken. Gonzales next to him had a .357 Magnum poked against his ribs. "Follow that to the city limits, and from there I'll tell you what to do."

With each passing block, they traveled farther away from the fashionable centers of town and into the real Colombia. As they reached the outskirts of the city, shacks made of corrugated iron and other scavenged objects became more evident. Droves of squatters milled about by the side of the road. The children, if they had on clothing at all, wore tattered and filthy rags, and they stared at the passing vehicle with blank expressions. Yet in the midst of all the squalor, a certain touch of festivity filled the air. Strung along some telephone poles and displayed in front of many houses were brightly colored, if a bit dingy, Christmas ornaments, still up even though it was early January.

They passed the city limits. From there, Neeley started keeping track of the distance to make sure Rodriguez didn't exceed the required ten-kilometer perimeter. After five kilometers, they entered the small village of Nueva Valencia and took a right turn onto a narrow cobblestone street, which became a winding dirt road leading up a large hillside.

They passed a small church on the left and, beyond that, a few farmers' shanties, but the road was deserted as they wound their way to the top of the hill. If Valdez himself was here, he might have ordered the road cleared until the conclusion of the exchange. The hill had a steep drop-off on the right side. With no crossroads, one could safely assume this road provided the only route in or out. Therefore, it made their destination a perfect trap.

CHAPTER SEVEN

Over the hill, they entered a small pasture in a slight valley with a high ridge of trees behind it. In the center of the field, pointed toward them, sat the same Mercedes 500 SEL they had seen yesterday, with nine other cars parked around the periphery. Five men stood beside the main car, but the other vehicles looked empty. Rodriguez instructed them to pull alongside the Mercedes, and Neeley did, the passenger side of the two cars facing one another like two neighbors stopping to chat. "This is good," Rodriguez said. "I'll get out and make sure everything is okay."

"You ain't going nowhere, you jerk." Gonzales shoved the Magnum deeper into the Colombian's rib cage. "Not until we tell you."

Jonathan glanced at the stony-faced men standing behind the Mercedes and commanded, "Rodriguez, tell your men to show us the Stingers and let us inspect them before we make the exchange."

Rodriguez yelled to them, and one of the men opened the trunk.

Putting the Cadillac in park but leaving the engine running, Neeley opened the driver's door and walked over to the other car. Jonathan slid behind the wheel and took Neeley's Uzi to cover him.

Without appearing too obvious, Neeley scanned the tree line adjoining the pasture for signs of gunmen. They were there, no doubt, but they kept themselves well-covered. Then, he walked with one of Valdez's men around to the back of the Mercedes to make certain Jonathan was getting what he'd paid for.

Jonathan sat in the driver's seat, staring ahead. He didn't envy Neeley's job, which forced him right into the middle of the cocaine thugs. Among the men standing behind the Mercedes, he saw a face he recognized from the newspapers and TV. Valdez was a short, squat man with a mustache, as burly as his cousin was emaciated.

I'll bet the DEA would give anything to get as close to Hector as I am now, Jonathan thought. He glanced in the rearview mirror at Rodriguez, who was, in turn, looking anxiously at Valdez. Gonzales stared ahead without blinking, and the jeweler sat nervously waiting to see what would happen next.

Valdez's henchman held up the spare missile, the one not inside the crate, and Neeley studied it for a moment, then he demanded that they open up the crate so that he could see the other three. They haggled back and forth for a minute, then the Colombian popped open the box. Jonathan caught a glimpse of one of the Stingers, and the thing looked ridiculously small and frail for all the trouble and expense it was taking to get it.

Finally Neeley walked back and leaned over the driver's side. Keeping his eyes on the unfriendly-looking crew with the Mercedes, he spoke to Jonathan in a low voice. "Stingers look okay to me. 'Course, we can't say for sure without actually firing one, but at least we know that it's not just empty launch tubes in the crate."

"Good deal," said Jonathan. He glanced back at the jeweler and nodded. The man got out, with Jonathan right behind him.

Emerging from the car, he looked straight into the face of Hector Valdez, who had strolled over with two of his men. Valdez studied Jonathan, and Jonathan studied Valdez. Jonathan wondered if anyone else could hear the wild pounding of his heart.

A long, long moment of silence ensued. Then Valdez, still keeping his eyes on Jonathan, asked the jeweler a question. The other man answered, and Valdez nodded his head.

"Those are the diamonds in this bag here?" Valdez asked Jonathan in perfect English, pointing to the briefcase attached to the jeweler's wrist.

Jonathan nodded his head.

"Then unlock the handcuffs so that he can give me the diamonds, and we can get on with the exchange." Valdez stared at him, smiling with his mouth but not his eyes, and added, "Please."

Jonathan, breathing very slowly, undid the cuff from the jeweler, who now backed away, rubbing his wrist. He walked toward Valdez, and one of the henchmen started to advance on him, but Valdez held up a hand. Carrying the briefcase, Jonathan came toward Valdez, the two of them staring one another in the eyes. He leaned forward to set it down. The henchmen watched, ready to pull the trigger at one false move. And then—

"*What the*—" Valdez exclaimed. He looked down at his hand, which was suddenly cuffed to the briefcase. In the blink of an eye, Jonathan had slipped the cuffs around Valdez's wrist and locked them.

Now Jonathan stood as close as he could to Valdez, so that no one could get a clear shot at him from any distance. Neeley and Gonzales, both armed and with weapons now visible, glared at their adversaries.

"I asked you what you did to my hand!" Valdez was screaming now.

Jonathan waited as long as possible—an agonizing ten seconds, during which Valdez looked ready to shoot him personally—before speaking. "I will explain."

Valdez looked at one of his men, who shoved an AK-47 toward Jonathan.

Jonathan glanced at Valdez. "I can tell you right now," he said, speaking slowly, "that you'll be very, very sorry if you let him do that."

Valdez hesitated. "You better explain this right now, *Cabron*," he hissed.

"Certainly. If you will allow my man there"—he nodded toward Gonzales—"to fetch me something . . . " Moving slowly, Gonzales walked around to the trunk of the Caddy and brought out a briefcase identical to the one Valdez had. He handed it to Jonathan, who held the case up and pointed to a letter *B* stenciled in white on the top of it. "You see this?" he asked Valdez. "I'll explain this in a minute, but first I would like one of your men here to take this briefcase and leave it over there behind that rock." He nodded toward an outcropping fifty feet away.

Valdez stared at him with a look of freezing hatred.

"I think you'll find this information helpful," Jonathan offered.

Valdez's men became anxious and began to move in closer to Jonathan, but both Gonzales and Neeley pointed their Uzis toward Valdez, and things seemed to quiet down. Valdez looked at Jonathan, then at Jonathan's two men. He was exactly where he didn't want to be—in the line of fire. He growled something in Spanish to one of his men, who took the second briefcase and did as Jonathan had instructed.

Meanwhile, Jonathan glanced at Rodriguez, who looked both a little scared and a little curious. Mostly he looked like he was in a hurry. He stood by, tapping his feet like he wanted to get things over with and get out of there.

So did Jonathan, but he couldn't afford to hurry now. With slow, deliberate movements, he pulled from his pocket a black box the size of a garage-door opener and marked with a white letter *B*. He showed it to Valdez. From another pocket he pulled a second box, marked *A*, and again showed it to Valdez.

"Yes, yes, I see that," Valdez said with anger.

"Don't rush me," Jonathan said. "This is very important. What letter is on the briefcase attached to your arm?"

"There's no—" Valdez looked down. "Oh, yeah, there's an *A* here." He looked up at Jonathan.

Jonathan held up the *A* box. "Watch how I'm holding down this button and activating this transmitter with the letter that corresponds to the one on your briefcase. Do you realize what this means?"

"Get on with it!" Valdez said furiously.

"And you can see, I am now activating *B* as well," Jonathan went on, pressing the button and holding it. He glanced over in the direction of the rock, behind which Valdez's man had placed the *B* case. "Suppose I were shot or something, and

93

my hand were to fall off of the *A* switch, let's see what would happen to you." He turned toward the rock outcropping where the men had placed the briefcase, then waited a second and glanced back at Valdez. "That *is* the *A* briefcase in your hand, is it not?"

With a murderous look, Valdez held the top of the briefcase toward Jonathan and pointed to the letter.

Jonathan shrugged. "Just making sure." Again, he started to let go of the button, then he paused once more. As if to make sure everyone was paying careful attention, he glanced at Valdez, at Neeley and Gonzales, at the terrified jeweler, at the impatient Rodriguez, at the henchmen who would gladly have killed him if they could figure out what was going on. He glanced at the two cars and beyond them at the hillside. He looked back at Valdez, who wanted his blood so much Jonathan could practically see it in his eyes. He raised the *B* black box so Valdez could clearly see the letter marking. And then he let go of the button.

As soon as he released the rocker switch, there was a massive explosion—equivalent to three sticks of dynamite—just beyond the rock outcropping fifty feet away. The sound was deafening. Everyone who hadn't figured out what was coming jumped in shock. Jonathan continued to look straight into the eyes of one of the most powerful men in Colombia. "Now do you understand what you are holding?"

"Yes," Valdez croaked, his mouth sounding dry. He cleared his throat.

"One other thing." His thumb on the button, Jonathan pointed the *A* box toward the handcuffs. "In case you get creative and try to cut those cuffs, I'm warning you. They're part of the circuit. If you cut them, the whole thing blows. Understand?" Valdez nodded. "Now, assuming you let us get out of here unscathed, I will deactivate this device in my hand as soon as we get down the road. We get to keep our missiles, you get to keep your diamonds."

Jonathan smiled and turned slowly toward Rodriguez, then he pulled a bag out of his pocket. "Oh, yeah, Rodriguez, I almost forgot. Here's your $200,000." He tossed him the little cloth bag from his coat pocket.

Valdez, with a murderous look in his eyes, started to move toward Rodriguez, but Jonathan motioned for him to stop. "You can deal with him after we're gone." He started backing toward the car, holding the little black box out in front of him as though it were a pistol.

Gonzales carefully loaded the four missiles into the trunk of the Cadillac. As he finished, Jonathan said to Valdez, "Remember, my thumb will stay on this rocker switch, and this device has a fifteen-kilometer transmission radius. If someone follows us . . ." He smiled and nodded his head in the direction of the pile of rubble where the rock outcropping had been a few minutes before. "Got it?"

Valdez nodded. "Don't worry about anyone following you," he said, clenching his teeth. Glaring at Rodriguez, he said "We have something else to deal with first."

Rodriguez stepped toward Jonathan, holding up the bag in his hand. "You gotta take me with you, man," he whined, his eyes pleading.

Jonathan burst out laughing, and Neeley and Gonzales laughed too. "You tried to double-cross me *and* your cousin over there," he said. "Why should I help you?"

Rodriguez held the bag toward Jonathan. "I'll pay you $200,000 for a seat in that car."

Jonathan jerked his thumb—his *other* thumb. "Get in the front and close the door."

"Hey Boltar," Valdez shouted, followed by a venomous string of what Jonathan could only guess were Spanish expletives of the vilest sort. "I'm gonna get you, man. Don't you ever turn your back again, 'cause I'm gonna get you. I don't care if I gotta go to camel land, I'm gonna have your blood."

Jonathan looked back at Valdez, who he knew would have killed him personally if he could have. "If you find me," he said.

"Oh, I'm *gonna* find you."

Rodriguez, looking like he was about to faint from gratitude, crawled into the front seat, Jonathan and Gonzales into the back. They closed the doors, and Neeley eased the car toward the road.

Looking behind him, Jonathan saw a fuming Hector Valdez, surrounded by some of the toughest thugs in South America. But as they drove out of the pasture, silhouettes began to appear along the ridge surrounding their meeting place. Thirty or forty snipers had been positioned to take out Jonathan and his men. But Valdez never gave the order.

Jonathan hadn't sold Rodriguez this Cadillac ride because he needed the money. And he certainly didn't do it out of mercy for the man who had tried to get him killed. He had another purpose in mind. "All right, Rodriguez," he barked. "Where are Valdez's men hiding?"

Rodriguez faced Jonathan and shrugged. "I don't know nothing 'bout no men hiding."

Gonzales brought his Uzi up against Rodriguez's chin. Rodriguez looked down at it, then up at Jonathan. "The first one is in less than a kilometer," he said slowly. "There should be three or four cars on the side of the road, and they've got radios. So if they've been given the signal by Hector, they will have blocked the road."

Up ahead, they saw nothing but a dusty road leading down the hill, with a steep drop-off to the left. "Looks like Valdez hasn't figured out how to deactivate the thing," said Jonathan. "Not yet, anyway. Okay, now where's the next checkpoint?"

Rodriguez seemed to hesitate. Then he must have realized there was no turning back now. "Another three kilometers down the road in the village," he said. "Past the church. Five vehicles with radios and automatic weapons."

Valdez stood, frozen in place, and watched the cars leave. For several seconds, silence descended on the field as his men moved forward, looking to him for instructions. Suddenly he seemed to snap out of his trance, and he barked at his driver, gesturing with his left hand because he didn't dare move his right. "The doors of this Mercedes," he demanded, "they bulletproof?"

"*Si,*" answered the driver. The other men had stepped back from him as soon as Valdez addressed him. "Nobody could shoot at you and hit you when you're in there."

"What about dynamite?"

"Huh?" The driver looked a little uncertain.

"To blow up this briefcase, fool!" shouted Valdez.

"I don't know. You heard what—"

"I don't care what the camel-jockey said. If somebody blows up a stick of dynamite outside the door, would I feel it inside?"

The driver shook his head. "I don't think so. But—"

"Okay, then," Valdez ordered. He nodded toward the car. "Open the doors on the other side of the car, and open the windows on this side." While the men were doing that, he yelled, "Now, bust out the windshield—there, do it, you heard what I said." A couple of men knocked out the glass, which was bulletproof but couldn't withstand sustained pounding with a rifle butt. "Good, good. Now." He looked at one of the men. "You got a tool kit in your car?"

The man nodded.

"Bolt cutters?"

"*Si.*" In their line of business, all sorts of tools came in handy at times.

"Get them."

While the man ran to do as he was told, Valdez leaned in on the driver's side, gingerly lifting the briefcase with his other hand. One of his men rushed to help him, and he snapped, "Be careful, idiot. You want to kill us all?"

As soon as he had placed the briefcase on the floorboard, he looked around from where he crouched beside the driver's seat. Scanning the group, he found the biggest, dumbest man and pointed to him. "You. Yes, you. Come here."

When the hulking thug came forward, Valdez motioned for him to lean down toward where he squatted beside the car. "Okay, here's what you're gonna do," he said in a confidential tone. "I'm gonna lie down, then I want you to lie on top of me with those bolt cutters in your hand." The big man just stared at Valdez, and there was total silence in the crowd. Nobody dared laugh. Valdez glanced at two other men, and said, "You, lay on top of him, and *you*, once we get into position on the ground beside the car, on my signal I want you to slam the door."

Everyone did as instructed by Valdez, who lay down on the ground. When the big man stretched out on top of him, and then the other one got on top, Valdez worried he was going to be crushed. But he needed all that cushioning in case anything went wrong.

He had no idea whether or not Boltar had told the truth about the handcuffs activating the charge, but he didn't plan on taking any chances. The first test would be slamming the door, and if that didn't break them, he would have the man on top of him use the bolt cutters. If and when the case did blow, having the opposite door open and the windshield busted out would diffuse the shock somewhat and send most of the blast out the other side of the car. At least he hoped so. If not, he still had two bodies on top of him for protection.

Before Valdez could give any further instructions, one of his top lieutenants leaned over and said, "What about the diamonds, boss?"

"What do you care about those diamonds, huh?" demanded Valdez. "You hopin' I'll be dead and you take 'em for yourself? Don't worry about those diamonds." From where he lay on the ground, not looking much like a fierce drug lord, he glanced around at the other men. "I'm gonna put somebody in charge of picking up the pieces while the rest of us go after our little friends. And after it's all over, my jeweler is gonna make sure that we've got exactly two million American dollars there, so don't nobody think about making a quick fortune." He looked at the man who had the job of slamming the door. "All right, let's do it."

While everyone else ran to hide, the third man crawled forward, reached up and slammed the door shut, then threw himself to the ground with his hands over his head. At the same moment, an explosion went ripping out the other side of the car, sending metal and fragments of the briefcase—plus hundreds of diamonds—scattering over a radius nearly as big as a baseball field. In spite of their precautions, the blast sent the door flying open on Valdez's side of the car, and it hung above him now, still attached on its hinge but just barely.

Within seconds of the explosion, Valdez stirred. He nudged the man above him, the one with the bolt cutters. "All right, cut me loose," he demanded.

But it turned out the man couldn't do it. He was dead—as was the man on top of him. The door had slammed into their heads. Their deaths were no loss to Valdez. He wouldn't have picked them if they had been essential. As soon as one of his men cut him loose from the handcuffs, he realized his throbbing hand was hanging limp. The blast had shattered his wrist.

Around them, the field lay littered with diamonds. A few men began picking them up, but Valdez ordered one man to take four others and do the job. "Keep this field secured!" he shouted as he raced to get in one of the automobiles, clutching his bad arm. "The rest of you, come on. We're gonna get that gringo's blood."

The remaining men sprang into action. Within moments, calls went out over the radios, and the group of nine vehicles tore out of the pasture.

The dirt road changed to coarse gravel, and the uneven surface made for some tough driving on Neeley's part, but he sped them along as fast as he could. Suddenly they all heard a gigantic explosion in the distance behind them, and Jonathan winced. "I'll bet he figured it out."

"What you mean, man?" asked Rodriguez, his hope rising. "Sounds to me like Hector's dead."

"That's why Hector's the boss and you're not," said Jonathan. "You watch. He's not dead. He's too smart. Okay, Gonzales, time to add a little lubricant."

"You got it." Gonzales turned a valve hidden underneath a decorative tissue box in the back window, sending two gallons of twenty-weight motor oil onto the road. He then leaned out the side window and tossed out two smoke grenades to camouflage the spill.

"Speed up a bit," Jonathan commanded Neeley. But he was already going as fast as the Cadillac could safely go on the rough road, especially with the steep drop-off on the left. As they rounded the next turn, Jonathan leaned forward while Gonzales loosened the back seat. Together they pulled it out. Gonzales threw open the door and hurled the seat onto the side of the road, then slammed the door shut again. Now they had ready access to the trunk, where they had stored dozens and dozens of two-by-four blocks with eight-penny nails driven in at different angles. No matter which way the spikes landed, several nails would be sticking up.

Gonzales began tossing them out on the road while Jonathan kept a gun trained on Rodriguez up front—just in case the idiot decided to make one last bid to get back into his cousin's good graces. "Hit them with the smoke," Jonathan ordered. "And some more oil."

Rodriguez, who already seemed a little bolder because his miserable little life had been saved for another few minutes, turned around toward Jonathan.

"Eyes to the front," Jonathan said, jabbing him with the Uzi.

"No problem," Rodriguez answered, turning around and putting up his hands. "I was just wondering what happened to your accent, Boltar. Thought you were from the Middle East?"

"You got more important things to worry about," said Jonathan. To Neeley, he said, "Pull over behind the church there."

The three cars at the first checkpoint came barreling around the corner after the Cadillac. The first driver slammed on his brakes when he saw the smoke, which was a mistake he would never have the chance to repeat. His brakes locked just as his tires hit the fresh oil, and he began sliding over the side of the hill and down the 200-foot ravine. His car bounced off a boulder and burst into flames.

The driver of the second car applied his brakes a bit more cautiously when he saw the smoke. But since he still didn't know about the oil patch, he swerved straight up the embankment on the right side. The move flipped his vehicle and sent it spinning across the road and down into the ravine after the earlier vehicle.

When the occupants of the third car saw the fate of their predecessors, they had better luck. They drove slowly through the oil and the smoke and one of them radioed back to the first of the vehicles leaving the pasture with Valdez. They sped up again once they left the oil patch—until they met the next turn and rolled over the tire shredders.

Seconds later, the lead car from Valdez's group came flying around the corner and ran into them. The car almost flipped over as its driver skirted the damage by driving up on the right embankment, but he regained control and continued in pursuit. As he hit the next bend, he too rolled over one of the tire shredders and came to an abrupt stop.

Valdez and the other six cars, two in front and four behind, slowly passed around the destruction on the road. He signaled for two of the other cars to assume the lead, and they moved on, picking up speed.

Jonathan climbed out of the car behind the church and retrieved a portable transmitter from the trunk, which he strapped onto his back. Neeley and Gonzales pulled out a giant sling and loaded it with the four missiles, as well as their other weapons, and together they assumed the burden.

"Okay, Rodriguez," Jonathan said. He tossed him the keys and motioned for Gonzales to give him back his Beretta. "You can take the car and find your own way out of here."

Rodriguez looked confused.

"You ain't coming with us," Gonzales shouted. *"Vamanos!"* He gestured with his Uzi to show he meant business.

"I'll see you again, man!" Rodriguez said as he jumped into the car.

"I don't plan on going where you're headed," Jonathan muttered as he double-timed after Neeley and Gonzales while Rodriguez sped away. They had just barely gotten off the road before seven vehicles in a row flew past the church in the same direction as Rodriguez.

Rodriguez pressed his foot down on the gas pedal as far as it would go. The Cadillac fishtailed as it spun around the corners of the winding country road. But there were two cars behind him now. And they were gaining on him.

Clouds of dust billowed on every side, making it hard for him to see, and he nearly ran down a flock of chickens crossing in front of him. He sped through the middle of the nearby village, a barely paved stretch between small shops and huts, and he swerved to miss a group of children playing in the street.

He cursed out loud. Sweat beaded on his forehead, but he didn't dare take his hands off the wheel to wipe it away. Every ounce of his concentration had to go into keeping the car on the road. His eyes burned from staring ahead through the dust without blinking. He wished he could have just one hit to help clear his head.

"What do I do? What do I do?" he shouted to himself. Up ahead he could already see a couple of men eyeing him from the checkpoint. They had four cars, two backed by two, blocking the road, and they were armed. There was no getting through their barricade.

At the last moment, he swerved left, crashed through a fence, and plunged into a pasture. But he still saw no way of escape. The two cars behind him spun off the road and across the pasture in his direction.

Rodriguez did a quick one-eighty and bounced back onto the road headed in the direction from which he'd come. By now, there were two cars blocking the other end of the village.

"Blast you, Boltar!" he shouted. He swerved off on a side road, knowing it would lead him nowhere. Up ahead, a group of men jumped to get out of his way. From that street, he turned off onto another, and then another, but they all led back to the main road. He swerved down an alleyway toward the central marketplace, only to spot two more vehicles approaching from the other end. In desperation, he jerked the car left into another alley—and he knew it was over. A brick wall loomed up ahead.

He jumped out of the car and sprinted toward the wall. Behind him he could hear the cars slamming on their brakes, doors opening. Running at full speed, he jumped up onto the wall, grabbing the top and pulling himself over. In doing so, he cut his hands on the cracked cement surface, but he paid no attention to his pain. Taking quick stock of what lay below him—a bare dirt yard with chicken coops and a small house beyond them—he jumped down.

The men from the cars scrambled up over the wall and spread out. Within moments, four of them had assembled in the yard, submachine guns ready. They stood looking at one particular chicken coop. Inside, they could see the top of Rodriguez's head.

An old woman ran out of the nearby house and shouted at them not to destroy any of her hens. "Don't worry, *Viejita*," one of the men shouted back at her, "there's only one chicken in there we want. If we hurt one of your hens, Hector Valdez will buy you a whole new hen house." At the mention of Valdez's name, she immediately ran back into her house.

"Rodriguez!" the leader of the hit squad called out. "You gonna come out, or you gonna stay in there and die like a chicken?"

Inside the little coop and surrounded by fretting hens that seemed none too happy about his invasion, Rodriguez reached into his jacket and took out his beloved cocaine spoon. Rodriguez knew this was the very last fix he would ever get.

He felt something else in his breast pocket. His Beretta, which Boltar's men had given back to him.

"Rodriguez! You listening to me, man?"

At the sound of the loud voices, the chickens around him started squawking.

Rodriguez looked at the pistol in his hands. "Yeah, I'll be out in a second!" he called back.

And then he pointed the 9-mm at his temple and pulled the trigger.

The three men raced up a narrow footpath behind the church and into a small open pasture. Gonzales and Neeley spread out in a defensive perimeter ahead of him while Jonathan began punching in a message on a keypad that accompanied his transmitter.

Three minutes after they last saw Rodriguez, they heard a gunshot ring out from down the road. Jonathan and the other two exchanged glances. Everyone guessed what it meant—and they all knew Valdez would come after them next, once he realized they weren't in the car.

Crouched beside some low sheltering shrubs, Jonathan laid down his weapon and placed a headset over his ears. He worked frantically at the keypad, punching in a code. "Come on, come on!" he pleaded in brusque whispers at the instrument.

Suddenly he glanced down and saw two feet in dusty peasant's sandals. Whoever stood next to him wasn't Neeley or Gonzales.

Jonathan looked up to see one of Valdez's henchmen pointing an AK-47 directly at his chest. The man said something in Spanish and grinned. He looked like a Jack-o'-lantern with his mouthful of missing teeth.

Jonathan took the headset off, laid it on the ground, and backed away.

The henchman reached down and grabbed Jonathan's Uzi, then pointed down the trail with his rifle barrel. As Jonathan began to move in the direction indicated, a voice came over the headset. "Bravo One, this is Bravo Two. Come in." The startled gunman, who like many of his comrades was an illiterate peasant, turned around to see where the voice had come from. As he did, Jonathan leaped off the trail and into the underbrush. The gunman fired a quick burst after him, but Jonathan scrambled away another ten feet.

The man ran after him, firing as he went. The area in front of Jonathan opened into a clearing. If he moved now, he wouldn't get another foot without getting shot.

The gunman approached Jonathan, weapon raised. Just then, a purplish-red spot formed on his forehead, his mouth opened wide, and suddenly he fell forward. A single shot rang out, and Neeley ran up out of the woods holding his Uzi.

Jonathan looked at Neeley, but there wasn't time for thanks. On the road, he could see Valdez's caravan. They had pulled to a stop in front of the church, probably because they had heard gunshots. Jonathan rushed back to the keypad and sent the all-clear message.

Valdez's men jumped out of their cars in front of the church and took up a firing position. But just then, over the tops of their heads, came a roaring sound—a chopper. The Colombians dove for cover. The breath of its rotors fanned the tops of the tall trees as a Huey UH-1H Iroquois buzzed over the heads of the Cartel death squad and headed toward the field.

Within seconds, the three men tossed the Stingers into the helicopter and, as the first of Valdez's men approached the edge of the field with automatic weapons blazing, the chopper bolted straight upward with both Gonzales and Neeley firing their Uzis from either side. The men out on the field hit the ground as the automatic weapon fire broke through the trees over them.

"Sorta makes a man think o' Saigon!" Sonny Odom shouted from the pilot's seat.

Later that night, they crossed the Venezuelan border, and Sonny returned the chopper to its owner, a drunk to whom he had slipped $20,000 for two days' rental. The man didn't even seem to mind that Sonny had repainted the helicopter, obscuring all of its identifying numbers.

After they arrived in Caracas and checked into the hotel, they ordered a huge dinner from room service, and Neeley and Gonzales shared a bottle of tequila. Seeing them drunk, Jonathan was glad they hadn't gone out on the town that night. He and Sonny only had wine, and after the other two passed out, they sat up talking for awhile. Thinking back on it later, Jonathan hoped that Neeley and Gonzales were really passed out. He had shared some fairly sensitive information with Sonny about his plans. Even so, he felt pretty confident that they were dead to the world— it *was* tequila, after all.

By the time George Watt got on the plane from Caracas to Miami two days later, his "machinery" had been shipped to Puerto Cabello, a harbor town seventy-five miles from Caracas. The pieces had been disassembled, and they were mixed in with some tractor parts, after-market pieces for the Pakistan and India agricultural market. In two weeks, the pallet labeled FARM EQUIPMENT would be shipped out on the S.S. Cordillera de San Blas, a freighter under Panamanian registry. It would travel across the Atlantic, through the Mediterranean and the Suez Canal, down the Red Sea, up the Gulf of Aden, and across the Arabian Sea to Karachi, Pakistan.

When the Stingers got there, Jonathan would be waiting for them.

Nearly 7,000 miles away on the other side of the world, two men returned from battle, but they did so on foot and not in a jet. Nor did they feel elated like Jonathan. One was wounded and limping. The other helped his comrade up the long, rocky path back to their encampment.

Khalid, the wounded man, was a simple farmer from the hinterlands of Afghanistan. Ali, on the other hand, had once taught history at the university in Kabul. They came from different nations, one of them a Tajik and the other a

Pushtun. But they were both Afghans, and they were both Muslims. And they both had the same vision of defeat fresh in their minds.

Just two days before, they had initiated an attack on a government outpost near the blacktop highway that ran between Kabul and Jalalabad, a road built by the U.S. Army Corps of Engineers back in the late 1950s. At first the battle had seemed to go well. After hours of heavy fighting, they had overrun the outpost, an ancient fortress with high battlements. They captured most of its defenders, many of whom defected to the mujahideen's side at once.

But just as they began to regroup and move out of the battle site, a group of Soviet Mi-24 Hind helicopter gunships swooped in from the west. The terrain in this particular part of the country should have allowed the men to see them from a great distance, but their appearance had been shielded by the glare of the setting sun.

The gunships rained fire across the captured battlements. Since the surrounding countryside offered no route of escape, but rather a series of wide, dusty plains encircled by mountains, Ali and his men had no choice but to take up a defensive position within the perimeter they had just breached. For a full hour, they endured attack after attack by the wave of Soviet-piloted helicopters. And if that weren't bad enough, when the choppers pulled out, a fighter wing of attack aircraft swooped in and napalmed their defensive perimeter.

The men fought with bravery, but they didn't have the weaponry to take out the Soviet aircraft. Rifles wouldn't do it. Their bullets just bounced off the heavily armored attack helicopters.

After softening the area, the Soviets dropped infantry squads onto a ridge behind the fortress, and advanced on the remaining mujahideen. They overran the battlefield and, in less than an hour, most of the mujahideen lay dead or wounded. The eight who remained, including Ali and Khalid, managed to escape only because darkness had come over the area.

"Just remember," Ali whispered to the younger man in a comforting voice, "those who died are *shahidan,* martyrs. While we continue to suffer here on earth, they are in Paradise."

"But why is it always our people who become martyrs?" asked Khalid, his eyes glowing with rage. He shivered from the cold as a sharp wind blew through the mountain pass.

"That I do not know, my friend," said Ali sadly. "Surely Allah has some purpose in it all, some purpose we cannot see."

"My brother told me the same thing," Khalid answered, wincing with pain, "the last time I saw him alive. I wonder if he felt the same when he fell into the hands of the Butcher of Kabul."

"Your brother is in Paradise," said Ali, "along with the rest of your family—and mine."

"I know," Khalid answered. "I only wish we had something to hope for besides death."

Ali held his comrade's shoulder as the two of them walked together, and in his heart he agreed with what Khalid had said.

On January 10, the following appeared in the personal section of *The Washington Post*:

Ray:
Had a great time shopping. I'm ready to go on vacation now. Are our reservations in order?

—Bill

Since Jonathan had not volunteered any information about himself—least of all his phone number—he didn't have the luxury of waiting for a phone call informing him of the date when the reply would appear. Instead, he had to buy the *Post* every day thereafter and wait for an ad to run from "Ray." Rashid kept him waiting a week and a half. And Jonathan had begun to get paranoid. He started varying the newsstands and bookstores where he purchased the paper, which was not an easy thing to do since there were only about a dozen locations that carried it in the entire New Orleans area.

But finally the message came, in the form of a simple request. *Bill: call Ray.*

So he did, using another one of the many anonymous pay phones around the city.

"I trust you secured the fruits of your shopping trip?" Rashid said when Jonathan had identified himself.

"They're safe."

"Good. I have made arrangements for you."

"And?" Jonathan wondered why Rashid had asked him to take the risk of calling, if that was all he had to say. He'd already given him the information before.

There was a pause on the other end of the line. "I only want to make something clear. There is no one to inspect your gifts. The man you meet there understands you are bringing radio equipment. No one, however, will test it till you reach your destination." Rashid didn't say anything for several more moments. "I just want to assure you," he went on, "that it would be unwise to attempt to fool anyone. At some point you will be expected to produce the presents you have brought, and I trust at that time it will not turn out you have been bluffing."

Jonathan yanked the phone receiver from his ear and glared at it. Here he had risked his life, not to mention spending a good two and a half million dollars, to obtain those Stingers—

But he held his temper. "You don't have anything to worry about," he said at last.

"Then may Allah go with you."

"I'm telling you, Frazier," said Rusty Wharton, "it's the strangest thing. They've been watching his house, bugging his phone—nothing. Either he's on a long vacation, or . . ." He stared at the man across the table, and it was clear what he meant by *or*.

They sat in the cafeteria. Hollis was eating with vigor, but Wharton just picked at his lunch.

"Big deal," said Hollis, cutting into his meat loaf. "Another Cartel killing."

"Yeah, that's what McGinnis said too," Wharton answered. "He told me they'd—we'd—have somebody in Colombia watching the deal go down. So when I found out Rodriguez never came back, I went back to McGinnis and asked what had happened."

"And?"

"And he just told me the full report wasn't in, so I should just sit tight," Wharton answered.

"So just wait then." Hollis pointed at his plate. "You know, the meat loaf isn't half bad today—you should try it."

Wharton leaned forward, poking his fork toward Hollis. "Doesn't it bother you we seem to be kept in the dark?"

"I'm just doing my job, is all." Hollis shrugged. "Why get so personally involved?" He held up a hand, counting off points on his fingers. "Here's what we do know. This guy Boltar, as he calls himself, makes a contact with Rodriguez to buy Stingers for Rashid—we assume. Boltar goes to Colombia, where Valdez and his men take him out. Rodriguez stays down there for a while, just in case Boltar's people come looking for him. The Stinger deal didn't go down, and that's it. End of story."

"Maybe," said Wharton. "And maybe not. Just before lunch, I talked to some agents over in DEA who've been watching *Señor* Hector for awhile. From what they say, he isn't actin' like a guy who just scored a major coup. In fact, from their report, he's keepin' a really low profile." He chuckled. "Got a broken wrist too."

"Interesting," said Hollis. "So you think Boltar somehow got the better of him?"

Wharton spread his hands. "Not likely, but anything's possible."

"Did you tell McGinnis about this?"

"Yeah, and he said the same thing as before—we just need to wait and see."

"Wait and see what?" asked Hollis.

"Beats me," Wharton answered. "Wait and see if the Stingers somehow wind up in Afghanistan, I guess. And by then it's too late." He sighed. "I keep feeling like there's some missing piece here."

"Yeah, but we're new on the case. We can't possibly know everything, right?"

Wharton shook his head. "We were new on the case back months ago. By now we ought to be up on everything that's going on, and we're not."

CHAPTER EIGHT

In March, Jonathan began preparing to leave for Afghanistan and, as before, he needed a fake identity and an assistant. Sonny put together another ID kit and offered Phil Neeley the job. Not only did Neeley have the crucial knowledge of Stinger missiles, but Jonathan's and Neeley's personalities also meshed well.

Neeley seemed enthusiastic about going, and Sonny worked up a fake passport for him. He would never pass for an Australian with his flat voice, so the best he could do was sound like he had no accent at all. Sonny turned him into "Joe McKenzie," a Canadian citizen who had spent much of his life in the United States.

Jonathan rented a cabin in a remote part of the Ozarks, and the three men went there to take Neeley's crash course on assembling and operating the Stinger Missile. Neeley built a Stinger mockup out of cardboard tubes and other unlikely objects in order to simulate firing the missile, while Jonathan watched. For five days, they worked patiently together. Neeley drilled Jonathan on the various parts of the missile and the firing procedures until Jonathan felt sure he could recite them backwards. The more he learned, though, the more he hoped he wouldn't have to fire the Stinger on his own.

Sonny drilled them in various survival tactics, and Jonathan and Neeley ran hundreds of miles together in anticipation of the arduous hiking a journey through the Afghan mountains would entail. They even managed to learn a few rudimentary bits of Farsi, the common language in Afghanistan and neighboring countries, and both men grew their beards out so that they would more effectively blend in with the natives.

During their time in Colombia, both Gonzales and Neeley had impressed Jonathan with their professionalism and the way they managed to keep calm in life-threatening situations. But he had grown to appreciate Neeley in a way he hadn't Gonzales. The difference had nothing to do with culture and everything to do with attitude. Gonzales displayed an attitude that bordered on flippant, which irritated Jonathan. Neeley had an uncomplicated sincerity, which he liked.

Because neither of them was prone to a great deal of talk, their friendship didn't develop quickly. But after a few days in the Ozarks, Jonathan began to form an image of Neeley as a wounded loner—someone who kept his own counsel, not because he had nothing to say, but for quite the opposite reason. From the look on his lean, handsome face, and from his quiet, soft-spoken manner, he seemed like a man who harbored a buried pain. Something had altered his life permanently.

Jonathan could sympathize.

One late afternoon after another exhausting day of training, the two relaxed outside the cabin, near the edge of the clearing. Jonathan sat on a stump and Neeley on a stone, while Sonny cooked dinner for the three of them inside.

"Hope you don't mind if I smoke, George." As Neeley tended to do, he said Jonathan's alias with a glint of humor in his eye.

"Go ahead," said Jonathan.

"Good, 'cause I was goin' to anyway." Neeley pulled a pack of unfiltered Camels from his sock, along with a lighter. He lit his cigarette carefully, deliberately, even though there wasn't any wind, and he inhaled in such a luxurious way, he made smoking seem almost appealing. Seeing Jonathan watching him, he said, "Man's gotta have a few pleasures."

"That's one I never took up," said Jonathan, picking up a stick and scratching the ground with it. He shrugged. "I guess danger's become my addiction."

"Can't say I ever had that particular habit," Neeley drawled as he took another puff.

Jonathan raised his eyebrows. "Then I'd say you're in a pretty strange line of work."

"Mmm, I don't know." Neeley leaned back. "I do what I'm good at, that's all, but I like stayin' alive."

Glancing over toward the cabin, fifty yards away, Jonathan could see Sonny's profile in the window as he stood over the stove. "You got any family, Phil?" he asked.

"Nope."

It wasn't the kind of response that invited further probing, but Jonathan didn't have anything else to do. And besides, he was curious. "I suppose you had some family at one time, right?"

Neeley stared up at the trees above them. "Had a wife from Vietnam. She left about six years ago, haven't seen her since. No kids. Two brothers—one's in prison, the other one I don't know what happened to him. I see my sister every few years, but we don't have much to say to each other."

"Your parents?"

Neeley looked at Jonathan coldly. "Are you interviewing me, George?"

"No, I—"

The other man chuckled. "Naw, I'm just kiddin'. How 'bout you?"

Jonathan chose his words carefully. "Both of my parents are gone, and I was an only child. I had a wife and child once . . . but they both died."

"Mm-hmm." Neeley took another drag on his cigarette. "What was your wife like?" He gestured toward Jonathan. "Rich man like you, I'm sure you could find you another wife if you wanted, no problem. She musta been special."

Jonathan looked down at the ground. "Yeah, you're right. She was special. So was my boy."

"What happened?"

"They were murdered," Jonathan replied. "That's why we're taking this little trip. The man who killed them is somewhere in Afghanistan. Once we hand off these Stingers, I'm going to track him down and teach him a lesson he won't forget."

"Sonny told me I had to ask you if I wanted to know what our mission was all about. All he would say was that you had a score to settle. Still, it seems a little risky. Are you sure it's worth gettin' yourself killed too?"

"Oh . . . it's definitely worth it." Jonathan declared. "That devil deserves to die for what he did to my family."

"Well, I don't blame you for wantin' to take justice in your own hands, but I hope you got a good plan and a cool head on your shoulders. Like I said, I like stayin' alive."

"Don't worry . . . I just need you to help me get into the country and put those Stingers in the right hands," Jonathan replied. "After that, you're free to get out of there if it gets too hot for you."

Neeley took one more long puff, then carefully put out his cigarette on the ground in front of him. After a long silence, he finally said, "Both my parents are dead too. My mother, uh"—he looked away—"my mother committed suicide while I was in Vietnam."

Another lengthy silence followed. The sun had set long before, and darkness gathered in the trees above them. Inside the cabin, Sonny had lit the Coleman lantern. Dinner would be ready soon.

"Well," said Jonathan, "I guess we—"

"She did it because of me," Neeley said. "Because I shot my Daddy."

Jonathan, who had been about to go back inside only a moment before, now waited for Neeley to continue.

"I don't come from the same kind of background as you," Neeley said, taking out his pack and lighting another smoke. This time, though, he did it fast, as though trying to calm himself. "My folks was poor, what a lot of people would have called 'white trash.' My daddy sure was, I'll say that. Mean. Drank. Whipped us all with the buckle end of the belt—the kids and Mama too." He drew in a breath. "That was how come I killed him."

Neeley let his voice trail off, and it sounded to Jonathan as though he choked back a rush of emotion. He made no other sound for several seconds, and the woods were quiet except for the chirping of the crickets and the clanging of pots and pans inside the cabin.

"Y'all come on!" Sonny yelled, and the noise startled Jonathan.

"Since I was six months shy of eighteen," Neeley seemed oblivious to Sonny's call as he continued, "I was tried as a juvenile. There were all kinds of what they called 'mitigating circumstances,' and they gave me the option of reform school or the Marine Corps. So it's obvious which one I took, or I wouldn't be sittin' here now." He put out his cigarette and glanced over at Jonathan in the twilight. "I'm sure you can't relate, but that's how some people's lives are."

"You'd be surprised just how much I can relate," Jonathan said. He made no move to get up. "Our stories are more similar than you think—only difference is I didn't kill my own father. He did that himself, the slow way."

"Now you got *my* curiosity up," said Neeley.

"It's gonna get cold if y'all don't hustle on in here!" Sonny was shouting.

Neeley stood up. "'Nother time, I guess."

"Yeah, another time."

During dinner that night, Jonathan didn't talk much. Sonny laughed as he helped himself to seconds. "Phil here's always quiet as a stump. Guess I gotta do the talking for all three."

But Neeley's story consumed Jonathan's thoughts. His own childhood had been rough, but to have killed one's own father before turning eighteen . . .

He couldn't quit thinking about the parallels between Neeley's experience and what had happened to him. They had both felt compelled to take matters into their own hands. They weren't the kind of guys who could just sit back and wait for someone else to act. Neeley had been forced to live with his mother's abuse until he took vengeance into his own hands and killed his father. Jonathan had to live with the death of his wife and son and was now taking vengeance into his own hands, planning to kill the one who gave the order for their death.

He hadn't built an international health care company by waiting to see what others were going to do. He saw what needed to be done and did it—which was exactly the mode he was in now. He was acting to correct an injustice. But he couldn't help but wonder if, when Drakoff was dead, he would feel any better. Did Neeley feel better for having killed his father? Or worse?

When it came time to go to sleep, Jonathan lay awake for more than an hour, even though he was worn out from the day's work. In his mind he replayed countless scenes from his childhood, feeling helpless as he watched his father beat his mother—then reliving the sensation of momentary power when, at the age of fifteen, he stood up to his father for the first and only time.

When he finally did drift off, he fell into a nightmare about Jennifer and Jon and the plane. He woke up sweating. The cabin was silent except for the sounds of the other men's snores and the crickets outside. For months after the crash, he'd had these nightmares every night—at least on the nights when he could sleep. But this was the first time since he began his mission that the dream had returned.

When it came time to leave the United States, Jonathan and Neeley traveled separately. Jonathan left Louisiana several days ahead of Neeley because he had some business to attend to stateside. Jonathan, disguised as George Watt, arrived in Paris a week later.

He felt a little shaky standing at the customs counter while a gendarme in a Charles de Gaulle hat peered at him with an expression of mild curiosity, comparing Jonathan's face to the one on the passport photo. But George Watt got through without any problem and melted into the streets of Paris.

The next day he met up with Neeley and they boarded a plane for Karachi as Steven Wright and Joe McKenzie.

They arrived in Karachi late in the afternoon, and throngs of people pushed their way through the airport, some of them accompanied by their goats and other livestock. Fans revolved lazily overhead, but they did nothing but stir the unbearable heat. Eastern music wailed over the loudspeakers. Jonathan and Neeley pushed their way through the crowds. At every turn it seemed someone thrust a cup of tea, a plate of sweets, or simply an open hand at them.

Jonathan felt relieved to get out of the terminal. Yet, as he hailed a taxi and gave the driver the address of a freight brokerage on the East Wharf, he felt his stomach tense. The moment of truth was upon them.

Sonny had set up the whole deal with the freight broker in Venezuela. The transaction involved $5,000 worth of palm greasing, and he'd forewarned Jonathan he might be expected to provide a little more in the way of financial favors. But it wasn't the money that worried Jonathan. *If anybody has the slightest inkling as to the pallet's actual contents,* he thought as he watched the passing swarm of people and animals out the taxi window, *they would immediately throw me into prison.*

Every doorway and street corner they passed seemed to have its own resident beggar. When they stopped at a light, a man wearing dark glasses walked up to the window of the cab with outstretched hand. "Blind," he said in English, "please give money." Neeley held up his hand to decline the request, and the supposedly blind man reacted to this visual signal by turning away. Jonathan and Neeley exchanged amused smiles.

Twenty minutes later, the two men stood in the front office of the Eastern Gateway Freight Brokerage, Ltd. A long, dark counter separated them from a bespectacled little man in a white shirt who worked behind an ancient, battered desk. Behind him was a glass-enclosed office cubicle such as a supervisor would occupy.

The man finished writing on a form, laid it carefully on a stack to his right, then got up, and came over to Jonathan. "May I help you?"

"Yes," said Jonathan, pulling out his bill of lading. "I wish to accept delivery of an overseas shipment—from the *Cordillera de San Blas* out of Venezuela."

Peering through his spectacles at the form, the man brightened and said, "Oh, of course. Yes. Your crates would be in the warehouse. I will go to get." He turned to leave, then picked up a sheet of paper from a stack on a nearby desk and handed it to Jonathan. "Please," he said, smiling and gesturing for Jonathan to sit down in the waiting area. "Only to fill out this form."

Jonathan took the piece of paper. The legal-sized sheet was densely printed on both sides with blurry English letters.

"Not too long, Mr. Watt," the clerk reassured him. "Please have a seat, and I will locate your—" He looked at the form. "—your farm machinery."

Jonathan labored through the form while Neeley sat in silence. Besides the backless vinyl couch the two of them occupied, which was a shade of green Jennifer would have called frightening, the area contained only a decrepit end table laden with an array of film fan magazines, all of them in Urdu. Looking up from his form, Jonathan noticed that, instead of going back into the warehouse as he had assumed he would do, the clerk stood in the glass cubicle talking on a clunky black 1950s-style telephone. He looked at Jonathan as he spoke.

Save your paranoia for when we get to Afghanistan, Jonathan told himself. *The guy's just doing his job.* Seeming to notice Jonathan watching him, the clerk hung up the phone and disappeared into the warehouse.

After several more minutes of wading through the form, Jonathan noticed Neeley was getting restless. He glanced at him.

"All right if I go grab a smoke, Chief?" Neeley asked.

"Sure," said Jonathan. "Just don't go too far. And hey, why don't you see if you can locate the rental truck that is supposed to be waiting for us. I'm sure Sonny did his part, but I'll be flat bowled over if it's actually here."

"Yeah," said Neeley with a grin, "that'd be a certified miracle if it was here *and* ready like it's supposed to be. I'll check it out."

"Don't stray too far."

"No problem."

More than fifteen minutes passed after Neeley left. Jonathan, having more or less completed the form and laid it on the counter, began to pace back and forth. No one had come in or out of the office, and he was wondering if the clerk would ever return when, finally, the man bustled in from the back.

"Come, come," the man said. "We have located your materials."

"Was there a problem?" asked Jonathan.

"No, no, no," the man insisted, smiling. He held open a hip-high swinging door so that Jonathan could pass behind the counter.

"Don't you want to see the form?" Jonathan asked, stepping through.

"Oh yes, of course." The man picked it up and casually looked it over as a tall, elegantly dressed gentleman entered from the street.

The clerk looked up at the man and nodded. The latter nodded back as he withdrew a notebook from his breast pocket. With his dark brown skin and his black hair, he would normally have assumed he was Pakistani. But seeing him next to the clerk, Jonathan wasn't so sure.

"Come, come," said the clerk to Jonathan. "We will go to get your things from the loading dock."

"Right," said Jonathan. He glanced once more at the man in the dark suit, who was alternately staring at him, then back at his notebook. But he followed the clerk on through the office, past the glass cubicle, and into the warehouse.

The warehouse was a large, open area, surprisingly empty. He easily spotted his pallet on the loading dock. There sat six wooden crates, each small enough to be carried by two men, with *Puerto Cabello-Karachi* stenciled on their sides. Why the clerk would have had trouble locating them, Jonathan didn't know. *Maybe I didn't grease enough palms,* he thought.

Just then, he sensed someone standing right behind him.

"*Boltar!*" a voice shouted.

Jonathan knew he should know the name, but it took a split-second for it to register. He wheeled around, keeping his head low.

The well-dressed man from the waiting area was now standing behind him with a .38 caliber revolver in his hand, pointed straight at Jonathan's nose. He jerked his head for Jonathan to put his hands up, then nodded to the clerk, who scurried back out of the warehouse, his job done.

Still keeping the pistol on Jonathan, the man pulled out a portable UHF radio and spoke into it. He shouldn't have been surprised to hear Spanish, but the full implications of *Boltar* hadn't sunk in yet. One word of the man's transmission stood out. *Hector.*

"Uh-oh," Jonathan muttered, remembering Valdez's words, *"I don't care if I gotta go to camel land, I'm gonna have your blood."*

"That's right," said the man in the dark suit, a devious grin stealing across his face. "Hector has been waiting for this moment two months now. We didn't know we would find you so soon, but didn't think you would leave those valuable pieces of farm machinery sitting idle for too long. Guess you weren't so smart this time, were you?"

Jonathan ignored the taunt. "How did you find me?" he asked, still holding up his hands. His nose itched from a bead of sweat that had trickled there, but he didn't dare scratch.

The man shrugged. "Wasn't hard to figure out you left by either Venezuela or Panama, and we knew you had to ship those rockets. We figured Venezuela was more likely." He made a slight bow as though to say *And we were right.* "We paid off some shipping clerks and were able to locate your shipment. Unfortunately, it had already left port. However, Hector was happy to follow the shipment here for the opportunity to retrieve his valuable items and have the pleasure of killing you, as well. Hector has been waiting quite patiently for you to arrive, but he is most anxious to meet you again."

Jonathan laughed nervously. "Seems like a lot of trouble to go to, just for one man."

"Tell that to Hector, *Cabron*," said the man, moving in closer with the pistol. "When you see him."

"Oh," said Jonathan, his voice cracking. "Are you taking me to him?"

"No," the man answered with a grin. "He's coming right here to see you. Then we figure out where we want to go." Looking Jonathan up and down, he sneered. "You don't look the same. And without that fake accent, I might not have known it was you. But when I called out *Boltar* and you turned around, I knew." Edging still closer with the pistol, he added, "So I guess you're not as smart as you think."

"Neither are you!" boomed Neeley's voice from the edge of the loading dock. The Colombian dropped to his left knee and wheeled around to point the revolver toward Neeley. Jonathan took this as an opportune moment to jump out of the way—just as Neeley fired a single 12-gauge slug. The blast knocked the man backward against the wall, and his lifeless body slumped, leaving a trail of blood.

"Good thing Sonny had us prepared!" said Neeley with a laugh as he jumped up onto the loading dock.

"Good thing *you* were prepared," Jonathan answered. "I take it you found our truck," he said, nodding toward the Remington 870 shotgun, which Sonny had arranged to have taped under the front seat for Jonathan's trek into Afghanistan.

"Unbelievable, but it's ready and waitin'," said Neeley. "Since when does anything ever work out according to plan?"

"Good thing it did this time," Jonathan answered, picking up one end of a crate. "Let's load these up and get out of Dodge—I don't think our friend Hector is too far away."

It took them ten minutes to load the crates, and just a minute more to don the Afghan-style clothing Sonny had arranged to have in the truck along with the shotgun. They put these on, complete with headdress, over their traveling clothes, and sped off down the alleyway behind the freight brokerage. Just as they pulled away, in the rearview mirror Jonathan saw five men running out onto the loading dock. "They're here," he said calmly to Neeley, who was driving.

As they pulled out of the alleyway and onto the street packed with vehicles, pedestrians, and animals, they saw a sleek, black limousine turning into the alley. Meanwhile Jonathan and Neeley, looking like a couple of locals, passed right by them in the rented panel truck and blended into the flow of traffic.

Jonathan looked back again at the limousine. He was sure Hector Valdez himself was in there. "That was too close!" he shouted.

"I've been in worse scrapes," said Neeley as he turned another corner.

"How do you think they found the shipment?" Jonathan asked, sitting back in his seat as Neeley steered them through crowds of people, none of whom seemed to understand the concept of crosswalks or any kind of orderly traffic flow.

Neeley shrugged. "Probably wasn't hard—not for a guy who was so determined to find you."

"But why?" Jonathan asked. "I'll bet he spent five times the value of the diamonds to find me."

Neeley took his eyes off the road for a second. "He couldn't afford *not* to catch you. Think how much face he's gonna lose with his cartel buddies."

"Yeah, I suppose," Jonathan said. "It just seems like a lot of energy and expense just to settle a grudge."

Neeley glanced at him and raised his eyebrows. "Not that you would know anything about that," he said with a smirk.

Touché, Jonathan thought. He had just been taken to school by his mercenary assistant. So far, Jonathan had spent nearly a year and several million dollars to settle a grudge, and he wasn't even close to being through. He could easily have been killed in Colombia, as could Sonny, Neeley, and Gonzales. Valdez had not invested near what he already had in energy or expense. This was a clear case, as they used to say in south Alabama, of the pot calling the kettle black.

By 7:00 P.M., they were pulling up in front of a dingy white concrete three-story building indistinguishable from those on either side. Getting out of the truck, Jonathan heard a voice behind him and turned around to see a handsome Afghan with a scar over his left eye and the long, sharp features of a figure from a Byzantine painting. "Welcome," he said. "I am Khalid." Without taking his eyes off Jonathan, he shouted a command, and seconds later, several stout young men materialized from the building's interior. Khalid barked a set of orders at them, then turned to his two Western guests. "They will bring the radio parts inside," he said, and motioned for Jonathan and Neeley to follow him.

Khalid seemed to glide rather than walk as he moved ahead of Jonathan and Neeley, leading them down a narrow dark hallway, which smelled of hot spices and human sweat. It seemed like they walked a long time, then suddenly they entered a courtyard bathed in the fading light of afternoon. Jonathan blinked his eyes. Several women sat in a circle and, when they saw the men coming, they covered their faces with scarves. He and Neeley had done painstaking study about how to behave toward women here. The rules were pretty simple, really. Never, ever, ever act as though they existed.

Through another doorway they walked, up a flight of stairs, and down a long corridor to a series of back rooms. Khalid showed them their room, which had two Western-style mattresses on the floor. "Is safe," he announced. "Leave your belongings here and continue with me." They followed him into a vast and dimly lit room. Men sat on couches and pillows around the periphery.

Khalid clapped his hands, and one of the men jumped up. After he told the man something and the fellow scurried off, their host held out his hand to Jonathan and Neeley and said "Please," motioning for them to sit on the floor. As they eased onto the cushions, he raised his eyebrows and said, "Tea?"

"Yes, please," said Jonathan, bowing slightly. He hoped the gesture was appropriate. It seemed like the right way to show respect. And there was something about the rugged, wind-burned Afghan that commanded it.

While they waited to be served, he surveyed the group of men sitting on pillows around the perimeter of the room. All of them wore beards, and most had on embroidered *pattoos*, or shawls, though one wore what looked like a woman's coat. It was. Used Western clothing was a major import in Afghanistan even before the war, and Afghan men, not knowing Western fashions, sometimes selected women's jackets.

Each man stood and introduced himself with a Western handshake, smiling at them in the same mysterious, half-trusting way as their host. Suddenly, Khalid looked around at the others and they scattered, leaving just himself, Jonathan, and Neeley in the room.

When the tea was served, Jonathan decided to try and pry their host for some information.

"Have you returned from Afghanistan recently?" Jonathan asked, taking another sip.

"You are asking if I am in the fighting?" asked Khalid, smiling with both his mouth and his chestnut-colored eyes. He had a trace of a British accent. "Yes, I have been where there is fighting." He said it like someone who had no urge to brag. Jonathan again noticed the scar just above his left eye. His left hand, which he rested on the floor to balance himself as he sat cross-legged on the cushion, was missing two fingers. "Since the time there is war, I am fighting," he went on, "until this year. And then, I am wounded. A friend takes my place while I am here in Pakistan. I bring the supplies. I am"—he brightened a little and smiled slightly—"tour guide."

A whale of an expensive tour, Jonathan thought, his mind on the "machine parts" stored somewhere in the vast building. *And not exactly the luxury package, either.* "I see." Jonathan nodded his head gravely. He glanced over at Neeley, who sat there, with his teacup in hand, looking very disinterested. He didn't want Neeley to do any of the talking. That was for sure. "Do you know anyone in America?" Jonathan said, turning back to Khalid.

By asking the question, Jonathan hoped to establish a clear line of authority between the people he'd spoken to in Washington and his present hosts. But either Khalid wasn't going to give up that kind of information to a virtual stranger, or else he genuinely didn't understand the question. All he did was shrug his shoulders, smile, and say, "I have never traveled any farther from my home than here in Karachi. Once I planned to go on *hajj* to Mecca, but that was before . . ."

Presently a servant brought them dinner, which consisted of fish, yogurt, lentils, and a flat, chewy bread called *naan*. Jonathan found the food quite tasty, although Neeley didn't appear to feel the same. Jonathan didn't care. Not for what he was paying him to go along on this trip. Neeley could eat dog meat as far as he was concerned. The main thing was not to offend their proud hosts.

"These radio equipments you have bought," Khalid observed as he chewed on a piece of *naan*, "they are a gift from Allah." Jonathan watched his eyes, still wondering if the man knew what they were really bringing. But no. He figured if he had known that, there would have been a flash of excitement that was missing in his expression. "I wish only that your government would give us weapons—or sell them to us. We could expel the *Shuravi* in a very short time." He waved his hand. "But it does not matter. I have mission, and I will fulfill it. My instructions are to deliver both the equipment and yourself to our commander." He paused, and Jonathan wondered if he was going to talk about Massoud.

"But there is something you should know."

"What?" Jonathan didn't like the concerned look on his face.

"It is really no problem," Khalid said with a feigned air of nonchalance. "You see, normally we go into Afghanistan by a certain route, through Chitral in north Pakistan. But we have problems these days. The *Shuravi* recently hit many caravans on this route, so we don't go that way this month. Also, there is the problem of the weather. In this time of year, the only way to get to Chitral is to fly on commercial jet. Snow and ice makes it so we cannot drive there. Even if we could, the pass into Afghanistan is also blocked until May."

"So how are we going in?" Jonathan asked.

"We have another route," Khalid said. "We will go in west of Khyber Pass."

At the mention of the famed pass, Jonathan felt a leap of excitement. But there was also a sense of danger, heightened when Khalid said, "Yet there is only one problem more."

"Which is?" Jonathan sat forward on his cushion.

"Which is, I do not know this route as well as I do the one through Chitral."

Oh, great, Jonathan thought. *What's our next problem going to be?*

After dinner, Jonathan and Neeley returned to their rooms to find the crates had been moved in. Working together, they retrieved the pieces of each missile and Neeley assembled, and disassembled one before passing it over to Jonathan. He repeated the process for his own education. Jonathan paused for a moment over the

Stinger. After all the time and money they had cost him, this was only the second time—other than a brief moment in Caracas—he had held the powerful weapon.

He surrendered the missile launcher to Neeley, who took it apart and wrapped it in a blanket. As he did, Jonathan took time to admire his special gift from Sonny, the shotgun he had arranged to have waiting for them with the truck. This weapon, which had saved his life, was a customized Remington 870 shotgun. Sonny had picked it out, along with two boxes of double-aught buckshot and two boxes of slugs. Encased in a leather holster made to strap onto a horse for easy access while riding, the "Competition" Trap 12-Gauge was a lethal-looking weapon, from the pistol grip to the sawed-off barrel.

Neeley smiled when he spied the weapon again. "Sonny does know how to pick 'em, don't he?" he asked.

Jonathan nodded his head. "I'm just glad you made use of it at the right time." He brought the gun up and pointed it at a picture on the opposite wall, something he and Neeley had chuckled over when they first inspected their room—a framed photograph of the Ayatollah Khomeini.

According to Sonny, the pump action on the 12-Gauge made it the most reliable and effective weapon available for the sort of close action they might encounter on the narrow mountain trails of Afghanistan. Not only that, but the short barrel allowed for easier handling and greater shot dispersion. *And if none of that impresses you,* Sonny had added with a wink, *just the sound of that baby goin' off will scare the stuffin's outta anybody.*

"You never know when something like this will come in handy so far from home." Jonathan set the gun down and enclosed the weapon in its leather holster with great care.

Off in the distance he heard the haunting and mysterious wail of the muezzin calling the faithful to their fifth and final set of prayers for the day.

They left early the next morning in a dusty old truck. Boxes of oranges completely covered the Stingers, now stored in a single crate positioned directly behind the cab. Besides Jonathan, Neeley, and Khalid, there were two Pakistanis who took turns at the wheel. The one who wasn't driving did a stint riding in back with Neeley while Jonathan and Khalid stayed up front.

They took the main road to Lahore, 750 miles northeast. From there, they would turn north by northwest to Rawalpindi, another 200 miles, and then northwesterly to the end of the road in Peshawar, 100 miles farther. In the U.S., a trip like this would take a good solid day of driving, but here in Pakistan, even on the main national highway, they could expect to spend nearly three times as long.

The truck bounced along on the bumpy road with such violence, Jonathan was sure it would flip over. Posted road signs were few and far between, and the occasional ones they did come across looked so old, their reliability seemed questionable at best. From time to time, the driver would have to swerve to avoid a particularly huge pothole—or a bus crammed full with people, some riding even on the front bumpers, and careening toward them at sixty miles an hour in the wrong lane. There were bicycles and bullock carts, behind which the driver would usually slow to a crawl before finally pulling around them.

And that was during the day. They had to drive all night, partly because of the need to cut the trip short and partly because there weren't any Holiday Inns along the way if they'd wanted to stop. Apparently, headlights were optional in Pakistan. Many times in the dark, Jonathan saw another vehicle come out of nowhere and careen past them in the other direction while the driver kept his face forward, apparently unperturbed.

There were bandits, too, more and more the farther north they drove, which gave them yet another reason not to pull over and stop along the way.

Jonathan sat up front in the cab. There was no radio and, because the engine was so loud and Khalid wasn't inclined to talk anyway, no conversation. He had plenty of time to think through his plan in the minutest detail possible and to relive all the experiences that had gotten him to this point. But after riding for three days—almost non-stop—he was extremely pleased to arrive, at last, in Peshawar, "the city of flowers," on the evening of the third day.

A mountain town, Peshawar stood at a critical juncture between the Indian subcontinent and the landmass of Central Asia. The magnificent city had been coveted by conquerors throughout history. But Jonathan wasn't up for any sightseeing. Besides, their destination was farther out, in a refugee settlement an hour's drive past the center of town.

Here the people lived in small drafty houses, made of mud or whatever materials they could find, without enough wood for fires or clean water for drinking. An influx of war refugees during the past five years had not allowed time for the building of sewers—even if there had been any money to build them, which there wasn't. So an unspeakable stench wafted over the wide plains. Children in tattered clothes darted back and forth across the road.

The truck made a sharp right and sped past a group of men carrying firewood. After a few more turns, they stopped in front of a long, low, mud building, from which a number of men now emerged, swarming around the truck.

When Jonathan disembarked after sitting for so long, he felt like a sailor trying to get used to walking on dry land. He was exhausted, not just from the ride, but from the fact that, for three days, he'd only slept as much as the bouncing, dusty, uncomfortable truck would allow him. Emerging from the truck, he found the crowd, the darkness, and the stench of cooking onions a bit overwhelming.

Four Afghans, each carrying AKMS 7.62-mm assault rifles with folding stocks, assumed positions at the four corners of the truck while another four jumped up on the bed and began lifting down the orange crate. Jonathan squirmed, but he held his tongue. The last thing he wanted was for anyone to realize what the orange crate actually contained.

Khalid showed them into the mud hut, where they found three men sitting around a dim oil lamp. Two of them jumped up to greet Khalid, and he chatted with them. But he didn't seem to know the third, who only sat in silence and carefully watched the others. One of Khalid's men began talking, pointing toward the third man, while Khalid listened and frowned. This last man looked younger than the others, perhaps in his late twenties. He stood, smiled at Khalid, bowed, and spoke to him for some time.

Neeley glanced at Jonathan. They hadn't spoken much in the past few days because Neeley had been riding in the back of the truck, which must surely have been even more unpleasant than the front. Neeley looked haggard, but his eyes burned with suspicion as he gazed around at the Afghans.

Meanwhile Khalid, appearing perplexed, continued listening to the man. Suddenly, he smiled and nodded.

"What's going on?" Jonathan asked him.

"This is Hamid," explained Khalid. "He is new with us."

"You mean you don't know him?" Jonathan spoke with a stiff smile on his face and did not take his eyes off Hamid.

"He has just come to the camp," said Khalid. "My men"—he stopped to introduce them—"received a wire in Peshawar from . . . well, it is not important who it comes from. But it was a friend and supporter." From the look Khalid gave Jonathan, he assumed Khalid must be referring about Rashid. "According to this message," he went on, "Hamid has located Chinese RPGs, and he brings these in with us."

Jonathan looked at Neeley to see his reaction to this news, but Neeley wasn't looking at him. He had fixed his gaze upon Hamid.

"So you're saying that . . . your supporter vouches for him?" asked Jonathan, glancing back at Khalid.

Hamid said something to Khalid, who turned to Jonathan. "Hamid says to come look. He has seven RPGs, finest quality."

"Yeah, I'll come look," said Jonathan. He stared suspiciously at Hamid, whose black eyes met his for only a second before he turned away.

CHAPTER NINE

The next morning, Jonathan found himself surprisingly alert and awake, despite the hard journey to Peshawar and the discomfort of the night's accommodations. At least the bare dirt of the mud hut floor had been better than sleeping in the cab of the truck. He had rested well.

He was the first one to awaken, or he thought he was, and he stepped over Neeley's slumbering body to the outside of the hut. He yawned and stretched in the cool morning air, then surveyed the camp. There weren't many people awake, just a few children here and there playing in a mud flat between huts. He startled when he sensed the presence of someone off to his left.

Hamid, the newcomer, squatted on the ground a few paces from the hut. "Oh, good morning," said Jonathan, even though he knew the man couldn't speak English. He looked around. "Do you know where the toilet is?" he asked, speaking slowly. "Toilet?"

The man shook his head, shrugged, and then seemed to comprehend. He jerked his head past the hut, and Jonathan looked to see a thatch wall fifty yards or more beyond the hut. He nodded to Hamid and strolled over there. As he got closer, the smell and the sound of buzzing flies confirmed he'd found the place.

The primitive toilet conditions weren't the only hygienic discomfort he could expect in the next few weeks. Usually the second thing he did in the morning was to brush his teeth, but fresh water was scarce, and what they had was for drinking. From the looks of Khalid's dark teeth when he laughed, oral hygiene—or any kind of hygiene—wasn't a priority with these people.

He trudged back to the hut and found the rest of the group had awakened. Jonathan followed Khalid over to the stable where he learned that Khalid's men had secured twelve horses for the journey. Jonathan selected a sturdy-looking black one. He loaded the Remington with six shells, alternating the double-aught with the slugs, while Khalid's man stood by, observing the shotgun with admiration. Then he placed twenty-four shells in his cartridge belt, put the rest of his ammunition in a saddlebag, and strapped the shotgun onto his horse.

Later, after they breakfasted on *naan,* Jonathan and Neeley relieved the stable guard of his duties, which gave them an opportunity to remove the "radio parts" from the crate and put them on the horses without anyone seeing what the crate actually contained. They secreted the bundled parts on two different horses, then added pouches of rice, dried fruit, *naan*, fodder, ammunition, a few water containers, and a first-aid kit. When they'd finished, no one, not even their four Afghan companions, would suspect the horses carried anti-aircraft missiles.

Just as they finished, Khalid came to the stable to show them their route on a map. They would avoid most of the heavily guarded Khyber Pass a few miles distant and, instead, go "inside," as Khalid called it, by a much slower but safer southwesterly route. Once they entered the country, they would pass through an area of open plains along the Kabul River, avoiding the cities, which were the enemy's chief stronghold.

"We have to be careful," said Khalid, as though Jonathan and Neeley did not know as much. "All along the way we have the opportunity to be killed by Communists, or . . . " He stopped.

"Or what?" Jonathan asked.

Khalid shrugged. "It's nothing."

"Is there anything else out there we should know about?" Neeley asked.

Khalid shook his head. "No . . . " He refused to say anything more on the subject.

As the hills rose toward the Khyber Pass, the terrain spread out wide on either side with low hills full of Pakistani Frontier Force encampments. The army guarded this area well. And though some Pakistanis and Afghans could pass with permission, the only Westerners allowed through were U.N. officials and some approved journalists.

On the road up from Karachi, Jonathan and Neeley had adopted Afghan clothing, a comfortable style of dress consisting of loose-fitting garments. Combined with their beards and the deep tans they had aquired, they looked, at least from a distance, like they could be Afghans.

Jonathan wanted the group to stay as close together as possible on the trail, but the narrowness of the road made riding abreast difficult. So, they spread out into a long caravan of six men and twelve horses. Khalid rode out front, with Jonathan directly behind him, then two horses carrying food and supplies, two more horses with Hamid's RPGs, followed by Khalid's two men, the two horses carrying the Stingers and, at the rear, Neeley and Hamid. Having seen the way those two had eyed each other on first meeting the day before, Jonathan had hoped to keep them as far apart as possible. But Khalid was in charge of the convoy, and this was the way he had set things up.

The air was fresh and cool, and Jonathan was glad it was March instead of August—and not just because of the temperature. The air at the camp in Peshawar was heavy with stench, so it was a relief to get out onto the trail, where the only smells came from his horse and the thinning plants and trees growing nearby. There was one other source of odor. Jonathan hadn't had a bath since they landed in Karachi more than half a week before. Whether anyone else noticed or not, Jonathan knew he reeked.

The dirt road zigzagged upward, climbing swiftly, the trail becoming more and more treacherous. Nothing, neither the road nor the spaces on either side, not even the horizon, seemed flat. Everywhere Jonathan looked he could see only sharp rises and jutting peaks. Around them, fewer and fewer trees grew. The ones that survived here were hardy, strong from withstanding ferocious winds and little rainfall. Jonathan doubted it ever got very warm here, even in the summertime. He could feel a cool breeze at his back that could easily turn icy. As he let his eyes roam over the steep hills, he realized just one false move and both he and his horse would tumble end over end for hundreds and hundreds of feet. There wouldn't even be any point to searching for survivors at the bottom of the ravine.

Jonathan leaned in and patted his horse on its dusty neck. "Good boy," he said softly into the horse's ear. "You just take it easy, now." The ear twitched as though the horse understood him.

As they rode, Khalid pointed ahead toward a bulky concrete guard facility in the distance. Several soldiers stood on watch, with a number of jeeps standing ready nearby. "What are we going to do?" Jonathan asked.

Khalid laughed. "We won't go that direction, I will tell you for certain." He pointed toward the southwest. "We go that way," he said. "We see the guards, but we will never be close enough for them to see us."

"How will we know when we're in Afghanistan?" Jonathan asked.

Khalid shook his head. "We won't. That is why we go this way. No one knows when we come and go."

They came to a crook in the trail and turned onto the detour that would take them away from the guards. Jonathan looked back at Neeley, riding close to Hamid, and the wind at his back felt colder.

The caravan picked its way onward through the pitch-black night. Jonathan could only make out the shadowy figures of his companions. A sliver of the new moon glowed faintly in the sky, and, beyond its dim light, the night hung around them as dark as the inside of a mine shaft.

During the past fifteen hours, they had traveled through a variety of topographies. They had covered thirty miles of windswept, bluish-gray wasteland. Then, they had entered the mountains. The terrain had changed from a treeless plateau to a maze of shallow canyons, seemingly endless in their monotony. They had ridden along the bottoms of these dry scars for what felt like miles and miles, their horses carefully treading over sharp rocks. Everywhere blew dust of a light brown color, the Farsi word for which was *khaki*.

From there they passed the first of the mountains, a "mere" 7,000-foot peak with patches of snow along its slopes. They rode ever upward. Beyond the valley, Jonathan could see a range of rocky heights, which seemed to shoot up almost at a right angle from the earth's surface. He watched the skies change from white to purple to black while the temperature, already cool, dropped a good ten or fifteen degrees.

When they stopped at one point, he pulled Neeley aside to confer. "How are you holding up?" Jonathan asked, stretching to get some of the soreness out of his thighs. He couldn't imagine how some of those out-of-shape journalists ever managed to make it into Afghanistan. The journey proved hard enough while riding a horse, even without the hardship of getting off and hiking when the slopes got too steep.

"Not too bad," Neeley answered, a little hesitantly. "I'll just be glad when we get where we're going." He paused to light a cigarette.

"Me too," Jonathan agreed. "I'm looking forward to delivering those Stingers."

"Yeah." Neeley thought for a minute. "You know, Chief, I—" He stopped in mid-sentence and shrugged his shoulders.

"What?"

Neeley shook his head. "It's nothing. Just a hunch." He jerked his chin almost imperceptibly in the direction of Hamid, who stood apart from the other three Afghans. "That one there seems pretty tense. Somethin' just doesn't feel right. How much do we know about him?"

But Jonathan didn't have a chance to answer because Khalid called out to them, telling them it was time to be on their way.

They rode on through the night for what seemed like an eternity. The darkness, the horse's rocking motion, the terrain, and his own sheer exhaustion, all blended together, and Jonathan fell into a half-sleep, half-wakened state of hallucination.

The mountains rose higher and higher and higher. He felt as though they might keep on going up through the top of the stratosphere. The Persian name for this range was Safed Koh, meaning White Mountain, and the 16,000-foot peaks that rose all around them kept their snowcaps all year long. Icy winds blew off the tops of the mountains and swept through the tiny caravan, chilling both men and animals.

At some points the path became so steep and narrow, each man had to dismount and lead his horse. In the middle of a dangerous narrow passageway, Jonathan's horse knocked a rock loose, and he listened as the stone went tumbling hundreds and hundreds of feet, kicking up other rocks as it fell. The miniature avalanche resounded like gunfire in the night until the stones finally came to rest far, far below.

Deep in the night, before the sky showed any signs of lightening, they reached a very steep section of the trail, which went winding around the side of a particularly treacherous mountain. Everyone dismounted, and Jonathan was speaking soothing words to his horse when he heard a commotion behind him.

What sounded like someone's saddlebags falling off was followed by the desperate neighing of a horse. And then—

The cold mountain peaks reverberated with the sound of a man's horrified screams, slowly dying off into the abyss far below them.

Jonathan whipped around and looked at Khalid. Just then, Hamid came scrambling toward them up the rocky trail, out of breath and shouting in frantic Farsi. A look of deep shock filled Khalid's face as he listened, nodding his head.

"What's he saying?" Jonathan demanded.

Gravely, Khalid turned toward Jonathan and told him to wait while he checked it out. Jonathan, ignoring the instructions, followed Khalid to the rear of the caravan. There stood Hamid, pointing off toward the steep side of the trail and speaking rapidly.

"What's happened?" Jonathan demanded, looking from Khalid to Hamid to the other two Afghans. But he feared he already knew the answer to his question. "Where's . . ." His question died on his lips as he realized who was missing.

"Your friend," said Khalid. "He must have slipped on a loose stone . . . this is what Hamid says. I am sorry, but these things happen in many trips over mountains. If a man is not careful enough—"

Jonathan shook his head. What he knew, but couldn't say, was that the man who had supposedly "fallen" was a Marine Force Recon veteran. Trained in rappelling, Neeley could climb up sheer rock faces. Guys like that didn't just simply fall off of cliffs.

"We have to go find him," Jonathan said, taking a deep breath. "It may be he's only injured. I'm sure he's still alive."

Khalid shook his head firmly. "The bottom of that cliff is a long, long way down. You would need many days to reach the bottom. No one could survive such a fall."

Still disbelieving, Jonathan brought out a flashlight and began to inspect the edge of the trail. The marks where the horse had lost its footing were evident, but it looked like there was something more to the story. Judging by the skids in the dust from one side of the trail to the other, where the tracks disappeared, it looked like there had been a struggle.

As he looked, he became aware of the four Afghans watching him. He glanced up and saw them gazing at him in the darkness. A fresh realization struck him. Now, for the first time, he was completely alone.

Just when the sun began to rise over the distant mountaintops, they reached a village where Khalid intended to stop and rest. But as they got closer, they noticed a clay hut in the center of the small settlement had been reduced to smoking rubble. Other dwellings closely surrounded the demolished one, yet they did not appear to have been touched.

At the sight of the caravan, several men ran out, pointing and shouting. They explained that a bomb—dropped seemingly as an afterthought from a Soviet Su-22 fighter-bomber—had hit the village. Due to the random nature of the raid, only three people had been killed and the one building destroyed.

Jonathan and the mujahideen rode on into the center of the village, toward the remains of the mud house. A number of other buildings, showing signs of recent damage to their walls, appeared to have absorbed some of the impact. Already the villagers had placed three bamboo poles with white flags on the bombing site to commemorate the three "martyrs" who had fallen there.

Khalid pointed upward, and Jonathan saw thin contrails from a high-altitude reconnaissance jet, which was probably photographing their movements. "You see now why we travel only at night," he said to Jonathan.

A group of children began to gather around them, curious at the sight of a non-Afghan, but Khalid shooed them away. A villager allowed them to put their horses in his stable, and someone else showed them to a mud house where they could all sleep. The floor was matted with straw, and a few blankets were spread out upon the straw. A sheepskin covering the building's one window kept out the morning light.

Jonathan felt dazed. The minutes he spent moving from the saddle of his horse to his makeshift bed passed in a blur. All he had been able to think about for the past few hours had been Neeley. He couldn't believe the man was really gone. He kept looking around for him. But the only men in sight were Khalid, Khalid's two soldiers, and Hamid.

As exhausted as he was, when he actually lay down on the soft straw, Jonathan felt keyed-up and restless. And when he did fall asleep, his nightmares were filled with images of Neeley, Jennifer and Jon, and Drakoff—always the leering figure of Drakoff laughing at him. In one dream, it was Drakoff pushing Neeley off the mountain—

Pushed! Jonathan suddenly jerked awake. *Neeley was pushed!* The expense of Jonathan's journey toward vengeance had just risen inestimably. A man whom he had come to depend on was now dead. And it was all Jonathan's fault. If only he had acted on his own preferences—or responded to Neeley's intuition . . . but if Hamid had pushed Neeley, wouldn't he be planning to kill Jonathan as well?

This isn't a movie script where the good guy always wins. He couldn't shake the troubling thought from his mind. This was real life. For the first time, Jonathan began to realize the full impact of the truth: It was entirely possible that he, too, would die before he could accomplish his objective.

When he opened his eyes, it appeared to be late afternoon. Someone had removed the covering from the window, and he saw the sky outside graying like an aging man. Jonathan felt a little sick to his stomach.

Khalid leaned over him and gave him a weak smile. "I let you sleep a little bit longer," he said. "I know it is hard if you are new to these mountains. Also, we will have to delay leaving tonight."

Jonathan sat up, rubbing his eyes. The inside of his mouth tasted like an old sock. "Why?" he asked groggily, looking around and seeing the others sitting in a corner of the room, talking to a couple of locals.

"The *Shuravi* are near. One of the men in the village was herding goats on a hill not far away, and he saw their soldiers on patrol. He said he thinks they are not heading into this direction. But until we can be sure they are gone, we must delay our departure."

So they waited for hours, the others talking amongst themselves in Farsi while a group of children gathered around the window to spy on Jonathan. He ignored them, and he might have grown bored if his mind hadn't been on Neeley and what had happened the day before. From time to time he would see Khalid talking to the others, and he was sure the man was talking about him.

Four hours passed and darkness had fallen when they finally started off again on their journey. But they only traveled a few hours before Khalid ordered them to stop at an abandoned house outside another village. "Why are we stopping again?" asked Jonathan impatiently. It was only three in the morning, and they still had a good four hours of darkness in which to travel.

"I do not think we can reach our next destination before morning," Khalid answered. "And it is too dangerous to travel in day with these patrols nearby. Since we already know this house from our other journeys, we will stop here and sleep again." Khalid smiled.

He seems more than a little condescending, thought Jonathan.

"Don't worry, my friend, there will be plenty of opportunity to become tired. Sleep now, for you will need it."

One of Khalid's men took first watch while everyone else went to sleep. Jonathan spread some straw around in a corner of the one-room dwelling and stuffed some more of it into a saddlebag to make a rudimentary pillow, much to the amusement of the rugged Afghans. As it turned out, Khalid was right about needing to rest again. As soon as he put down his head, Jonathan was asleep. This time he didn't dream about Neeley. In fact, he didn't dream about anything at all.

It seemed as though he'd just dropped off when Jonathan heard people around him shouting, and at first he thought he was dreaming. He was back at the International Trade Mart, facing off with Tchinkov, only this time everyone stepped aside to give him a clear shot. And yet just as his fist hit the Russian's face, he was jarred awake by the loud *ba-rak-ak-ak-ak* of an automatic weapon. With Khalid shouting in his ear, he jumped up.

"What?" he demanded. Caught between his dream and reality, Jonathan wasn't sure exactly where he was, but his heart was pounding.

"Keep your head down!" Khalid whispered angrily, pulling him swiftly to the ground.

"What's going on?" Jonathan asked again. He glanced at his watch. It was only a little past four in the morning. He jumped when he heard more automatic weapon fire outside, and quickly he rolled over to retrieve his shotgun.

Beside him he heard Khalid breathing heavily. The two crouched on the ground, facing the open door of the house. Outside the moon had risen, but its light only faintly glimmered in the dark night.

"I don't know." Khalid shifted slightly to get a better view through the door. "I wake up hearing gunshots, and I look up, and the door is open."

Jonathan looked around. One of Khalid's men lay motionless against the wall of the house. He gestured wildly, "Khalid—what has happened to him?"

"I don't know." Khalid started to move toward the body of his friend when suddenly, *Ba-rak-ak-ak-ak! Ak-ak-ak-ak!* The firing continued for a few more bursts, and Khalid and Jonathan threw themselves against the doorframe for protection.

"Quick," Jonathan said, pointing. "You stand there, and I will take the other side." They took their positions on either side of the door.

"Ssh!" hissed Khalid. He pointed outside, where they could hear the distinct sound of footsteps just beyond the door. The feet seemed to hesitate, and then began running in their direction.

Jonathan leveled the barrel of his shotgun at a ghostly silhouette coming through the open door, but Khalid shouted, "No! It is Hamid!"

Glancing in Jonathan's direction, Hamid proceeded to speak frantically with Khalid. "You stay!" Khalid ordered Jonathan, turning around. "I will go and check."

While he crept off, Jonathan and Hamid sat facing each other. Time slowly crept by, and the only noise for several minutes was their ragged breathing. After what seemed an eternity, they heard Khalid shouting to them from outside the house, announcing his return so they wouldn't shoot him by mistake.

"Well?" said Jonathan.

Without a word, Khalid sat down on the ground and shook his head, seemingly unable to speak.

"What happened?" Jonathan demanded after several futile attempts to get him to say something. "Where is the guard?"

Khalid shook his head again. "Dead."

"Dead?"

"There has been an attack, and whoever did this thing has slipped off in the dark." He shook his head over and over.

Hamid broke in and spoke to Khalid for several seconds.

"What's he saying?" Jonathan asked.

"He wants to know if he should take the first watch."

Jonathan glanced at Hamid, who was looking at Khalid and not at him. "No," Jonathan said. "I can't go back to sleep. Tell him I'll do it."

Khalid relayed this to Hamid, who looked at Jonathan with hard eyes but said nothing.

So Jonathan went outside, shotgun in hand. They were on a small plateau, and it didn't look like the kind of place where someone on guard could have been easily ambushed. He glanced around, walking the perimeter and gazing down the rocky slope. Somewhere he could hear a stream running.

Suddenly his foot struck something, and he nearly cried out. It was the body of the guard, leaned up against a post. The head drooped to the front, and the chest was covered with blood. Apparently someone had slit the man's throat. Jonathan moved the head slightly to get a better look at the wound. The cut was the work of a professional assassin—very surgical. Whoever did this knew what they were doing.

So this was the one who had been ambushed. Jonathan looked around, still thinking that it seemed unlikely anyone could have sneaked up on the guard without being heard . . . when it suddenly occurred to him that the other man had been killed *inside the house* while he slept. First Neeley; now these two men. There was no way this was just a coincidence. He pondered how he might relay his extreme suspicions to Khalid.

Jonathan looked up to see Khalid coming toward him, his head hanging low. Jonathan watched him in the pale moonlight, and he knew the man's heart was heavy. Behind him followed Hamid. In stark contrast to Khalid, Hamid held his head high.

Khalid looked up at Jonathan. "My friend inside too is dead, his throat slashed. These men were my brothers, though we had different mothers and fathers. I have lived with them, worked with them, and fought beside them for almost seven years." His eyes blazed. "Whoever has done this thing will surely die—*Insha'Allah!*"

"Khalid," Jonathan said softly. "I was just thinking—" He motioned for Khalid to come closer. Even though Hamid supposedly didn't understand English, he felt safer not taking any chances. Watching Hamid, who stood staring into the darkness with his hands behind his back, Jonathan said, "Doesn't it seem strange that the guard was taken by surprise so easily? And that one of us was killed *inside* the house?"

Khalid shook his head. "It all seems strange."

"No, but I mean, doesn't it seem odd that somebody was able to sneak up on us and kill two men?"

"Yes," said Khalid somberly. "And they might have killed you and me as well, if Hamid had not woken up and chased them away with his AK-47."

Jonathan looked at Khalid, then at Hamid. He nodded his head and went back to standing guard while Khalid sat by and Hamid went back into the house for a few hours' sleep.

As the sun rose, the few people still living in the nearby village began to move about, several of them coming to a well just a few dozen yards from the house. Khalid walked down to question them about the previous evening.

From where he and Hamid sat in silence at the front of the house, Jonathan could see him talking to locals. When Khalid returned a few minutes later, bearing a full canteen of fresh drinking water and some bread and fruit, he shrugged and said, "They heard nothing—only the gunshots. They say there are no government troops in this area for months now."

He looked around. "I do not like this. But before we talk of it further, I must . . ." He broke off as he turned and walked over to kneel beside the dead body of his friend. It was the man who had been inside. Hamid had dragged his corpse out and laid it on the ground beside the guard. Khalid, his face showing signs of exhaustion, looked up at Jonathan. "I must prepare them for burial."

"You want me to help?" Jonathan asked cautiously.

"Thank you," said Khalid. "But no." He turned to Hamid and gave him an order, and the other man hurried off. Khalid looked at Jonathan apologetically. "Only Muslims can take part in burial," he said.

Jonathan nodded his head, and squatted down on the ground to watch what they did.

First they disrobed the bodies, then washed them with water from the well. Hamid went down to the village and got some white linen to wrap their bodies, and while he was gone, Khalid gave Jonathan a task which an "infidel" could do just as well as a Muslim—dig the graves.

The villagers loaned them shovels, and they proceeded to dig about thirty yards from the house, behind a thicket of scrubby bushes.

"We must reduce our load," Khalid said as he pushed his shovel into the hard ground with his boot. "When we started, we had six men and twelve horses; now we are only three men. Let us take our three horses, with four others to carry supplies, and give the other food and five horses to the men in village. Then when we return, we will get the other horses back."

After he had worked for a while, Jonathan stopped digging for a moment and planted the shovel in the earth. He squinted as a droplet of salty sweat ran into his eye. "Khalid," he ventured cautiously, "what do you know about Hamid?"

Khalid shook his head. "I know only he comes with recommendation of our liaison office."

Jonathan gestured toward Hamid, who they could see down in the village, talking to a group of men. "Remember that first day in Peshawar when we met him? I asked you if . . . your liaison office really vouched for him. But before you had a chance to answer, Hamid told you he wanted to show us the RPGs he'd brought." He looked Khalid in the eye. "It was like he understood what I was saying. And have you noticed, he's always looking at us when we're talking? I'm telling you, it's like he understands." As though in confirmation, they saw Hamid, hundreds of yards away and well out of earshot, stop talking to the villagers and look up toward them.

Jonathan looked at Khalid. "And think about this," he went on. "Three men are dead, all under strange circumstances. And every time, Hamid . . ."

"Was there." Khalid nodded. "Only *he* saw your friend fall, and only *he* saw last night's intruder. It is possible he is telling the truth, and then again . . ." Khalid let his voice trail off and, for a moment, he shoveled on in silence. "I will draw you a map to our destination, in case something should happen to me," Khalid said in a solemn voice.

"But Khalid," Jonathan said. "I couldn't find my way through this country in the daytime, let alone at night."

"As one man," said Khalid, "you would be too small to be seen from the sky. You could travel freely during the day."

"*That* makes me feel reassured," Jonathan answered.

"Now," Khalid continued, "we are many days from our destination. There are villages between, and I will give you descriptions of each so you can recognize them. There are, of course, no signs to tell you where you are going. People who travel this way already know where they are." He withdrew a piece of paper and a stub of pencil from his pocket and began sketching out a map. "I will give you the name of a contact at each location, and a letter from me instructing them to take care of you. I must confess. I do not know these people well because I rarely travel this route, but they are allies. Now, at the final destination, my friend Ali will be looking for you."

Seeing Hamid coming back toward them, Khalid spoke rapidly. "There is also one very important message to learn in Afghanistan," he explained. "In our code of honor, we have this word, *nanawatai,* and if you say it, you are asking a man to give you his hospitality and his mercy. Normally a man of honor will respect this request. But it is a risk. If you say it to a man, you bring shame upon yourself, and the other man is not obligated to help you. An Afghan who uses this term must present his wives without their veils. So, my friend, if you are in a situation where you cannot communicate, and you have tried everything else, invoke this word." Khalid studied Jonathan's eyes. "*Nanawatai,*" he said again. "You never know when it may be very important to use it."

CHAPTER TEN

Days—or rather, nights—passed. They slept out the former and traveled during the latter, which meant they didn't make as much headway as they might have. And on top of darkness and the threat of the enemy, they had weather to contend with. Monsoon rains blew north from India, and one night they didn't cover two miles before they had to stop.

Food proved scarce wherever they went. For the most part, they survived on the dried fruit they'd brought along with them, a favorite mujahideen food because of the high sugar concentration. There were also nuts, pistachios, walnuts, and almonds. But none of these things really satisfied the stomach. As for meat, they couldn't bring any with them because of spoilage, and chances of finding any were slim. After 3,000 years of hunting, there were no deer left in the Afghan mountains, and the best they could hope for was a rabbit or a duck—if they were lucky. They weren't. In some parts of the country, boar ran wild. But, because Muslims wouldn't touch them, they might as well not have even existed. As hungry as he was all the time these days, Jonathan wouldn't have minded a ham sandwich himself, but he wisely did not express this sentiment to his hosts.

Khalid and Jonathan always rode side-by-side behind the four packhorses with Hamid out front, his back to them. "It has only been seven years, my friend, since these troubles began," said Khalid to Jonathan one night as they rode along on the rocky trail. "No one knows how many men have died because of the Soviets since they come, but I know of four. My father and my three older brothers."

"They were shot by the government?"

Khalid shook his head. "My father and two brothers were so lucky, but another brother went to Pul-i-Charki—that is prison in Kabul where government take men to die. I never saw him again after he went in, but I have heard stories. They beat people and torture them. One man was put in a room full of dead bodies, and just the smell of them almost killed him. Another was put in water with electric shock. I do not know what happened to my brother, but I am sure he has died."

Jonathan shook his head. "What kind of creatures can do things like that to other people?"

He had meant it as a rhetorical question, but Khalid answered him. "They say he is called the Butcher of Kabul."

"Who?"

"The man who interrogated my brother." Khalid leaned away from his horse and spit onto the ground. "The man who killed my brother. He is the most evil of the *Shuravi*. If I could ever find him alive, I would . . ." He finished his sentence with a sigh. "I only need to say, I would take pleasure in watching him die slowly." He glanced at Jonathan. "Perhaps you do not understand this kind of hatred I feel for this man."

"Oh, I do, Khalid—believe me, I do." Jonathan smiled at his companion. "We are not so different as you might think." He pointed to himself. He thought of Drakoff, who was somewhere in the same country as he. "There was a man who harmed my own family, and I have devoted my whole life to finding him." In his mind Jonathan could see the man's imaginary face. *I am so close to him now. In the same country even.* Jonathan looked at Khalid. "And when I do find him—" Jonathan was caught by surprise at his failure to finish his own sentence. He was too close to his objective to be having any doubts now.

"He will wish that his father had never known his mother," Khalid finished, nodding with approval.

"Yes," said Jonathan with a forced firmness, as though Khalid was the only one who needed convincing of his intentions.

Nine days out of Peshawar, they were beyond Kabul, having skirted around it about thirty-five miles to the east. Only one more day to Massoud's camp, and then this interminable journey would be over. It was five o'clock on a Wednesday afternoon, and, in accordance with their practice of traveling at night, they were just beginning preparations to get underway after having slept for the whole day in an isolated hut.

Jonathan had just put all his gear together and stepped out of the hut when he heard a gasp. He ran to find Khalid kneeling on the ground, a dark red spot growing on the surface of his white shirt.

"Khalid!" Jonathan rushed toward the slumped figure, but he was too late. His own knees buckled under him as the blood rushed from his head. He knelt beside the dying man, taking him into his arms. Khalid, his lungs already filling with blood, managed to rasp, "Hekmatyar—I should have known."

"Khalid?" Jonathan asked frantically. "What does that mean?" He looked down at his friend, whose eyes rolled back in his head as blood began to gurgle from of his mouth. "Hekmatyar? The mujahid leader, Hekmatyar?"

Khalid mustered the strength to say, *"Allahu akbar!"* before his body went limp in Jonathan's arms.

In preparing to hit the trail, Jonathan had already strapped his Remington 870 onto his shoulder, and he instinctively reached up to pull it out as he laid down Khalid's lifeless body.

But he froze at the sound of Hamid's voice behind him, speaking perfect English.

"Don't, you infidel!" the voice said. "Drop your weapon to the ground."

Jonathan did as commanded. He stood up slowly as Hamid came around beside him and, out of the corner of his eye, he stared at the other man with sudden, growing hatred and fury.

"I see that look," Hamid said. "If I were you, I wouldn't waste my energy on anger." He had an AK-47 in his hand, and he thrust the barrel toward Jonathan's chest. "Lift your hands above your head," he ordered.

Jonathan raised his hands slowly. *So this is how it ends,* he thought, his anger now mingling with fear.

But several minutes—or at least what seemed like several minutes—passed while Hamid walked slowly around him, and the realization dawned on him that if the man meant to kill him, he would have done it by now.

Hamid was chewing *naswar,* which resembled snuff, and he spit a black wad onto the dusty soil. "You're surprised I speak English?"

Jonathan shrugged.

"I worked at the American Embassy for three years in Kabul while I was at the university, then I went to graduate school at Columbia University. Watching your American television improved my English even more." He added with a sneer, "It taught me how to kill as well."

"So why did you kill the others?" Jonathan kept his voice hard and steady.

"They were in the way," Hamid answered with a nonchalant shrug. "Three of them are happy. They are martyrs." An evil grin twisted his face, exposing a mouth with three teeth missing. "However, your friend the infidel . . . he is perhaps not so happy where he is."

"Okay, so we've established that you're not on Khalid's side." Jonathan pointed his chin toward the body. "Does that mean you're an agent of the Communists?"

Hamid spat again. This time the brownish glob of sputum grazed the tip of Jonathan's boots. "Do I look like a Communist to you?"

Once more Jonathan heard Khalid's dying words, *"Hekmatyar—I should have known—"*, and comprehension finally began to dawn on him.

"No," he said with a knowing smile, "you're working for Hekmatyar, aren't you? The one who will kill his own people sooner than he kills the Russians?"

"You talk too much," said Hamid, and Jonathan had all the confirmation he needed.

Now, if he could just figure out how to get away from his captor. Testing Hamid, Jonathan moved one hand to swipe a ticklish stream of sweat that had trickled down his forehead.

"Hey!" Hamid barked, jerking the barrel of the AK-47. "You move only when I say so, understand?"

Jonathan held his hands higher. "Okay, okay!" he said. "Now why not tell me what it is you want from me?"

"You know exactly what I want, Yankee. The equipment you've brought."

"Radio equipment?"

"Don't play the fool," Hamid said angrily. "Maybe you could get Khalid and his friends to believe you, but not me. I know all about the Stinger missiles. And now I'm prepared to get them to their proper destination. You know, if I wanted to I could kill you and take them right now—" he swung the rifle directly at Jonathan's chest, then moved it away. "But instead, I will let you show me how to operate the missiles."

"So how did you know about the Stingers?" Jonathan asked.

"None of your business." Hamid gazed off in the direction of Khalid's body. "But let's just say we have important friends in Washington."

"Rashid?" Jonathan asked, picturing his contact in D.C.

Hamid hesitated, and then he nodded slowly. "Yes," he said. "Yes, it was Rashid."

"He said he was working for Massoud."

"Of course. Our leader Hekmatyar is not popular in the West. Massoud, on the other hand . . ." Hamid spread his arms wide, and assumed a facetious tone. "Well, Massoud is honorable! Massoud is a hero! Massoud looks good in photos!" Hamid chuckled, a most disagreeable sound. "But no matter. Just rest assured, these weapons will find their way into the proper hands and will end up serving Allah."

Jonathan ignored the taunts. "Why should I show you how to operate the missiles, when that means I become expendable?"

"Oh, I'm not worried about you. Once I have the missiles, I'll let you go," Hamid said with a leer.

Sure you will, thought Jonathan.

"You don't believe me?" demanded the other man, reading Jonathan's face. "Oh, I *would* kill you, certainly, but I don't have enough time for the kind of slow death that you probably deserve. So I'll let the peasants do it for me. Once I let you go and they catch you wandering around the countryside, they'll take you for a Russian and skin you alive. They're simple folk, you know, and they won't know the difference between a 'good' Yankee and a 'bad' Russian."

Jonathan just stared at his captor.

Hamid pointed toward one of the horses carrying the alleged radio equipment. "Now," he said, "you go fetch a missile and show me how to operate it, then I will let you go."

"It's more complicated than that," said Jonathan irritably. "I've practiced with them a lot of times, and I'm here to tell you, it was only after a lot of practice that I was ever able to hit a moving target." It was a lie, but he hoped Hamid wouldn't know it. "Take me where you're going, and I'll fire them for you. I just want to kill Russians, and I don't care who I'm with when I do it."

Hamid narrowed his eyes. "We shall see. You will still explain to me how to operate them, but I may let you come with me and fire them. I warn you. If these missiles fail to operate, I will hold you accountable. And you know what that means."

Jonathan nodded.

"All right, then," said Hamid. "We are ready to move, so let us go." He walked over to Khalid's body and, with a twisted smile, spoke down to it in a loud voice. "However, Khalid, I'm afraid we have had a slight change of destination."

"Can't we bury him first?" asked Jonathan.

"No." Hamid looked up angrily. "Who are you, an infidel, to bury one of ours? Besides, we have no time. The villagers, they will take care of it." He glanced at the body of the man Jonathan had begun to know as a friend, and as an afterthought added, "Leave them his horse also—we don't need it slowing us down. Now, move!"

Hamid forced Jonathan to ride up front. "And you better not think about anything other than staying on the trail," he ordered his captive. "My weapon is no more than ten feet from the back of your head, and you have absolutely no place to go."

Of course he was right. Jonathan would be lost in the darkness. And without a weapon, it would just be a matter of time before Hamid tracked him down. Even if he did get away, he would be alone in the dark in the middle of Afghanistan. It was almost better to remain a captive—for now at least. Jonathan would wait for the right moment to make his move. In the meantime, he kept Hamid's mind occupied with questions.

"Hamid?" he called back to his captor.

"What?" demanded the Afghan in an irritated voice.

"I still don't understand. If your people, Hekmatyar's people, have the same enemy as Massoud's people, then why—"

"Just because you and I have the same enemy does that mean we are friends?" Hamid snapped. "The Russians and their puppets, they are just a speck on our history. What endures are the rivalries between ourselves, and those will continue long after all you foreigners are gone."

"But why Hekmatyar and not Massoud?" Jonathan asked.

"Because when this war is over," Hamid said bitterly, "and Hekmatyar is in power, he will return our country to us, and keep the foreigners—*all* the foreigners—out. Is that a good enough answer?"

Jonathan thought for a moment as his horse jostled him slowly along the trail. "You're obviously very well-educated," he said finally, "and you speak English about as well as I do. You must have been a top-notch student at the university . . ."

"Don't try to flatter me," Hamid answered. "And I know what you're getting at. You're asking yourself how an educated man could believe these 'uneducated' things? Because I am not like one of you Westerners, who have no souls and nothing to believe in. Now shut up and keep riding."

Some time later, after having ridden uphill for a long while, Hamid announced they would stop and sleep until daybreak, still several hours away. From here on, he said, the trail would get steeper and narrower, and they would have to travel in daylight. Just before bedding down, he tied his prisoner's hands and feet, then attached a rope connecting the two of them.

Not long before they stopped, Jonathan casually asked Hamid how much farther they had to go to reach their final destination. Hamid beat around the bush at first, but finally said they would meet his people within a day or two, and then it would be another couple of days before they got to camp.

Therefore if Jonathan planned to get out of Afghanistan alive, he had to do something soon. Right now it was just he and Hamid, but once Hamid had a half-dozen or so friends with him, that would be the end of any chance for escape.

Once Hamid had been still for about half an hour, Jonathan tested the ropes, shifting against them carefully in various ways. He had a knife hidden in his combat boot, a place Hamid hadn't thought to search him, and if he could get to it . . . But Hamid had tied the ropes so that he couldn't move much without waking him. He then considered the various ways he might try to escape when Hamid went to untie him in the morning.

But he should have known his captor would be smarter than that. After Hamid woke up and stretched, he reached over to untie Jonathan, with the barrel of his AK-47 pointed straight at Jonathan's heart. He quickly cut the ropes binding Jonathan's hands, and then he stepped back and instructed Jonathan to untie his own feet.

They got going and, as Hamid had warned, the trail became much steeper and narrower now. Both men walked, Jonathan in front and Hamid ten feet behind, each of them leading his own horse. Behind them came the four packhorses.

A sheer rock wall rose on one side of them and, on the other side, a steep drop-off. They couldn't see more than a few feet ahead because the trail curved around the mountainside, following its rugged, rocky contours. A couple of times, Jonathan glanced over the side at 1,000 feet of empty space below. A shudder ran through him when he thought of Neeley's demise. Now, here he was in almost the same situation—with Hamid behind him. But there was a big difference. Hamid needed him. And more importantly, Jonathan had a plan.

Just when they got to a particularly narrow, rocky spot, Jonathan stopped and turned around.

"What are you stopping for?" Hamid demanded. "Keep going."

"Okay," Jonathan said. "But look." He held up the leather water bag he kept slung over his shoulder and shook it out to show that it was empty. "I'm not going anywhere until I get some water." Jonathan figured it was safe to make this kind of ultimatum. What was Hamid going to do, shoot him? He needed Jonathan's help firing those Stingers. Then he would kill him. As though in agreement with its master, Jonathan's horse turned around and looked straight at Hamid.

Hamid shook his head. "Americans. Worse than women. Very well, you may drink of mine. Don't move—I'll come to you."

There was little room to maneuver. But in the area where Jonathan stood, a small platform widened a bit on the cliff-hanging trail. Hamid made his way toward Jonathan.

"Do not try anything," Hamid warned. "You know the consequences."

"Of course," Jonathan said in exasperation, sounding offended. "I just need some water."

Hamid held his AK-47 fully against Jonathan's rib cage as he handed him his water bag. But this actually gave Jonathan an advantage. If he could divert Hamid's attention for a split-second, the positioning would give him much greater control over the weapon than if Hamid held it back away from him—particularly since Hamid's finger wasn't on the trigger.

As Jonathan drank from the water bag, he looked off down the trail curving back behind them in the distance. He stared in that direction, squinting as though trying to make something out, then stole a look at Hamid out of the corner of his eye. He looked off down the trail again and glanced slyly at Hamid once more.

Once upon a time, Jonathan had loved to play this little trick on his son. It worked every time. Just like little Jon, Hamid had his curiosity—and his suspicions—aroused, and he couldn't withstand the temptation to look back down the trail.

The moment Hamid's eyes moved, Jonathan brought his left hand down onto the weapon, pulling it aside. The startled Hamid responded by trying to yank the rifle back, almost losing his balance along the narrow drop-off. A six-round burst shot off into midair.

But Jonathan still had a grip on the barrel end with his left hand, and he brought his right hand up and grabbed Hamid's throat. Hamid made a gagging sound, but he held onto the weapon and tried to wriggle out of Jonathan's grasp.

They fell to the ground in a scrambling knot, struggling for possession of the AK-47, and slid toward the edge of the 1,000-foot precipice. The loose, gravelly surface of the trail had begun to slide under them, rolling them closer toward the edge of the abyss, and both men instinctively dropped their grips on the assault weapon to get a better handhold. The rifle bounced away over the cliff.

Jonathan pulled himself back up and, just as he was about to reach out and push Hamid, who hadn't yet fully recovered his position, he saw the other man pull out what looked like a 9-mm Beretta. He could do nothing but run, so Jonathan made a beeline around his horse, startling the creature and almost making it lose its balance.

He didn't know what lay ahead on the trail, but with a head start of mere seconds, he knew he could get to safety behind a rock outcropping. As he worked his way around the rough cliff, now out of Hamid's line of sight, he heard the pinging sound of the pistol firing twice behind him. The two bullets ricocheted harmlessly off the solid rock wall up ahead, the shots echoing in the stillness.

The main path continued up to the right, but he noticed a narrower trail branching off to the left, up over a boulder and out of sight. Jonathan scrambled down the path, repeatedly losing his footing and gaining it again as broken particles of rock scattered under his feet. Several times his feet slipped, throwing him painfully to his knees, and once he almost went careening over the side. But he could hear Hamid coming after him, and that kept him moving.

Next to a steep, sheer drop to the left, Jonathan found a spot behind another outcropping just as another bullet ricocheted from the rocks above.

"Yankee, come back!" Hamid yelled, his voice echoing in the windy valley below. "I will forget this incident. Remember, I need you for these missiles. All will be forgiven." He paused. "But that trail, you cannot go anywhere on that trail. There is no other path off this main one, and those little ruts are dead ends. You'll see!"

Jonathan feared Hamid was right. Moving cautiously, he rounded the next outcropping and saw the already narrow trail got narrower still up ahead. Too busy walking and looking at the same time, he let his foot slip on a loose rock, which threw him off-balance and sent him sliding toward the edge. Quickly he grasped a hole in the rock just above his right shoulder, and even though his left foot had gone out from under him, the sheer strength of his right hand alone kept him from falling over the edge.

His heart pounding, he stopped to gather his breath and regain his footing. He looked ahead around the corner, and to his horror he saw that the trail simply petered out into the side of the cliff. He glanced up at the hole in the rock he had grabbed, and an idea occurred to him.

"Hey, Yankee," Hamid shouted. "You want to know how I found out about the Stingers?"

"You said you knew Rashid," Jonathan shouted back. "Are you changing your story now?"

He reached down into his boot and retrieved the small throwing knife he had stashed there. Thank God Hamid had never searched his boot. He pulled a roll of adhesive tape and two gauze packs out of a first aid kit strapped to his belt, and used the tape and gauze to cover most of the hole in the rock, thus creating a pocket with a small open space at the bottom.

"Rashid is nothing!" Hamid taunted. "He is a pawn. The real power is your own CIA!"

"What?" Jonathan yelled back. "You're insane."

"It is true!"

It was hard to tell, but he sounded serious. For a moment, Jonathan felt disconcerted. And then he realized that Hamid was just trying to rattle him. Two could play at that game. "I'll bet you're not even a real Muslim," Jonathan said. "I'll bet you're really an infidel."

That got Hamid back on the defensive, and the absurd shouting match resumed while Jonathan continued to work. Hamid had confiscated his shotgun, of course, but he had made Jonathan carry the extra shells in the bandolier, probably thinking he'd let his American prisoner bear the burden of all that weighty ammunition. Jonathan took one shell from the bandolier, tied it to a length of surgical thread from his first aid kit, and stuffed the shell into the hole at the bottom of the pocket created by the gauze. Then, he cut the ends off half a dozen of the other shotgun shells, dumping their contents carefully into the pocket.

The new pocket quickly filled up with double-aught buckshot, almost like ball bearings though not as hard. He moved away from the hole, spooling out the surgical thread as he went.

Hamid continued to yell at Jonathan in the meantime. In order to know where his enemy was at all times, Jonathan yelled back that he questioned Hamid's motives in obtaining the missiles. Hamid took the bait, and thus Jonathan managed to engage his adversary in a pointless dialogue, which bought him a little more time.

When he no longer needed to carry on this discussion, Jonathan quit responding to Hamid. He stood very still, waiting patiently for Hamid to close in on him. Off in the distance he saw vultures circling, as if sensing an impending meal.

Eventually, as Jonathan expected, Hamid started to come after him. As he listened in the stillness, he could hear the other man's footsteps up the trail. When he judged they were close enough, he shouted, "Hamid! I've got a knife!" In the stillness, the words echoed down the canyon below him.

Hamid fired a shot as though to say, *"So what?"*

"No!" Jonathan shouted. "You see, I came prepared! I knew I might meet up with someone like you, and so I prepared this knife especially for you. You know how?" He waited. "I rubbed it in pig lard, and kept it wrapped up with that lard all over it. I may be an infidel, but I know that if I stab you with this unclean knife and you die, you'll endure eternal torment. You'll be *unclean* in the eyes of Allah! How do you like that?"

After almost a minute of silence, Hamid shouted back, "I don't believe you! And even if it's true, there is no way you can gain the advantage." But he sounded rattled, and Jonathan smiled to himself. To an orthodox Muslim, even the possibility that he might die in contact with something unclean was terrifying.

"I can see why you people hate pigs!" Jonathan shouted back. "When I went to a pig farm back in my country—the place where I got the lard for my knife—I saw just how filthy those creatures are. It even disgusted me, and I'm an infidel." He waited a moment. Meanwhile, he cut open a packet of ointment from his first aid kit and rubbed it on the knife. "Oh, did I mention that when I was at the pig farm, I also collected a specimen of pig dung for the very same purpose? It was terrible. I kept it wrapped up and enclosed in three layers of plastic bags, which I've carried all this time. Crazy, I know, but it sure is coming in handy now. I'm rubbing it on the knife even as we speak, and in a minute I'm gonna stab it in your gut."

Jonathan waved the knife around the side of the outcropping so that Hamid could see it, then quickly pulled it back, just seconds before a shot from Hamid's pistol bounced off the side of the cliff beyond him.

Standing nearly 15 feet beyond the makeshift pocket that held the buckshot, Jonathan waited, listening very closely and keeping a loose grip on the piece of surgical thread attached to the shotgun shell. Hamid was moving quietly and slowly, but he could hear him. Just as Hamid rounded the outcropping next to the pocket, Jonathan yelled, "Have some pig dung, Hamid!" and threw the knife straight at his adversary.

The blade stuck into the man's left shoulder, inflicting what would normally have been a very superficial wound. But these were not normal circumstances, and the effect couldn't have been more dramatic. Hamid yelled, and when he felt the slick ointment on the knife, he screamed, quickly pulling the vile instrument out of his body.

At that moment, Jonathan yanked on the string, pulling the shotgun shell from the bottom of his jerry-rigged pocket and releasing the buckshot onto the rocky precipice in a shower of metal balls. In struggling with the knife, Hamid had already gotten slightly off-balance and, as his foot came back down, it landed on top of the scattered buckshot. It was like stepping on marbles. His feet slipped out from under him, and he lost his balance completely.

Hamid's pistol went flying down the side of the cliff. Hamid hung on with his bare hands to a piece of rock along the edge. His eyes looked up at Jonathan with mingled terror and hatred. In that moment Jonathan felt strangely merciful, even though he knew Hamid would never have shown him mercy if the tables were turned. It was too late anyway. Hamid lost his grip, and screamed out *"Allahu akbar!"* as he plunged thousands of feet to his death.

Jonathan stood for a long time, looking over the side of the precipice as though somehow he would be able to see Hamid's body on the windswept rocks below. He felt no exhilaration of victory, only a numb sense of relief.

CHAPTER ELEVEN

Jonathan trudged back up the trail, taking care not to slip on the ball-bearing surface he'd created. With the edge of his boot sole, he pushed a few stray buckshot pellets over the side before setting his foot down on the rocky path.

He soon reached the main trail and slowly crept down toward the horses. He breathed a sigh of relief to find them still standing there quietly, staring off into the distance. A couple of them grazed on tufts of grass growing out of the rocks. Earlier, when he and Hamid were engaged in their shouting match, he thought he heard the stamping of restless hooves. The thought had crossed his mind that, because they were tied together, if one of them got spooked and bolted, all the others would be forced off the precipice.

As his heartbeat slowed, he had to fight a fresh panic rising up in him. Here he was, alone and in an empty, hostile country, with no companionship but his horses. He had no idea how far it was to his destination, or how many obstacles he would meet along the way—Soviets, Afghan Communists, or even mujahideen. And there were the suspicious villagers Hamid had alluded to, the ones who would kill him simply because he looked like a European.

Trying to get his bearings, he looked up at the deep blue sky. From the position of the sun and the shadows across the brown rocks, he guessed it must be three in the afternoon, which meant he had only three more hours before darkness began to set in. He refused to think about what that would mean. Right now, he had to get himself and the horses off of this cliffside. But which direction should he go? Then he remembered, *Khalid's map!*

He pulled the document, folded many times into a tiny piece, out of his saddle-bag, where he had hidden it from Hamid's prying eyes. This was the first time he'd really looked at it since the day Khalid had given it to him, and it didn't look like it would help him at all. At first it was hard to even identify it as a map, drawn as it was on a piece of brown paper that already had a lengthy message in Farsi printed on it. It looked more like a doodling. Was it some kind of code?

But after straining his eyes, poring over the scribbles for several minutes, he began to discern a pattern. And once he saw it, he slowly understood the route. It showed them going northeastward into the Panjsher Valley, stopping at a village called Chil Khanna, which meant *forty houses* in Farsi.

For a second, he felt relieved. It was all starting to make sense, and he was sure he could reach Chil Khanna, especially with all the milestones marked out by Khalid. They had already come a long way since he'd drawn the map, and it appeared to be another day's ride to Chil Khanna.

He looked up at the horses, and he was just getting ready to mount up when he stopped. A sudden realization hit him like someone kicking him in the chest.

The map was worthless. Hamid had taken them far off-course, and there was no way to get back on the right path since he didn't know where he was now. In frustration, Jonathan made a fist and drew back, wanting to hit something but not finding anything around to hit but the rock wall. He let his fist drop to his side, and he gazed out over the windswept valley in disgust.

Then he had another thought. And his hope rose again. *I can just hike back the way we came—back to where Hamid killed Khalid.* All he had to do was backtrack a day's hike to the spot where they had left Khalid's body—if he could find it—then start from there.

It wasn't a very promising possibility, but under the circumstances it felt like a relief. Certainly he'd be better off to go back and start over than he would be if he simply started out from here and hoped to find his way by the sun or the moon.

So he set out finally, leading his own horse and the two bearing the Stingers. He released the other three to reduce his profile.

All around him was a vast, yawning emptiness, the sheer upward slope of the rocks on one side and the canyon drop-off on the other. Even in the best of times, this was not a very hospitable land. And these were hardly the best of times.

He couldn't think about that now. Right now he could only think about getting himself and his horses to a resting-place by dark. And when he got there, then he would find a way to get some sleep.

Even though he found a fairly secluded and relatively comfortable spot, where a ring of boulders made a natural shelter, Jonathan didn't sleep a wink that night. With every wisp of wind or crackling of a twig, he started awake, looking around for intruders. From 3:00 A.M. on, he just sat still in the chilly darkness, waiting for dawn to come.

As soon as the sun rose, he started moving. By the time he stopped to eat a few nuts and drink some water, he had come down off of the high cliffs into a lower elevation.

During a whole day's travel, he never once saw another living soul. A couple of times he glimpsed a farmhouse or a village in the distance, but he never got close enough to see if they were inhabited. He guessed many were not.

The horses had obliged him by being good, patiently walking along tethered to one another, contentedly grazing and watering when they were allowed, and otherwise giving him little trouble. He was thankful for that at least.

When he finally did get back to the spot where Khalid had died, he was startled to see that someone had already been there. Near where the body had lain, he saw a freshly dug grave with a white flag marking it. There were footprints all around, suggesting two or maybe three men. But if they had buried Khalid, then they must have been allies and not enemies.

Or, he thought with a shudder, they could have been Hamid's men. Suddenly he had an intense desire to put this place behind him.

By now it was late afternoon. But, after studying Khalid's map, he began to believe he could find his way to Massoud's camp within a day, two at the most with a lot of hard riding. So he got the horses going again, and they traveled as far as he could on the fading light of day, not stopping until it was absolutely pitch-black. He had entered a farming area, and since Khalid's map seemed to indicate his destination lay close to a farm, he took it as an encouraging sign.

But he still had a long way to go, and there was no way to know exactly how far. Khalid had never gotten that specific about the situation, nor had he made any kind of notation on distances.

After finding a secluded spot behind some rocks and letting the horses graze, he sat down to eat. His supper consisted of dried fruit and almonds. These days, he expended far more calories than he took in, and just by looking at his chest and arms—he hadn't seen a mirror in weeks—he knew he must look emaciated.

But he wasn't too hungry to sleep. After his almost complete sleeplessness the night before, he was exhausted. He drifted off the moment his head hit the hard ground.

Just before dawn, a sound woke him. Voices. *Voices!* He suddenly remembered his situation, and his eyes shot open. Beyond the rocks he could see a light, and he heard men speaking in low tones. His heart pounding, he looked around for the horses. They were all there, resting calmly. He just hoped none of them suddenly snorted or whinnied.

He listened and recognized what they were saying. They were speaking Russian. It sounded like there were four of them. From their conversation, he gathered their vehicle had overturned farther back, and they were walking toward a main road.

Just as they were passing by, one of them said something about a girl in Odessa, and it made the others laugh. At the sound of the laughter, one of the horses beside

Jonathan pricked up his ears. Jonathan, his face pressed to the earth, looked around at the horse. *Please,* his eyes pleaded with the animal. *Please don't make any noise.*

But the horse let out a loud snort, and Jonathan quickly covered his face. "Listen!" exclaimed one of the Russians. "Did you hear that?"

"What?" asked another.

"Sounded like a horse."

They listened for a moment, and Jonathan once again looked over at the horse, which seemed to have lost interest in whatever was out there in the darkness. In a split second he processed the whole issue he had considered on the plane to Colombia—whether God would hear the prayer of a person like him in a desperate moment. He decided this was a good time to risk it. *Please, God,* he prayed.

"There is nothing," came the first Russian's voice finally. "You must be getting senile." Then they laughed and walked on.

Jonathan lay there for a long time, with his head on the ground, listening as their footsteps died out. Then there were no more human sounds. *That's it,* he thought. *I'm not sleeping again until I get there. Even if it's another two days' ride.*

Before he got off the ground, he found himself muttering an awkward prayer, thanking God for saving him from what would surely have been death at the hands of the "Butcher of Kabul." By himself, the Russians would have probably shot him on the spot. But when they discovered an American was packing Stingers into Afghanistan, he would have been taken to Kabul for interrogation—and torture.

Jonathan Stuart found himself in an unfamiliar spot. A man who had survived the Vietnam War and American corporate wars now found himself with three horses and four Stinger missiles, surrounded by multiple enemies in the middle of Afghanistan. He had little food and water, a scrap of a map, and barely a clue as to how to find Khalid's contacts.

Jonathan stood and listened—still no sound but the wind. Yet, somehow, he felt a new strength to move ahead, a new conviction that if he would walk, the path would unfold itself in front of him.

It *was* two days' ride—two full days, and they were the longest days of his entire life.

Many times, especially at night, he heard a noise beside or ahead of him and felt certain he had wandered into the midst of hostile forces. But each time, he discovered he'd only spooked himself. He became so fatigued he began to hallucinate. The sound of tanks turned out to be a babbling brook. Marching feet were nothing more than branches brushing against one another in the wind, and gunshots dissolved into the pelting sound of hard, under-ripe berries falling off a tree.

As he rode through the dark night, a stern, icy wind blew around him, chilling him to the bone and shrieking as it whirled by in funnels of dust. He covered his face with his *pattoo* shawl and rode on.

Over the hours, initially without his noticing, he fell into a delirium, resulting in part from his hunger and in part from his jarring memories of the past few days, but mostly from complete exhaustion. The hypnotic rhythm of the horse's gait combined with the whispering wind around him and produced a drug-like effect. At times, he didn't feel sure where or who he was. There were voices, too, including those of his dead wife and child, and they spoke to him in the wind, sometimes urging him to sleep and sometimes telling him to turn back. Several times he had to shake himself to snap out of his stupor.

He could have eaten his meager rations while riding, but the animals needed rest from time to time. He stopped every few hours to let them graze on scrubby growth or drink from a stream if he found one, not always an easy thing in a barren country like Afghanistan. Somehow the animals seemed to understand they were not allowed to stop for long, and they walked on through the night without a great deal of coaxing.

The landscape began to flatten even more, and a couple of times during the day he saw farmers tending their fields. They looked up to see him going by, but no one called out to him and he saw no troops of any kind. He didn't bother to stop at any of the villages Khalid had drawn on the map. He was taking the express route. No detours.

At one point, he got a scare when he saw what appeared to be a fortress in the distance. But as he came closer he realized the group of buildings were abandoned. What he'd thought were rifle emplacements in the walls turned out to be merely slits where farmers could hang grapes to dry into raisins.

The whole time, he could only think about what Khalid had drawn on his map— a star with the words *Chil Khanna—village* beside a well on the right side of the road. The name, Khalid said, meant "forty houses," but he didn't really expect to find forty. One would do, as long as it was the right place.

Finally, at a little past three in the morning after the second night, he almost rode past a well on his right when his mind snapped to attention. Up ahead he saw the darkened silhouette of a village, or the remains of a village, and beside the well he saw a small stable. He hadn't really expected a welcoming party, not at this hour, but he wished he could have found someone to report to, someone who knew Khalid or at least had contact with the mujahideen. He had no idea if the houses up ahead were even inhabited, so he decided to take his chances and bed his horses and himself down in the stable.

The next thing he knew, bright sunlight was glaring off his face, and half a dozen men were standing over him with drawn rifles.

At least they were mujahideen. He could discern that much from their clothing and their appearance. But no one seemed to speak English, and they didn't appear to respond to his body language when he sat up and held up his hands in a gesture of both greeting and surrender. They just stared at him with hostility in their eyes.

He only knew a smattering of their language, and he wasn't ready just yet to pull out the *nanawatai* trump card Khalid had given him. Khalid had said the use of it meant a loss of all respect, and he couldn't afford that with the mujahideen.

He certainly didn't want to speak Russian, and if he tried German or French or Spanish, each of which he knew well enough to order food, he figured he would only confuse things. So he sat there with his back propped up against the wall of the stable while three fierce-looking men stood guard over him. He wondered what had happened to the Stingers.

He was just about to attempt another sign-language conversation when another man stepped into the stable. This one was a mujahid like the others, but he looked older—perhaps forty-five—and he had silvery hair and beard, with spectacles that made him look studious and not exactly like a soldier.

"Good morning," said the man in English, as he sat down cross-legged facing Jonathan. "We have searched your horses, and we know who you are."

"Good," said Jonathan, feeling a little odd. Didn't they know he was their ally?

"Allow me to introduce myself," the man said. "I am Ali."

Jonathan was sitting too far away to stand up and shake the man's hand without it seeming somewhat awkward, so he just waved. "Steven Wright."

The Afghan smiled at the name, and said, "Of course. Now, Mr. Wright, we are of course very grateful for the . . . radio equipment you have brought us, but we find that something is missing."

"Excuse me?"

Ali sat forward expectantly. "Some time ago, I took over this command from my good friend Khalid, and I am looking forward to seeing him. Where is he?"

"Dead," Jonathan said quietly.

After several seconds of silence, Ali said, *"What?"*

"He's dead," Jonathan answered. "He and all the others."

"Dead?" Ali asked, pushing his glasses up on the bridge of his nose. "All four?"

"Yes—" Jonathan stopped. "Don't you mean three? There were three from your army, plus an assistant I brought with me. He was the first to go, then the other two men with Khalid, and then Khalid. After that it was just Hamid and me, and I killed Hamid."

Ali shook his head. "I do not know this Hamid."

"A soldier of Hekmatyar," Jonathan said in weary reply. "He infiltrated the group. Said he had some RPGs. But what he really wanted was the equipment we were carrying."

"I see," Ali replied. "Hekmatyar, you say?"

Jonathan nodded his head.

Ali turned around and said something in Farsi to one of his men—a giant who looked like he stood a good six and a half feet tall. Hearing what Ali told him, the man looked at Jonathan with an expression of renewed hostility.

Jonathan wanted to ask Ali what was going on, but he considered it best to sit and wait for the Afghan to speak.

"Mr. Wright," Ali said, smiling without humor, "we sent a man to Peshawar to pick up some RPGs and to meet Khalid and his men." He nodded toward the giant, who stared at Jonathan with simmering anger. "He was a close friend of Abdul's here, and Abdul says his friend's name was not Hamid."

Jonathan held up his hands. "I can't say much more. All I know is this guy's name was Hamid, and he was posing as a member of your army, but he was working for Hekmatyar all the time. I guess he somehow managed to intercept your man in Peshawar, but . . . I really don't know."

"You don't know," Ali repeated, glancing at Abdul, then apparently relaying this information in Farsi. He turned back to Jonathan. "There are also things I do not know. For instance, if Hekmatyar had these other men killed, how did you survive?"

"It was no small miracle, I assure you," said Jonathan, meaning it more than Ali probably thought he did. It had begun to feel very hot in the little barn, and he was conscious of the men's eyes on him—especially the big one, Abdul. The smell of stale hay made him want to sneeze.

"Yes," said Ali suspiciously. "Yes, I'm sure you are telling the truth."

"Well, I—" Jonathan stopped. He looked straight into Ali's eyes, and at that moment he realized how all this appeared from the other man's perspective.

"Mr. Wright, please understand that your story seems a bit strange," Ali said finally. "Those three men had gone in and out of Afghanistan many times together, and they were quite experienced at preparing for danger." He stopped. "Or should

I say, four men, counting the one who went to get the RPGs. But you say that man also was killed by Hamid—is that what you say?"

Jonathan stared at Ali for a moment. After risking his life to get the Stingers here, it seemed absurd that the mujahideen were about to kill him. And they probably wouldn't even offer him a last meal. "Look," he said finally, reaching into his pocket to pull out Khalid's map. One of the mujahideen jerked his AK-47 toward him, but Jonathan held up a hand impatiently. "If my word isn't good enough for you, then perhaps this will convince you I am telling the truth."

He handed the map, with its messages and phrases handwritten by Khalid, to Ali. The latter studied it for a long time. Finally, he raised his head. His expression was different now. "I recognize the writing and the words of my brother Khalid," he said gravely. "He says here, 'protect my friend Steven Wright, in the name of Allah, and of . . . ' then he names his brother who was killed by the Butcher of Kabul." Ali nodded his head, then said to Jonathan, "Please accept my apologies for doubting your word. You must understand. With the sort of dangers we face, we do not know who to trust."

Too exhausted to waste energy on offended honor, Jonathan held up his hands. "I understand. Now, can you take me to Massoud?"

.For the amount of riding he had done since he crossed the Khyber Pass almost two weeks before, Jonathan figured he ought to be in Tibet by now. And yet, even when he was sure the journey was over, he had another eight hour ride with Ali to get to Massoud's camp. Apparently the mercurial leader had already moved on. He never tarried in the same place for two nights in a row for fear the Soviets would find him, so they now had to catch up with him.

The contingent—a dozen mujahideen, Ali, and Jonathan—moved up the Panjsher Valley in a northeasterly direction. Unlike Jonathan on his own, they went on a well-trafficked route, passing villages and other travelers, many of whom seemed to know them. These others gave Jonathan a suspicious once-over, then ignored him.

Many miles from their point of origin, they turned off the main course of the river valley and up into the hills. Soon they came to a place with a solid rock wall on one side and a series of caves on the other, like an Indian village in New Mexico. Jonathan almost jumped out of his skin when, from out of nowhere, a dozen men materialized. Poorly clothed and apparently ill fed, they shouted out a greeting to the men on horseback, and Ali dismounted and embraced one of them.

But for Jonathan, who had come nearly seven thousand miles to be here, there was no fanfare, no special welcome. He'd half-expected to ride into Massoud's encampment and find cheering crowds with banners waving, firing rifles into the air to greet him while Massoud, himself, stepped out to welcome him. Instead, he wasn't completely sure that they had actually arrived, because the "camp" wasn't any camp at all, but rather a collection of caves. The place seemed deserted, populated only by a motley crew of disheveled, half-starved men. Looking at their gaunt figures, Jonathan's hopes for a substantial meal dissolved.

A general atmosphere of untidiness and poverty prevailed about the place and the men who now swarmed their caravan. One man wore a shirt made of little more than rags, and he shivered, though the air was not particularly cold. Most others wore ragged versions of the traditional loose-fitting shirt and pants. A couple of the more fortunate ones had what looked like Soviet army jackets. One, with his arm in a sling, even had on a Soviet officer's dress hat with hammer-and-sickle insignia.

They rode through the encampment, and then Ali signaled for them to stop before a group of men sitting in a circle in front of a particularly large cave. The men in this group looked healthier than the ones they had met earlier, and Jonathan realized they must be the key leaders, or "commanders" as the mujahideen called them.

Ali approached a man in the middle, who was tuning in a portable short-wave radio while talking to the others. He had on Soviet fatigue pants, Afghan Army boots, and a flat traditional woolen cap. Over his shirt he wore a fishing vest with an array of pockets, and a Spanish pistol in a holster. Ali said something in Farsi to the man, who looked up at Jonathan.

The bearded and dark-headed man was virtually indistinguishable from the other mujahideen. The man gave Jonathan a quick, curt wave, then went back to his radio.

Jonathan realized Ahmad Shah Massoud, one of the century's great military leaders and perhaps his nation's equivalent of Patton or MacArthur, had just acknowledged him. When Ali returned to Jonathan's side, he announced, "Massoud says he is very grateful for the missiles you have brought."

"He can thank me after we've wiped out about three or four of the *Shuravi's* gunships," Jonathan said, nodding in the direction of Massoud, who had looked back at them. "They won't know what hit them."

He glanced at Ali. The man seemed to have a more welcoming expression in his eyes, and his lips curved into a slight smile—but just beneath the surface, he was certainly as suspicious as ever, and Jonathan didn't feel very welcome here. "We have already arranged for you to participate in the next mission two days from now," said

Ali. "You will go with my group. And, if I decide the time is right, we will let you use these missiles." He jerked his head. "Come. I will show you to your quarters."

As they rode through the camp, Jonathan saw a group of dirty children dressed in rags. They stared back at him through sunken eyes. The sight of a boy, five-years-old going on fifty, reminded him of little Jon. Ali pointed out the camp hospital, housed in a tent off to the side. Beyond the hospital lay more caves, out of which several soldiers peered. Farther on they came to a smaller cave, which Ali claimed as his.

Ali assigned two men to guard the Stingers and sent the others on their way, then he led Jonathan into the dark interior of the cave. Though dank, the space seemed comfortable enough, with a threadbare rug on the floor, a lamp, and a bookshelf containing perhaps thirty volumes. Jonathan leaned over toward the books, all of them ancient hardbound copies, and he was surprised to see several titles in English. He pulled one down—H.G. Wells's *Outline of History*—and thumbed through it for a second before putting it back and glancing at Ali.

"I was once a professor of history at the university in Kabul," said Ali quietly. "Then the war came. Some of my colleagues fled, but I could not. My faith and my people—they came first."

Jonathan nodded his head.

"You are surprised to learn I am an educated man?" asked Ali. He sat in the mouth of the cave, staring back at Jonathan, his dark silhouette framed in the infused light. "You wonder why a man of learning would go to war for his faith?"

"No," said Jonathan, shaking his head and smiling. "But somebody just the other day used almost the same words as you did just now."

"Yes?"

Jonathan told him about his discussion with Hamid and how Hamid had said that after the Soviets were gone, there would still be no peace—the Afghans would simply fight one another.

At these words, Ali nodded with the seriousness of a sage. "There is truth in what this Hamid said." Suddenly he interrupted himself. "Forgive me. I'm sure you are hungry?"

Jonathan nodded his head, and Ali pulled a piece of *naan* from a basket in the center of the cave. While Jonathan gnawed on the hardened and slightly stale bread, Ali continued to talk. "Of course you know there is no such thing as an Afghan," he said. "There are the Pushtun, which I am—we're the largest group. There are Tajik, like Massoud, there are Uzbeks . . . And then there are the regional loyalties too. For instance, Massoud and I are of different nations, but we both come from the Panjsher Valley."

"But you're all Muslims," said Jonathan with his mouth full. "Doesn't that count for something?"

Ali shook his head sadly. "Not enough. Everyone wants to be in control. We have been fighting amongst ourselves for a thousand years, and if I had to make a wager, I would guess we will still be fighting a thousand years from now." He shrugged. "Conquering nations come and go—Alexander the Great, the British, and now the Soviets—but our hatreds remain in place. We unite long enough to defeat the enemy, and then . . ." Again he smiled sadly.

Jonathan leaned his head back against the wall of the cave and closed his eyes.

"But because that is the case," Ali was saying, "it is a good thing you have placed these Stinger missiles in the hands of Massoud. This will greatly increase the power and influence of our army, which could help us defeat the Soviets. And then, when the Soviets are gone—"

Jonathan heard no more as, exhausted from being on the run for days and days, he fell fast asleep.

On Tuesday morning, Rusty Wharton returned from a long weekend out of town with his family and sat down in his office to get the latest information from Frazier Hollis. Hollis ran down the list of their latest cases and their current status, little of which had changed. But there was one name missing from the list, a name that had been on Wharton's mind that morning.

"So what about Rashid?" Wharton asked.

Hollis shrugged. "What about him? He goes out to eat here, he goes out to eat there. We follow him. We photograph him. Nothing. He gets fat; we get bored." He opened up a folder and started to read. "Want to know what he's done since you went out of town? Let's see. Thursday night, dinner with some Mideastern types—but before you get too excited, forget it. We checked them out and they're squeaky-clean. Friday, a luncheon with an Afghan trade delegation, one that we've already established has connections with the mujahideen, but nothing new came out of the meeting, as far as we could tell." He looked up at Wharton. "Should I go on?"

Wharton shook his head. "No, no, you made your point. There's nothing new."

"That's right," said Hollis. He studied Wharton's face. "Should there be?"

Wharton nodded toward the door, and Hollis shut it.

"McGinnis called me at home this morning," Wharton said in a low voice, leaning across his desk toward Hollis. "Said he wanted to know if I enjoyed my time off, asked how the kids were."

Hollis raised his eyebrows.

"Yeah, that's what I'm thinking," Wharton replied, nodding his head. "Total nonsense. When has he ever shot the breeze unless he wanted to find out something, right? So I let him fish around, and finally he gets to the subject of Rashid. Asks me what's going on, have we picked up anything from our surveillance? I say no, of course not—he'd be the first to know if we did. Then he asks me—get this—do I have any more leads about the Stingers Boltar was supposed to have purchased in South America."

Hollis raised his eyebrows.

"Pretty weird, huh?" Wharton acknowledged.

"So then what?" asked Hollis.

Wharton threw up his hands. "So then he just tells me have a nice day, et cetera, he'll see me in the office, blah, blah, blah."

Hollis shook his head, mystified. "Wonder what's up?"

"I don't know, Frazier," said Wharton, tapping a pencil on his desk and staring off into space. "But if I'm any kind of investigator, I'm gonna find out."

CHAPTER TWELVE

Jonathan fought the war in Vietnam from the skies, which meant he seldom got to see either his enemy or the innocents who suffered. Only in occasional nightmares, when he was plagued by visions of napalm bombing, did the physical reality of those decades-old battles strike home.

Here it was different. Here he was with the guerrillas—a smaller, lesser-equipped, but much more mobile force that wreaked havoc on a larger, more exposed enemy. The government controlled the main cities and highways, but the countryside and villages belonged to the mujahideen. Due to its fear of attack, the government ran its convoys only in the daytime.

Of course the mujahideen attacked these convoys at every opportunity, and they had developed a successful formula over the years. First, the attacking rebels needed to knock out the convoy's communication abilities so that nobody could call in combat reinforcements or air support. They usually targeted the command vehicle, normally a jeep with a long whip antenna protruding from its rear bumper. And usually they gained the added benefit of taking out the convoy commander in the process. Attacks had to be swift, clean, hit-and-run operations and, to ensure success, the rebels needed to ambush smaller convoys—the smaller the better. Once they had done what they came to do, they needed to move away from the scene as quickly as possible, because when the reinforcements came, there would be a hefty price to pay.

Of course, they did not operate in a vacuum. Eventually the Soviets had gotten wise to these tricks and begun counteracting them. Starting as far back as late 1981, the enemy began clearing away trees, walls, houses, and any other possible sniper hiding places within 150 to 200 meters on either side of the main roads. They also started running longer convoys—a typical one stretched for more than a kilometer and consisted of no fewer than twenty-five vehicles. Nor did they come unarmed. One-fifth of all vehicles had ring-mounted machine guns, and they assigned at least one armored vehicle for every ten trucks, not to mention at least two BMPs per convoy.

The BMP, a mechanized infantry combat vehicle on tracks, was like a more mobile, even more deadly, version of a tank. They carried both a 73-mm gun and a 7.62-mm machine gun mounted in the movable turret. Three men operated the

BMP and, in back, it carried something tanks didn't have—an eight-man infantry squad, ready to pour out and rain death on their enemies while the big gun on the turret provided cover.

The final piece in the arming of the convoys came from the air. High above the field of combat flew Il-76 Mainstays, large airborne warning systems similar to the U.S. AWACS. A radio call to one of these flying command centers would bring in bomber and fighter reinforcements, not to mention airborne infantry. Even so, a convoy had to be big enough to defend itself until help got there.

Ali's unit had the job of looking for suitable convoys and ambushing them. But as Jonathan would discover, much to his exasperation, the commander proved to be painfully conservative about committing his troops to the attack. He was apparently wary from demoralizing experiences in the past, which meant the unit took up much of its time just trying to find suitable targets. Once they did, there would be endless deliberations between Ali and other commanders, and usually they would end up calling off their plans before commencing the attack—even though the troops had spent hours setting up for the kill.

After two days in the field, they found a suitable ambush site. Two thousand meters up the road to the north lay a small village through which the convoy would pass on its way to Kabul. Ali sent two men toward the village as forward observers to identify and count the vehicles as they approached. It was a highly communication-sensitive job, but Ali could only afford to give them one radio to share. This meant if the man without the radio saw something, he had to signal to the other to call in to the reinforcements down the road. It was the best Ali could do. That single radio represented one-third of all those available to his unit of fifty-seven men.

Another two-man team took the back door. They watched the south end of the road, 3,000 meters away from the kill zone, to make sure no enemy troops came up from that direction. They, too, had a radio.

The kill zone itself comprised a 200-meter long strip of roadway in the middle of a short, but narrow, mountain pass. The spot was ideal for their purposes, positioned such that the enemy's vehicles would be climbing, and therefore slowing down and bunching up together as they climbed. On the west side, the shoulder dropped off several hundred feet into a ravine and, on the east, a rocky hillside rose up steeply. The hillside, covered with heavy boulders, offered great cover for Ali's men, and the majority of them took up positions there.

A few more placed themselves on narrow ledges just off the road to the west, safely out of the way should any vehicles run off. They were there to thwart any enemy escape. That wouldn't be a problem if everything went as planned. The deployment of men, and the landscape, put the Soviets between a rock and a hard place—literally.

At the north end of the kill zone, between the main unit and the forward observers, Ali stationed one of his leaders with three riflemen. This forward combat unit had already prepared the road with a few surprises for their guests—mines, which were calculated to take out the lead vehicle and thereby block the road.

Sometimes in similar situations, a rebel contingent would use RPGs—Soviet-made grenade launchers popular with the mujahideen. But they preferred using mines, especially because one of the men up front had special training with them. A defector from a Communist incendiary unit, he had adapted a World War II-era Soviet anti-tank/anti-personnel mine, the PMZ-40. Shaped like a huge bottle cap nine inches in diameter, the mine consisted only of a main body and outer case, inseparable from one another, with a pressure plate locked by a spring clip inside the mine. Four pressure-plate stud bearings on the top kept it from reacting to a load of less than 500 pounds. But when something larger rolled across it, the pressure plate would drop and crush the igniter head, firing off about eight pounds of TNT.

At the south end of the zone, to the rear, sat a squad of six men, including Abdul, the big man whose friend Hamid had killed when he stole the RPGs in Peshawar. Jonathan had been watching Abdul for some time. It was hard not to, since he stood a good six-foot-five-inches tall, probably weighed 275 pounds, and had a distinctly unpleasant expression on his face. On the truck ride from Massoud's encampment, he caught the giant glaring at him. When he turned away and looked back a minute later, he saw Abdul still continuing to stare at him without blinking. The experience was not a pleasant one.

Abdul and the other five would block any possible escape and contain all vehicles within the kill zone. Ali had ordered them to use their machine guns first. Only as a last resort were they to fire off one of their RPGs.

The RPG was essentially a rocket launcher without an internal guidance system; a poor man's Stinger, virtually worthless against aircraft unless they were stationary. It was easy to fire, though. The user screwed a cardboard cylinder containing propellant onto the missile, lined up the grenade inside the muzzle, found his target using the optical sight, and pulled the trigger. It fired a 2.25-kilogram grenade with stabilizing fins that sprang out once it left the launch tube. Seconds after firing, a rocket motor kicked in, increasing the grenade's velocity. And it could do some damage. The PG-7 grenade could penetrate a solid foot of armor. The only problem with the RPG, in fact, was that its fuse had a tendency to short out easily, rendering its warhead inoperable.

Jonathan waited beside Ali, who held the third and last radio, near the middle of the zone. The remainder of the men took up strategic positions all along the area.

All of them prepared to conceal themselves once word came from the front that the convoy was up ahead. But even then, Ali might opt not to attack if the target didn't seem viable. If he didn't give the order for his forward combat unit to detonate the mine and open fire on the drivers, there would be no battle.

For most of the day, time passed without event. Several motorized caravans passed through this major road. But they were all too big, and Ali never gave the signal. Then, late in the afternoon, the forward observer alerted Ali that he saw a small convoy up ahead—probably a straggler, which had splintered away from a larger group because of a breakdown. This mini-convoy consisted of only four trucks and, since there were no antennas visible, it probably didn't possess any communications relay ability.

The target looked good, and Ali raised his hand to give the signal to his forward kill team. Jonathan tensed.

Whole minutes seemed to pass in the half-second it took for the tires of the lead vehicle to roll over the spot where they had set the explosive. But just as the rear axle crossed the line, the mine exploded with a blast, instantly killing the entire crew and sending the vehicle flying over to the side of the road. At almost the same moment, Abdul and his men opened fire on the truck in the rear, annihilating its occupants.

Then, everything went dead silent except for the hissing radiator of the immobilized vehicle up front. Jonathan shook his head in amazement and admiration. In less than thirty seconds, Ali and his men had taken out two vehicles and their crews.

Now the drivers and the assistants in the other two vehicles, all of them Afghan Communist troops, got out, their hands above their heads, begging for mercy. Ali ordered several of his men to tie them up and load the prisoners into the middle truck. Even with the time it took to do this, the whole operation lasted barely ten minutes. And not once did the enemy have an opportunity to return fire.

Two dozen men rushed in and surrounded the hull of the lead truck, which still contained the bodies of its driver and rider. Rocking the enormous vehicle back and forth with their combined strength, they managed to dislodge it from its resting-place and send it careening over the side of the ravine. The truck fell several hundred feet before coming to a loud, dusty halt at the bottom.

Breaking into shouts of victory, the men began to board the other trucks. Those at the rear of the kill zone scurried down from their high perches and jumped onto the sides of the vehicles, which stopped and picked up the forward observers on the way out.

With a nod of congratulation to Ali, Jonathan hoisted himself up into a truck full of laughing mujahideen. Nobody paid him any attention except for the sullen, suspicious Abdul, who still trained his hard gaze on him. Jonathan looked away, down the road at the yellow and brown land behind them. He swallowed, and his mouth tasted like dust.

Ambushing convoys also served the purpose of re-supplying the mujahideen armies. Therefore, they were disappointed when they discovered the convoy wasn't carrying weapons, ammunition, or medical supplies in any quantity—only food and clothing.

After they tossed the dead bodies from the third truck over the edge of the ravine, the three trucks full of mujahideen bounced over the rocky road toward town, a few miles away. There, they distributed the supplies to the grateful townspeople, who rushed to tear into the boxes of food and uniforms.

Jonathan stood back and watched the Afghans together, mujahideen and villagers talking and embracing and swapping stories. These were their people, not his, and he felt completely detached from what was going on around him. Ali was the only one who would even bother with him, and he wasn't exactly the most talkative sort.

The trucks, now empty, remained hidden until sunset. Once it grew dark, Ali reassembled the men, and they headed out to another ambush site in another valley. There they hid the trucks again, parking them behind a large rock outcropping, and set up camp for the night.

They had kept several boxes of the Soviets' rations, and now they feasted on them. Most of the rations looked like indistinguishable slop, resembling food Jonathan had refused to eat on visits to the Soviet Union. But now he ate as greedily as any of the Afghans and, when he was done, he sat back and listened to them telling stories in Farsi. They sat around a fire, and several of the men smoked pipes. Although he didn't understand a word they were saying, he found something comforting in it. For a few hours that night, Jonathan didn't feel so much like a stranger.

Yet, if he could judge by the looks Abdul gave him, these Afghans were just waiting for one false move on his part. *Good thing I brought them two million dollars' worth of Stingers,* he thought. *I'd hate to see what they would have done if I had shown up empty-handed.*

Abdul clearly suspected Jonathan was a *Shuravi,* or at the very least an outsider. Therefore Jonathan noticed with irony that one of the big Afghan's best friends seemed to be Sergei, a Russian who had defected to the mujahideen eighteen months before. Sergei was young and fair-skinned, at least as Western-looking as Jonathan—but there was a big difference. Every night at the appointed hour for prayers, Sergei joined the others in bowing toward the setting sun, in the direction of Mecca. He was a convert. Jonathan, on the other hand, could bow his head and pray if he wanted to, but in their eyes he was still nothing more than an infidel.

He had tried to befriend the Russian, but Sergei seemed to view him with every bit as much suspicion as the others did. Occasionally, though, he would let down his guard a bit, and this evening he made small talk with Jonathan in English for a minute or two before moving on to share a joke with the Afghans in their own language. Jonathan longed to ask him if he had ever heard of an officer named Drakoff, but he wasn't ready to bring up that name just yet. All he could do was wait.

Eventually it came time to bed down, and Jonathan slept on the hard earth with the other warriors. Ali was off somewhere, sitting up with a couple of his officers, planning strategy. Jonathan had not been invited.

Two more days passed, with nothing to show for them.

By now Jonathan had begun to look more and more like an Afghan. His skin was brown, not only from the sun, but from layers of dust. He hadn't had a bath since days before, somewhere back down the trail, when he and Khalid and the others had stopped at a mountain stream.

One convoy went by each day, but both times it was too large for them to attack, so they hid in the hills above the road and let it pass by unhindered. Then late on the second day, the forward observer radioed back to Ali that he saw five trucks approaching.

From what the observers could see, the convoy didn't have anything but light arms, and Afghans, not Soviets, operated it. The soldiers—probably conscripts—would not put up a fight if given the opportunity to surrender, so all the mujahideen had to do was destroy the lead vehicle.

Jonathan, squinting ahead into the dust and the sunshine, watched as the trucks came up the road below them, gears grinding as they climbed. Suddenly Ali gave the signal to move. Six men jumped out in front of the convoy and fired their rifles into the air, while beyond them another mujahid pointed his RPG without firing. No need to waste a valuable grenade if they could make the point without using it.

"*Tasleem ya'a marg!*" the mujahideen shouted—surrender or die. The terrified truck drivers chose surrender, and they came out with their hands up.

Ali's men captured the entire convoy without shedding so much as one drop of blood. Aside from new supplies, they now had ten more potential soldiers, a total of fourteen prisoners.

While Jonathan watched, the mujahideen broke up into little groups of three or four men, each of them interrogating a prisoner. After several minutes there was a commotion, and Abdul emerged from the crowd, dragging a captured soldier by the hair. Even without understanding a word, it was obvious to Jonathan that the screaming man was begging for mercy. But apparently he'd been identified as a Communist informant—as opposed to someone who'd just been drafted into the army to serve against his will—and there was no mercy to be had. Abdul pulled the man off behind a rock, and after several minutes he returned alone, rubbing his right hand along the side of his coat as though to wipe something off. Keeping his left hand behind him, he glanced up at his comrades and gave them a sinister smile. He then brought out his fisted hand to show the trophy it held—the severed head of the informant.

This had the immediate result of showing the other thirteen prisoners the mujahideen meant business. They were given the opportunity to become probationary soldiers in Ali's unit, and since the only other option was to join their dead comrade, they readily accepted. After administering a solemn pledge of loyalty to them, the mujahideen separated their new conscripts, and assigned each one a guardian. Once the new soldier proved himself in battle by killing a Soviet or Afghan Communist soldier, he would be allowed to operate on his own. Until then, though, he had a vested interest in the safety of his guardian. If the guardian were killed, the probationer—whether or not he had anything to do with it—would pay with his own life.

Even better than the thirteen new conscripts, the convoy had come with a sizable cache of small arms and ammunition, along with more food and medicine. Ali sent two trucks containing weapons and ordnance back to Massoud's camp, and distributed the rest at another village.

As much as he enjoyed witnessing these small victories, Jonathan started to feel a little depressed, even disillusioned. He wanted to use his Stingers, and now seemed as good a time as any. Out here on the highway, he could create a small but shocking incident that would cause rumors to spread. In that way, the missiles would have impact far beyond the moment. By the time word of their existence got back to the Soviet High Command—and the CIA—Jonathan would be long gone.

Yet, in order for him to deploy the Stingers, a convoy had to call in air support. Each time a convoy had appeared over the past few days, he had set up a missile in preparation for the enemy air assault that would give him reason to fire. But no such opportunity appeared, and he began to wonder if, given Ali's methods of operation, one ever would.

Jonathan waited to approach Ali until after the evening meal, which consisted of a stew called *korma*—much tastier than the Soviet rations. He calculated the man would be in the best of spirits then, what with the day's victory and a full stomach.

The commander crouched on a boulder by himself, looking off in the direction of the dying sun across the barren, windswept rocks and plains to the west. He had a stick in his hand and made motions as though he were writing.

When Jonathan walked up behind him and called his name, Ali turned around, startled. In that split-second look, with his spectacles and his hawk-like nose, Jonathan could almost see the man as he had been before the war, a professor lecturing his students about history.

"Another victory," said Jonathan, coming and sitting beside him. "I'm impressed with how well you lead your men."

Ali, still gazing off into the distance, nodded his head.

"So," Jonathan asked impatiently, "Is this the way all attacks will be conducted?"

"Why do you ask?" Ali glanced sideways at Jonathan, looking him up and down in suspicion. "Are we not successful in our attacks?"

"Oh, you're successful, all right," Jonathan answered. "A little *too* successful."

Ali considered this comment. "Perhaps my English fails me," he said dryly.

"All I'm saying is, you're hitting them so hard and so quick, there's no chance for them to call in air reinforcements. And that means no chance for me to use the missiles."

"Ah." Ali nodded his head. "Your missiles. That's because we have no desire to bring down their gunships on our heads. We have to fight this war like jackals, not lions, because we're weak and the enemy is strong. We have to *strike quickly*—" He clapped his hands together. "And move, always a step ahead."

"Hmm," said Jonathan. "So you don't really plan on encountering any air power this week?"

Ali tossed a pebble off into the distance. "This week, this month, this year. I hope to never encounter their air power. But if I do, you will be there, yes?" He smiled at Jonathan. "If you can wait long enough."

Controlling his exasperation, Jonathan searched for a way to make his point. "You see that truck over there?" he said, indicating one of the captured vehicles. "Let's say you and I and the rest of your men had to push one of those trucks for a kilometer. The majority of our effort would go into getting it moving, and once it was rolling, it would be much easier to keep it going. But if we tried to stop every few meters, then it would become difficult because we would have lost momentum."

"I have some understanding of physics," said Ali in a slightly condescending tone.

Jonathan held up a hand. "Okay, if I may be so bold, the same applies here. By going up against small convoys, you're getting a victory here, a victory there, but never anything that really strikes fear in the hearts of those *Shuravi*. But what if we tricked them into sending a group of their gunships? Then we're talking about serious damage." He waited until Ali nodded his head slowly in agreement. "You said you fight like jackals, not lions—so instead of hitting the enemy head-on, we lure him into a trap." He sat back. "Then he finds out you're lions after all."

Ali listened to all this without smiling. Finally, he said, "I don't know about this plan. It seems you are proposing we stir up a nest of cobras. If we invite their firepower, they can destroy us even before we use the missiles."

"Of course there's a risk," Jonathan answered. He looked down over the group of men, some of them sitting around the fire, others attending to their weapons. "Isn't there always a risk in war?" He glanced at Ali. "You're right to be careful, but think about this. *Why* are you cautious?"

"It's obvious," said Ali. "I am cautious because I am not a fool."

"And?"

Ali threw up his hands. "What a question. And because I do not want my men to die. What do you—"

"And?" Jonathan stared at Ali, holding his gaze.

Ali looked away. "I don't know. Because I've seen what the enemy can do in battle."

"There you go," said Jonathan with a triumphant smile. "Just like you hesitate because of what you've seen the *Shuravi* do, you can make them afraid by showing what *you* can do. I guarantee you—the Russians will be ten times less likely to engage in an air strike after we hit them with these missiles. And they'll think twice about entering a battle zone if they believe your soldiers now have this kind of firepower."

"This could be so," said Ali, sounding as though he were wavering just a bit.

"And consider this," Jonathan went on. "There could be another long-term effect that would really make a difference in this war. I'm sure Massoud has considered this. If you can demonstrate to my government how effective your people are with these missiles, then maybe you would have some leverage toward convincing Congress to supply you with them directly." He didn't tell Ali at this point, but he had brought a camera with him, and he planned to have someone record the Stinger attack. Later he would mail the unexposed roll to Washington.

"Yes," said Ali. "Sometimes it seems like a paradox. They will not give us the missiles because we have not demonstrated how effective we could be with them, and how can we demonstrate their effectiveness if they will not give us the missiles?"

Jonathan spread his arms. "What you're doing right now is brave, it is noble, but you take much risk for low reward. Maybe you get a few trucks and some supplies, and a few government troops defect, but you're not really making the *Shuravi* suffer. You're not doing anything that would really break their will and cause them to want to pull out of Afghanistan. If anything, you're just making them mad and more determined to stay. But those Stingers, they can turn the tide of this war."

Ali only sat nodding his head, not meeting Jonathan's eye. After a long silence, he finally said, "What do you propose to do?"

"All I'm suggesting," Jonathan answered, "is that we ambush one of the main supply caravans and be prepared for an air attack. In the event of such an attack, your men would remain concealed, and I would blast those devils out of the sky with the missiles."

"Yes, but what if those missiles do not work?" Ali said it as though he had discovered the one flaw in Jonathan's plan. For as much as the mujahideen said they wanted the Stingers, there was yet a reluctance to turn away from the ancient ways of battle in favor of modern, space-age technology. "What if my men are exposed in the open, and this trap suddenly swings the other way and we become the trapped instead of the trappers? If my men are slaughtered, how can you ever repay me for my losses?"

There was a bitter taste in Jonathan's mouth when he swallowed. "Well, I can't give you more men." He shook his head. "I don't know how I'd repay you if the missiles didn't work, but if they *do* . . . but I risked my life to bring these missiles here, so my level of commitment . . ."

He stopped, and Ali looked over at him. "What?"

"Do you see that big one there?" Jonathan pointed down the hill, toward where Abdul stood with a group of other men.

"Abdul? Yes. What of him?"

Jonathan thought for a second more. Gathering his courage, he looked at Ali. "You take Abdul, who I can tell isn't particularly fond of foreigners—or maybe he's just not fond of me—but you assign Abdul to me and let him be my loader. Then if I fail, you tell Abdul to shoot me on the spot."

Ali squinted at Jonathan. Jonathan saw a troubled look in his eyes, as though he didn't feel comfortable with the ante Jonathan had just thrown into the game. There was still a trace of suspicion, but there was a hint of something else, something new. Could it be respect? "I will think on this," Ali said simply.

They spent the next day watching two large convoys come and go. Jonathan waited for a signal from Ali, but none came.

The day after that, yet another large convoy passed. Still there was no go-ahead from the commander.

An hour later, Ali received word from the forward observer that a small group was on its way—seven vehicles without combat support or visible communication antennas. Jonathan watched as Ali ordered his men into position and again prepared to spring the trap. He didn't even bother to arm his missile launcher.

Instead he took a position next to Ali and settled back to watch through a pair of binoculars as the vehicles crept through the valley below. First came three trucks, medium-sized Ural-375s. Each had a canvas covering over the bed, a tarpaulin supported by a frame. In the middle of the convoy rode a "low boy" tractor-trailer of the type used to carry heavy equipment such as earthmovers, and it had the same canvas-covered frame on the bed.

Jonathan started to check out the last three vehicles, when something caught his attention. He pointed his binoculars back at the "lowboy." Something didn't seem right.

Then he realized what it was. The frame with the tarp. Ordinarily, a truck that big didn't have anything covering the bed, because the frame was cumbersome. Besides, the big trucks didn't usually carry the kind of loads that needed to be protected from the elements, and if they did, the driver would simply sling an ordinary tarp over the load.

There was something else. Normally there would have been a good six inches of vertical space between the body of the wheel-wells and the wheels themselves, but from what Jonathan could see, the truck body and the wheels—both front and back—appeared to be almost touching one another. Clearly the vehicle was carrying an unusually heavy load, one far beyond its ordinary capacity.

The truck itself seemed to make an incredible amount of noise, as though its axles were enduring great stress. Nor did it bounce on the bumpy road the way the ones to the front and the rear did. It simply rolled forward, leaving deep ruts in the road. A couple of times the rear vehicles nearly got stuck in these ruts, and the sound of the lowboy's complaining axles mingled with the straining gears of the other trucks.

Jonathan touched Ali's arm. "Ali," he said hoarsely. "Call off the attack. We're in some serious danger here."

"What do you mean?" Ali demanded. "This is an ideal convoy, and we're ready to attack."

"Please," said Jonathan. "It's a decoy. You'll be sorry if you attack this one."

The convoy, creeping like a short, fat snake, slowly approached the end of the kill zone, and the forward man watched Ali for the final go-ahead.

As the first vehicle inched forward, Ali raised his hand. The point man on the forward combat team took careful aim. Ali glanced back at Jonathan.

Jonathan shook his head again and held up his hands.

Ali started to make the signal but then he slowly lowered his arm to call off the attack.

The vehicles continued on out of the kill zone and over the hill, and Ali turned to Jonathan with a perturbed expression on his face. "Now, explain the meaning of this."

"Come with me." Jonathan started scrambling down the rocky hillside toward the road, and as they walked out into the dirt, he stepped in one of the ruts. It was more than ankle-deep—shin-deep was more like it. "You see how deep these impressions are? They were carrying something heavy—too heavy."

Ali's face darkened. "All the more reason why we should have fired on them. They were probably full of artillery shells and mortars."

Jonathan shook his head. "No. They must have learned this from Vietnam. Sometimes the American troops would place an armored personnel carrier on a truck in the middle of a convoy, hidden away. Of course the APC weighed about three times what the truck was supposed to carry, and after three or four runs it would destroy the truck. But if the convoy got ambushed, *boom*—it was like they had a tank, and they could blow the Vietcong away." He pointed down at the deep lesions in the road. "You don't make these just by carrying ordinary mortar shells. This was a tank. I'm willing to wager. A T-72, maybe. If we had ambushed them, they would have pointed that gun up on this hillside and blown us away."

Ali shook his head in consternation. "One moment you are aggressive, the next you back away."

Jonathan shrugged. "I never said I wanted to walk us into a trap."

Ali's radio crackled, and Jonathan heard a voice saying something in Farsi. Ali listened intently, replied, and signed off. He stared down at the tracks, then slowly glanced up at Jonathan. "That was our rear observer. He says one of the trucks broke an axle just after it passed him and now the enemy is unloading a tank from the back of this truck."

"Like I said—" Jonathan began.

"However," Ali interrupted, "you are wrong about one thing. It was a T-62 tank under the tarpaulin, not a T-72." Then he smiled slightly and said, "Let's talk about what it will take to execute your plan."

Jonathan had just opened his mouth to speak when more chatter broke in on Ali's radio. The commander, holding up a hand, spoke into it, and suddenly he shouted something to a group of men nearby, who all dove for cover. He yelled into his radio, then grabbed Jonathan and pulled him behind the shelter of a large rock.

As he crouched down beside Ali, Jonathan watched the commander's face for some indication of what was happening. Then a split-second later, he heard them. Choppers.

Ali pointed in the direction of the noise, toward the forward observer's station. "A patrol of gunships is passing over our forward observer now," he said. "Obviously they are following that deceptive convoy." Within a few seconds, the whir of rotor blades filled the air, and a squadron of six Mi-24 Hind gunships passed over.

The dust flew, and tufts of scrappy grass bowed down as the monsters roared by just a hundred feet above them. But the mujahideen remained hidden.

When the choppers had gone, Ali looked at Jonathan. "You were certainly right about the convoy. Without you, we would all have died. We are in your debt."

Jonathan smiled modestly. Maybe they would trust him now.

"However," said Ali, holding up a finger, "I have not forgotten your promise. Abdul blames you for the death of his friend, even though I have explained that you had nothing to do with it. He also seems convinced, despite my efforts to prove otherwise, that you are a *Shuravi* spy working undercover. And as you have seen, he likes to use his knife. It is said that he has killed twenty of the enemy with his bare hands." He shrugged. "I hope you know what you are doing."

So do I, Jonathan thought. He wondered if he would be pushing his luck if he asked God for help a second time. He didn't like the thought of becoming Abdul's twenty-first victim.

CHAPTER THIRTEEN

They planned the ambush for the next afternoon.

At this point Ali's force was seventy strong. Fifty-seven had left the camp to go on this mission, and they had added the thirteen probationary soldiers. Together they possessed some forty AK-47s, assorted sidearms, a handful of the makeshift land mines, the eight RPGs Jonathan's caravan had brought up from Peshawar— and four Stinger missiles.

Ali selected an ideal setting in a place called Qudar Canyon. Approximately half a mile long, the canyon had a steep ridge on one side, rising almost 1,000 feet, with a smaller ridge of about 100 meters on the other side. Down the middle ran a narrow road, another supply route, which curved as it passed out of the canyon. The morning was clear and crisp and a little on the chilly side—typical for Afghanistan. For most of the day, clouds threatened, but by mid-afternoon they had parted and the sun burned hot on the men's backs as they watched and waited on the ridge. Several convoys passed through, but not the right convoy—one small enough to fit entirely within the canyon at one time.

This time, the forward observers were positioned much farther away, ten kilometers up the road. Other men held positions all along the trail, the majority of them on the higher mountainside, dug in and well-concealed behind large rocks and boulders.

At 3:45 in the afternoon, Ali received the signal that a convoy of thirty-one vehicles had just passed the forward observers. The configuration sounded good. It was mostly Ural-375 trucks, with only three BMPs.

They had thirty minutes to prepare before the convoy would arrive in the valley, and Ali sent out the signal for all troops to take up the ready position.

The men in the rear set off a stick of dynamite above the bend in the road at the far end of the canyon, knocking thirty tons of rock, dirt, and debris onto the road and making it impossible for the convoy to pass the mound of stones. This also meant the mujahideen had committed themselves to the ambush.

Jonathan brought out his camera, a 35-mm Leica, and Ali assigned one of his men to the job of taking pictures. If everything went as planned, the photographs would provide a record of destruction. What they would not show, on explicit directions from the camera's owner, was Jonathan's face.

Jonathan sat high on the hill above the canyon with stone-faced Abdul at his side. He smiled at the unfriendly giant, but that only made Abdul frown even more. Shrugging his shoulders, Jonathan looked out over the valley in the direction of the convoy's approach, and mentally reviewed Neeley's instructions for operating the Stingers.

It was a warm afternoon, but that had nothing to do with the steady stream of sweat trickling down his back. Up here the wind blew strong and made his loose-fitting Afghan shirt flutter. He felt a chill.

Almost precisely at 4:15, the convoy entered the kill zone. Below him, Jonathan could see the trucks and the men in them. He could hear the sounds of their engines straining and the gears shifting, and he smelled the pungent diesel fuel and the dust they kicked up as they plowed their way into Qudar Canyon.

Two minutes later, he heard the screeching sound of brakes as the first vehicle rounded the turn at the far end of the canyon, just before the roadblock of boulders and dislodged stones. One by one each vehicle squealed to a stop, several of them rear-ending each other, until they came to a dead standstill.

The mujahideen waited.

Gradually men from the convoy began to cautiously get out of their vehicles. There were sounds of doors creaking open and slamming followed by a lot of shouting back and forth in Farsi. Jonathan wished he knew what they were saying, but he could guess.

A small, lightweight, armored car, probably belonging to the commander, skirted around the trucks to the front, then stopped before the wall of rocks. A couple of officers, clearly Russians, got out of the armored car to inspect the damage while four Soviet infantrymen covered them. One of the officers, most likely the commander, yelled out an order, and within a minute the troops began setting up a defensive perimeter, gathering around the three BMPs with their weapons drawn.

One of the BMPs moved past the commander's vehicle, toward the pile of rocks and dirt. Like a giant dune buggy, it began to climb upwards over the rubble, presumably to inspect the far side of the heap.

What none of the men in the convoy could see was that, in rising over the boulders, the BMP had exposed its underbelly. However, one of Ali's men, hidden and waiting on the other end of the pile, saw it perfectly. In the split-second that the giant armored vehicle sat teetering at the top of the rock pile, he fired his RPG.

In a flash of light, followed an instant later by a high-pitched whining sound, the missile found its mark in the lightly armored underbelly of the BMP. It ripped a giant, gaping wound in the steel skin, undoubtedly killing at least two men. The first casualties were the lucky ones. The interior of the vehicle erupted into a flaming death-trap, and soldiers frantically scrambled to get out. In the panic, several men suffocated or burned to death. The few who did get out were charred beyond recognition.

By then, the mujahideen stationed in the forward position had set off another dynamite charge. When it blew, it covered the convoy's rear escape route with rocks and stones. Three trucks stopped short of the choke point and found themselves outside the trap. Their drivers reversed rapidly down the road, nearly running into one another. The truck in the very rear ran over a land mine, which a mujahid, now hiding beside the road, detonated. The vehicle exploded into flames. The other two trucks following careened into it, so that all three of them became a single, burning chunk of metal.

High on the hill above, Jonathan watched this for a moment, then looked back toward the center of the action. The twenty-seven vehicles between the front and the rear found themselves in the middle of an inferno. All around him, the mujahideen opened fire with everything they had, raining death on the poor souls below.

But Ali's unit had their casualties too. A man up on the cliffside fired his grenade launcher into the front of the second BMP, but the projectile bounced off the heavily armored portion of the vehicle. The infantrymen inside scrambled through the rear door while the gunner turned the smoothbore gun on the man who'd fired at them. In an instant the mujahid on the hillside, along with the conscript who served as his loader, had been obliterated.

The BMP kept moving forward, raking the hillside with heavy machine-gun fire. But by now, the mujahideen had had time to react and move out of danger. The men operating the armored vehicle suddenly found themselves in an exposed spot broadside of another RPG team, who fired on them at point-blank range.

The vehicle lunged forward one last time, coughed, spluttered, and died. As smoke billowed from the engine compartment and command cupola, the front hatch flew open, and the driver rose up to extract himself, only to fall back like a lifeless mannequin as multiple rounds penetrated his chest. There was a chance—but not a likely one—that the men firing had failed to notice the white kerchief of surrender he held in his hand.

Far above them and many miles to the south, two MiG-23Bs out of Bagram Air Base roared over the Afghan sky.

"Scorpion, Falcon 1." It was the Mainstay surveillance aircraft, some 30,000 feet above them. "Come in, Scorpion."

"Falcon 1, Scorpion, over."

"Scorpion, convoy under attack at Qudar Canyon, approximately 100 clicks north of Charikar." Falcon 1 relayed the coordinates to them, and ordered the two MiGs to the site of the battle.

"Cobra," Scorpion asked, "did you copy?"

"Affirmative, Scorpion. En route." There was a pause. "Preparing to rain destruction on *cherno joppi*. Like shooting fish in barrel."

Both pilots laughed.

Down below, some of the vehicles in the center of the convoy began circling like covered wagons, protecting their flank. Only one BMP remained, and it turned sharply toward the attackers and started to shower the side of the mountain with 73-mm gunfire. From its rear, a squad of Soviet infantrymen dropped like worker ants from the queen's abdomen, and promptly set up a human perimeter inside the ring of vehicles. Now the BMP began rotating its smoothbore cannon, searching out concentrations of machine gun power.

Jonathan tensed as he watched the BMP move along, its blasts coming nearer. At any second, he would have to jump back or the cannon would turn him to powder. But turning, he saw Abdul holding his ground, fierce as ever.

Just 100 yards away, two mujahideen manned an American 50-calibre machine gun. They maintained fire even as the cannon pounded the hillside just below them. Jonathan was just thinking the two soldiers had better take cover when the cannon hit their position. Instantly, the men disappeared in a crash of metal.

He didn't know how many of the eight RPGs they still had left. One had taken out that first BMP, two more had obliterated the commander's scout car, and two others had removed the second BMP. Besides that, Abdul behind him held one, so that was six. That meant surely they had two others, but in all the smoke and noise and confusion, it was hard to be sure.

Down below, the BMP moved up through the valley. It fired like an angry, brainless beast, raking the stony cliffsides in the hope that it would hit one of its invisible attackers. And it did.

Suddenly a mujahid below Jonathan—and in full view of him—took a heavy cannon round in his chest. The dry earth all around him turned red with fragments of heart and lungs. *Another martyr for the cause,* thought Jonathan as he watched, grim-faced.

Abdul had a clear shot at the top of the armored vehicle, and he fired his RPG as it passed underneath. The BMP was so close below them that Jonathan instantly took cover, knowing the upward blast could knock the rocks loose around him.

But nothing happened. As the grenade hit its target, its fuse shorted, and the projectile failed to explode.

Now they were in the worst possible position. The commander of the BMP now knew their location, and they didn't have anything·to use against him. A heavy peppering of machine-gun fire followed, then some concentrated blasts from the smoothbore gun. All around Jonathan the earth was churning. Shells exploded in the dirt. Rocks flew by. It was only a matter of time before the cannon would zero in for the direct hit.

He watched helplessly as the vehicle began to move up the hillside off to the left to get a better angle on their position. He could see its turret rotating in his direction, and in seconds there would be a clear shot. He tried to scramble around the upper side of the boulder behind him, toward safety. A shell went *woomph*—not ten feet from him. The heat of the ensuing fire in the weeds and dry grass singed the hairs on the back of his neck.

This is it, he thought, but he wasn't ready to die. He kept his eyes open—and then he saw something very strange.

Instead of everything going black, the BMP exploded into flames. Apparently one of the men with an RPG had crept back along the far ridge and was able to fire into the vehicle.

Jonathan panted with relief, but the danger was far from over yet. He looked out over the golden late afternoon sky, and he wondered if anyone from the convoy had managed to call in reinforcements. By now the mujahideen had knocked out all the enemy's communications, but they had taken at least fifteen minutes to do so. Surely somebody was coming.

Just then two MiG-23s roared in over the valley from the south.

Up ahead, Scorpion could see a narrow canyon lined with high walls. Devastation filled the canyon floor.

"Scorpion, Falcon 1," came the voice from the Mainstay up in the clouds. "Give report, over."

So Scorpion described what he saw as best he could—smoke and fire, destroyed equipment, a few wounded, crawling vehicles, a lot of others burning or blackened. And bodies. Dozens of them. "Canyon extremely narrow," he concluded. "Will proceed with caution. Uncertain as to capabilities of enemy."

"Scorpion, proceed into canyon. Over," came the voice from the Mainstay.

The implication was *"Of course* you're uncertain—move on anyway." But the pilot's battle instinct told him the mujahideen were up to something more than their ordinary tricks.

In a daring and acrobatic move, Scorpion led the way for Cobra into the valley. Just when he was about to fire on the enemy positions, though, he realized that with such a narrow field below him, he was just as likely to hit his own wings as he was mujahideen. He let a few shots from his twin-barrel gun bounce harmlessly off the dusty cliffs, hitting no one. "Cobra, hold your fire," he said into his radio. "Canyon too narrow."

"Affirmative, Scorpion," said Cobra.

After they had passed through the attack area, Scorpion got back on the radio. "Falcon 1, Scorpion. Impact zone too contained to drop ordnance without injuries to friendlies. Have vacated, awaiting gunship support, over."

"Gunships en route, Scorpion. Hold pattern at 1,000 meters."

"Affirmative. Scorpion out." Scorpion switched over to his low-frequency transceiver for communication with his wingman. "Viktor, do you read me?" he said.

"I'm here, Misha," answered Cobra. "Haven't seen anything as tight as that canyon for a long time."

"I say we do another fly-by overhead, observe, and hang back," Scorpion announced. "The men on the ground should be able to deal with them."

Cobra readily agreed. He had a family, and only thirty days till demobilization. He didn't want a medal. The only certificate he really wanted was a discharge.

Jonathan watched the fighters streak by. Their engines sounded like screaming demons, and the sight of them filled him with alarm. But he also felt a certain childlike awe. *Now the* real *battle begins,* he told himself.

The mujahideen, under machine-gun cover, moved back up the hill and fired on the enemy below. From the advantage of higher ground, they worked on the center of the convoy, pounding the enemy's defensive perimeter.

Most of the remaining drivers had taken cover, but a few trucks had 7.2-mm machine guns mounted on them, and they returned fire. They produced little more than a sideshow. One by one, the mujahideen took out the trucks and their crews. In a few minutes, Soviet choppers would come with reinforcements. In the meantime, the Afghans maintained their rain of fire.

One of the trucks exploded with three times as much noise and smoke as the others before it, and, despite the ongoing shots and cannon bursts, Jonathan jumped—Abdul too. Apparently the vehicle had held ammunition.

The one immediately in front of it also caught fire, and Jonathan watched the driver trying to escape, screaming frantically. But just as the man opened the door, the truck blew up.

The canyon roared with the blaze of burning trucks, exploding ammunition rounds, and the screams of the unfortunates caught in the middle of it all. One by one, the remaining trucks started going up in flames.

In spite of the spreading conflagration, no one fired on any vehicles, only on the soldiers themselves. If they could save just one truck full of valuable munitions, it could keep the unit supplied for months.

Jonathan estimated there had been about one hundred men in the convoy. Now it looked like they only had two dozen remaining. With the mujahideen, it was harder to say, but he guessed there had been only about a dozen casualties out of seventy men.

The Soviets on the ground had only one hope—quick chopper support. He waited patiently for them to arrive, listening for the sound of their rotors. But he couldn't hear anything above the din on the canyon floor.

The choppers came in with the sunset behind them, black blotches against the western sky. The group consisted of four Hip transport helicopters, containing a total of eighty-two airborne assault troops, and two Mi-24 Hind gunships. Hinds and Hips—sometimes called the "master of ceremonies"—were a killer combination. To Scorpion and Cobra, who had just swung back over the valley, there could have been no better sight in the world.

"Scorpion, this is Black Widow," came the chopper unit commander's voice over the radio. "Proceeding into hot zone. Have lost communication with ground. Request your reading on the situation. Over."

After Scorpion reported on the most recent round of explosions, the assault commander said, "Those *cherno joppi* just bit off more than they can chew. Proceeding to shove fire down their throats. Over."

"Go to it, Black Widow," Scorpion laughed. "You guys have all the fun. Good luck." Then he got back on low frequency and said, "Viktor, let's head up to 7,500 meters and circle around while our good friends stir up the pot a bit down there."

"Good idea. See you on top."

It was almost time. Jonathan put on his earphones, which would make it possible to hear the low-key tone that the Stinger emitted when it was ready to fire. He had placed the missiles themselves in a crate hidden in a shallow cave behind him, and now he took one out.

Even through the earphones and the noise from the valley below, he could hear the rhythmic *whomp whomp whomp* of helicopters approaching. Soon he could see them coming over the cliffs.

He expected the first hit to come from the Hind gunships, which would probably rake the area with devastating force for several minutes to clear a landing zone so that the Hips could drop off the troops. Then the transports would join the attack, pounding the hillside with machine guns and 30-mm grenade launchers.

He was right. The two attack helicopters moved out in front of the others and bore straight into the valley, their fire showering the cliffs on either side. Normally in such a situation, it would have been time for the mujahideen to make an orderly retreat, firing behind them. They might eliminate a Hip or two, but their small arms could have no impact on the heavily armored attack helicopters. To take out a Hind, they needed a surface-to-air missile—something along the lines of the weapon Jonathan now held in his hands.

Instead of retreating, the mujahideen dug in, ceasing fire and seeming to disappear into the rocks. This left the choppers without any viable targets. Even so, the gunners in the Hinds raked the sides of the hills for several minutes. Without any return fire, though, the situation must have seemed baffling to the chopper crews.

The four troop carriers moved toward the landing zone. As the first two came down and deposited contingents of twenty heavily armed soldiers each, the gunships kept up their fire.

One of the Hinds passed close to Jonathan's position, hovering as it pounded the opposite hillside.

He rose into firing position with the first missile and listened for the tone indicating that its infrared/ultraviolet seeker mechanism had locked on the target. He flipped a switch that released argon to keep the seeker cool, enhancing its sensitivity—something he didn't need to do at this close range, but he only knew how to follow the instructions Neeley had given him. The tone now came on clear and unbroken. He locked on. There was no backing out now.

In front of him, the chopper pilot had spotted his movement and turned his craft to face him. Tracers edged toward his position, flashing and crashing against the hillside around him.

He had to act now.

Jonathan pulled the trigger.

Nothing happened.

He glanced over his shoulder at Abdul, who looked ready to kill him then and there. But fortunately for Jonathan, the helicopter's gunfire swept over their position and forced the two men apart as they sought shelter behind separate rocks.

Jonathan wanted to throw up. *What on earth did I do wrong?* He frantically went back over the process in his mind. *Got to stay calm . . . Got to figure it out . . .*

At least when he'd taken cover, he had wound up within reach of the missile crate. Forcing himself to move slowly, even though he could feel panic rising up in him, Jonathan exchanged the first missile for another one. His mind was spinning feverishly, desperately, but he made himself focus. He crept down the right side of the truck-sized boulder as the gunship's fire swept over to his left. The enemy couldn't see Jonathan, but he could see the enemy.

Now he aimed.

He pulled the trigger.

Swooshhhhh! The missile flew off from his shoulder and, literally in the blinking of an eye, it hit the intake port of the jet turbine.

Time seemed to freeze for a split-second, then the chopper burst into flames as the rupture spread through its system. A few seconds later, it exploded with a crash of fire and metal.

Jonathan and Abdul both dove for cover behind the same boulder, and above him Jonathan could feel the radiating waves of intense heat from the blast. On top of the first explosion came a resounding crash as the burning mass fell to the rocky canyon floor, smashing a truck filled with munitions, and causing another eruption.

Jonathan waited ninety seconds—until there was no more noise but the roaring of the flames and the sound of the other choppers' rotors as they pulled back. Then, he ventured a peek around the side of the boulder. He saw heads popping up all along his side of the hill. Several feet away stood Ali, and he was doing something Jonathan never thought he would see him do—grinning from ear to ear.

Ali called out something, but Jonathan couldn't hear him. He couldn't hear much of anything, as a matter of fact. The blast had left his ears ringing mercilessly. Seeing Ali pointing, Jonathan looked over at Abdul, who for the first time no longer looked ready to kill him. In fact, it was hard to tell what Abdul was thinking. He appeared to be in shock.

Jonathan scrambled back up behind the boulder, picked up another Stinger, and moved to the top of the rock. He took aim at the second gunship, which had turned back as soon as its pilot saw the fate of the first one. But because the shot had come from so close by, it wasn't clear where the danger was, and inadvertently the chopper pilot was steering right into the mouth of destruction.

"Come on," Jonathan whispered as he raised the Stinger. *Swooshhhhh* went the sound of the missile as it flew from the launcher. First he saw the chopper—the second and last Hind—burst into flames, and a tremendous explosion followed. A second later, the Hind crashed against the side of the mountain in a heap of fire and metal.

Jonathan was about to let out a whoop when he saw something that made the shout die halfway up his throat. As the doomed chopper fell against the cliffside like a sinking ship, it had landed squarely on the spot where two of Ali's men had hidden.

He felt sick, horrified at what he'd done. Until he saw Abdul's face. The Afghan was nodding and smiling, shaking his fist in what he must have thought was a gesture of approval. Apparently nothing could take the edge off sweet victory, not even the deaths of comrades.

In the past two minutes, Abdul's opinion of Jonathan seemed to have undergone a complete transformation. Now he eagerly handed Jonathan another Stinger, and Jonathan—as uncomfortable with the new Abdul as he had been with the old one— nodded his thanks.

Jonathan had jumped down from the boulder at the moment of impact, and now he crept back to the top, where he saw the first two Hips had unloaded their squads and lifted off to begin an air assault on the hillside. Meanwhile, the other two entered the landing zone to bring in the remainder of the troops.

That left him with a difficult decision. He only had one operable Stinger for dealing with the four remaining choppers. Doing some quick thinking, he took aim on one of the two choppers entering the landing zone. He could do more damage on it, because it still had twenty combat troops on board.

One more time, he unleashed the deadly force of the hardware on his shoulder. This time he was so close, the missile never even had an opportunity to assume strike velocity. Instead, it reached its target before anyone even realized it had been fired.

The Hip leapt thirty feet up into the air as it exploded, throwing bodies out onto the landing zone below. The blast sent its tail hurtling into the rotor of the other chopper, knocking out its anti-torque rotor.

Black Widow, in the second Hip, didn't sound so confident now. "We're hit," he yelled over the radio. "The chopper is out of control. No, we're going down. Pull up—" Then the transmission went blank.

The pilot tried desperately to bring it back to a proper altitude, but the chopper spun out of control. It lifted up fifty feet into the air, tilted on its side, and slammed into the earth, killing most of its occupants.

⌇

"Ye-e-e-s!" Jonathan exclaimed as he watched the Hip come crashing to earth. "Two for one." The roaring of the blaze filled the valley of death below him.

High above, Cobra and Scorpion couldn't see who had been hit. They radioed Black Widow to find out. "Widow 1?" called out Cobra. "Widow 1, this is Cobra—come in, over. Do you read me, Widow 1?"

"Cobra, Widow 2," said a voice into the radio. It was from one of the two remaining choppers. "Four craft down . . . enemy missiles . . . evacuating . . . Repeat. Four craft down, enemy missiles, evacuating the scene."

"Widow 2, clarify 'missiles.' Referring to RPGs, over?"

"Negative!" shouted Widow 2, sounding desperate and a little crazy. "*Missiles*—heat seekers of some kind, I don't know. They're like something from outer space. Can't tell where they're coming from. You don't stand a chance in that valley—it's a death zone! We're getting out, suggest you wipe out the entire area!"

Prior to the Stinger attack, two squads of infantrymen had been let off by the transports. One squad was an Afghan unit, the other was made up of Soviet soldiers. The Afghans, finding themselves stranded, threw down their weapons and ran with arms raised in surrender toward their "brothers" on the other side. A few of them were shot by the Soviets, who had dug in and begun fighting back.

"Misha," Cobra asked on the secure channel, "what do you think that chopper jockey meant by heat seekers?"

"It's impossible," Scorpion replied. "Those bandits just got off some lucky shots with a couple of RPGs."

"Maybe." Cobra didn't sound convinced. "But I wish we had some flares." Shooting off a magnesium flare could confuse a heat-seeking missile because the flares burn with a higher intensity than the MiG's engines. But unused flares were a fire hazard, and since Soviet intelligence *knew* that the mujahideen didn't possess any heat-seekers, the Soviet Air Forces had stopped carrying such items more than two years before.

"Scorpion, Falcon 1," came the voice from the Mainstay above them. "Commence bombing run on target area."

This order took Scorpion by surprise. "Falcon, repeat, over?"

"Reenter canyon, bomb all visible targets."

"Falcon 1," answered Scorpion, highly annoyed. "No room to maneuver in valley. High chance that ordnance would fall on friendlies."

Falcon's voice came back without missing a beat. "Scorpion, proceed as ordered. Convoy commander says position being overtaken, requests bombing run. Says this is his only chance. Repeat, proceed to target as ordered."

"Affirmative, Falcon 1. Proceeding as directed."

Scorpion and Cobra could communicate on the low-frequency channel, but neither man dared use it as a forum for expressing his doubts about the orders they had just received. There was no telling who might be listening in—the man in the Mainstay, perhaps, high in the sky above them. Both men knew Falcon was lying about the convoy commander. If the commander was even alive, which was doubtful, he hadn't had any communications capability for half an hour now, or the two pilots would have heard him on their radios. Clearly Falcon had written off the convoy and all the men in it and didn't want any equipment left in the hands of the rebels. But neither Cobra nor Scorpion could acknowledge this fact.

"Cobra," Scorpion announced, "let's make one dry run and check out the positions."

"I'm with you, Misha."

The two jets peeled off and swung down into the valley, firing their 23-mm guns at the canyon walls as they made their subsonic pass down through the kill zone.

Each Stinger had cost Jonathan in excess of $550,000, and he might have been upset that the first one hadn't proven operable. But given the fact he'd bought them from Hector Valdez, he was just glad three of them worked. And those three had been such a success, he was willing to write off the loss. Besides, later on when the battle was over, he could take a closer look at the remaining one and see what the problem was.

His job done, he once more became a spectator. He watched the carnage unfolding on the ground below him as the battle continued and the mujahideen moved in to surround the Russians who remained. The return fire indicated no more than fifteen or twenty enemy troops remained, and the mujahideen began to work their way down into the canyon, closing the noose on the enemy.

Suddenly he heard the roar of the two MiG-23s, magnified many times over by the echo on the walls of the narrow canyon. Their guns were blazing, spitting heavy fire on the sides of the cliffs.

They're coming in again! The realization hit him full-force. *Got to do something.* He looked down at the defective Stinger and suddenly had a burst of insight.

Quickly, he unscrewed the back plate with his knife and opened the firing mechanism. He was hoping to see something obviously amiss, though he had no idea what. As soon as he peered in, he saw a small wire had come detached from the triggering mechanism. There seemed to be only one loose screw, so he reattached the wire, tightened it down with his knife, and put the plate back on.

Meanwhile the jets pulled up and circled around again.

"My God!" shouted Scorpion into his radio. "There's no maneuvering room down there!"

"Maybe Widow was right," Cobra answered. "Only heat seekers could have done what we saw."

"You may have a point," conceded Scorpion. "Not sure of anything anymore. If it's true, we're in trouble. Our planes weren't made for this kind of thing—all we can do is take out the convoy."

"Waiting on your directions," Cobra replied.

But Scorpion didn't have a clue. "Uh . . . looks like many of the vehicles haven't been hit yet. On this next pass, you take the lead, and we'll try to hit a couple. They should be full of ammunition, and when they explode, they'll destroy the others around them." He stopped for a second, and both pilots were horrified at the thought of what they were about to do to their own comrades. "I just don't see any way we can save those guys on the ground," Scorpion went on. "Let's just hit 'em with everything we've got and get out of here."

"Okay," answered Cobra. "I'll take out the vehicles at the top end of the convoy, and you follow up with the rear."

"Agreed. I'm right behind you. Let's switch back to open frequency."

They flew into their second bombing run, Cobra in the lead, firing both guns at either side of the canyon.

On the ground, a mujahid rose up from behind a rock with a missile on his shoulder.

As Cobra approached the front of the convoy and prepared to drop his ordnance, Scorpion behind him saw the fireburst and its vapor trail heading in the direction of the forward aircraft. "Viktor!" he screamed into his radio. "Pull up, pull up! Missile to your left! Pull up!"

Viktor pulled up, but he didn't even have time to reply. He was never going to see his wife and child again. In a flash of light, the projectile rammed right up his tailpipe, and a second later, the aircraft exploded and cartwheeled toward the canyon floor.

Scorpion pulled back on the stick and kicked in his afterburner, and his plane leapt out of the canyon like a grasshopper. As he climbed to a safe distance, he kept looking back for more signs of the heat-seeking missiles, but they never came. When he got out of range, he had to take a lot of deep breaths before his heart stopped pounding louder than the sound of his engine.

He got on his radio. "Falcon 1, Scorpion. Cobra is down! Valley full of heat-seeking missiles. Canyon is impenetrable by low-flying aircraft. Suggest high-altitude bombing."

After a moment's silence, Falcon 1 came back. "Scorpion, Falcon 1. No bombers in the area at this time. Continue with bombing runs as directed."

Scorpion thought for a moment. Trying hard to mask his fear, he said in a calm voice, "All ordnance is expended." As he spoke, he released all of his cluster bombs over an empty valley below him, several miles away from the hot zone. "Running low on fuel. Request permission to return to base."

Again, there was a moment's silence as Falcon 1 apparently consulted with his commander. "Permission granted," Falcon 1 announced finally.

Scorpion sped up and turned on his afterburner so that his plane would burn more fuel. "Scorpion on way in, over."

As soon as he had signed off, he fired his cannons into the air so he wouldn't have an ounce of remaining ordnance. "This is getting to be a really scary war," he said aloud in a trembling voice.

And it was true. For the first time in nearly seven years, the Soviets truly had something to fear.

CHAPTER FOURTEEN

The explosion of the aircraft was the last straw. The few remaining Soviet infantrymen threw down their weapons and put up their hands. The mujahideen roared down into the valley with shouts, quickly gathering their prisoners in the center. Ali wasted no time in ordering his men first to clear an exit, then to take the remaining vehicles and move out.

Jonathan walked slowly down the hillside, his knees shaking so badly he could hardly walk. As he reached the bottom, with Abdul right behind him, the mujahideen raised a cheer in his honor.

"This is no longer Qudar Canyon," said Ali, coming out and embracing him. "We will always know this as Wright Canyon."

For a second, Jonathan had no idea what he was talking about. In the adrenaline rush of the moment, he'd forgotten his pseudonym. But when it came back to him, he nodded with appreciation. He felt light-headed and wanted to sit down, but he had become the center of attention.

The men around him wore broad grins and greeted him with newfound respect. As for Abdul the *Shuravi*-hater, he reached over, picked Jonathan up, hugged him, and kissed him on both cheeks. Then, in a loud voice he shouted something to the other men, and they all nodded in agreement. "He says," Ali translated, "even though you are . . . not Muslim, you are still a messenger from Allah." Jonathan nodded gratefully to Abdul, who looked like he might come over and give him another one of those painful bear-hugs.

Besides the stunning blow they had dealt the enemy and all the prestige such a victory carried with it, they now had a great cache of arms and ammunition and thirty-two captured troops.

Within thirty minutes, the group assigned to clear out the exit had completed their work, and the remaining twelve trucks were on their way out of the canyon. They found a secondary road off the main highway and hid the newly captured vehicles in another canyon ten miles from the ambush site. There they waited until dark. Then, still in high spirits, they boarded the trucks again and drove all the way to Massoud's camp.

Jonathan rode in the same truck with Ali and Abdul. Abdul looked at Jonathan and said something to Ali, who translated for Jonathan, "Abdul insists on being your personal bodyguard for as long as you are in this country."

Embarrassed, Jonathan said, "Tell him thank you, but that's not really necessary."

"You had best accept," Ali cautioned, looking at his enormous compatriot.

"Okay," Jonathan answered, turning from Ali to Abdul, "if you say so."

When he had first arrived just a few days before, he had been made to feel like an intruder at best, and maybe something much worse. But when Jonathan returned with the mujahideen to Massoud's temporary cliffside fortress, he came—thanks to an apparent radio call from Ali reporting what had happened in the canyon—as a hero.

By the time they pulled in, riding shoulder to shoulder in the truck, it was two in the morning and pitch black on the long road leading from Qudar Canyon up into the mountain where Massoud and his forces hid. But a crowd gathered to greet them and, when they saw the trucks coming, they sent up a cheer.

Jonathan looked around at the others in the truck. It seemed a little incongruous to him that they would all celebrate so loudly and so openly when the whole purpose of this remote camp was to stay hidden from Soviet eyes and ears. But they must know what they were doing.

By now they were in the middle of the camp, which was lit up like broad daylight. Cheering people surrounded them, firing weapons into the air. A group of younger men jumped off another truck and swarmed the one in which Jonathan rode. They grabbed him and literally pulled him off of it onto their shoulders. Held aloft by the other men and gripped by their hands on his arms and his legs, Jonathan was ridden around the camp like a king.

He let them carry him—he really had no choice—but the whole display embarrassed Jonathan. "No, no, no," he kept shouting, laughing, and trying to be heard above the noise of all the others. And still they carried him on their shoulders back and forth, singing something halfway between a song and a chant.

The whole thing made him feel a little giddy—and a little worried. He remembered Kipling's, *The Man Who Would Be King*, about how an adventurer like himself—though one with low motives—had come into this country thinking he could rule it, yet he ended up losing his head, quite literally. It all could have happened much the same for Jonathan—if those Stingers hadn't fired.

They finally lowered him down in front of Massoud's cave, and the commander came out, greeted him with a smile, and kissed him on both cheeks. Shouting to be heard over the din, the leader spoke in rapid-fire Farsi. Jonathan just smiled and nodded his head. Even if he could have understood, he certainly couldn't hear.

"Massoud says," a voice shouted up close in his ear, "that you are a great defender of our people." Jonathan wheeled around, and there stood Ali—still looking like a schoolmaster, beaming with approval at his star pupil. In response to something Massoud said, Ali looked at his leader and asked him a question, then listened and bowed his head gravely. He turned toward Jonathan. Something in his expression caused others around him to go quiet. "Massoud says he is granting you the honorary title of commander in his army."

Jonathan, taken aback, bowed slightly as well.

". . . And," Ali went on. "He is promoting me to the rank of general commander."

All this news raised another round of cheers from the crowd. The mujahideen didn't have officer ranks—there were just commanders and general commanders, and now Ali had the same rank as Massoud, though it was obvious who the leader was.

Jonathan, impatient to speak, finally raised a hand. When it got quiet enough for him to be heard, he said to Ali, "Tell him—Massoud, you have made a wise decision in making Ali a general commander. He is an outstanding leader of men."

"Thank you," said Ali, with a warm look in his eyes.

"Tell him." Jonathan gestured toward Massoud, and Ali did as he was asked. Massoud smiled when the message was relayed to him.

"And tell him," Jonathan went on, "that I request the opportunity to discuss how I might continue to contribute to the liberation of your people." He looked at Ali. "Make that, *humbly* request."

Ali fired off the words to Massoud, who replied that Jonathan could come to his cave and speak with him whenever he wished, but for now it was time to celebrate, not to worry over strategy.

And celebrate they did. The men who had fought, Jonathan among them, went off to sleep until mid-afternoon. But, they awoke to the smells of a feast. The women—and there were several of them in this camp, although as always in Afghanistan, they were seldom seen or heard—had killed the fattest of the lambs and cooked it along with a steaming vat of rice and huge loaves of *naan*.

This kind of feast was virtually unheard of in these lean days, and Jonathan would have been embarrassed if he thought it were only in his honor. But the people were celebrating their victory, the victory all of them had gained. And much like Americans, the Afghans couldn't resist a good cookout.

As the sky grew dark that night, they built a bonfire. An impromptu band played traditional songs on homemade sitars and tambour similar to the instruments of India, though much simpler. Young men and old sang and danced around the fire while Jonathan, sitting with Ali on his right and Massoud on his left—the place of honor at the leader's right hand—watched them. One of the minstrels chanted the same two lines over and over, which Ali, in his pedantic way, explained as a *landai*, a traditional song composed of a single two-line verse in strict Farsi meter. They sang songs of great heroes in ages past, from the days of Alexander the Great to medieval times—to the heroes living still.

As one dancer left the center of the bonfire to loud cheers, everyone startled to see big, tough Abdul enter the ring. This brought up another cheer from the crowd, and he smiled and waved before he started to sing in a hesitant, flat, and very deep voice. But he gained confidence and, as he began chanting, the *landai* took shape. Suddenly he broke into full song. It was as though his big bass voice had to get off the ground like a giant airplane, because now it was soaring, and the men cheered wildly.

A grinning Ali clapped his hands. "I had no idea Abdul had such poetic talent," he said loudly to Jonathan.

"What's he saying?"

"He says," Ali translated, "'Commander Wright shoots craft from the air as boys shoot birds with slings. Now the *Shuravi* have no place to run, and the skies belong to us.'"

Jonathan smiled, touched by the fact that the man who had been ready to slit his throat just thirty-six hours before was now quite literally singing his praises. He nodded his appreciation toward the giant, who smiled back as he danced around, making the motions of an aircraft flying through the sky and exploding as it entered Wright Canyon.

The wildly enthusiastic way in which the Afghans could celebrate amazed him. And they did it all without one drop of alcohol. Instead he sipped a yogurt drink with a quite appealing sour, salty taste. He had stuffed himself on lamb and rice pilaf and sweet pastries similar to baklava. When Ali tried to force more on him, he smiled and crossed his arms in front of his chest, palms out, to indicate he could take no more.

"I gotta get a little fresh air," Jonathan said, standing up as Abdul finished his song.

"Everything is all right?" asked Ali, looking concerned.

"Yes, I'm fine." He just wanted to be by himself for a minute, to walk off some of his dinner, and maybe take a look at the moon. He had much on his mind—thoughts of what had brought him here to Afghanistan and of the unfinished mission, of Sonny and the man who should have been here celebrating with him, Phil Neeley, dead at the bottom of some mountain pass on the way in from Pakistan.

"So," said Ali as Jonathan got into the saddle of his horse. After three days of recuperation, he felt rested and ready for the long journey out of Afghanistan. "I am glad to know we will see you again."

Abdul, sitting on a steed beside him, grinned as though he understood this.

"Yes," said Jonathan, squinting into the morning sun. He couldn't help dreading the trip down, just because of what he'd gone through on his way in. But Ali had told him that with just two men riding, they could travel during the day, and they would make Peshawar in less than a week. "I think for now it's best we keep this just between you, Massoud, and me."

"Of course," said Ali. He stood looking up at Jonathan through his spectacles, shielding his eyes from the sun.

"There's something on your mind," said Jonathan. He pulled an object out of his saddlebag and put it in the breast pocket of his coat—the roll of film taken the other day at Wright Canyon. Once he got back to civilization, he planned to mail it to CIA Headquarters in Langley, Virginia.

"I'm just wondering," said Ali, clearing his throat. "You have enjoyed such great success during this time with us . . ."

"And you're curious why I would risk coming back in?" asked Jonathan.

Ali nodded his head.

Jonathan's horse snorted and shook its head, and Jonathan pulled back slightly on the reins. "Let's just say I'm not doing this for sport." He looked over at Abdul, who again smiled back.

"I assumed not," Ali answered. "But I do not think it is because you are one with us in heart either. We may hate the same enemy, but we do not worship the same god."

Jonathan gazed at the mountaintops ahead of him. "We are more alike than you may think," he answered. "If I understand anything about you and your people, after this time I've spent here, I know that you don't just fight for religion, or for your tribe, or for Afghanistan. You fight because of Khalid and all the other friends and loved ones you have lost in this war, isn't that so?"

"Yes, of course," Ali answered. "And you?"

"And the Koran," Jonathan went on, turning and looking down at Ali. "Does it not speak of retribution—something like 'an eye for an eye'?"

Ali nodded shrewdly. "I see. So it is revenge, then?"

Jonathan tasted dry dust in the back of his throat, and he thought about the long trail ahead. "It's not important why . . . just know that when I return, it will be . . . shall we say, a grand entrance."

"That it will, if it happens as you have told Massoud and me." From the way Ali said it, he clearly doubted he would ever seen Jonathan again.

"Oh, it *will* happen as I said," said Jonathan. At that moment, he felt total confidence in his own abilities, even though he had experienced enough to doubt the feeling. He was on a high now, he knew. Who wouldn't be? But eventually he'd have to come down and face the reality of what lay ahead.

It was time to go. "Abdul will take good care of you," Ali said, glancing at the other man, "and will see that you get safely to Peshawar." He looked at Jonathan and smiled. "And now, my friend, *Khodai paman*—go with the protection of Allah."

Jonathan turned back to the man who had distrusted him just a few days before, yet who was now his friend, and waved goodbye. Then, he and Abdul set off on the long, long trail out of the mountains.

Rusty Wharton poked his head into McGinnis's office. "You wanted to see me?" There was someone sitting in a chair in front of the desk, facing the boss.

"Yeah, Rusty," said McGinnis, looking up and smiling. "Come on in."

McGinnis had plenty of faults in Wharton's eyes, but being ostentatious wasn't one of them. His office wasn't much bigger than Wharton's or Hollis's, and Wharton had to squeeze in because McGinnis's visitor blocked the doorway.

"Rusty, I'd like you to meet someone I've told you about before," said McGinnis with an affable tone.

Wharton gave his chief a look of suspicion. He was being too polite—always a sign he was up to something. Glancing at McGinnis's visitor, Wharton saw a Hispanic man in his early thirties with a military-style haircut. Dressed in jeans, combat boots, and a ratty tee shirt, he slouched sullenly in the chair. "Rusty Wharton, meet Jose Gonzales," McGinnis was saying.

Wharton looked at McGinnis in confusion.

"Jose was in Bogotá with our friend Boltar in January," McGinnis explained.

Wharton raised his eyebrows, then turned to Gonzales. The two nodded to each other.

"So go back to what you were saying," McGinnis prompted Gonzales.

Gonzales shrugged. "There ain't much more to tell, Mac. It's all in the report—you read it, didn't you?"

"Sure, sure," said McGinnis. "I just wanted Rusty to meet you."

"Well, hold on a second," said Wharton, looking from McGinnis to Gonzales. "This trip to Colombia was three months ago—how come I've never seen that report?"

Gonzales gave Wharton a sneering look. "Ask him," he said, nodding toward McGinnis.

"Uh, Rusty," McGinnis said, running a pudgy hand through the thin, almost nonexistent hair atop his head, "Jose here isn't uh . . . he's not with the Agency. He's just—"

"Employed on an ad hoc basis," Gonzales interrupted, looking at Wharton defiantly, as though to say, *You got a problem with that?* "Advisory capacity. Strictly ad hoc basis."

Wharton folded his arms. "All right, then," he said, looking from one man to the other. "What's in this report of yours that I never got to see?"

"I just had to wait until I could get Jose in here," said McGinnis, "to debrief him." He opened a drawer and pulled out a manila envelope. "Now you're the first guy to see the report." He winked at Wharton.

The wink confused Wharton. "Help me out here," he said to Gonzales after a moment's deliberation. "Did the purchase go off? Did the Stingers make it out of Colombia?"

Gonzales snickered and, still looking at McGinnis, gestured at Wharton. "Sounds like your boy's kind of behind schedule, Mac." Sighing, he said, "Read the report. George Watt, or Boltar, or whatever you want to call him, purchased four Stinger missiles from Hector Valdez. I was there."

"You and who else?" Wharton demanded.

Gonzales shook his head. "I don't rat out my friends, man."

"You ratted out Boltar," said Wharton. "Or George Watt."

"George Watt's just a dude who hired me, okay?" asked Gonzales. "I ain't got no loyalty to him." He looked at McGinnis. "Can I go now?"

"Yeah, sure, Jose," said McGinnis, standing up.

Gonzales stood up too, and Wharton, more confused than ever, followed suit.

As soon as the visitor had left, Wharton turned to McGinnis. But before he could ask any questions, his boss held up both hands.

"I know, I know," McGinnis said. He gestured for Wharton to sit down. "These things are a little more complicated than you might initially guess."

"How so?" asked Wharton.

"Well," McGinnis began, opening up the envelope on his desk. "It was a priority to get Gonzales in here—"

"To deliver a report three months late?" asked Wharton. "Who is this guy, anyway?"

McGinnis waved a hand. "Ah, he's nobody. Mercenary type. You'll never see him again. But we needed him to corroborate a theory about what's in these pictures."

"Pictures?"

"We picked them up through the Keyhole," McGinnis replied. The Keyhole was the nickname for the KH-11 satellite, which could make high-resolution, real-time images of events on the ground.

"*And?*" asked Wharton impatiently.

"And," McGinnis went on with a self-satisfied smile, "we got some great shots over the northeastern quadrant of Afghanistan, in a place called Qudar Canyon, maybe 100 clicks north of Kabul." From the envelope he extracted a dozen or more photographs and a few sheets of paper from a dot-matrix printer and slid them across the desk to Wharton.

Wharton studied the photographs, black and white enlargements of pictures made by the KH-11. From what he could see, it looked like some serious devastation in that canyon—maybe five helicopters down, though it was hard to tell from the jumbled scenes of wreckage the photos showed. One of the choppers could actually be a plane. He just couldn't be certain. Around them were the remains of a convoy.

"Pretty impressive, huh?" McGinnis prompted him.

"Absolutely," Wharton mumbled as he thumbed back through the pictures. "So how come you're so certain it was Stingers that did this—and *our* Stingers at that?"

"Look at the printout," said McGinnis, and Wharton unfolded the dot-matrix pages, held together by a perforated strip along the edges. "We picked this up from a listening post on the Pakistan border. It looks like Stingers to me, and the information from Gonzales confirms a timetable that would be compatible with—"

But Wharton wasn't listening. He was busy reading the printout, which appeared to be a series of transmissions back and forth between two pilots. This must have been a translation, because he quickly picked up from the names—Misha and Viktor—and their references to various items of Warsaw Pact equipment that they were Russians. As he read along, he started to realize what McGinnis meant. From the way the pilots described the situation below them, this piece of work had to be that of the Stingers. One of them as much as said so. And they both protested the fact that they were obviously being sent in to kill their own comrades on the ground—probably trying to destroy the position of whoever was firing on them. After that, it appeared one of them got shot down himself, and the other one—certain his wingman had been taken out by a surface-to-air missile—hightailed it out of there.

"Wow," said Wharton aloud. He looked up at McGinnis.

McGinnis nodded his head. "Listening post got another transmission a few hours later," he said. "Apparently another squadron of MiGs entered the ambush zone, made several passes, and determined that most of the convoy had disappeared. They found four helicopters destroyed on the ground, plus one MiG-23."

"Hum," said Wharton thoughtfully.

"What's on your mind, Rusty?" asked McGinnis.

"Well, I'm just thinking," he said. "Wasn't it supposed to be *four* Stingers Boltar purchased down in Colombia?"

"Yeah, that's what Gonzales reported," said McGinnis.

"The force on the ground uses four Stingers to knock out *five* aircraft?" asked Wharton. "Since when does that happen?"

"What are you saying?" asked McGinnis, sounding irritable.

"Just that I'm wondering if maybe our man had more than four Stingers."

"I don't know," McGinnis sighed. "The point is, he's fired them." He pointed to the photographs, and suddenly his tone changed. "Do you understand?" he asked sternly. "The missiles have been fired, and they were used against an enemy of the United States, not an allied power. It's finished."

Wharton studied McGinnis's face. "Isn't there going to be some serious fall-out from this?" he asked.

"Why? What fall-out?" McGinnis spread his hands. "Those weapons were made in the U.S., but we didn't have anything to do with the shootdown of those choppers and that plane. There's not going to be any press on this, believe me, because the Soviets wouldn't want anyone on either side to know they were rendered so vulnerable."

"The mujahideen won't get the word out?" asked Wharton.

McGinnis snorted. "How? Through the Afghan News Network? Forget it—they're living in the Stone Age."

"They can't all be that backward," Wharton said calmly, "if they're in contact with Rashid. And what about this Watt guy, the missing link between Rashid and the Colombians?" He pointed at the pictures. "Maybe between the Colombians and *this*? What if it turned out he were an American citizen who just decided to conduct his own diplomacy?"

McGinnis shook his head. "Like I said, there's not gonna be any press on this, so what does it matter now? The deed is *done,* Rusty." He pointed to the photographs spread across the desk. "The deed is done."

"May I have your attention, ladies and gentlemen. At this time we request that you extinguish all smoking materials and put your seat backs in an upright position." The sound of the captain's voice woke Jonathan from a nap. Funny thing, ever since he had made it out of Afghanistan, after the most grueling month of his life, he couldn't get enough sleep.

"In a few moments we will begin our final approach to New Orleans' Moisant International Airport. Out your windows you will see the twenty-four mile Lake Pontchartrain Causeway, the longest bridge in the world." Jonathan looked out at the blue water with a ribbon of gray asphalt running through it. The sight of familiar surroundings gave him a strange feeling of déjà vu, as though he were entering a city he knew everything about but had never actually visited.

"Our latest weather report has a clear eighty degrees, with no chance of rain. If you are stopping in New Orleans today, we wish you a pleasant stay, and if you're traveling on with us—"

Thank God, Jonathan thought. *No connecting flight.*

An hour after his plane touched down, he stepped out of a taxi in front of his home on St. Charles Avenue. The gardener had kept the lawn perfectly manicured and, once he'd fumbled for his keys and gotten inside, he saw that the interior looked immaculate, thanks to his housekeeper.

Before he left, he had told her he was going mountain-climbing in India, the same story he had used with anyone he figured ought to have some idea of his whereabouts. It was close to the truth, and it made it easy to explain why he couldn't be reached during the past month.

Jonathan left his bags in the foyer and walked through the rooms. The place was clean, all right. So clean he could have run a white glove along the baseboards at the back of the deepest closet and found no dust. But it was empty. It had no life, and seeing it now for the first time in a month, he felt just how long it had been since the laughter of his wife and child had been heard inside these walls. Opening the door to the garage, he looked out at his two cars—the stately black Mercedes he had driven back when Jennifer was alive and the Porsche he had bought after her death.

He looked in the master bedroom cautiously, as though it belonged to someone else and he were just housesitting. Jennifer's big walk-in closet stood empty except for a few hangers pushed to the very back. He'd gotten rid of all her clothes soon after her death. Even his own closet, with its neat rows of suits and crisp dress shirts, seemed foreign. Jon's little room, once decorated in a Sesame Street motif with a giant stuffed Big Bird in the corner, had been stripped bare of all furnishings long before, but he still couldn't bring himself to go in there. Even the sight of the doorway gave him a catch in his throat.

After he unpacked, he checked the refrigerator. His housekeeper had obviously gotten the phone message he had left her on his way back through London. The fridge was stocked.

He popped open an orange juice. He hadn't been back to civilization long enough yet to take for granted the convenience and cleanliness of good ol' processed, packaged, American food. He looked at the label on the bottle for a moment, savoring the taste of reconstituted O.J.

"What next?" he said aloud in the empty hallway as he wandered into his study. A neat stack of magazines and mail waited on the library table in front of the double windows, with about a week's worth of the *Times-Picayune* in the basket beside his favorite reading chair. Jonathan took a handful of mail and several of the most recent magazines and papers and settled down to read. A quick flip through the mail revealed nothing interesting or urgent. He had long ago given his accountant charge of his bills via an escrow account, and he didn't have any personal mail—no letters, anyway.

He stopped when he saw an engraved invitation with a familiar return address, and he rummaged around in his desk drawer until he found his letter opener, then popped it open. "Well, whaddaya know?" he said aloud as he read that the parents of Miss Kimberly Welch were pleased to announce her upcoming marriage to . . . He vaguely recognized the guy's name, an investment banker in town. *She sure didn't waste any time,* he thought as he set down the envelope.

A flip through the local newspaper revealed an interesting tidbit about yet another wedding. Annelise Revier, sister of the late Jennifer Revier Stuart, had gotten married the week before. He looked at the picture of the bride and groom and her smiling family, the "best" of New Orleans society. *Guess I'm still not good enough to mingle with you people,* he thought to himself. Even Kim had invited him to her wedding—although the invitation was probably more out of spite than anything else.

The house seemed as quiet as a tomb, so quiet he could hear the clock ticking in the living room. The sound brought him back to that night, now six months past, when he had first gotten the idea for his Afghan odyssey. Sitting there in the silence with a pile of papers in his lap, he smiled at the memory. Then, as he listened, it seemed as though the ticking clock was speaking to him. "Dra-koff," it said. "Dra-KOFF . . . Dra-KOFF . . . Dra-KOFF."

He shook his head and said to the empty room, "Brother, what's wrong with me?" He glanced at the phone, and thought about calling Sonny to let him know he was back in town. But what he really wanted was to get out of the house.

Within half an hour, he stood drinking a Dixie beer at the bar of the Acme Oyster House on Bienville in the French Quarter. Across from him, a jovial black man named Mo shucked oysters faster than he, or any other customer, could down them. He knew he was taking a risk, coming out to a place where he was likely to run into acquaintances. He had already chatted with several. But what did he have to hide as far as they were concerned? He had been away, that was all.

Just as Jonathan peeled back the head of a fresh broiled crawfish and popped the tail into his mouth, he felt a large presence over his right shoulder. He glanced down at the shadow it cast over him. Looking out of the corner of his eye, he said, "Hi, Len."

A smiling Leonard Krygowski put his big, beefy hands on Jonathan's shoulders and said, "Jonathan Stuart! It's been awhile. How ya doin', partner?"

"Doing fine," Jonathan said nonchalantly, taking another sip of beer.

"Mind if I join you for a mud bug or two?"

"Help yourself." Jonathan waved a hand at the plate piled with bright red crawfish.

"Hey, Mo," Krygowski called loudly over the zydeco blaring from the dining room, "gimme an order o' crawfish and a dozen oysters—oh, and a Dixie too." He turned to Jonathan. "So what have you—say, that's quite a tan you got there, boss. Been soakin' up the sun and fun in the Bahamas or someplace?"

Jonathan smiled. "No way, Len—you oughta know I'm too much of an action and adventure type to go just lie around for a month."

"I didn't ask you how long you'd been gone."

"No, you didn't." Jonathan, who had turned toward Krygowski, faced the bar again.

"I'm sorry, where'd you say you went?"

"I didn't, but I was mountain climbing—in the Himalayas."

"Oooh, ain't that somethin'," said Krygowski as he took his beer from the bartender. He thought for a second. "I noticed you say 'Him-a-*LAY*-as,' and I thought those in the know said 'Him-*AL*-ayas.'"

Jonathan shrugged. If this deputy-dog wanted to catch him in a lie, he was going to have to do better than that. "Guess I'm not as sophisticated as you, Len."

"Well, I see you followed my advice and did some traveling." Krygowski propped an elbow on the bar and turned to face Jonathan. "Looks like it suits you, too." He nodded his head. "So—where else you been? I know you ain't been in the mountains this whole time, and I haven't heard too much about you for, oh, six months or so." He looked at his watch in that odd way people do when talking about time periods of months or years.

Jonathan wondered if Krygowski's appearance here tonight was just a coincidence or if, for some reason, he'd had an eye out for Jonathan's return. The thought was a little unsettling, but he remained nonchalant.

"Well, Len," he said, "you know how time just slips away from us, and you look back and don't even know how you spent it all." He launched into an explanation of all he had gone through in selling off his company, filling his story with lots of boring details calculated to make Krygowski lose interest.

But Len stayed right there with him, asking intelligent questions. After listening for awhile, he said, "You still didn't tell me where you went."

"Gee, Len," said Jonathan sarcastically, "I'm flattered by your interest in me."

Krygowski shrugged. "You forget, Jonathan. I had some firsthand evidence of just how . . . upset you were last fall." He stood back and gestured toward Jonathan. "Now you seem, you know, less tightly wound. I'm just wondering what you did to get yourself straightened out. Just asking as a friend, that's all."

"As a friend," Jonathan repeated, and Krygowski nodded his head and smiled.

Jonathan proceeded to tell Krygowski a long story about his travels to places such as London and Paris, filling them with details he remembered from earlier visits with Jennifer. When he was finished, Krygowski, sounding suitably bored, said, "Sounds like an interesting few months there, Jonathan."

Krygowski's fading interest made Jonathan relax a bit, and from there they fell into small talk. He asked Krygowski about the Saints and whether their owner, John Meacom, had managed to get them sold off. Krygowski gave him an earful about the perpetually losing team and Meacom, who he said couldn't run a shoeshine shop. They talked about Villanova upsetting Georgetown in the championships, and about the first woman ever winning the Iditarod sled race in Alaska. They discussed the new Coke formula, introduced just the day before, which Krygowski said tasted like flat Pepsi.

"So whaddaya think about that new Soviet leader?" asked Krygowski offhandedly.

"New—?" Jonathan wracked his brain. He'd heard something since he'd been back, but hadn't really paid attention. After a month on the dark side of the moon, there was no telling what had happened in the real world without his knowing it.

"Yeah, you know, Chernenko took the dirt nap, and they've got this young guy, Gorbachev." Krygowski popped a crawfish into his mouth and washed it down with a big swallow of Dixie.

"Oh, yeah, of course," Jonathan lied. "I know what you're talking about now. He seems okay to me."

"Yeah, they say he's kind of a liberal, by Soviet standards." Krygowski thought for a moment. "Some people say he might even pull them out of Afghanistan."

Jonathan, who had relaxed, suddenly tensed at the sound of the country's name.

Krygowski looked at him. "Say, that reminds me," he said. "Didn't you and I talk about something to do with Afghanistan last time we saw each other?"

Jonathan shrugged and tried to think quickly. There was no way on earth Krygowski could know what he'd been up to. Sure, he was an FBI agent, but that didn't mean much when it came to international activities. Quickly he rehearsed his response. Of course he would remember their conversation about Drakoff and Afghanistan. It would seem suspicious if he claimed he *didn't* recall it. So he nodded his head and said, "Yeah."

"That's right," said Krygowski, as though it were all coming back to him. "I was right, wasn't I? The place *is* like going to prison, isn't it?"

Jonathan did a double take. "What?"

His face suddenly flushed, Krygowski said, "Um, I just, uh, meant that, you know, I've heard things are really bad there."

"Yeah," said Jonathan, puzzled now. "Yeah, I've heard that too. I mean, I wouldn't know, but that's what I've heard."

"Sure, sure," said Krygowski. "Listen, Jonathan, I gotta get going."

Jonathan watched Krygowski make a hasty exit, his huge body moving through the crowd and toward the door with amazing speed. *I wonder what that was all about?* he asked himself.

CHAPTER FIFTEEN

Jonathan adjusted the shade on the window in his study and looked across the desk at Sonny. "So," he concluded, "I'd say all in all, it was quite a productive little vacation."

Sonny shook his head. "Yeah. I was gettin' a little antsy till I got that cable from you in Pakistan last week."

"I'm making some arrangements to get some money to Neeley's sister on his behalf," Jonathan added.

"You think that's a good idea?"

"I can do it anonymously, through an attorney," Jonathan answered. "There's no exposure, and . . . well, I feel responsible for what happened."

"I do too, Bubba. Phil and I go way back. Way back. He was like a son to me." Sonny stared at Jonathan. "But I'm tellin' you, as good-hearted a gesture as that is, givin' survivor's benefits to his sister, I'm just not sure how wise that'd be."

"Are you afraid somebody's going to come asking you about Phil?"

Sonny shook his head. "Not necessarily. Just wantin' to be cautious."

"How about mutual acquaintances?" Jonathan asked.

Again Sonny shook his head. "May be hard for you to believe, but Phil and I didn't have that many mutual acquaintances. I liked it that way."

"Well, what about Gonzales? Aren't you likely to see him?"

"Gonzales?"

"Remember," Jonathan said with exasperation, "the guy you hired to go with me to Colombia back a few months ago?"

"Oh, him," said Sonny, slapping his forehead. "Naw, Bubba, I didn't know him."

"*What?*"

"Relax, relax. He came on Phil's recommendation," said Sonny, holding up his hands to signal that Jonathan should stay calm. "And Phil was a good judge of character. He thought *you* were all right, didn't he?"

"True, true," said Jonathan. "But still, if anybody comes asking you about Neeley, you better have a story."

"My 'story' is that I ain't seen him," Sonny answered. "What's so hard about that?"

"Fine," Jonathan answered. He thought for a minute. "Hey, another thing. Remember Len Krygowski? The FBI guy who tipped me off about Drakoff back in September?"

"Sure. What about him?"

"Well, I ran into him the other night when I got back in town, and he said something kind of strange." With that, Jonathan told the story of their recent encounter.

"Hmm," said Sonny. "Almost like he knew what you were doin' all along?"

Jonathan nodded his head. "You think he's on to me?"

"I don't see how FBI *could* be up on what you're doing," Sonny answered. "Not if you were overseas. CIA maybe—but not FBI. But still, it's worth checkin' into. I'll ask around, discreetly, with some folks I know who might be able to shed a little light on your friend Krygowski."

"Good," said Jonathan. "Okay, now, I want to talk to you about—"

"I know what you wanta talk about," Sonny grumbled.

"—Phase Two," Jonathan continued. "I used to always say in business, don't ever just rest on what you've done. You gotta face the next challenge."

"Yeah, I used to feel the same way as a Marine. Only difference was, I didn't go out looking for that next challenge. But I've been busy, for sure. About a month ago, I called my old friend Paul LaVallee, who runs the simulator facility out at Luke Air Base near Phoenix. Paul and I go way back to Vietnam, and we always kid each other about him bein' a Flyboy and me bein' a Jarhead. You know, all that." Sonny pointed a finger at Jonathan. "But he's also a Yankee, suspicious as the day is long, and even with me, it don't sit well why Willa's son, a civilian—"

"Did you tell him I was former Air Force? Vietnam?"

"Dadgum right. I played every card I had. Anyway, it took awhile to get him comfortable with why you needed to come out and play on his MiG simulator. But I told him you were writin' a book. Anyway, he finally went for it. You're scheduled to report to him Monday morning." He looked Jonathan in the eye. "But I'm tellin' you, Bubba, be on your best behavior with him. If he was to ever suspect what you're really up to . . . "

"Ever heard the expression, 'déjà vu all over again,' gentlemen?" asked McGinnis, waving his hand over an envelope on his desk and looking at the two men seated before him.

"Kind of redundant," Hollis said.

Wharton thought he knew what was coming. "What you got, Chief?"

"These," said McGinnis, popping open the envelope with a flourish and letting the pictures spill out across his desk.

Wharton and Hollis leaned forward to look at them, and Hollis was the first to speak. "Would ya look at that!" he said. "It's just like what you said—" He turned to Wharton, but Wharton was absorbed in what he saw.

He had seen it all before, of course, in grainy black-and-white pictures taken from a spy satellite. But this was a gorgeous set of color prints, apparently taken on the ground with a high-quality camera. There was no question he was looking at the same scene, only from a much more intimate view. He could see the downed choppers, the carnage on the valley floor, cheering mujahideen, Soviet soldiers being rounded up . . . and most of all, the live-action photographs of exploding aircraft.

His mouth fell open in shock and he looked up at McGinnis. "How . . . ?"

"They arrived courtesy of Federal Express this morning," McGinnis explained, "addressed to CIA, ATTN: Afghanistan." He grinned.

"With Fed Ex," said Wharton, thinking out loud. "You'd have a tracking number." Eagerly he said, "It wouldn't take us fifteen minutes to find—"

McGinnis held up a hand. "Save your energy, Rusty. We've already tracked it. The envelope came from a Fed Ex outlet in Phoenix, Arizona."

Hollis looked at McGinnis, then at Wharton. "So now," he began cautiously, "I guess we—"

"We do nothing, that's what we do," McGinnis answered abruptly, sweeping the photographs back together and straightening them in his hands like a dealer shuffling cards.

"But Chief," said Hollis. He looked at Wharton, who wore an amused smile. Wharton waved as though to say go ahead. "Look," Hollis went on. "If this envelope was sent from Phoenix, that means there's someone alive in the U.S., walking around out there on the streets, who knows exactly what went down with the Stingers. Don't we need to find that guy?"

McGinnis looked at him the way he would have looked at someone who had make a stupid remark without knowing they'd said anything wrong. "And then what would we do, Frazier? Would we go up to him and say, 'Excuse me, sir, can you confirm what we already know?' Is that how we should spend our time?" He shook his head. Dropping the pictures back into the envelope and sealing it, he went on. "Like I told Rusty already, the deed is done."

"But still," said Hollis. "If we've got something on this guy, we could—"

"We could what, Frazier? We don't have law-enforcement powers within the U.S. borders."

"We're not, strictly speaking, what you'd call a law *enforcement* agency," Wharton interjected. He seemed almost amused by what was going on.

"No," said Hollis, answering McGinnis, "but the FBI does."

McGinnis shook his head.

"You just don't want to share your info with the FBI, is that it, Chief?" asked Hollis defiantly.

"When you have as much field experience as I do," McGinnis said in a stern tone of voice, "you'll be in a position to question my decisions. But until then, you'll do what I say." He looked from Hollis to Wharton. "And I say we've got better things to do with our time than chasing after some vigilante when the damage has already been done."

With that, he dismissed them from his office, and Hollis and Wharton didn't speak about the matter again until late that afternoon. Both men's wives were out for the evening, and since they had the care of their children, they agreed to meet at a shopping mall outside Alexandria.

Hollis had a little one in a stroller, and he kept her while Wharton's kids, who were older, shepherded his other two off to the video arcade. After chatting about various things, Hollis was the first one to speak about what they had seen that day. "The important thing to me," he said, "is that whoever sent these photos is still out there—and has a direct link to George Watt."

"You heard what Mac said," Wharton answered with an amused smile. "We got better things to do."

"How come you're so blasé about this, Rusty?" asked Hollis.

"Because," said Wharton, "I've made up my mind I'm going to keep investigating this thing, no matter what."

"Even when McGinnis told you to stop?"

Wharton made a face. "He didn't tell us to stop—he just didn't encourage us to go on." He laughed. "If he told us to stop, that would be a little . . . *obvious,* don't you think?"

Hollis leaned forward to say something, but just then a woman came over to look at Hollis' baby. As soon as she was gone, he turned to Wharton. "What do you mean, obvious?" he asked.

Wharton tapped his forehead. "That's Mac," he said. "He only tells you what he wants you to know. He saves the best stuff for himself."

"So what do you think's going on?"

"I don't know," Wharton answered, "but I've got a hunch how we can find out."

Colonel LaVallee fit Sonny's description right down to his extremely conservative military "buzz" haircut. He stood about five feet ten inches, with graying temples that gave him a distinguished appearance. Jonathan could easily imagine him chewing up and spitting out a subordinate if he felt it was warranted. After Jonathan got to Luke Air Force Base, they went to the colonel's office and exchanged pleasantries for a full ninety seconds before LaVallee began to grill him on the book he was supposedly writing. But Jonathan must have given satisfactory answers, and he certainly gained LaVallee's approval when he told the colonel he had served a tour of duty in Vietnam.

The colonel offered to personally oversee Jonathan's week of simulator instruction. This may have been because he'd taken a liking to Jonathan after he found out he had spent thirteen months with the 355th Tactical Fighter Wing. Either that or he just wanted to keep an eye on him.

Whatever the reason, Jonathan found himself in a briefing room alone with LaVallee, seated at a long oak table surrounded by numerous maps, photos, and diagrams.

"This," began LaVallee, as he pulled down a diagram of a plane, "is a jet."

Jonathan groaned internally. It was clear that when it came to instruction, this guy was a "fundamentalist." He wanted to raise his hand and remind the colonel about what they'd discussed earlier—how he, Jonathan, had logged hundreds upon hundreds of hours flying F-105 "Thunderthuds" in and out of Takhli in Thailand, or how he had flown his corporate Lear jet for many years.

But it seemed wisest of all to just listen and take notes. In fact, much of what the colonel said was highly informative. Jonathan learned new information about Mikoyan and Gureyvich, the Soviet design team whose initials provided the nomenclature for generations of fighter planes under their design. There was the MiG-15 "Fagot," which saw service in the Korean War; the MiG-23 and MiG-27 "Floggers"; and the MiG-21 "Fishbed," the '57 Chevy of Soviet fighter planes. The Fishbed had the longest active life of any combat aircraft, from its official introduction in 1958 straight through 1985, and it had served the Soviet Union, its satellites, and various client states all over the world.

But Fishbed was a dogfighter, and the Soviets wanted something faster—an interceptor. So did Jonathan, and his ears perked up when LaVallee got to his main interest, the reason he had come here to Luke AFB: The MiG-25.

During a pivotal air show in 1967, the Soviets introduced the interceptor, which NATO dubbed "Foxbat." Initially, U.S. observers believed the Soviets' claims that the MiG-25 could attain a speed of Mach 3—until they discovered the so-called Mach 3 planes were actually drones, remotely piloted vehicles that only incorporated some elements of the MiG-25 design. But there was no question Foxbat was fast, very fast—Mach 2.8, almost 2,100 miles per hour. And in 1973, it set a record for flying at an altitude of almost 119,000 feet, more than twenty-two miles up.

From one of a series of wall racks, LaVallee pulled down a tri-view of the MiG-25, which showed it from the front, top, and side. "Now, Foxbat is a combination of steel, aluminum, and titanium," he said, "which is used in areas of high thermal stress. It runs on T-6 fuel, which has both low freezing and high flash points, and is powered by a couple of Tumanski R-31 turbojets—you see the wide rear fuselage? It's a simple engine, driven by a single turbine, and at low speeds it's not particularly efficient."

Lavallee studied the diagram for a moment before going on. "They basically intended Foxbat to do nothing but go up quickly, knock intruders out of the sky, and come back down just as quickly. It's no good for anything else except guzzling fuel. In essence, it's a rocket with wings. And these—" He pointed to a couple of mean-looking missiles visible on the overhead view. "—These are its payload. Acrid AA-6 missiles, which are made to inflict heavy damage on targets at a high altitude."

As LaVallee explained, every facet of the plane was designed with its "up—shoot—down" mission in mind. Hence the radar, for instance, only picked up signals from a very short range. But within that range, it was jam-proof, the most powerful radar ever installed in a bomber or interceptor.

"Given these facts about the MiG-25," said LaVallee, turning to Jonathan with just a ghost of a smile on his face, "it's understandable that the Soviets would have figured it to be the last plane on earth that one of their pilots would use to defect. Especially given the Soviet practice of providing just enough fuel for their mission and not a drop more, it was hard to imagine somebody escaping in this gas-guzzler. But Viktor Belenko gave them a surprise—and gave us a major gift—when he took off from his air base in Siberia in 1976, headed for Japan. We didn't get to keep the plane, but we took it apart and studied it before sending it back in pieces to the Russians."

"I'll bet they loved that," said Jonathan.

"I'm sure they did," said LaVallee. "But in the course of taking it apart, we learned some interesting stuff about the way they do things. Put simply, Soviet design is primitive technology brought to an incredible level of sophistication. They have an analog computer from *1959* in that Foxbat—but it works." LaVallee counted off points on his fingers. "You'll find, more often than not, they use vacuum tubes instead of microchips, steel instead of titanium, two inefficient engines instead of one powerful, efficient engine—but it all works. The guys taking the plane apart saw a bunch of rivets sticking out on all sides, and they had a big howl over that one. How could the Soviets be so stupid? Didn't they know that would produce wind drag? But when they went on and researched it, they discovered the rivets were positioned in such a way as to create no resistance while at the same time strengthening the plane—brilliant, huh?"

Jonathan nodded his head.

"One of our experts about a decade ago said it was the best interceptor in production at the time," LaVallee added. He pulled down on the three-point and let it roll away to the top. "The Soviets never exported it to the WarPac nations in Eastern Europe, and, after Belenko's defection, they made some changes on the original to keep for themselves and started sending the old ones to countries like Libya and Syria." He sighed. "So, to some extent, yours and my interest in the MiG-25 as a significant Cold War weapon is academic."

Jonathan smiled up at the colonel, but he was thinking this was anything but academic to him.

"Now," said the colonel, "what you're going to be working with are two things, a mockup and a simulator." He motioned for Jonathan to precede him out the door of the briefing room. "The mockup is nothing fancy—just a re-creation of the cockpit of a MiG-25 from data recorded by our technicians and the Japanese in 1976. From that one you'll get the placement of the instruments, the feel of the controls—even the feel of the seat—but what you won't get is how it flies. That's what the simulator is for."

They walked down the hall, LaVallee now leading the way, past rows of mysterious, unmarked doors. They came to a place where they could only turn right, and entered another long corridor. "So," Jonathan said, "I've heard about the Goodyear simulator for F-15s, or the Hughes F/A-18 simulator—how does yours compare here?"

"No comparison," said the colonel brusquely. "This thing is absolute state of the art. Nothing like it. Those others can perform the function of one aircraft only, whereas this one has computer programs for over sixty planes, both NATO and WarPac. You can even program in your surrounding landscape—360° view—and we've got movement built in, thanks to some hydraulic valves installed in the floor.

You actually *feel* the acceleration when you kick in the afterburner. And that's not to mention the illusion of movement created by the landscape view."

After several more turns, they emerged in front of another unmarked door, just like any of the others. LaVallee took out a set of keys and opened it. The inside was dark and cool and quiet, with no sound but the gentle hum of air conditioners. At the front sat an enlisted man at a desk, working by the light of a single lamp, and he stood to attention when the colonel entered. LaVallee snapped back a salute, signed Jonathan in, and took him into an adjoining room to look at the mockup.

The mockup chamber contained ten different black boxes, five on each side of a central corridor, and each box, slightly smaller than a Volkswagen Beetle, contained a mockup of a different aircraft cockpit. They walked to the third one on the left, and LaVallee opened the door for Jonathan to look in. "Thanks to Belenko," he said, "we have an extremely accurate model of a MiG-25 front office, all the way down to the pea-green interior."

Jonathan looked in. The color was a sickly shade, the sort of thing one would expect to see in a Communist country. "Looks like puke-green to me," he observed.

"You'd be surprised," LaVallee answered. "They came up with this color after extensive research into what was most soothing. Remember, the Soviets don't treat their military pilots the way they would some loser working in a vodka factory— they're like prize thoroughbreds, pampered."

As LaVallee watched, Jonathan got in the chamber and sat down. The padding on the seats did seem awfully comfortable—quite un-Soviet, as a matter of fact. And the cockpit was extremely impressive in its lack of clutter. The designers had assembled simple and well-ordered rows of buttons, dials, and gauges such that the pilot didn't have to go through a lot of mental strain in the heat of combat.

"Any idea what happens if you push this button?" asked LaVallee, pointing to a red one.

Jonathan read the word *Danger* in Russian on the button. "I don't know, what?"

LaVallee shrugged. "We don't know either. Supposedly it activates an ejector seat. But Belenko and other pilots were pretty sure that the Soviets wouldn't want a pilot ejecting and his plane possibly falling into enemy hands. They believed that pushing this button would actually cause the aircraft to explode."

As he sat there a little longer, Jonathan began to realize the seat wasn't as comfortable as he'd initially thought. It seemed as though there wasn't enough padding above the steel bracing to comfortably support the weight of the pilot. And as he touched the controls, he noticed they felt rather chintzy. They didn't give the kind of almost imperceptible resistance that really well-made instruments do.

He mentioned this to LaVallee, who shrugged. "It's still the Soviet Union we're talking about here. Thank God *they're* our chief military rivals, and not the Japanese. We'd be in a world of hurt then."

He leaned over Jonathan and pointed at the instrument panel. "All right, let me just go over this real quick, then I'll show you to the simulator and let you get started. Here you have your altitude indicator/flight director . . . your HSI . . . tape instruments for air speed." He pointed to each in turn. "There's your vertical velocity, altitude, throttle quadrant, primary com radio, autopilot controls, transponder . . . Ah, and here we go." He pointed to a button labeled with a Russian word and read it out loud. "*Voroozhyonniy.* That means 'armed.' This is for your Acrid missiles."

When LaVallee had finished, Jonathan got out of the cockpit. "Pretty impressive," he said.

"It is," LaVallee agreed. "And it's a lot to keep track of if you're doing research, I know. I'm sorry our rules prevent you from bringing in paper and writing instruments."

"Well, of course," said Jonathan. "Those *are* the rules."

"You sure this is the place?" Hollis asked. They stood on either side of the stairs, just barely under the shed of the twin duplex garages, so that the spring rain fell heavily on the tips of their shoes. No one coming down the stairs from the townhouse above could see them, but thanks to a handheld mirror—the kind used by dentists to look inside people's mouths—Wharton could see who was coming.

"What are you talking about?" Wharton asked. "We've seen him come here dozens of times—every week, right to this place."

"I *know*," Hollis answered. "But isn't this kind of a tender moment for him?"

"Shhh. Here he comes."

Hollis could hear the footsteps clattering on the wooden stairway and, with his tiny dentist's mirror, Wharton saw his target sauntering down the steps.

As soon as he had reached the ground and started walking toward his car, Wharton signaled Hollis, and the two began following the man. They were halfway to the car, and the rain was kicking up, when Wharton said loudly and distinctly, "Rashid Amal?"

Terrified, Rashid spun around.

"Ray Whitfield, FBI," Wharton announced, showing him a badge. He gestured toward Hollis. "This is my partner, Forrest Hall. Could we have a word with you, sir?"

Still looking frightened, Rashid put up his hands.

211

"No, no, no," said Wharton irritably. "That's not necessary. Let's go to your car." He gestured toward Rashid's Mercedes, and Rashid, still not speaking, fumbled for his keys. Meanwhile Wharton looked over his shoulder, back at the townhouse. "Come on, come on," he said.

"I know who you are," Rashid said as he unlocked the door. "But I don't know why you're coming to me—this way."

Puzzled, Wharton glanced at Hollis on the other side of the car. "No, Rashid," he said, "I don't think you do know who we are."

As soon as they had gotten inside the car, Hollis in front beside Rashid and Wharton in back, Rashid said, "I was just visiting my lady friend. Is there a crime in this?"

"Depends on what you and your wife have worked out," said Wharton. "But that's not our concern."

"Then what—?" Rashid looked at Wharton, and again it seemed he knew something he wasn't saying.

"Why do you *think* we're here, Rashid?" Wharton asked.

"I—" Rashid looked back at Wharton, and his eyes narrowed. "You are trying to take advantage of me, Mr.—?"

"Whitfield."

"Mr. Whitfield. I know how your system works. I don't have to guess why you're here—you have to tell me." Seeming indignant, he straightened up and looked from one man to the other. "I would like an explanation as to why I, a private citizen with a valid visa and business license, am being subjected to this harassment."

From his breast pocket Wharton withdrew a photo of Rashid with "Boltar" in front of the Old Country Deli the previous fall. "Tell me who this is in the photo," he said, "and we'll be on our way."

Rashid studied the picture. "This photograph is doctored. That is me, of course, but I have never seen this man in my life."

"Didn't you talk about Stinger missiles that day?" asked Wharton.

Rashid glanced suspiciously at him. Then, he seemed to have a look of recognition on his face. "I see what you're after," he said. "Mr. *F-B-I.*" From the way he said it, it was clear he could see through their ruse. "Are you acting on your own, or on orders from your superiors?"

"I think we're not communicating here," said Wharton, glancing at Hollis out of the corner of his eye. Rashid was trying to put him on the defensive, and he couldn't allow that to happen. "We need your help tracking down the man in that photograph."

"And?" asked Rashid.

"And then we'll leave you alone."

"I have a right to be left alone anyway," answered Rashid, but by the look in his eyes, it was clear. He was scared.

Wharton, seeing this, pushed ahead. Leaning forward so that his face was very close to Rashid's, he said, "You've lived in this country long enough to know—if we want to make your life difficult, it doesn't matter if we've got anything on you or not. We can revoke your visa and deport you. We can drag you through the court system till you lose so much money and waste so much time, you'll promise to do anything we want just so we'll leave you alone. My guess is that you do *not* want to anger us."

Rashid waved a hand. "All right, all right." He pulled a pack of cigarettes from his pocket and brandished a lighter. "I don't suppose it matters, since you people know so much more about this than I." He lit up in a big puff of smoke that made Hollis cough because the windows were still up. "Why should I care what you do with this . . . William Masters was his name, if I recall."

Wharton glanced at Hollis. Even though Wharton didn't put much store by the name—it was just another alias to add to Boltar and George Watt—he pulled out a pen and a scrap of paper and wrote it down. "I'm sure you know more than that," he said. Rashid, smoking in deep, nervous puffs, eyed him in silence. "You spent close to half an hour with him."

"Hmm," said Rashid, who looked up as though straining to remember something. "Yes, I recall he took out a pack of matches," he said. "From a place called Anthony's in—"

Wharton and Hollis sat forward.

"Or was it Antonio's?"

"What city was it in, Rashid?" Wharton demanded.

"Antoine's, that was it!" said Rashid triumphantly. "Yes, Antoine's—in New Orleans, Louisiana."

Wharton looked at Hollis. They had gone over Rashid's and Rodriguez's phone records for the pertinent months, no easy task because both lines had a high number of incoming and outgoing phone calls. Among the promising-looking leads had been a series of calls from a number of different pay phones in the New Orleans wharf area.

"Anything else?"

"Just one other thing," Rashid said. "I remember this man was driven by a deep and strong hatred of Russians." He looked at the two agents. "Now," he said, starting the engine, "I would be most grateful if you would allow me to go on about my business."

Jonathan spent five working days at Luke AFB. Every night back in his motel room, he worked on a scale diagram of the cockpit, erasing and adjusting after he went back each day and saw some detail he had remembered incorrectly the night before. By the end of his time there, he had located every instrument within the "front office," or cockpit, and he set about memorizing the location of every single gauge and control.

Hour after hour during that week, he practiced takeoffs and landings, feeling the kick of the afterburner and a thousand other details that helped to re-create the actual sensation of flight. It helped him get reacquainted—or really, just *acquainted,* since the technology had changed so much in the twenty years since he had flown in Vietnam—with flying a military plane.

For one thing, he was used to a situation in which he had to *fly the plane,* operating the throttle and doing the other things a pilot of a small aircraft has to do. But combat jets were a breed all their own. In order to move at Mach-plus speeds and maneuver inside tight circles, they had to be designed with shortened wingspans, sharpened wing sweeps, and a number of other adjustments that made it a full-time job just to keep the plane aloft, let alone guide it. Therefore they utilized "fly-by-wire technology." A computer, rather than the pilot himself, did most of the work of flying.

But the designers—even the Soviet ones—understood that human pilots needed the tactile sensation of flying the old-fashioned way. So, they had installed a stick on the floor, which operated electronically rather than hydraulically, moving a bit at the touch of a hand in order to give men the illusion of controlling the plane directly. Jonathan liked that, and sometimes when he was "flying" in the simulator, he would touch the stick and think to himself, *Ah—the illusion of control over one's destiny.*

He was even able to "go up" in a dual simulator against an Air Force hot shot—who beat him in twenty out of twenty simulated dogfights. But that was only partly due to Jonathan's rustiness compared to the skill of the twenty-five-year old fighter jock. It also had to do with the fact that the MiG-25 had never been designed to engage in dogfights. In fact, the fighter pilot, who used a McDonnell-Douglas F-15 Eagle, kept insisting Jonathan change simulations.

"Why you want that Foxbat?" asked the pilot after his eighth victory. He had an annoying way of smacking his gum, which Jonathan figured was an unconscious habit intended to intimidate others in a very subtle way. "I mean, why take on a handicap like that?"

"I like the challenge."

"Suit yourself," the fighter jock said as he got back in his simulator.

In the next fight, they had climbed to ten thousand feet and flown at each other just like they were playing chicken with two cars. Somebody had to move, and the other pilot did. At the time, Jonathan thought it was a stupid gambit. When he took off at a forty-five-degree angle to Jonathan's starboard, gaining altitude as he went, the man left his underside exposed, offering the MiG a clear shot at him.

It would have been a clear shot, that is, if Jonathan could have turned his Foxbat around and locked on his missiles in time. But by the time he did, he saw only empty sky up ahead—no F-15.

The 360° display on the simulator allowed him to "check his six"—to see what was behind him—and there he saw the Eagle, gaining on him. At any second, a red button on his control panel would flash and a buzzer would go off, indicating that he had been locked on.

He had to move quickly. By no stretch of the imagination could he outmaneuver the Eagle, especially with it closing on his tail. At their current altitude, he was losing fuel at an alarming rate, as the digital gauge indicated, and he needed to climb so he could conserve gas while he figured out what to do. For a split-second, though, he considered going into a dive just because it would be such an unorthodox move for a Foxbat, and might throw the other pilot off for a few precious seconds. But he chose to go up instead.

In a few seconds, he had attained maximum rate of climb—41,000 feet per minute—but the other pilot was gaining on him. And then at 65,000 feet, they passed through the Eagle's service ceiling, the point beyond which the plane could no longer rise except very slowly and with a high cost of fuel. Suddenly Jonathan and his high-flying MiG had the stratosphere all to themselves. *That* was why he had chosen the Foxbat.

After slowing down and circling around for a minute or so at 80,000 feet, he decided to come back down and find the Eagle. Sure enough, he saw the other pilot about twelve miles off. Laughing to himself, he prepared to arm his Acrids as he approached his opponent's location, but before he'd even completed lock-on, the Eagle had circled around, locked on *him,* and fired. A message flashed on his screen. *Sorry, Ivan—Superior Maneuverability Wins Again.*

Jonathan's performance in that engagement, even though he lost, won the other pilot's respect and, after that, he didn't ask again why Jonathan insisted on flying the MiG-25.

But fight after fight only proved what everybody knew. The Foxbat was no fighter aircraft. With full tanks, it could withstand no more than 2.2-g, whereas the

Eagle could handle more than four times that much, turning easily within the range of the fixed-geometry MiG wings. Even the MiG-25's much-touted speed had to be taken with a grain of salt. When Jonathan tried once to pass through Mach 2.5, it set off a message flashing across his screen, "Caution, MiG pilot! your plane will ignite if you increase velocity!"

To top it off, American missiles had so much greater range than their Soviet counterparts that an American could blow an East Bloc opponent out of the sky without even coming close enough to see him. Hopefully he wouldn't have to worry about American planes, though—just MiGs. And there was no MiG as fast as the Foxbat.

"Hey, Rusty," McGinnis called as Wharton walked by his office door. "Can you come in here for a minute?"

"Sure, Mac," Wharton said.

"Shut the door."

Wharton knew he was in trouble, but he tried to seem nonchalant. "So what's up?" he asked.

"You tell me," McGinnis replied. "I just got a call from an FBI agent in New Orleans named Len Krygowski."

"Uh-huh?" Wharton asked, keeping his face a blank.

"Uh-huh," McGinnis answered, looking Wharton in the eye. "Seems you sent his office a photo, and asked him if he could identify it."

"Oh, that," Wharton said. "You mean the photo of the guy with Rashid in front of the deli?"

McGinnis nodded.

"Yeah, well, I was just thinking that, you know, we had picked up a pattern of calls to both Rashid and Rodriguez from New Orleans." Wharton looked at the floor. "Really, I shoulda checked with them down there months ago."

"That's fine," McGinnis said, leaning back in his chair. "But why is it I get the feeling you're going around behind my back?"

"I wasn't going around behind your back," Wharton protested. "I was just—"

"That's fine, that's fine," McGinnis said, holding up a hand. "Save it. But just don't go to another agency for help like that without consulting me."

"Okay," said Wharton, feeling chastised. "Is that all you wanted to tell me?"

"Not quite," said McGinnis, switching his tone. "See, Krygowski told me something else. He thinks the guy in the picture is a fella from down there named Jonathan Stuart."

"Oh yeah?" asked Wharton, leaning forward in his seat.

McGinnis nodded. "Krygowski says that although he looks different in the photo, which is likely a disguise, there was something that made him suspect he knew him. Turns out that when KAL 007 got shot down in '83, this guy's wife and child . . ."

And so McGinnis told Wharton everything he'd heard from Krygowski about Jonathan Stuart. Wharton listened, fascinated. McGinnis concluded by saying, "Krygowski's setting up a stake-out on Stuart's house even as we speak." He smiled like a father giving his child a gift at Christmas. "How soon can you leave for New Orleans?"

On Friday afternoon, Jonathan once again sat in LaVallee's office. "As I told you before," LaVallee observed, "The Foxbat MiG-25 is a fine piece of machinery in its own way—when used properly as an interceptor and not a fighter. But their technology is no match for ours." He smiled faintly. "I hear you did some impressive flying against one of our guys—particularly impressive considering he does this all the time and you don't."

"Well, I appreciate it, colonel," said Jonathan with a modest bowed head. "Just wanting to learn as much as I can so I can write more effectively."

"You know, Mr. Stuart," said the colonel, this time with a conspiratorial grin, "When you're writing your book, I would appreciate it if you would downplay the inferiority of the MiG. Otherwise, it might create the impression that the Soviets aren't really as powerful as they are, which could negatively impact our funding situation. I'm sure you wouldn't want to do that."

"Absolutely not," said Jonathan.

"I didn't think so." The colonel smiled. "And anyway, as you've now seen for yourself, the MiG-25 is a mighty fine, if simple, piece of equipment."

Thank God it is, thought Jonathan, remembering his painstaking re-creation of the cockpit on paper. "Much less can go wrong that way," he said out loud.

"Exactly my point," said the colonel, pleased that Jonathan was such a good student.

Jonathan stood up. "Well, I'm due back in New Orleans," he said, extending a hand. "Thanks for all your help."

"Don't mention it," answered the colonel, standing and shaking Jonathan's hand. "Glad you got to experience the trainer—there's a lot of folks, both civilian and military, who would kill for the chance. After all, it's the closest any of us will ever get to flying a real Foxbat."

"Yeah, I suppose you're right," said Jonathan; but he was thinking, *That's where you're wrong.*

There had been no traffic to or from Jonathan Stuart's house for the first few days of surveillance, and Wharton had wondered if they were looking in the wrong place. But late on Friday night, he got word from Krygowski that the agents in the field had spotted what appeared to be a white male, speeding down St. Charles in a black Porsche and whipping into the garage, closing the door before anybody could get a good look at him. They had contemplated going in that night but decided it would be wiser to move in mid-morning on Saturday.

So, at a few minutes after 10:00 A.M. Saturday, an FBI agent stood at the front door of the Stuart home with a clipboard in his hand, listening on his ear piece for the signal that it was time to go in. When he got the order, he raised his hand to ring the doorbell.

From a catering delivery truck parked across the street, Wharton crouched beside Krygowski and watched the man at the door through a set of binoculars. The delivery truck had a compartment over the cab, and they had stationed a sniper in the compartment to cover the front man. There was a jogger coming from the other direction—another agent, this one with a 9-mm pistol in his fanny pack. By the time the door opened, the jogger should be just abreast of the house. And out back, beyond the swimming pool, there were more men, all of them waiting for the moment when the suspect inside opened the door.

The forward man pushed the doorbell.

He waited fifteen seconds, and when he didn't hear any noise from inside, he rang the bell again. Then, the door suddenly opened, and a stocky, athletic-looking man in a bathrobe appeared.

The man waited impatiently as the undercover agent hesitated. "Uh, sir," he said, glancing at the clipboard, "My name is Randy Westheimer, and I'm in your neighborhood soliciting donations for the Children's—"

Suddenly a man's voice shouted *"Freeze!"* and a black-clad agent sprang into action out of nowhere, with his semiautomatic rifle trained on the front door.

CHAPTER SIXTEEN

Exactly one week after leaving Luke Air Force Base, Jonathan stood on the curb in front of the international airport in Tripoli, waiting for his ride.

Based on a strangely worded telegram he'd gotten from Sonny at Luke just before he left, he had decided to head overseas straight from Nevada. *Look out, Bubba,* it had said. *Bears at the back door. Do not pass go, do not collect $200. See you in T'ville.* Since he wasn't due in Tripoli—T'ville—until tonight, he had spent the past week relaxing in London. Or at least, trying to relax. All week long, he had been worried over what might be going on at home. He hoped Sonny wasn't in trouble.

He had first travelled to Libya several months before, on his way to meet Neeley in Paris before the two of them headed for Afghanistan. Some time before that, he had located—through intermediaries—a certain Libyan named Abdel Aziz who, through important family contacts, had the capability to market various products to his country's air force. Posing again as George Watt, marketing rep for an Australian supplier of jet climate-control units, Jonathan had contacted Aziz, and then, in March, had visited him in Tripoli.

At that time, he'd had a good series of meetings with the Libyans. Aziz turned out to be an ideal contact, always free with the kickbacks and payoffs—*baksheesh,* as they called it here—which made him extremely influential within the bureaucracy of the Libyan People's State. He also seemed, as Jonathan got to know him, to have little loyalty to anyone other than himself and his family, which was fine with Jonathan.

On the last morning of Jonathan's earlier visit, Aziz had arranged a meeting with his cousin, who was a general at Oqbah ibn Nafi Air Base outside Tripoli. Along with the cousin, whose name was General Saddiq, there had also been a Soviet advisor at the meeting. It had been a tense few moments for Jonathan, especially when he walked in and saw the Soviet uniform. The two officers had seemed a little skeptical about George Watt and his product. But George, who spoke with a subdued Australian accent and had a warm, reassuring manner, soon overcame their doubts.

The officers asked a number of questions about his other clients. They clearly wondered whether the Americans used these units on their air bases.

With a nonchalant air, Watt said a friend of his had sold forty of them to the U.S. By the end of the meeting, General Saddiq had invited Watt to return in three months and install a trial unit at Oqbah ibn Nafi.

Now, Jonathan stood on the curb in front of Tripoli International at dusk. A warm breeze blew in from the direction of the Mediterranean to the north. Cars pulled in and out in front of the terminal, mostly small Italian models, but he didn't see Aziz's Fiat among them. He looked at his watch, wondering if there had been a miscommunication. Just as he thought it might be a good idea to catch a cab, Aziz whipped in, nearly running up over the curb in front of where Jonathan stood. The Libyan threw open his door and jumped out, the sounds of Western pop music blaring from the interior.

"George!" Aziz shouted, embracing him and kissing him on both cheeks. From his manner, one would never have guessed that they hardly knew each other. "You are looking well! Did you have any problem with customs?"

"Thanks to you, no," Jonathan answered. At the conclusion of his previous trip, Aziz had given him a typewritten letter in Arabic, which identified him as a friend of General Saddiq at the air base. Aziz had also suggested—just to hedge his bets with the bureaucracy—that he "accidentally" leave a package containing a quart of Johnny Walker Black Label Scotch at the immigration desk.

"The system is the same everywhere," Aziz said, grabbing Jonathan's carry-on bag and setting it in the trunk of his car. "One just has to know how to operate it."

"I have a feeling I could learn a lot from you, Aziz," said Jonathan with a grin.

"More than you can imagine, my friend. I have some good news to share with you."

He had gestured for Jonathan to get in, but Jonathan stopped and looked at Aziz. "What good news? Has the consignment cleared customs?"

"Oh, that? Of course." Aziz made a face that said getting the equipment through customs was child's play—which it had been, since George Watt's money had greased the wheels of the bureaucracy in a big way. "Yesterday morning we picked it up, and you have an appointment at Oqbah ibn Nafi tomorrow at 9:00 A.M. to begin the installation."

"Terrific."

"That is not the only good news," Aziz continued with an impish grin. "But to learn more, you must join me tonight for dinner."

Jonathan had grown more or less used to Aziz's driving the first time he had visited Libya, but this time it seemed his Libyan associate had become even more reckless. Aziz flew up the highway into Tripoli at speeds in excess of a 130 kph, or

80 miles an hour, which felt much faster due to the road conditions—not to mention the small size of the vehicle and the loud music on the stereo. Jonathan just sat back and watched the brown landscape careen past the window.

Later, after checking into the hotel and cleaning up a bit, he joined Aziz for dinner at the latter's favorite restaurant, the Swan. They ordered and began eating their soup, at which time Aziz told him the big news. "George," he said with an edge of excitement in his voice, "I have talked to some of my contacts in the armed forces—" He waved his hand as though to indicate it wasn't important to name names. "—And I have arranged to sell new climatized storage units to every military air base in the country, assuming your test units work as specified."

"That's fabulous," said Jonathan, taking a spoonful of soup.

"You do not realize how fabulous it is!" Aziz said, gesturing with his right hand. "These commitments come to 250 units, each selling for £3,500. With a cost of £1,600, that leaves a wide profit margin." Again he waved his hand in a dismissive gesture. "Of course we must split some of the proceeds with my military contacts, but even so, you will make about $400,000 U.S."

"Wonderful, wonderful," said Jonathan. *Too bad I won't be here to collect it,* he thought. He raised his teacup. "Aziz, I toast your marketing brilliance."

"Thank you, thank you," said Aziz. He glanced at the cup, then looked around. "Later we will go to my house, and you can make that toast again with Napoleon brandy."

Just then dinner arrived, a main course of *bezzin,* or maize with lamb in tomato sauce.

"Yes indeed," said Jonathan, reaching for a red sauce in a glass canister on the table. "Just like Bogart says in *Casablanca,* this could be the start of a beautiful friendship." He spooned just a bit of the sauce onto his plate.

"You will not like that, I think," said Aziz, watching him take the sauce, a puree of ground red peppers called *harisa.* "And I do not feel like interrupting my meal to drive you to the hospital. Yes, I think we can make lots of money together. And"— he leaned closer—"I would like you to take some of that money, money I will give you, and place it in a Swiss bank account for me." Raising his voice now, he added nonchalantly, "It is not that I do not trust the banking system of my own country, it is just . . ." He shrugged and laughed.

"Sure," said Jonathan. "I can take care of that for you. And I'm glad you trust me."

Aziz laughed dryly, but it was apparent that underneath his jovial demeanor lay a steely resolve. "Of course," he said. "It's simple. If I ever thought you were trying to take advantage of me or my respected associates, I would cut your throat."

Jonathan's product, the climatized storage unit or CSU, was a whole system—two giant polyethylene bags the size of an airplane, relative humidity meter, humidity sensing equipment, and a dehumidifier/air filter. With its modular construction, if one part had to be replaced, then a crew could simply do so without having to replace the whole system. It could run on 220 volts, and each CSU could control the environment of two aircraft. The plane would be stored fully fueled and loaded, and when it was time to take off, the bag could simply be ripped away in a matter of seconds.

The units removed six pounds of moisture an hour. Here in the desert, of course, moisture wasn't a problem. But Aziz, who stood to make 15 percent of any business Jonathan did, didn't seem to think that ought to prevent them from doing business with the Libyan military. Besides, they were also effective for keeping the plane free of dust and sand, which could destroy a jet engine.

The next morning, Jonathan went to install a trial unit at Oqbah ibn Nafi. He and Aziz arrived at the air base promptly at 10:00 A.M. Already it was so hot out on the runway, Jonathan was sure he could have seen steam rising off the tarmac if there had been any moisture in the air.

A Libyan Air Force captain rode in with them, and they met five men in coveralls guarding the crates, which stood alongside two MiG-21s ready to be outfitted. With Aziz acting as interpreter, Jonathan had them dismantle the crates, place the bags over the two Fishbeds, and hook up the CSU to an electrical outlet. The process took well over ninety minutes in the sweltering heat.

He was glad he had practiced all this beforehand. As he stood out there on the runway, no air stirring except the hot blasts generated by the planes taking off and landing nearby, Jonathan felt convincing in his role. He could almost have fooled himself.

Once they had gotten everything set up, he shouted to Aziz over the roar of an ascending plane, "I'm going to need to come back every day for the next week to make sure the equipment is calibrated properly."

"Okay," said Aziz with a smile. "You do what you need to do."

"And another thing," Jonathan shouted, wiping a fresh sheet of sweat from his brow. "For the first three days, I need to report to the base at different times during the day so I can make sure there are no differentials occurring at various times. Can you get me clearance for that?"

Aziz held up a hand and turned around to speak with the air force captain. Then he looked back at Jonathan and said, "It is done."

Jonathan watched the Libyan captain, who stared at him suspiciously.

"He said to tell you, if you will call ahead, he will meet you at the gate and escort you throughout your visit to the base," said Aziz. "If he is not here for some reason, he will assign an enlisted man to you."

The captain barked something else at Aziz, who actually looked a little embarrassed when he turned around and said, "But George, he wants to make sure you know that when you are on base, you stay where you are supposed to be and enter no unauthorized areas." Aziz shrugged, looking a little embarrassed.

"Of course, of course," said Jonathan. He smiled at the Libyan airman, but the man didn't return the favor.

Wharton looked up to see the robust figure of his boss in the doorway. "I'd like to speak with you for a minute," McGinnis said coldly.

"Sure, fine." Wharton stood up, but McGinnis, closing the door behind him, motioned for him to sit back down. "Have a seat," Wharton said, motioning to one of the chairs in front of his desk, but McGinnis shook his head.

"First you go to the FBI behind my back," McGinnis began in a hoarse whisper, "and I said that was okay—just don't do it again. So what's this I hear now about you tracking down Rashid Amal and questioning him?"

"Rashid Amal?" asked Wharton. "You know he's under regular surveillance. I don't know what you're so upset about."

"Don't play dumb with me, Rusty," McGinnis advised, now taking a seat. "I know that's how you got your lead in Louisiana."

"Fine," said Wharton, sounding a little angry himself. "You caught me—okay, fine."

"Why didn't you go through me?" McGinnis demanded. "Rashid is a pretty slippery character. It's important to make contact with him only under dire circumstances. You could have blown someone's cover—you never know who could be watching him, and now you've raised his suspicions." His anger subsiding slightly, he added, "You should have just come to me. I would have gotten the information you needed."

"Would you, Mac?" Wharton asked sarcastically. "You've been such a help on this whole case." He threw up his hands. "Case? What am I talking about? We don't have a case. Not after what went down in New Orleans the other day."

"Are you blaming me for that?" McGinnis demanded.

"All I'm saying," Wharton answered, "is that I've been kept in the dark this whole time, and nobody will tell me squat. I don't expect somebody like Sonny Odom to tell me anything . . . " He let his voice trail off, and he turned to look out the window as he spoke. "*That* character," he said with a chuckle. "*He's* got a past for sure, and I'll bet you anything he's mixed up in this."

"But we've checked him out," McGinnis cautioned. "To be honest with you, Odom knows stuff *I* don't know. I don't think he's anybody to mess with."

"There you go again," Wharton said, pointing at McGinnis.

"Who do you think you are, Ronald Reagan?" McGinnis snorted.

"You just keep deflecting the pursuit of this investigation," said Wharton. He looked away when he said it, because it was a pretty serious thing to say to his superior.

"Regardless of what you may think I'm doing," McGinnis said, "you've gotten way out of line, Rusty—going to the FBI. And before that, Rashid."

"You know what I think?" said Wharton, gaining in confidence. "This whole investigation of him and of Stuart—" He made a sweeping gesture with his hands. "—Is all just a put-on. There's no investigation. We're not trying to stop anybody. Just the opposite, in fact. I'll bet the Agency was working to make sure the missiles got to Afghanistan, and you were using me to cover it up."

McGinnis laughed. "That's the biggest bunch of malarkey I've ever heard."

"Which means," said Wharton, standing his ground, "that it's probably true."

McGinnis waited for several long seconds before speaking, then finally he said, "All right, all right. I gotta hand it to you, Rusty. You're a better investigator than I thought."

"You picked me for this case 'cause you thought I wouldn't figure it out, is that it?" Wharton asked.

"Aaah, not necessarily," said McGinnis, but his sheepish expression belied his words. He leaned forward. "Here's the deal," he rushed on, his voice dropping to a whisper. "I'm only going to tell you this once, so you better get it now. If you ever ask me again, I'm going to deny we had this conversation."

"What conversation?" asked Wharton, leaning in closer to hear.

"Good. Okay. The fact is, Congress wouldn't authorize the delivery of those Stingers, but we knew it was important to put them into the hands of the mujahideen in order to even out the balance of power in the region. We figured if we get three or four Stingers into Afghanistan in such a way that we could fully deny our involvement, and then have the mujahideen use 'em against the Soviets, we would be able to show how effective they could be. And maybe that way, we'd get Congress off dead center." He smiled. "As a matter of fact, copies of those pictures have gone to Capitol Hill. Rumor is, several members of the Armed Services Committee are taking a pretty serious look at them."

"So what about Stuart?" Wharton asked. "Is he working for us?"

"Stuart's working for himself," McGinnis answered. "He's a crafty devil, that's for sure. We had the missiles earmarked for one group of mujahideen, but Stuart decided they should go to Massoud's people instead." He paused. "In spite of the fact that Hekmatyar's guy tried to kill him to get the Stingers."

Wharton raised an eyebrow. "Were we—you, should I say—behind that too?"

"We just let the Afghans sort things out," McGinnis said with a shrug. "For one reason or another, the State Department has decided to put its money on Hekmatyar, so that's who they wanted the Stingers to go to."

"Well," Wharton chuckled, "don't you think Stuart ought to have some say in that? After all, it was his money spent down in South America—more than two million, if what Gonzales says is true."

"Hey! Stuart wouldn't have even thought about the Stingers—or Afghanistan, or any of it—if it hadn't been for us," said McGinnis. "We were the ones who planted the idea." He smiled. "Took advantage of an incident involving Stuart and a Soviet diplomat to interview him for the job, so to speak." He snapped his fingers. "Then planted a story about Rashid in the press, and let Stuart figure it out from there."

"I wonder what Stuart would think if he knew he was being used by the CIA the whole time?" wondered Wharton.

"I don't know. But I meant what I said. You better forget we had this conversation, Rusty. Just forget the whole thing."

Unlike Colonel LaVallee at Luke AFB, the Libyan Air Force captain did not become any friendlier toward Jonathan. But Jonathan did manage to get a lot accomplished over the next week in spite of the hostile environment—much more than Aziz would ever have guessed.

On Wednesday afternoon, six days after his arrival, Jonathan had returned early from the air base. He was sitting in his hotel room reading when his phone rang.

"George Watt."

"Mr. Watt?" asked a nasal-sounding Englishman's voice. "Dave Duffy here. Would you mind coming down and joining me for tea in the lobby?"

Jonathan smiled. "Not at all, Mr. Duffy." He set down his book and grabbed a shirt. "I'll be there in two minutes."

As he stepped into the lobby, he saw Sonny standing there in a khaki shirt with sweat stains under the armpits. He nodded toward him as he walked past.

When they had gotten out the front door, Jonathan turned and said, "Shall we have a stroll, Mr. Duffy?" "Mr. Duffy," who had still not spoken except on the telephone—with a pretty bad imitation of an English accent, as Jonathan had known it would be—simply nodded.

When they had gotten down the street, Jonathan dropped the Australian voice and whispered, "What bears are at the back door?"

"Federal bears," Sonny replied. "The kind with SWAT teams and high-powered rifles."

"What?"

Sonny told him what had happened and about how he had managed to play things off with Wharton and Krygowski.

"So while they had me," he continued, "they asked me a few questions. I could have said I didn't have to tell them anything, but under the circumstances it seemed better to appear like someone with nothing to hide. I told them you were headed for Europe." He laughed. "Which was actually true, thanks to that warning I sent you after I realized they were stakin' out the place. Anyway, I said you were over there and wouldn't be back for another month. I was just watchin' the house for another few days, I said, before I headed out myself to the Virgin Islands."

"I knew they had to be watching," Jonathan said. "I figured they'd get wise to what was going on sooner or later." He squinted off into the distance. "I just want to finish the mission, and I don't want you to get caught up in this any more than you are already."

"I think," Sonny answered, "they're kind of on the defensive now, because they were so sure they had you in New Orleans, and I ended up making them look like fools. So we're okay for now, but . . ." He shook his head. "You were right about Krygowski being bad news."

"Oh yeah?" asked Jonathan. "Do tell."

"Didn't learn much, but what I did pick up was interesting. According to information I gathered from the folks I know, Krygowski's FBI, all right. But he's rogue FBI."

"Rogue?"

"Meaning he's employed by the FBI, gettin' his paychecks from them, but he's really working for the CIA."

"What?" asked Jonathan. He stopped in the middle of the road and looked at Sonny. A man leading a donkey passed them by on one side while a Volkswagen, horn honking, pulled around them on the other. "That means—" A thousand thoughts raced through his head.

"That means," Sonny said, "back when he told you the CIA agents said such-and-such about that Russian you whupped up on, he was really talkin' about himself—he was the CIA agent. At least that's what I think."

"Wow," said Jonathan. "I can't even think about what that means right now."

"Well, combined with the fact that they were trying to raid your house," Sonny said, "I'd say it means you might want to plan on laying low for awhile."

"Yeah, I guess you're right," Jonathan answered. He knew he wouldn't be able to return home for a long, long time—if ever—but he couldn't think about that now, either. "In the meantime," he went on, trying to sound cheerful and get his mind back on track, "we've got plenty to occupy our attention. How long have you been here?"

"Four days, just like we planned."

"Excellent. You been staying busy?"

Sonny grinned. "You know it, Bubba. Dave Duffy may be here on business for BP, but he's one busy fellow, that's for sure—and nosy too."

"I'm surprised you fooled anybody with that south Alabama version of an English accent," Jonathan observed.

"Yeah, coulda been a problem at the airport," Odom agreed, "but it seems I had this extreme case of laryngitis, and needed to talk real low. Between that and your trick about leavin' them a fifth of Johnny Walker, weren't nothin' to it."

As they walked along, they wound up at a large empty building across from the Nasser Mosque. Actually, it wasn't a building at all, just an open series of massive Gothic archways that would have made for some great photographs if they had come for that purpose. But it was also a good place where they could stand and talk—looking like tourists—and still observe anybody who might be in the vicinity.

"Okay," Jonathan announced. "I arranged it so I could go to the base at odd hours, and I'm pretty clear on what their routines are now. Their missions depart like clockwork, and thanks to a lot of 'fine-tuning' trips I've made out there, I've gotten a fairly detailed understanding of how the base is laid out, how it operates, et cetera. I also figured out where the security strong points are, plus the location of the active MiG-25s and the times of their departure. Looks like reconnaissance flights take off exactly every three hours, beginning at midnight."

"Good deal," said Sonny. With a thoughtful expression on his face, he looked down the street. The light of the sun bounced off the white stucco buildings and made him squint behind his sunglasses. "You figured out where their operations room is?"

"No," said Jonathan with biting sarcasm. "I was more concerned with the PX. *Of course* I scoped out their operations room." He knelt down and drew with his finger on a patch of sand at their feet, laying out a map. "Okay, Flight Ops is here, and several times I saw pilots going in this door wearing their regulation uniforms and coming out later from this door." He indicated the other end of the building. "And they were wearing their flight suits, with their helmets and oxygen masks hanging to the side."

Still looking out across the empty square that separated them from the mosque, Sonny said, "And that's where we need to get you into."

"Exactly."

"It won't be hard gettin' you in," said Sonny. "The key is to get you out." He kicked the dust at his feet, obliterating the map. "All right, here's what I've done so far. Months ago, when you told me about this plan, I arranged a supply line through a fella I used to know in the Moroccan army. When I showed him some green, he remembered me real well, and he helped me arrange to ship some things in via the Tuareg Pony Express."

"Tuaregs?" asked Jonathan, amazed at what Sonny could achieve when left to his own devices. "The nomad guys?"

"You got it. They deal in contraband all over the Sahara. As long as you pay 'em well, they don't ask any questions that don't need asking."

"You sure you trust them?"

Sonny shrugged. "Why not?" He looked at Jonathan. "It wasn't really a matter of trust; it was a matter of money. I paid 'em half up front, the other half on delivery. That way, I knew I could trust them—especially because I made sure we did the transfer in a place that was public, without being *too* public. Which was hard, you know, because—"

"Sonny, I'll hear about it later," said Jonathan, holding up a hand. "Time is limited. So you got the uniforms?"

"Affirmative."

"Passes too?"

"Yep," said Sonny with a grin. "Thanks to a Tuareg pickpocket I hired. I've already arranged to insert your picture and mine."

Jonathan shook his head, amazed. "And all the other goodies?"

"You bet."

"Sonny, you're truly a giant among men." He looked at his watch. "So, let's say 2230 hours tomorrow, in time for a midnight takeoff?"

"Sure. Now let's talk about our backup plan. I had those desert cowboys bring in a couple of small-caliber revolvers with silencers, and—"

Jonathan shook his head. "Uh-uh. Nobody gets hurt—if we can help it, anyway."

"That's real nice, Jonathan," said Sonny. "Real nice and real stupid. What you got here is a war. This ain't no game. If you aren't prepared to deal decisively with anyone who threatens you, you will rue the day. And that's a promise, son."

"Maybe," said Jonathan, watching a group of women veiled in the traditional Libyan *barracan* walking by at the other end of the square. "But that's a risk I'm willing to take."

"Yeah, well, then you ought to be the only one taking the risk," Sonny shot back, clearly angry.

"Now, Sonny," said Jonathan in a gentle voice, "I know, first of all, that you're not one to put innocent people in danger—"

"Bubba, nobody's innocent in a—"

"And furthermore, you are the most resourceful person on the planet and could probably find us some kind of . . . I don't know, a gas-operated dart gun with some kind of sedative?"

Sonny turned toward Jonathan with a look of annoyance. But there was a twinkle in his eye, and he broke into a smile, then laughed aloud. In spite of himself, his laughter echoed off the stone walls of the ancient building.

"Would you mind letting me in on what's so funny?" asked Jonathan, now a little irritated himself.

"I'm sorry," said Sonny, still chuckling. "A *dart gun?*" He laughed again.

"Thanks for the vote of confidence," Jonathan said, his attitude souring.

"You won't see those dart guns nowhere but the movies," Sonny went on, taking out his handkerchief and wiping his eyes, then blowing his nose. "They take up to a minute to work, and by the time they do, you're dead. Nah, what you'd need is a direct injection of something like sodium pentothal or amobarbital or maybe even scopolamine."

"Sounds good," said Jonathan. "And I know you can find it for us."

"By tomorrow night?"

Jonathan studied Sonny's expression. "I'll bet you could."

Sonny shrugged. "Well all right, Bubba, you got me. Seems I came prepared, knowin' you'd pull some kind of stunt like this on me. Yeah, packed in with all the other goodies is an epée pen with a thousand milligrams of ketamine. It's made to produce twenty to forty minutes of amnesia, with a fairly long period afterward before the victim gets back his full fighting strength. Since you allow five milligrams for every pound of human weight, I figured a thousand for a grown man."

"Excellent," said Jonathan with a smile. "Now, since we got that straightened out—" He stopped. "What's wrong?"

Sonny looked serious again. "My advice to you, Bubba, even though you didn't ask me for it, is that if you're gonna be in this game, you better be in it all the way—no last-minute change of heart. Like I said, you're in a war, and it's either them or you. And I'd hope you'd be looking out for my hide too."

"Believe me, that won't be a problem. I'm seeing this thing to the finish line—no matter what," Jonathan replied gravely. "And I've grown kinda used to having you around over the last several months, so I'll definitely do my best to keep track of your hide."

The next day was Jonathan's last at the base. He completed his routine there, said goodbye to Aziz's cousin General Saddiq, and promised he would return in three months to install more CSUs. Late that afternoon, he made his way to the Red Castle, the place where, during the Tripolitan War, the Tripolitanians held prisoner the crew of the U.S.S. *Philadelphia*. Shortly after five o'clock, Sonny pulled up in a rented Peugeot and picked him up.

"Now, of course we ain't going on base with this car," said Sonny as he waited for a man leading a camel to cross at a stoplight in front of him.

"I wouldn't think so. What did you cook up for us?" asked Jonathan.

"Oh, it ain't no big deal," Sonny replied, making a turn. "It appears there's a Russian officer whose car has malfunctioned and had to be towed in for repairs. The vehicle's settin' in the repair yard even as we speak, waitin' for us to come pick it up."

"How'd you swing that?" Jonathan asked as Sonny negotiated the car through the narrow streets of Tripoli.

"Another job for my Tuaregs. The one boy that speaks English, I got him to show me a bar where the Russians go. So, then I found a car with base ID, and I arranged for it to get a short in the ignition—something I doubt the mechanics here can find in three days, but which I know I could fix in a minute and a half. I paid the boy to stick around and watch when the tow truck came. He wrote down the name of the place, so now all we have to do is run over and pick it up."

"Simple as that," said Jonathan, amused but also taken aback at the idea of stealing a car. Of course, he was planning to steal a MiG-25 as well, but somehow that was different.

"We'll be wearing our uniforms, of course." Sonny jerked a thumb toward the trunk of the car, where he had stored them. "Don't doubt for a minute these Libyans hop to it when a Russian officer's around. Of course you'll have to do the talking, since you're the only one that speaks Russian. Plus, you're gonna be the officer, and I'm just a lowly enlisted man, according to the rank on my uniform."

They drove out to a secluded spot near Gharian, high on a mountaintop to the southeast of town. It was a picturesque place, almost like something from the Painted Desert in Arizona, but they weren't here for sightseeing. They rushed to change out of their street clothes and into the uniforms the Tuaregs had smuggled in for them.

After he put on his uniform, Jonathan walked around nervously. They were parked a few yards from the edge of a precipice, and he could see for miles. A cold wind blew in from the desert, and the uniform didn't seem to offer much protection. In fact, the material of his shirt and pants felt chintzy. Of course, that only confirmed they were the real things.

"Jeez," said Sonny as he slipped on his pants, "what do they make these things out of, fiberglass? They sure didn't have Libya in mind when they did." He glanced at Jonathan. "Well, look at you, Bubba—ain't you the picture of a Soviet officer?"

"Thanks," said Jonathan, pulling back his scratchy collar with his finger.

"Ain't nervous, are you?" asked Sonny.

Jonathan shook his head.

"No reason to be," Sonny said. "Look at all you've already done in the past six months. This is simple. All it takes is panache."

Where'd he learn that word? Jonathan wondered. But it had the effect of getting his mind off his uneasiness.

Dressed in their uniforms with their ID badges attached, they drove to the repair shop, and Jonathan got out. The place looked like a typical junky auto-repair shop back home, but the Arabic sign on the front combined with the music and the smells coming from the interior to give this one an exotic flavor.

"There it is," Sonny mumbled, nodding toward a dark blue Renault 18i wagon. "Your car."

"Got it," Jonathan answered through clenched teeth.

Stepping smartly and looking very much like a Soviet officer, he walked toward the door of the dimly lit shop, which smelled of oil, various types of spicy foods, and body odor. An unkempt man met him at the door, speaking rapidly, probably trying to tell him that there was no one else there at that hour. By now it was long after closing time and exactly the situation Jonathan and Sonny had hoped for.

Jonathan looked the night operator up and down, then addressed him sternly in Russian, demanding he receive his automobile that very moment. Of course, the man didn't understand what he meant, but he obviously had the idea and responded in an imploring tone. Jonathan ignored him and just kept right on talking, an easy thing to do since he didn't know a word of Arabic.

In the meantime, Sonny had walked over to the car, slid behind the driver's seat, and removed the pin that had penetrated the ignition wire and shorted it out. Both Jonathan and the Libyan stopped talking when they heard the sound of the motor cranking, and Jonathan looked at the Libyan with raised eyebrows, then turned and walked over to the car.

Sonny, the enlisted man, gestured toward the steering wheel and grunted a few nonsense syllables before getting out. His superior, Jonathan, broke into a big grin and turned toward the Libyan, thanking him profusely for applying his mechanical genius to the problem. Then he did something that crossed all linguistic barriers. He reached into his pocket and gave the man twenty-five dinars—about seventy-five dollars.

The Libyan took the money, smiling broadly and no doubt thinking how easy it had been to cheat these dumb Russians out of their money. Meanwhile Jonathan barked some orders at Sonny, who already knew what he was supposed to do. He got back in the rental car and followed Jonathan to the spot where they had changed clothes.

From there, they hid the rental car and headed for the base.

As he drove them toward Oqbah ibn Nafi, Jonathan asked, "So you aren't nervous at all, Sonny?"

Sonny nodded. "I can tell you're pretty uptight. Don't try to think of it all as one big job—just think about what we've got to do tonight."

"Yeah, sure."

"Don't worry, Bubba," said Sonny. "Like I said, all it takes is panache. You can bluff your way through anything. The guy who wins out ain't necessarily the smartest one, or even the strongest one, but the one with the most testosterone. Like a fella I read about in the paper one time, walked into a Sears store and strolled out a couple minutes later with a boat and trailer, just as pretty as you please. Even got the manager to hold the door open for him. Wasn't till much later they realized they'd been had—reason being, he was so gutsy and seemed so confident, nobody would have thought he was stealing."

Jonathan tried to smile. "I wonder how long it'll be before the owner of this vehicle figures out *he's* been had."

"Ah, I wouldn't worry about that," Sonny drawled. "The Soviets are used to things not working, and it's only been since yesterday. It'll probably be a week before he even thinks it should be ready. And even if he does go over there sooner, it'll take them a few days to figure out what happened. By then, Dave Duffy and George Watt will have hit the trail." He pointed ahead. "That the main gate?"

"Yeah, that's it," said Jonathan, swallowing hard.

Across the single inbound lane was a red-and-white striped bar, which stayed down until the guard pushed a button to lift it. Four men armed with AK-47s stood at ease in front of the guard shack, which was decorated with a solid green Libyan flag and a bunch of signs in Arabic and Cyrillic lettering.

He pulled up, and the Libyan airman on guard gave him a half-hearted salute. The airman looked at the windshield and, after observing they had all the proper identification decals, stood back and saluted—a little more smartly this time—to indicate they could pass. As he drove onto the brightly lit air base, Jonathan looked in his rearview mirror at the airman, who didn't even give them a second glance. It seemed awfully anticlimactic after all the effort and preparation.

"Like I said, Bubba," said Sonny with a smile as he watched Jonathan. "Panache."

After a couple of turns, they arrived at the flight operations center. Jonathan got out of the car and glanced back, but he didn't say anything. He just closed his door and watched Sonny drive off in the direction of the air base perimeter. Then he walked into the Flight Ops center.

Jonathan tried to maintain an air of casualness as he walked in, thinking, *panache, confidence—all it takes is confidence.* Maybe if he said it to himself enough, he could get psyched up.

From past experience, he knew there wouldn't be any guard at the door or any pass procedure. The Libyans must have figured anybody who got this far had already gone through security barriers and wouldn't pose a risk.

He kept a measured pace as he entered the well-lit hallway, walking down it past darkened offices and conference rooms. The walls were painted an institutional gray-green and were sparsely decorated except for a few photographs here and there of military men, each with inscriptions in Arabic. A bigger frame held a photograph of *al-Qaid,* Muammar al-Qadaffi, looking grim and stern.

At 11:15 P.M., long after most people had left, but too early for the midnight formation, the place was practically empty. A Libyan sergeant came out of one of the doorways and yawned, startling Jonathan for a second. When he saw Jonathan, he simply nodded to him. Though the man should have saluted an officer of an allied force, Jonathan had no intention of going back and correcting the NCO's mistake.

So far, so good, he thought as he rounded a corner. His footsteps sounded uncommonly loud in the empty corridor, and he walked the length of the hallway before turning again. This time, though, he could hear voices coming from a large room down toward the far end of the hall. *It's show time,* he said to himself.

A few seconds later, he walked right past the open door of the room. Keeping his face forward, he glanced quickly from the corner of his eye to see half a dozen pilots sitting behind desks. Two officers, apparently a Russian and a Libyan, stood up front, probably briefing the pilots.

He continued down the hall and turned left into the locker room, which functioned as a changing area for the pilots. Cautiously opening the door, he saw two rows of lockers with a bench in between and, at the far end, a shower and toilet facility. Directly adjacent to the toilets was a door.

Somewhere a faucet dripped and, though he tiptoed in, it seemed to him that his boots made a loud *tap-tap-tap*—much louder than the faucet—as he strode past the benches. The place smelled of cleaning fluid. When he got to the door next to the toilets, he opened it, and as he'd hoped, it was a janitor's closet. The door had a hasp in place, but no lock of any type to secure it. Best of all, it was the kind with slats, so that anyone inside could see out, while anyone standing outside could not see in.

He glanced around for a second, listening to the faucet dripping. Then, he walked back out. He headed down the corridor, again passing the briefing room. This time he happened to look in just as the Soviet officer at the front of the group looked out at him, and their eyes met. The man was gray-haired, handsome, with brown eyes and a thin face. Jonathan felt sure, from that instantaneous look, he could recognize the man anywhere if he saw him again. Which probably meant the Soviet officer could recognize *him* as well.

Stay calm, he said to himself, as he turned his eyes forward and picked up the pace slightly. *Just . . . stay . . . calm.* He kept walking, and behind him he heard a series of loud snaps as the pilots closed their binder notebooks almost in unison, then prepared to go out on tonight's mission.

Moving quickly down the corridor, he stepped around the corner and watched the pilots leaving the briefing room. Talking and laughing, they headed into the latrine area.

He kept waiting and watching, and soon he saw the men begin to stream back out of the latrine one at a time, walking down the corridor and out the main entry to flight operations.

Jonathan turned around and started walking, aware that he needed to put as much distance as he could between himself and the Soviet officer from the briefing room. He held his breath as he walked, picking up the pace just slightly. In just a few more seconds he would be home free—

"Hello!" said a voice behind him in Russian. "Is there something we can help you with, Comrade?"

Jonathan kept walking, acting as though he hadn't heard.

The voice said something more, this time in Arabic, and Jonathan just kept walking. He could hear the officer's footsteps behind him, and he forced himself to maintain a steady pace.

It sounded like the officer was still talking, but by now, Jonathan was out the door, his heart pounding.

Midnight had come and gone, and suddenly he heard the roar of two fighters springing down the runway and into the night sky. Thirty seconds later came another roar as the second squadron took off. Then another, thirty seconds later. The third would be the squad that had just been briefed. As they rose into the air, they split off in three directions—two northward, in the direction of the Mediterranean; two eastward, headed toward the Egyptian frontier; and two toward the southwest, to patrol Libya's Saharan back door.

He was early for his rendezvous with Sonny, but he set off walking toward the spot where they were supposed to meet. He didn't want to hang around Flight Ops another second. As he walked, he tried not to think about his narrow escape, but he couldn't help it. At least he wouldn't have to come to the base with Aziz the next day, and face the possibility of being noticed by this same Russian. But what if the man happened to be on duty tomorrow night?

A blast of desert wind stirred up behind him, cooling the river of sweat on his back and giving him a slight chill. He wanted to find Sonny and get out of there as quickly as he could.

CHAPTER SEVENTEEN

While Jonathan had been inside Flight Ops, Sonny had kept himself very busy with some activities of his own. "Now let's hope everything stays extremely inconspicuous till you need it," he said to Jonathan as he finished up his handiwork, "and then, just when you need it to work, let's hope it gets very conspicuous."

The clock read well after 2:00 A.M. by the time they made it to their remote mountaintop location and changed clothes. Sonny then dropped Jonathan off back at the al-Wahdan Hotel. Therefore, Jonathan wasn't too thrilled when his bedside phone rang at 7:00 the next morning. He was even less happy when he heard the voice on the other end of the line.

"Aziz," he said, sitting up in bed. "Is something wrong?" He had already said goodbye to the Libyan the day before, insisting that he didn't want to trouble him by making him drive him to the airport. Of course Aziz had been equally insistent that it was no trouble, and they had fought back and forth. Aziz had finally relented—or at least, he seemed to.

But apparently not. "George! I thought you would be up, getting ready for your flight," said Aziz. "You said you were leaving early."

"Well, not till this evening," Jonathan answered groggily, "but I wanted to get rested up, because it's going to be a long one. Tripoli to Cairo to Colombo to Adelaide . . . thirty-six hours in transit." He put his feet on the floor. Already his hotel room felt stiflingly hot, even though there was a fan turning overhead.

"Yes, I suppose you would want to be rested up before such a long flight," said Aziz jovially, but with perhaps just a trace of suspicion. Not that he would ever in his wildest dreams have suspected what George Watt was really up to. But the previous day he had entrusted Jonathan with a great deal of money, which he wished to have deposited in a Swiss account.

"Well, if there was time, I figured I'd stop by the air base and check on the equipment one last time," lied Jonathan. He did plan to go to the air base once more, that much was true. But not during the daytime—and not as George Watt.

He regretted what he'd said as soon as he heard Aziz's reply. "Wonderful! Then we will meet, have a long lunch, and go to the base together. I think General Saddiq has some good news for us. He asked if we could meet in his office this afternoon. And then, I will take you to the airport."

Just great! Jonathan thought. But he had to play it cool. "Well, sure, Aziz," he said. "I'd love to go hear the general's good news. But as far as the airport, I'd really be fine just going by myself."

"Oh, nonsense!" Aziz laughed. "What kind of a host would I have been if I let you leave alone?"

"Very well, if you insist," Jonathan said. All of a sudden the room had become unbearably hot, as though the walls were pressing in around him.

As he put the phone back in its cradle, he yelled an expletive. He quieted for a moment, then cursed again. The action seemed to clear his head, and he quickly rang up Sonny, which wasn't an easy task with Tripoli's antiquated phone system. "Hello, Mate," he said into the receiver. "How soon can you be at the place where we met the other afternoon?"

Sonny sounded groggy too. "Uh, fifteen minutes, George," he answered.

"Make it ten."

Just a little more than ten minutes later, Jonathan stood waiting impatiently under one of the arches when Sonny strolled up.

"You look like half a mile of bad runway," said Jonathan.

"I'm gettin' too old for this, Bubba. This afternoon, I'm hoppin' that plane as *you*, or should I say George Watt, and then it's on to—"

"That's just the problem." Jonathan held up a hand. "Aziz wants to take me to the airport—in fact, he insists, and I couldn't get out of it. So how can you be me if he's walking *me* through?"

"Now that's a stumper. Hmm." Sonny thought for a moment as they began to walk. Squinting at Jonathan in the bright sunlight he said, "Well, we'd better come up with a new plan real quick. But I'm gonna need some coffee before I can think this one through. I don't suppose you have any ideas."

"As a matter of fact, I do."

"Well, all right then, Bubba—let's hear 'em."

At noon, Aziz met Jonathan in the lobby of his hotel, the al-Wahdan, and they went to lunch.

When Jonathan had arrived more than a week before, Aziz had told him that 250 units were as good as sold to the Libyan Air Force. But since then General

Saddiq, Aziz's cousin, had gotten cold feet and dropped the order down to just twelve. Now Jonathan informed Aziz that he planned to have the units shipped out in sixty days.

"Very good," said Aziz, grinning from ear to ear. "But hold your order until we speak to the general."

"Why—is he going to go for more?" asked Jonathan. He genuinely didn't care, just like he had no appetite for the food he was forcing himself to eat.

"Yes," said Aziz, raising his glass in a mock toast. "The whole 250!"

"That's terrific, Aziz," said Jonathan.

"Yes," said Aziz, who suddenly looked troubled. "George—?"

Jonathan, sensing the cause of his concern, smiled. "Not to worry. I have your personal property safe and secure, and as soon as I get back to Adelaide, I'll have it wired to Switzerland." He really did plan to take care of Aziz, assuming he made it out of Libya alive.

Ninety minutes later, they were entering the same gate Jonathan and Sonny had driven through the night before. Jonathan might have been more nervous, but he was pretty sure the guards on duty the previous night would be sleeping right now. As always, non-Soviet, non-military personnel had to go through a security check, while the guards simply waved Soviet vehicles through. Just past the gate they saw the Libyan Air Force captain who had been Jonathan's official "minder" during his base visits. The officer was standing around and, when he saw them, he greeted Aziz warmly in Arabic before getting in the back seat and riding with them to see General Saddiq.

This struck Jonathan as rather strange, and he felt even less at ease when the officer said something to Aziz, who translated. "The general is not in his usual office. We will have to go find him in another place, where he sometimes goes to give briefings."

With a sick feeling in his stomach, Jonathan realized they were going to the Flight Ops center. What was going on? Were they just playing with him, waiting to see when he would crack? He glanced out of the corner of his eye at Aziz, but Aziz seemed just as jovial as ever and, as for the officer, he had a stern expression on his face when Jonathan looked at him, but he had been that way all week.

As they walked into the building, Jonathan's head felt light, and his stomach felt heavy. There were a number of Russians milling about just inside, and he scanned their faces for the one he'd seen last night, even though he knew he wouldn't see him. Like the guards and everyone else on duty the previous evening, the officer would be off today. Ahead of him, the Libyan captain walked quickly, with Aziz one step behind. Neither man looked at him or said anything. Bits and snippets of Soviet and Arabic conversation wafted from this room or that. At one point he thought he even heard Spanish—a Cuban advisor, perhaps. And then he heard a voice he recognized—the Russian officer from last night.

He rounded a corner, and just as he had done the night before, he was staring the man in the eyes. The officer looked disheveled, as though he'd been up all night. Jonathan could only hope his exhaustion would slow his reaction time.

The man stared at him, as if trying to recall when he'd seen him before. Jonathan looked away.

"Aziz," he asked, "how many units was it we discussed?"

The Russian officer had stopped talking as they walked by.

"George," Aziz laughed nervously, "you know how many units we discussed."

"Oh," said Jonathan, trying to keep Aziz engaged in conversation so that he would make himself look less out of place. "I was just thinking whether I should subtract the twelve he said he was already going to get. Is it only 238 more, or 250 more, for a total of 262?"

"Well, no." Aziz sounded a little exasperated. "250 units. It's that simple!"

"Of course," Jonathan answered, and he didn't ask any more stupid questions because by now they were down the hallway and out of danger.

Heart pounding, Jonathan followed Aziz into General Saddiq's office, where the general greeted them with smiles and handshakes. With Aziz acting as translator, General Saddiq praised the CSUs and confessed that it was hard to get good equipment from the Soviets, no matter how much money they paid, because they were too suspicious that someone would try to steal their technology.

Jonathan hardly listened. In his mind he could picture the Soviet officer bursting in at any moment and demanding to see his identification papers.

His mind was so preoccupied, he didn't even notice when the general made his big announcement—that they would be ordering the 250 units as originally planned.

"George," Aziz prompted him, "my cousin says he's ordering 250 units. Isn't that good?" Aziz glared at Jonathan, obviously annoyed that Jonathan's apparent lack of surprise would give away the fact that Aziz had already spilled the beans about the order.

"Oh, certainly, certainly," said Jonathan, smiling at the general. "Please give him my thanks, and let him know we'll start fulfilling the order in sixty days."

After a great deal of banter and chit-chat, all of it agonizing from Jonathan's perspective, the general stood up, shook hands with both of them, and showed them to the door.

Jonathan dreaded going back out into the hallway, but he wanted more than anything to get out of there, so he held his breath and ventured down the corridor with Aziz at his side.

"You are in a hurry?" asked Aziz, walking fast to keep up with him.

"Shouldn't I be?" Jonathan replied, not breaking his stride. "We've still got to swing by my hotel and pick up my luggage before we go to the airport."

"Your luggage?" asked Aziz. He looked perplexed. "I didn't even think about it this morning. Why didn't you bring it with you to begin with? We would have saved time."

"Well," Jonathan replied, "I just thought we were passing by the hotel anyway, and I figured we had plenty of time."

Aziz looked at his watch. "Well, all right then . . . we can just make it if we go now."

At about the same time Jonathan and Aziz were exiting the base, the assistant supply chief for the Soviet section at Oqbah ibn Nafi received a frantic phone call from his wife. Apparently, she couldn't find her ID card, and she suspected she had left the card in the family car. But there was a problem. The car had recently developed an electrical problem and had to be taken to a local repair shop.

After the officer got off the phone, he called in one of his subordinates who spoke Arabic. Looking a little embarrassed, he explained the situation and asked the enlisted man to call the shop and see if the ID card was in the Renault.

The enlisted man did as he was told, but he came back several minutes later with some perplexing news. According to one of the men who worked the late shift at the shop, the officer had already picked up the car the day before.

The officer grew concerned after hearing this news and made a number of frantic calls to the garage and the base security office. By the end of the afternoon, the officer realized his car had been stolen. He demanded something be done about it. To humor him, the Libyan Air Force authorities promised that the guards at the front gate of Oqbah ibn Nafi would be on the lookout for the car, a dark blue Renault 18i wagon, license plate NZ 8015.

But to the man whose car had been stolen, this wasn't enough. Whoever had taken it wouldn't try to come on base—nobody could be that foolish. They would take it into Tripoli somewhere and have it stripped for parts, or get it repainted and sell it on the black market.

The Soviet officer called his commander, who listened with appropriate concern. The commander went to base security, but after a meeting with the Libyan officer in charge, he wasn't able to get much better results. The Russian made it clear that he wanted to get the Tripoli police involved, but the Libyan was sure it was a problem for base security. For years, he explained, he had been requesting permission from General Saddiq to beef up the security procedures at the gate. As things were now, if a car had the proper decal on its windshield, the guards just gave it a quick visual inspection and then waved it through—which meant all kinds of infiltrators could get in using a Soviet decal.

"And just who, exactly, are you expecting will try to sneak on the base in this fashion?" asked the irritated Soviet commanding officer.

"Our country is under attack from many forces," the Libyan answered. "Zionists are always trying to infiltrate our installations."

"I see," said the Soviet. "Zionists, you say." He stood up. "Very well, then. Thank you for your time."

"We will post a double guard," the Libyan officer said, calling after the Soviet.

"I beg your pardon?"

"We will have the ordinary checkpoint at the front, and if the intruder comes through, he will feel safe. But what he will not know is that there will be a second checkpoint, and by the time he finds out, it will be too late for him."

"Fine," the Soviet officer answered in a condescending tone. "You put your double guard on the job."

"Don't worry," said the Libyan. "We'll find it—a dark blue Renault 18i wagon, license plate NZ 8015."

"Best of luck," replied the Soviet commander, not even turning around. He left the Libyan's office shaking his head, disgusted at these backward Libyans. Didn't they know the man who had stolen the Renault would never try to bring it on base? What kind of fool would do that?

The al-Wahdan Hotel was named for a type of gazelle that populates the hinterlands of Libya, a stuffed replica of which sat in the lobby. As Jonathan and Aziz walked in the front door, a porter emerged from behind the animal and, seeing Jonathan, said, "Yes, Mr. Watt, I will get your luggage immediately." While the man went to get his bags, Jonathan strolled over to the front desk to check out, and Aziz sat patiently in one of the plush chairs near the door.

As he stood at the counter waiting for the clerk to finish up with another guest, Jonathan watched a hall porter walk by with a handwritten sign on a placard, ringing a bell. He called something out in Arabic, but Jonathan could pick out one word. *Aziz.*

Hearing this, Aziz, looking very startled, jumped out of his seat. He took the message and ripped it open, reading it quickly, then looked over at Jonathan.

"What's wrong?" asked Jonathan.

"I do not know," Aziz said, obviously very troubled. "It is from my wife, saying for me to meet her at the Omar al-Mokhtar, the hospital downtown. She says she is on her way. I don't know what this could mean—I wonder if someone is injured . . ."

"I'm terribly sorry, Abdel," Jonathan said. And he really did feel sorry. It was a low blow, scaring the man this way, but Aziz had been so insistent about taking him to the airport that it had required extreme measures. "Is there anything I can do to help?"

Aziz shook his head. "No, George, there is nothing." He paused. "Perhaps she has not left the house yet—I will try to call her at home."

"Yes, maybe you should try that," Jonathan said.

Aziz ran to the pay phone and quickly dialed his home phone number, then cursed when the line turned out to be busy. In the booth next to Aziz, Jonathan could see Sonny Odom, who had just dialed the same number and engaged it so that Aziz's call would not go through.

Aziz ran back to him. "George," he said, "I don't know what to do. The line is busy. Perhaps—"

"Now, calm down," Jonathan said in a soothing voice. "I believe you should go to the hospital. I've got plenty of time—I'll just catch a taxi to the airport."

Aziz nodded thoughtfully. "Yes, perhaps you are right. You know your way through the airport now, yes?"

"Certainly," said Jonathan, patting Aziz on the shoulder. "You go on to the hospital and look after whatever is wrong."

After Aziz left and the coast was finally clear, Jonathan and Sonny met briefly, then took off in separate cars. They didn't make much of a ritual of saying goodbye, though if all went well tonight, they would be seeing each other again under very different circumstances.

Jonathan drove up to their meeting spot on the mountaintop, where he tried to take a nap. But it was useless, just as he had known it would be. He had his mind on tonight's mission, and even though he needed to rest up, he couldn't make himself do it.

He finally sat up in the car and stretched, looking around him at the barren, desolate landscape of the mountaintop. The surroundings only added to his feelings of isolation as he contemplated what lay before him.

Finally he glanced at his watch and got out a bag of food he had packed for himself, some cheese, bread, fruit, and water. He forced himself to eat, because he didn't know when he would eat again. He wasn't hungry, though, and it was all he could do to choke the food down.

It occurred to him, of course, that this simple little meal could be the last one of his life. For the first time, he realized he wasn't so much afraid of dying as he was of getting caught. Torture in a Libyan prison might well make death seem positively attractive.

He put those thoughts out of his mind as he donned his Soviet officer's uniform and mentally prepared himself for tonight's mission. Stuffing several items into a canvas bag, including a .38 pistol with a silencer, he checked himself out in the mirror and started the engine.

His mouth felt uncommonly dry. Sweat stained his shirt under the arms. He rolled down the windows to let in a little fresh air, took one more drink of water, then popped a piece of gum into his mouth and headed for the air base.

At five minutes to eleven, he pulled in behind a line of cars in front of the Oqbah ibn Nafi gate. He noticed right away that they had stepped up security by a considerable margin, and he wondered why. Just then a guard behind the gate walked across the road, and he realized they had posted two extra sentries in the guard building. Something was definitely up. But to break ranks and run now would only invite pursuit and capture. He held his breath.

The vehicle in front apparently passed inspection, and it drove on through as the guards turned their attention to Jonathan's car. One of them walked behind it, studied the license plate, then spoke into a portable radiophone.

Who's he talking to? he wondered as he watched the sentry through his rearview mirror.

His survival instinct screamed for him to get out of there and abort the whole mission, but there was no way to go except forward. The guard at the gate had already motioned him forward. It would be suicidal to turn around now.

As he came abreast of the gate, the sentry looked into his car, just as he had last night, then studied Jonathan's ID badge and the decal on the window.

Jonathan braced himself. Any second now, the guard might shout something to one of his comrades and, then, a siren would go off. *They're not taking me alive,* Jonathan thought. *I'll do a 180 and peel out of here and just take whatever comes before I'll let them catch me.*

The sentry raised his arm and waved him through.

CHAPTER EIGHTEEN

Just remember what Sonny said, he thought. *All it takes is panache.* He passed slowly through the gate in first gear. But then he saw something that made his heart stop.

Directly in front of him sat a ring of military police cars waiting in the dark, their lights off. His car moved forward into the nest of armed guards. About half a dozen of them stood around smoking and talking, their AK-47s propped against the sides of their vehicles.

A double guard, he thought. *These Libyans are smarter than I gave them credit for. Or maybe it was some Russian's bright idea.*

He drove past slowly, ready to stop—or to take off at a high speed in the opposite direction—if someone motioned to him. But the guards just glanced casually at Jonathan going by in his light green Saab. He wondered if they were looking for a dark blue Renault 18i station wagon, license plate NZ 8015.

Sonny, you're worth every penny I pay you, he thought as he passed by in the rental car. *I never met a more resourceful guy.* Upon their return from the air base the previous night, Sonny had applied wet towels to the decal on the Russian's windshield. After twelve hours of soaking, it was easy to slide off the precious sticker, place it on a thin piece of adhesive plastic, and reapply it to the windshield of the Saab.

By the time he'd parked the car about a hundred yards from the Flight Ops center, it was well past 11:00. Clutching his canvas bag, he walked quickly and purposefully toward the concrete block building. Once inside, he let the door close quietly behind him, and he walked softly down the hall. Just as last night, most of the doors on either side were open, and though the rooms were dark, he passed each of them with trepidation. Everything was so quiet, he could hear the hum of the fluorescent lights overhead and, far down the hallway, muffled sounds came from the briefing room.

He was sure if the Soviet officer who saw him today had been on duty last night, and then somehow up at two o'clock in the afternoon, he wasn't likely to be here tonight. Or was he? His palms were sweating as he turned the last corner and saw the lit doorway of the briefing room up ahead on his right. Holding his breath, he walked a little faster as he approached it, and turned his head as though looking at something off to the left. He moved quietly but swiftly—in moments he was past the briefing room, and he didn't hear any voice behind him.

With a sense of relief, he reached the locker room. The next few steps went without a hitch, and he moved quickly. Things seemed almost too good to be true. The room was unoccupied as it had been the night before, the janitor's closet was likewise empty, and he quickly situated himself inside the closet to wait. Once he stopped moving, he heard the beating of his heart, and it was deafening.

He checked the lighted dial of his watch. The briefing would end some time around 11:30, and the pilots would make their final pit stop here before departing to mount their jets, which sat in readiness on the tarmac. He sat in the darkness, watching through the slats while his watch ticked off the slow minutes. The smell of cleaning fluids was oppressive, and the closet was cramped; he wished the pilots would hurry up.

From his vantage point, Jonathan had a commanding view of the entire toilet area, which consisted of nothing but two holes placed side by side in the tile floor against the wall. The Libyans called these *haman*. Suddenly he thought of how it might seem if somebody caught him right now. The thought almost made him chuckle, another indication that he was half-crazed from the tension of the moment.

Finally, at 11:28, he started hearing movement and voices in the hallway as the men began to enter the locker room. They had a relaxed air about them as they laughed and talked loudly, entering the toilet two at a time. He hoped somehow their sequence would fall out of order, and they'd end up not leaving all at once, because his only chance lay in catching a straggler. But the first two finished at almost precisely the same moment, backed away from the *haman*, buttoned their pants, and walked off laughing and joking.

Next, two more men stepped up, and virtually the same order of events happened. *Great!* Jonathan thought as those two walked off and the last two entered. He hadn't really thought this part of the operation through, he realized now, and had based his plans on the idea that the men would trickle out of here to their planes until there was just one left, as they had done last night. If that didn't happen, he would either have to think of a new plan quick, or abort the whole mission after coming this far.

But before the last two began, a voice called from off to the side, beyond Jonathan's range of vision—probably one of the earlier pilots, coming back in from the hallway. The pilot to the right of the *haman* stopped and said something in reply, then walked over to his locker. He pulled out a pack of cigarettes, and gave it to the person in the background. Then he and the unseen smoker exchanged a few words before the latter left.

Meanwhile, the other pilot had finished and said something to his buddy—who was now in front of the toilet—as he walked out the door.

Now. Jonathan opened the door, taking care not to make any noise. In front of him, he saw the back of the pilot, who was whistling. After a moment, as though sensing someone nearby, the pilot looked over his shoulder and suddenly grew quiet. For an instant, Jonathan could clearly see his dark skin, prominent nose, mustache . . .

Then he was at the pilot's back. In one swift motion, he placed his hand firmly over the startled man's mouth while sticking the barrel of the silenced .38 into the side of his neck. Just in case the man failed to get the message, for a split-second Jonathan held the pistol out where the pilot could see it, then put it up against his jugular again.

The Libyan didn't attempt to resist. Without saying a word, Jonathan motioned him into the janitor's closet, pulled the door closed behind him, and shoved the man's face into the wall. Holding the struggling pilot with one arm, he reached down with his other hand to remove the epée pen full of ketamine from where he'd stuck it down his boot.

Quickly he pulled off the top and slammed it into the man's hip, but as he did, the pilot wheeled around and tried to hit him. The pilot's movement broke the needle where it was lodged in his hip, and the man opened his mouth to scream in pain, but Jonathan hit him so hard on the side of the head with the barrel of the .38 that the silencer broke off.

The pilot slumped to the floor, and Jonathan quickly jumped on him with a knee in his solar plexus and the revolver pressed against his nose. The man was out, and before he came to, the Ketamine would take effect.

Swiftly Jonathan undressed the pilot and put on his g-suit, boots, and flight jacket. They weren't exactly the right size, but close enough. Jonathan stuffed his own clothes in his bag and, taking care to close the closet door behind him, he stepped out of the room and stole down the corridor toward the runway.

It was now eighteen minutes till midnight. All the other pilots would be on the flight line about 200 yards from Flight Ops. Up ahead he could see five occupied MiG-25s and one with the flight crew waiting around. That was his plane.

The flight crew hadn't seen him yet, and since pilots always walked to their planes either carrying their helmets or wearing them with the oxygen mask hanging to one side, he would look suspicious coming out onto the tarmac with his mask covering his face. But he had already thought of this long before, and had prepared a distraction—or rather, Sonny had prepared it. He just planned it.

As he walked out the front door of Flight Ops, helmet on and mask hanging to his right side, he reached in the canvas bag and pulled out an electronic transmitter. He pushed activator button number one, setting off the first of the goodies Sonny had planted the previous night. A split-second later, a satchel charge exploded along the perimeter of the fence approximately a quarter of a mile from his location.

Before anybody on the field could even react to that, he pushed buttons two and three, activating two other satchel charges closer by, which made it look like the explosions were mortar fire marching toward the planes on the runway. Certainly it must have appeared that way to the frightened Libyans. A general alarm went out all over Oqbah ibn Nafi. Sirens came on at full screaming volume, emergency lights flashed, and people began running out of buildings, scrambling to positions.

Jonathan moved briskly toward his aircraft, pushing more buttons as he ran. Three more explosions went off, seemingly moving toward a storage area about 500 yards away. A seventh blast tore into a fully loaded and fueled MiG-21, which in turn touched off explosions in two adjacent MiGs. A deafening explosion of jet fuel sent weaponry and machine parts flying. Flames shot hundreds of feet into the air, and even from his position Jonathan could feel the heat searing his skin. The noise around him was deafening, and people were running everywhere.

He had timed the explosions in such a way as to cause as few casualties as possible. Hopefully, the flight crews would get the message. And it seemed like they did. Out on the flight line, he saw men closing up cockpits and scrambling toward the safety of the nearest bunker. The other MiG-25 pilots, eager to get themselves and their valuable hardware out of there, began taxiing away minutes ahead of schedule.

When he came within fifteen yards of his plane, Jonathan saw the crew huddled, waiting for him. He pulled the oxygen mask over his face and snapped it closed, but he hardly needed to bother disguising himself this way. His crew just wanted their pilot to hurry up and take off so that they could get to safety.

As he ran toward the plane, he saw the crew chief signaling frantically for him to hurry up. Still clutching his bag, he pushed four more buttons, setting off blasts closer and closer. With one last charge, he blew up the rental car a quarter-mile away. It was all the crew could do to stay with the plane as Jonathan bolted up the ladder and into the cockpit. The crew chief, looking terrified, helped him into his seat and jumped down before Jonathan could even turn around.

Once inside and with the seconds ticking away, Jonathan worked to quickly recall the appropriate sequence of switches he had to flip. He looked out the still-open cockpit at the man on the ground and signaled, by rotating his index finger clockwise as he had seen the Libyan pilots do over the last week, for the external power cart to begin blowing compressed air into the small turbines of the engines.

As soon as the two turbojets had reached fifteen percent of full RPMs, Jonathan moved the throttle to the idle position. Fifteen seconds later, he had generated enough speed to kick off the main turbine. Within another fifteen seconds, he had reached 45 percent power.

But that was only for one engine. He had to repeat the same process with the second one. In an instant the electrical generators were functioning, and that would bring the inertial navigation system, or INS, to full operational capacity within ninety seconds.

While he waited, Jonathan finished strapping himself in. He connected the hose of his g-suit, his parachute harness, his lap belt, his oxygen hose, and, though he didn't plan to use it, the communication line on his helmet. Then, he did a quick flight check, moving the control stick and pedals, testing the aircraft's ailerons, flaps, and rudder. Everything was exactly as he had learned under Colonel LaVallee's guidance at Luke, a course of study he had reviewed every night in his motel room off base.

He looked over and could see at a distance the flaming debris of the MiG-21s, and he heard more sirens as fire trucks moved in to douse the flames. As soon as the INS was fully operational, he signaled to his crew chief to remove the chocks, and as he began to taxi forward he pushed the activator button that slid the cockpit screen down. Approaching the runway, he armed his ejection seat and taxied toward the far end.

On his radio he could hear what sounded like directions for him to take off, but of course he didn't respond. He would simply follow the course he saw the other MiGs taking, and fall right into formation. Within thirty-five seconds, he had reached the end of the runway. He circled about, aligning himself properly. He locked the brakes, revved the engines up to 80 percent power, and checked his oil gauge to make sure that no warning lights had come on. He did this more out of habit than anything else. Regardless of what any of the gauges said—his plane was going up, no matter what.

Looking around one last time, he determined the coast was clear, and he pushed the throttle to 100 percent and released the brakes. He began rolling down the runway and, when he hit the afterburner ten seconds later, he could feel the power of the engines with their 20,000 pounds of thrust hurtling him forward. He pulled back on the stick, and the plane leaped into space, the force of its power pushing him back into his seat. Immediately, he raised his landing gear and retracted the flaps. As he began to climb, he looked over his shoulder at the fires and flashing lights on the ground.

In all his years of flying, he had never experienced a takeoff like that. If he died tonight—and there was a good chance he would—he would die knowing that nothing could ever exceed the adrenaline rush of the last few minutes. He would have loved to top it off by shooting thousands of feet into the air, but he had to conserve his fuel, so he shut off the gas-guzzling afterburner and took a slower climb to altitude.

He took a deep breath. It seemed to him as though he'd forgotten to breathe for about five minutes now, because he kept inhaling and inhaling—filling up his empty lungs. Then he finally exhaled, and as he did he broke into a laugh. *He had done it!*

Moments after Jonathan cleared the runway, the pilot in the closet woke up in the dark, wondering where he was. Struggling to move thanks to his semi-drugged state, he looked around him.

Reaching up, he touched his head and felt the blood, still warm and sticky, over an enormous knot a few inches above his right ear.

The memory of his assault came back to him, along with scenes of the struggle. He remembered the needle. . . . So, that was why he had been passed out for—he looked at his watch—five, maybe ten minutes. Feeling a stabbing pain in his leg, he realized that the needle had broken off in the midst of the struggle, and for that reason he hadn't gotten much of the drug in his bloodstream.

Outside, he heard a loud commotion—running feet, sirens, even what sounded like explosions. Could this have something to do with the attack on him? He had to report to his commander. He tried to rise to his feet and, as he did, he fell on his face. He managed to grab the door handle and collapsed onto the floor of the pilots' lounge. *"Feesa!"* he shouted. *"Ta'al! Feesa!* Quickly! Come help me! Quickly!"

Half a minute later, several men crowded around him, firing questions.

Outside in the hall, a Soviet attaché stopped a frightened-looking lieutenant running out of the latrine and demanded to know what was going on.

As soon as he had heard, he rushed to the control tower.

One of the many panicked air-traffic controllers there reported that Wing-A had taken a westerly course, and Wing-B was moving out over the Mediterranean. But whereas one of the two aircraft in Wing-C was flying in an easterly direction as ordered, the other was approaching 10,000 meters and heading out north over the water.

The Soviet officer demanded to be patched through to the first pilot of Wing-C, and ordered, "change course to three-six-zero degrees, intercept stolen MiG-25, and destroy." He knew the renegade pilot would probably hear the order—they were speaking in Arabic, and presumably the thief understood the language—and so much the better if he did.

Then the officer informed Wing-B, the one headed out over the sea, that they had a traitor headed near their direction, and they should change to an interception course.

"Affirmative," came the reply over the crackling airwaves. "Coming about to a heading of zero-nine-zero degrees in pursuit of traitor. Will intercept and destroy."

With a grim face, the Soviet officer looked into the night sky. Last night and again today he had seen a suspicious-looking man at Flight Ops, once dressed in a Soviet uniform. In spite of his lack of sleep, which muddled his thinking a bit, he was sure the man he saw today was the same one he had seen last night. And he was sure it was the same one who had now taken off in a Libyan Air Force jet.

The Soviets and Libyans weren't the only ones who took an interest in the events above Oqbah ibn Nafi that night. Far out to sea sat the U.S.S. *Enterprise,* and somewhere above it, at 45,000 feet, rode an American AWACS. The radio operator on board the surveillance aircraft, who went by the call name *Popeye,* had just begun his nightly report to the carrier far below when he received word of strange activities at "ONAB," or Oqbah ibn Nafi.

"*Enterprise,* stray craft heading directly toward your coordinates," he announced. "Suggest you scramble two F/A-18s to meet him at your back door—expect him there by 0020 . . . Apparently two other aircraft now on interception course with stray. Be on alert for all three making run toward you."

But before the *Enterprise* radio operator had a chance to confirm, Popeye relayed a message from his commanding officer. "*Enterprise,* go on full alert—scramble eight more Hornets."

"Roger that, Popeye. Fighters have been dispatched, will maintain our perimeter. Any bandits crossing into zone will be splashed, over."

From the periphery of his vision, Jonathan could see what looked like flashes of fire. Glancing over his shoulder, he realized that it really was cannon-fire—coming from another MiG-25 just a quarter-mile behind him.

"What the—!" he shouted. He pulled his plane into a tighter arc, and began climbing higher.

The only good thing about his pursuer's close proximity was that he wasn't likely to get a missile fired at him. At such short range, the Acrid probably wouldn't arm, and even if it did, the other pilot had to know that the explosion of Jonathan's aircraft would destroy his as well.

Now at 22,000 feet, Jonathan winged over and began a power dive in a steep, sharp left turn, trying to shake the other plane off his tail.

He could feel the g-forces mounting, and pretty soon they would get to fatal levels. The Foxbat was so heavy, especially with its fuel, that high-g maneuvering could get dangerous. But even before the point where it threatened the plane, the pilot himself might pass out from the sheer weight on his body. At least he had on a g-suit, which constricted the blood vessels and would prevent the blood from completely draining out of his brain.

To complete this maneuver successfully, he had to strain as though he were sitting on the toilet in the middle of a bout with constipation. Flexing his face and neck muscles, Jonathan began to grunt loudly, one long sound that grew in volume to a scream, resounding in his ears even over the noise of his engines. His head was starting to feel light, and he knew he couldn't take the pressure much longer.

When he couldn't stand it any more, Jonathan pulled out of the dive and found himself alone in the empty black sky. The g-forces must have been too much for the Libyan pilot on his tail.

Wimp! he thought with derision. But just as he regained altitude, his radar-warning receiver flashed on. Someone had locked on him, and he looked down to see two blips on his screen. "No rest for the weary!" he said aloud.

Two more aircraft approached in formation from 215 degrees apart, flying toward him. But instead of evading them, he pointed the nose of his MiG straight toward a point where his plane's trajectory would intersect with those of the other two.

The Libyans were twenty miles out, but everything was converging at a rate of one mile every four seconds. That gave him less than a minute and a half until he would be looking down his nose at two bogeys.

He had Acrid infrared homing missiles on both his inboard and outboard pylons, and he hoped his adversaries didn't have the more dangerous semi-active radar homing version. His kind, the heat seekers, only worked when fired into the rear or side of a target, whereas the radar kind had proven effective from eight miles out in a face-to-face dogfight. But they were only six miles away now, and he didn't see any more blips on his radar screen to indicate a missile headed toward him.

As the three vectors began to converge, he reached down to arm one of his four heat-seekers. If it worked like the simulator, he should see the message *Voroozhyonniy*—Armed—on his heads-up display. But this was the real world, and there wasn't any message, which meant he didn't have any way of testing the missile without firing it.

The fighter to his left, just four miles away, began peeling up and to the right. Jonathan made a split-second decision to continue on course toward the remaining fighter, reasoning that if he turned toward the one on the left, the one on the right would have a direct shot into his side.

Jonathan aimed his own craft directly at the MiG on the right, intending to pass as close as possible to constrain the other pilot's firing room. But to his surprise, he saw a flash of cannon fire. *Idiot!* he thought. *Doesn't he know that if my plane blows this close to him, it'll take him out too?*

The gap had now closed to 200 feet, which was a little like two cars travelling seventy miles an hour pulling up close enough to touch side-mirrors. Jonathan rolled his aircraft up and to the left, slicing, and slowing so he could get behind his adversary and thereby gain the advantage for a firing position.

This left the Libyan only two choices. He could follow Jonathan in the same turn or make the reverse. But he couldn't maintain his same trajectory, because Jonathan was rapidly moving into position to blow him away with his heat-seeking missiles. The Libyan elected to duplicate Jonathan's turn. But if he thought he could somehow catch Jonathan now, he was in for a disappointment. The two aircraft had the same corner velocity, or maximum speed for the maximum degrees of turn per second—400 knots—and Jonathan's momentary head start created a gap that became more and more evident with each passing second.

A rush of exhilaration flooded over Jonathan. He had been a civilian for twenty years, yet combat flying felt every bit as natural to him now as it did in Vietnam. He hadn't even flown a fighter then, or an interceptor. But he felt as though he'd been born to do this. He knew he was living some of the finest moments of his life— even if they might be his last.

Suddenly the Libyan must have realized Jonathan was about to get a side-angle shot at him, because he fell off. In doing so, he slowed and, within fifteen seconds, Jonathan had brought himself around till he was directly on the Libyan's tail.

His heads-up display showed him that the target was in sight. A moment later he heard the buzzing sound of the target acquisition. He pushed the *Fire* button of the Acrid missile—and nothing happened.

"Help!" He pushed again, and still nothing happened. Rapidly he went back through the firing sequence, keeping locked on the other MiG in spite of the fact that the pilot was maneuvering wildly to shake him off his tail. Jonathan turned the activator switch on and off, but this didn't do anything either. He was out of time, and he had to use the cannons instead.

To his relief, the red letters spelling out the words *Mozhno voroozhyt'*—Cannon Armed—appeared on the heads-up display. As he began to bring the target back into his crosshairs, he quickly looked to the rear for any sign of enemy aircraft. It was a good thing he did, because he saw the second MiG firing its cannon off to his left. The other pilot, who had disengaged at the beginning of the dogfight, couldn't fire his heat-seekers. At this close proximity, he might just as easily hit his comrade's aircraft as Jonathan's.

Jonathan threw his Foxbat into idle and extended the flaps. The plane shuddered and slowed, rapidly losing altitude. The Libyan on his tail followed suit. Now Jonathan nosed over, lifted his flaps, and pushed the throttle to maximum power, hitting the afterburner. Nose pointed toward the water, he began to accelerate as he hurtled downward with the Libyan in hot pursuit.

His pursuer locked on him again and quickly fired two Acrid missiles before pulling up to avoid crashing into the Mediterranean. Without a second to spare, Jonathan fired two flares, whose heat drew the missiles off of him. Then, he pulled up as well. Just a few hundred feet above the water, the missiles exploded harmlessly.

Jonathan took advantage of the momentary confusion to change course and began to resume altitude. He couldn't see anything for the cloud cover, but he wasn't flying by sight anyway.

He could hear the two Libyans talking on his VHF radio. Suddenly, he thought he heard three voices, and he realized that the very first pilot—the one who had chickened out of the high-g dive—had rejoined them. A moment later, they reinitiated the pursuit from ten miles out.

They had the advantage of altitude, which gave them greater speed, a factor that would only increase as they accelerated in their dive toward him. Swiftly the Libyans closed the gap to three or four miles, more than close enough for missile lock-on. There was no way Jonathan could escape three aircraft with exactly the same flight characteristics as his own.

The AWACS far above watched all of this with interest.

"*Enterprise,* this is Popeye," came the report. "Unusual maneuvers taking place. Either Libyans are playing a game, or three Foxbats engaging a fourth in dogfight. Fourth is in the lead, the three still in hot pursuit. Will be within your zone in thirty seconds. We have identified their command frequency as 135 MHz—suggest you switch over to AM air traffic control frequency. Be prepared for any possibility—intent of Libyan aircraft unclear at this time."

The Hornets, which the *Enterprise* had dispatched against the four incoming Foxbats, were no faster than their Soviet counterparts, but much lighter and more maneuverable, with better instrumentation and armaments. As soon as the F/A-18s switched over to the frequency identified by the AWACS—American forces communicated on the wide range of 225 to 400 MHz, but the Soviets did their talking on a much narrower space, 118 to 136.975 MHz—one of the pilots announced to the MiG-25 in the lead, "Attention, intruder! This is the U.S.S. *Enterprise*. Do not enter this airspace, or you will be shot down. Repeat—turn back or you will be shot down!"

Great! Jonathan thought when he heard the transmission in English. *Looks like an Oreo—and guess who's the cream filling?*

"Repeat—Libyan aircraft, you are entering restricted zone! Turn back now!"

"American fleet!" Jonathan shouted back. "This is the MiG-25 headed your way. I am defecting. Repeat, I am defecting. Bogeys on my tail. Request assistance. I will follow you to any base. Have shut down my radar—repeat—have shut down my radar."

If he had shut down his radar, he couldn't lock on another aircraft with his missiles. In the skies, it meant the same thing as coming out with your hands up and waving a white flag.

Over his radio, he could hear the Americans conferring. "MiG pilot could be American, from the sound of accent . . . or Russian with language training. How could he be an American . . . ?"

Then Popeye broke in. "First bogey at oh-nine-oh, three more directly behind. I have them at ten miles from your location . . . options are running out . . ."

"American Carrier Group!" Jonathan called out. "Repeat—MiG-25 defecting. Will drop to 5,000 feet. Knock these bogeys off my tail."

" . . . Give him the benefit of a doubt," one of the American pilots was saying. "All four have entered no man's land."

" . . . Have to do something quick," came a reply. "Looks like they've locked on him."

And they had. Once again Jonathan dropped two flares and performed a quick left turn with full air brakes to bring the aircraft quickly about—and once again, the two Acrids went flying harmlessly into the water.

As he came out of his turn, he heard the F/A-18 squadron leader announce, "Attention, Libyan MiGs! Fall back, or you will be shot down. Repeat, fall back, or you will be shot down. Giving you five seconds. Five, four, three—"

Soviet technology was no match for the Hornets and their deadly AIM-7 warheads, and the Libyans knew it. In unison they switched off their radars, turned downward, and peeled to the left. Once they had completed the 180° turn, they hit the afterburners and fled.

As he pulled back onto his eastward course, Jonathan got on the radio. "Thanks for the help, fellas," he said. "Couldn't have done it without you."

"MiG-25!" came the reply. "You're headed the wrong way. Change course to two-four-five degrees, over."

Jonathan didn't say anything back, but after another fifteen seconds, they came back on. "MiG-25, do you read? Come in, MiG-25. MiG-25, are you defecting or not?"

"Sorry," Jonathan replied. "I can't right now."

"What do you mean you *can't?*" He could hear the pilot's anger in his voice, and he couldn't blame him. "MiG-25, give identification, over."

"Bond," said Jonathan in a phony British accent. He grinned, feeling giddy with relief. "James Bond."

"Who is this guy?" one of the American pilots demanded. They were relaying on a higher frequency, out of Jonathan's range. "Suggest we splash the bogey."

"That's a negative," came the squadron leader's reply. "MiG is out of restricted zone. We no longer have the authority."

CHAPTER NINETEEN

As soon as he found himself out of danger—at least, the danger posed by the Libyans and the Americans—Jonathan plugged a set of coordinates into his inertial navigation system. 32°37'44"N 40°58'16"E. He had become airborne at about four minutes after midnight local time and spent about fifteen minutes evading the Libyans and the Americans. According to his calculations, he should reach his destination somewhere around 0320 Libyan time—assuming his fuel lasted. The majority of his flight plan took him over the open Mediterranean. The hard part would come after he made landfall.

When he had planned his route, using aviation maps and every piece of information he could lay his hands on, he had charted a course that carefully avoided Israel, the country with the best air defenses in the region. Instead he would fly over Lebanon, southwestern Syria, a corner of Jordan, and into Iraq.

It was a dangerous route, but he had several things on his side. For one thing, he was going so fast, and the nations were so small—Jordan would fit easily inside of Louisiana—that he wouldn't be over one country for very long. A minute over Lebanon. Just under six minutes above Syria. A little more than two in Jordanian airspace. Nor did they know he was coming. By the time he entered a nation's airspace and they scrambled their interceptors, he would be far out of their reach. Besides, he knew the Syrian Air Force had MiG-25s of its own, which meant that his aircraft wouldn't stand out the way a NATO jet would.

The only thing he hadn't fully taken into account was the amount of fuel he would burn evading the Libyan pursuers. At least the Americans hadn't come after him too, or he would have really been in trouble. As it was, he kept his eyes on the fuel gauge, and he maintained a high altitude, which not only conserved fuel but gave potential interceptors that much less chance of catching up with him.

Alone in the cockpit of that MiG-25, he felt a solitude like he had never experienced before. He felt power at his fingertips—the power of controlling this beautiful piece of machinery, and the power of having gotten away with one of the most daring heists in history. What was the Great Train Robbery or even D.B. Cooper's getaway compared to this? He had stolen a MiG-25 interceptor from a Libyan air base! This would have made a great adventure story. Too bad neither he nor anybody else would ever get to tell it.

In the quietness of the moment, Jonathan reflected on what he was doing. His Bond-like exploits shocked him less and less the more he accomplished. The thrill of victory had not quite become commonplace, but he did gain confidence with every escape from a near miss. He started to think more about *why* than *how*.

All questions aside, he had told Ali he would return to help them, and he intended to keep that promise. He had developed an unexpected affection for the mujahideen and their struggle to live free of Russian control. He likened it in some way to America's own revolution against British tyranny, and he wanted to help them. His conscience was clear about doing whatever he could to assist the rebels in throwing off the yoke of their oppressors. He considered their war a just war, and if stealing an airplane in order to play a small part in their fight for freedom was required, then so be it.

He also planned to return to Afghanistan to face the object of his hatred. As far as he knew, Drakoff was still alive and well, and Jonathan still had intentions of dealing with him personally for having ordered the death of his wife and son. He would use the MiG to avenge his loss if necessary.

Just over the joint boundary of Syria, Jordan, and Iraq, two suspicious-looking dots on his radar interrupted his thoughts. He couldn't do anything about them, so he continued on his course. When he glanced down a second later, the dots were moving closer.

And then, just as he began to really worry, they suddenly disappeared. He wondered for a moment if they were hiding from him, lurking in a blind spot like a state trooper in a speed trap. But, then, his instrument panel gave him something much more pressing to worry about. The Russian words *shyest' minoot* flashed to tell him he had only six minutes of fuel left.

Forcing himself to stay calm, he considered his position versus his destination. He calculated he could go another 190 kilometers. Already over Iraq, he should make it—provided his INS guided him correctly to the spot.

He nearly jumped out of his skin when he heard the recorded voice of a woman telling him, "*Ostorozhno!* Caution! Caution, 483!" she announced. "Your fuel supply has dropped to an emergency level. You are in an emergency situation!"

Despite all he'd been through tonight, nothing had scared him like that. The guys who built the simulator hadn't included this detail, probably because few pilots had ever heard it and lived. Too bad he couldn't go back to LaVallee and tell him about it. "Thanks, Sweetheart," he said out loud, trying to calm himself. "I'm about to bring her down."

He began his descent, conscious of the fact he was running on fumes with more than thirty kilometers to his destination. The desert below him wouldn't have been the worst possible place for making an emergency landing—but then what? He would be alone, in the middle of a hostile landscape—in Iraq. He might as well crash-land on the moon.

His INS told him he had reached the vicinity of his destination, and he started to look for his visual marker. But instead he saw only the darkness of the desert. He held his breath. *Please God—*

Then, below him he saw a group of eleven flares in a row. With exclamation of relief, he began flicking switches, dropping flaps, and setting the landing gear. He knew a surplus airstrip lay exactly fourteen kilometers east of this marker, and all around him now he saw lights. Just ahead lay the airstrip.

He thought he felt the plane lurch a bit, probably about to give out of fuel completely. But now his wheels were down. As he flew in, he touched earth with a sharp jolt.

Bouncing down the runway, Jonathan pumped the brakes so hard he felt like he was leg-pressing a thousand pounds. Up ahead he could see the edge of the tarmac and, beyond that, the vast emptiness of the Iraqi desert. He skidded to a halt several hundred feet shy of the end.

As he slid his cockpit open, the warm desert air rushed in, and even though the air filled with petroleum fumes—the lights came from burning off the uneconomical sour-gas byproduct of oil field production—it smelled sweet to him. Beyond the edge of the light, he saw shapes moving and a lot of shouting, then several dozen men dressed in burnooses came running up to the side of his plane. For a second, he wondered if he had landed in the right place. *What if . . .*

And then he heard something off in the distance that told him he had definitely found the right place. Willie Nelson's voice warbled from a stereo somewhere, singing "Amazing Grace." He grinned as he got out of the cockpit, stepping through the men swarming around it. His legs felt wobbly when he touched the concrete, and for a second he thought he might pass out from the sheer adrenaline rush of the past few hours.

Sonny Odom stepped out of the shadows. "Glad to see you, Bubba."

"Not half as glad as I am to see you," Jonathan replied, swallowing hard and holding his stomach.

"Just go on and puke if you need to," Sonny chuckled. "You've earned the right."

Jonathan shook his head. Looking around at the other men, who had now pulled a fuel truck up to his plane, he nodded with admiration. "Pretty good setup you've got here," he observed.

"Yeah," Sonny shrugged, "it's amazing what a couple of Iraqi Air Force generals will do if you offer 'em a few hundred thousand to borrow a few men and a slab of concrete for an hour or two."

"I don't even want to know," said Jonathan, holding up a hand and laughing, feeling like he might lose the bread and cheese he had eaten just a few hours ago—a few hours that seemed like a lifetime. As he recovered, he stood and watched the men working on the plane, gassing it up with fourteen tons of fuel and another half-ton of alcohol for coolant. Other men stood by to pump oxygen into the life-support systems and to check the electronic equipment. *That thing's not a plane,* he thought as he looked back at the hulking MiG-25, *it's a spaceship.* "Long as you feel like you can trust these guys," he added.

"Why not?" Sonny asked. "Your money guarantees their loyalty, not to mention the fact that they've got plenty of reason to make sure everything goes well. Can you imagine if it ever got out that they'd used Iraqi government fuel to help an American who'd stolen a Soviet jet from Libya?" He shook his head. "Naw, they've got a major stake in seeing to it that all goes well." He looked down the runway. "But you did almost have you a problem. We lit the lamps at 0300, thinkin' you'd get here then, and the fellas around here started gettin' antsy about being detected. I finally got them to agree to leave 'em on till 0330—five more minutes, and you wouldn't have been able to find us."

"That's okay," said Jonathan. "Five more minutes, and I would have been dead anyway."

While they watched the men working on the plane, Jonathan gave Sonny a quick rundown on his escape from Oqbah ibn Nafi. "And you know the ironic thing about it?"

Sonny shook his head.

"The whole reason I took that sucker was because of its shootdown capability, and in the middle of a dogfight, come to find out, I couldn't get the missiles to arm."

"That ain't gonna work," said Sonny. He whistled to the crew chief and waved him over. "Don't worry, Bubba. We'll get you squared away."

Long after he took off again, the realization dawned on Jonathan how strange it was that he and Sonny had stood around talking as though they were back home—only they were in the middle of the Iraqi desert. But now he had plenty else to think about.

This second leg of the journey took him across the Iraq-Iran border, site of the bloodiest war since 1945. He started to tense again as he approached his roughly calculated coordinates of the border. Watching his radar, he periodically looked around to "check his six."

Over his radio he heard scattered bits of Arabic chatter, but nothing that seemed particularly menacing as far as he could tell. He kept listening for the point when the Arabic of the Iraqis changed to the Farsi of the Iranians, but since he didn't know either language—and because of his preoccupation with staying aloft and alive—he never noticed any particular change. It would have been a hard thing to do, as he later learned, because the Iranians were talking on a higher frequency.

At one point, he heard some men speaking rapidly, and he wondered if they were talking about his aircraft. Just when he wheeled around to look behind him, he saw a flash of fire. For a split second, he thought he was being attacked . . . then, he realized it was a meteor.

Flying over Iran rattled him more than any of the other countries, not only because they were at war and therefore more likely to be on guard against planes coming out of Iraq, but also because he spent more time over their airspace than any country yet. The fighting, however, was mainly in the south, and he flew across the central part of the country, avoiding Tehran by a wide margin and heading out over the Great Salt Desert at about sixty degrees east.

Soon he would enter Afghan airspace, one of the easiest air borders to cross. Most of Afghanistan's defenses lay to the south near Pakistan. But up here there weren't any borders. Ahead of him, he could see only the dark night sky—black as a pot of thick Afghan tea.

He glanced at his fuel gauge. Only 1,300 kilograms of fuel left, which meant within the next ten minutes, the fuel warning light would come on and, soon afterward, he would again hear that Russian woman's voice in his headset, telling him once again that he was about to flame out.

From his original reckoning, he anticipated about twenty-five minutes of flight time from this point to his destination. But he'd gotten a bit behind schedule because of unusually high headwinds this morning. By the time he touched down, he'd probably have little more than two hundred kilos of fuel, which would be like running a car's gas down to the last ounce. But in his case, the stakes were a lot higher. He couldn't just find a gas station. He had to locate a makeshift airstrip—one much less sophisticated than where he had landed in Iraq. And if he failed to find it, he wouldn't have the option of pulling over and filling up with a gas can in hand.

When he left Afghanistan in April, he and Ali had planned out the first landing for what Ali had affectionately dubbed, "The Mujahid Air Force." Together they had located a site, and Jonathan had given him loose instructions as to how to prepare the field—for instance, he knew that he needed 1,700 meters of runway to make a safe landing.

They had selected a spot far enough inside mujahideen-controlled territory to likely still remain in rebel hands when Jonathan returned at the end of May. After Ali's men prepared the field, Jonathan had said, they should cover it with scrub brush until the five-day period from May 30 to June 3.

He had left Ali with a homing device and a VHF receiver. For a period of four hours on each of the designated nights, they would send out a transmission to Jonathan, who would have a companion instrument installed by Sonny's men in Iraq. Once his directional finder homed in on the frequency of the beacon, Jonathan could easily plot the course of his destination. Then, when he approached the airfield, he would use his VHF transmitter to send a predetermined signal to the ground, and the men there would answer by the ignition of lanterns marking the runway.

Of course, if the directional beam or Jonathan's receiver failed to work, he would keep on flying and probably crash into the rocky plateau when his fuel ran out. Or if the VHF receiver on the ground malfunctioned, the men wouldn't know to light the fires, and he would fly right past the airstrip. Even under the best of conditions, landing on a dirt airfield could be risky, particularly when those who'd done the preparing really had no idea of the requirements for minimum safety.

He didn't let himself think much about that. Not yet, anyway. As he drew closer, his receiver began to pick up the faint sound of the incoming directional beam. *That's hurdle one crossed,* he thought. The inboard computer quickly calculated the distance to the signal, and Jonathan corrected his course accordingly. He would be on target within eight minutes.

He began to signal the ground with a series of dots and dashes. As he approached from one minute out, he slowed his speed down to 400 kilometers per hour and lowered his altitude to 2,500 meters, which put him about 500 meters above the ground. He watched below him for signal fires along the runway, but he saw only darkness.

And then several chilling thoughts raced through his mind. *What if Ali wasn't down there at all? What if he'd been captured or killed? And what if the airstrip had fallen into the hands of the Communists or—even worse—Hekmatyar's men? What if they were just waiting for him and his airplane?*

Involuntarily, he made a face like somebody who has just tasted something bitter, and he quickly put the disturbing thoughts from his mind.

He dropped to 2,300 meters, or about 300 meters above the ground. He was less than three kilometers away and, by now, he should be seeing some flares. What had gone wrong? He turned on his landing lights, even though he knew they wouldn't do him any good by themselves because Ali's men wouldn't know from the lights alone that it was him and not a Soviet or Afghan Communist.

Maybe they hadn't received his signal—or maybe he had just flown himself into a trap. Either way, he had no choice. He had to get the plane on the ground, or crash.

He began flashing his landing lights off and on, using the original Morse code signal of dots and dashes. No answer. His movements became more and more frantic as the seconds ticked by. Now the Russian woman's voice burst into his ears, warning Pilot No. 483 of danger: *"Ostorozhno, Chyet'rye-vosyem-tri!"*

"Come on, come on!" he pleaded as he kept flashing his landing lights. He was only sixty meters above the ground; how could they possibly not see him?

In just a few seconds, he wouldn't have any choice but to go ahead and land. He dropped the flaps, slowed down the landing speed, and continued flashing his lights. Suddenly he saw a flash in response.

Gunfire, he thought with a sinking feeling.

But a split second later there came another flash, and another, and he realized the lights were moving from side to side, waving at him—not gunfire, but torches! As he came closer in, he saw more and more of them coming on in the darkness, making a line to mark the runway.

By the time he saw the outline of the runway, he'd overshot it. So he pushed forward on the throttle, accelerated, and pulled up and away.

Now the Russian woman's voice was back on his headset, with her second, even more dire warning. There probably wouldn't be a third one.

He pulled up to 300 meters over the ground and, looking over his shoulder, he could see a clearly lit runway. He circled back, dropped altitude, lowered the landing gear, and touched down.

Now he skidded along the pockmarked surface of the runway, his craft bumping and careening with so much force, for a second he was afraid the whole thing would go up in flames. He could feel the tires struggling in the hard-packed earth, trying to stop—and finally, the plane came to a halt so abrupt he would have gone flying into the instrument panel if he hadn't been strapped in.

For several long seconds, he just sat there in the cockpit, heart pounding and adrenaline pumping. Then, he stood and slid open the canopy. Only then did he remember his fear that it might not be Ali and the others who had come out to meet him.

Too late now, he thought, as he saw a Soviet-made vehicle pulling out in the distance, its headlights moving toward him. He didn't move, but stood there watching as it rolled down the runway. As it did, the torches on either side went out one by one, leaving the early morning in purplish blackness except for the two headlights in a cloud of dust coming toward him.

As he stood there in the cockpit with the turbine engines still idling, he could make out the vehicle now, a GAZ-69, something like a Jeep. A man stood in the back seat, like a political leader in a parade. With relief, Jonathan realized it was Abdul, the fierce giant, wearing a grin wide enough to eat a banana sideways. He saw Ali in front, beside the driver, smiling and waving.

When they got within a few feet of him, they turned the vehicle around and motioned for him to follow. He began to taxi behind them, laughing at the sign someone had put on the back of the jeep, bold letters spelling out *FOLLOW ME*.

At the end of the taxiway, the vehicles and jet stopped. Actually, the vehicles stopped and the MiG just died—completely out of fuel. Jonathan had made it without two seconds to spare.

The other mujahideen began running from all directions and, as he stepped out of the aircraft, he nearly fell to the ground.

Ali rushed out and embraced him, holding up Jonathan's suddenly weak body. "We are sorry for not turning on the torches sooner," he said hurriedly. "A problem with the batteries. We tried the signaling device yesterday and it did not work, and we had no back-up battery, so we had to pull the one from the receiver."

"I don't . . . " Jonathan's words trailed as his thoughts drifted into a haze and he began to feel dizzy.

"I thought it would be better to send a signal to you telling you our position than for us to be able to receive a message from you." Ali stopped and studied Jonathan's face and then put one arm around him for support. With the other hand, he pointed off beyond the airstrip. "We have set up a temporary camp only a 500 meters away, and I am sure you will want to rest."

"Rest?" said Jonathan, repeating it like it was a foreign word.

"Come with me," said Ali gently, like a father helping his injured son off a football field.

Behind them, Ali's men draped the Foxbat in camouflage netting stolen from an overrun Soviet base. Others rushed to cover the runway with brush, which they would also throw on top of the plane. In just a few minutes, the scene wouldn't look any different from the area around it.

Meanwhile, Jonathan and Ali arrived at the makeshift camp, and Ali pointed Jonathan toward a tent.

Inside, Jonathan lay down on a cot, vaguely aware that Ali was still there, watching him. The thought occurred to him that he had just accomplished something truly remarkable. What he had done ranked as more amazing than anything he'd ever managed to do in Vietnam or in his career in business. It was even greater than bringing the Stingers to Afghanistan and shooting down five Soviet aircraft. Yet he could never tell anyone about having done it—anyone besides Sonny, that is.

"Sleep well, Commander," Ali was saying.

Jonathan mumbled an unintelligible response. By then, he had already fallen into a light, troubled sleep, full of dreams of narrow escapes.

Jonathan had known from the beginning that Massoud and Ali had greater expectations for their new "Air Force" than he could possibly deliver—or anybody else, for that matter. This fact became even clearer to him on the ride to Massoud's camp the day after he arrived. Ali began talking in enthusiastic terms about how they could use the Foxbat to hit selected targets over and over. Jonathan just listened and smiled.

He got a hero's welcome in Massoud's camp, and the leader himself greeted him with a big bear hug. Once Massoud, Ali, and Jonathan sat down to talk, they discussed various things, including the fact that Massoud's men had "acquired" a sizable amount of jet fuel from a Soviet air base for use on the MiG, which remained camouflaged and guarded at the spot where Jonathan had landed. But soon the leader came to what Jonathan knew was his main interest. "Massoud asks," Ali translated, "when your Air Force will be prepared to strike?"

"Tell him I'm prepared now," Jonathan replied. That much at least was true.

"Good," replied Massoud through Ali. "Then we shall discuss targets." He unrolled a wrinkled map, spread it before them where they sat on the floor, and began to sketch an elaborate aerial war plan—which would have been wonderful if they had possessed five or six more squadrons of Foxbats.

When he appeared to have finished, or at least stopped to take a breath, Jonathan nodded thoughtfully as though considering all that the leader had said. Then he turned to Ali with a question for him to interpret for Massoud, "Let me ask you something. How many Soviet generals have you killed in the field?"

"I can answer that myself," said Ali, making a zero sign with his thumb and forefinger. He repeated Jonathan's question to Massoud, who shrugged his shoulders and looked away.

"Exactly," Jonathan replied. "But until you strike at the very brains of their operation, they will just keep winning this war. So tell me. How would you like to wipe out a significant portion of their command structure, including possibly several generals?"

"How would you do that?" Ali demanded before he translated Jonathan's question for Massoud.

"I believe they have transports periodically, which fly officers from Kabul back to *Rodina*, the Motherland, so that they can rest and visit their families."

"Of course," said Ali. "But we never know which flights are officer transports, so what good does—"

"No, maybe you don't," Jonathan replied. "Up until now, it's never really mattered if a transport carried half the top brass in this country, because you could do nothing about it." He looked Ali in the eye. "But now it's time for a little fact-finding mission to Kabul, to go listen around the markets to what the Soviets are saying." He had something else in mind—something, or rather, *someone* he hoped to find in the capital—but he didn't share that fact.

"You?" asked Ali, incredulous.

"Well, I will need a guide," Jonathan admitted. He brightened. "There are all kinds of clues, if you look carefully enough—for instance, when officers are preparing to leave the country, they would probably be buying certain items to take home. If I take a leisurely walk around and observe what people are saying and doing, I believe I could learn when such a flight would take place. And when we know that, we could be in a position to blow it out of the sky."

Massoud looked a little troubled by what Ali translated from Jonathan. "So you will just go to Kabul, like that," said Ali sarcastically. He gestured toward Jonathan's white face, and then as his own dark complexion. "You don't exactly fit in, you know."

"Certainly," Jonathan replied coolly, "but who said I intended to go as an Afghan?"

"You mean—?" Ali turned and whispered furiously to Massoud, who shook his head.

"Ali, I speak fluent Russian," Jonathan said. "And I'll bet you've got a Soviet officer's uniform I could wear."

Massoud, without even waiting for the translation, shook his head *no*. But Jonathan sent an imploring look at Ali. "Have I been wrong yet?" he asked.

Ali looked at Jonathan, then began speaking with Massoud. The conversation between the two became louder and more animated. At first, Massoud sounded adamant, but Ali seemed to argue his case well. After a while, Massoud began to nod his head slowly and stroke his beard. Finally, Ali looked back at Jonathan. "You will go to Kabul," he said.

Jonathan smiled. "Tell Massoud he has made a wise decision, and I will not let him down."

Massoud said something, and Ali added, "Sergei will be your guide. The two of you will fit in well as *Shuravi*."

"Sergei?" asked Jonathan.

"You remember Sergei," said Ali.

"The Russian defector?"

Ali raised a finger and smiled grimly. "The Lithuanian defector. Calling him Russian is a bit like calling Massoud or me an Iranian."

Jonathan nodded his head. "You sure we can trust him?" He had been assuming his guide would be an Afghan.

"Like I trusted Khalid," answered Ali. "Remember, Sergei has converted to Islam." He said this as though it should settle any doubts. "In fact," he went on, "his name now is Saeid, but we still call him Sergei." Seeing Jonathan's skeptical look, Ali said, "And his loyalty has been tested many times. I dare say he has killed more of the enemy than all but the fiercest of my men. In his mind, we are brothers against the *Shuravi* because they invaded our country just as they did his, during the Great War against the Nazis."

"All right, if you say so," Jonathan replied.

Ali conferred with Massoud, then said, "It will take approximately one day of travel. And since the best time to infiltrate the city is around sunset, you should plan to leave tomorrow night, travel Tuesday, and arrive there Tuesday night. We have what you call a safety house, and, of course, an officer's uniform."

Jonathan smiled. "You mean a safe house."

Ali waved a hand. "Yes, whatever. A place where you can stay the evening and make your tour the next day. You can stay two, three, four days, but I told Massoud you will be back by next Monday."

"No problem," Jonathan replied, though he wasn't at all sure he could get the information they needed in that short span of time—or complete his primary mission. "Meanwhile, you need to ask your observers to begin plotting the landings and take-offs of large passenger-type aircraft and military transport planes from the Kabul airport, from Bagram Air Base—wherever else you can do surveillance."

"Yes, we will do that." Ali looked at Massoud. "I will inform Abdul when you will be leaving."

"Abdul?"

"He will come with you to protect you, of course," said Ali.

Jonathan shook his head. "We're posing as Soviet officers. How is it going to look if—"

"He is not actually going to be *with* you," Ali replied. "But he will be nearby. Watching."

"Okay," Jonathan said with a shrug. "If you think it'll be helpful."

"One never knows what one may find in an unusual city, and I am sure you will find Kabul very helpful." When he translated these words for Massoud, the leader nodded gravely, studying Jonathan with his deep-set eyes.

Rusty Wharton walked into the locker room of the gym at CIA headquarters. In mid-afternoon, there wouldn't be anybody here except for a few others like him, taking time off from work to clear their heads with a little activity.

As it turned out, he seemed to be the only one in the locker room. He had his gym bag and, after taking off his suit and tie and the rest of his clothes and hanging them in his locker, he began putting on his workout clothes.

He turned to head for the weight room when McGinnis came in, sweating and puffing from a workout. Wharton greeted his boss and tried not to look amused at the fact that the other man was covered with sweat and visibly fatigued. McGinnis smoked, and he always ate huge meals. No wonder he was so out of shape.

But he was surprisingly chipper, and he chatted with Wharton about various affairs of the day as he undressed and prepared to head for the shower. Wharton, on the other hand, was antsy to get on a weight machine or a treadmill, and he was about to tell McGinnis as much when his boss said, "Oh, by the way—I've got something interesting to tell you."

"Yeah?" said Wharton with impatience showing in his voice.

"Thought you'd like to know about something that came over the wire from Defense Intelligence." McGinnis now had a towel wrapped around his large, hairy stomach. He lowered his voice. "Seems that an AWACS above the Mediterranean recorded some transmissions between a Libyan defector in a MiG-25 and a couple of F/A-18 Hornet pilots."

"Yeah?" Wharton sat back down on the bench.

"This turned out to be an aborted defection," McGinnis went on. "In fact, what they think is that the guy flying the MiG was *stealing* it."

Wharton raised his eyebrows.

"It's the kind of thing that would be considered a major international incident," McGinnis went on, "but no one wants to admit it happened." Before Wharton could say anything, he added, "Defense Intelligence is sure that the thief was an American. The pilot spoke perfect English—with a slight Southern accent."

Stunned, Wharton said, "You think it's Stuart?"

"Who else could it be?" asked McGinnis. "I told them to check the passenger lists of inbound flights to Tripoli, and—"

"Boltar?"

"George Watt," said McGinnis. "Plain as day, right there on the passenger list."

"The guy didn't even bother to change aliases," Wharton said with a tone of wonder.

"Maybe he figures he doesn't have anything to worry about," McGinnis observed.

"What do you mean?"

"Stuart's not Superman, Rusty," said McGinnis, pulling his towel tightly around himself. "That's a suicide mission if I ever heard of one. Where could he go with that aircraft? Afghanistan again?" He shook his head. "Impossible. A Foxbat can't fly half that distance. That sucker's dead, man." He looked in the direction of the showers. "Listen, I better get cleaned up here—just thought you'd like to know."

"Yeah, thanks, Mac." But Wharton did not get up from the bench immediately. He sat there thinking for a few moments, wondering who understood Stuart better—McGinnis or him. He had a hunch he knew what Stuart was going to do next, *if* he was alive. But that was a big *if*. Maybe Mac was right. Wharton sighed, stood up, and headed for the weight room.

CHAPTER TWENTY

Jonathan didn't know exactly what he'd expected—something more exotic, perhaps—but when he saw Kabul for the first time, the city seemed benign, almost drab. As his and Sergei's horses topped the last ridge, the three-thousand-year-old city stretched out below him, all brown and gray, even in the sparkling light created by the sun's reflection on the ever-present swirls of dust.

Among the buildings sprawled across the hillsides, he saw gleaming mosques shining here and there above the surrounding structures. A bigger temple, bright blue, rose near the center of town. He looked out over acres and acres of corrugated rooftops, and farther away, blocks of dreary Soviet-built apartments. In spite of these, and a modern TV tower shooting up from their midst, the town looked ancient and dusty, and most of its dwellings appeared to be nothing but huts of dried mud.

Just outside the city they met their two guides, part of the "pipeline" for smuggling people in and out of Kabul. The two men escorted them into the heart of the city. Everywhere he turned, Jonathan saw men carrying guns—Soviet soldiers, Afghan soldiers, police, and civilian militia—much like the Wild West. The narrow, dusty lanes stank of open sewers, unwashed bodies, and the exhaust from the occasional Soviet automobile. Just walking down the street posed a risk, as Jonathan soon discovered.

He and Sergei walked along, leading their horses behind the guides, all of them dressed like ordinary Afghans with their eyes fixed on the ground so nobody would notice them. Ahead, Jonathan saw a Soviet GAZ-69 coming toward them with two enlisted men in the back, holding rifles. He knew the men would come within a few feet of him on the narrow street. In order for the Soviets to pass his party, one of the two groups would have to make way.

The Soviets barreled on, with small boys and chickens scurrying to get out of their path. Jonathan's hand tightened on the reins of his horse. At the last moment, the mujahideen reined their horses over the edge of the *juie*, the foul-smelling sewer that ran alongside the street. The Russians drove on past, honking their horn and scowling, and Jonathan distinctly heard one of them hurl a crude, offensive insult toward him and his companions. He glanced at Sergei, who had obviously heard it too.

Eventually, they came to a tiny shop, and their two guides motioned for them to follow around the side of the building. There in a courtyard at the back, they found a stable. After putting their horses up, they slipped into a tailor's shop and down a flight of stairs.

Jonathan and Sergei found themselves in what appeared to be a sewing factory. Even though the building didn't look very big from the street, the lower portion was spacious—perhaps 1500 square feet. The expansive area was open, except for several rows of antiquated sewing machines with a table for the foreman up front—like a teacher's desk at the head of a classroom. The shop stank of machine oil, cheap cloth, and sweat, but compared to the street outside, it smelled like the perfume counter at Macy's.

Abdul Rasul, the tailor, proved to be a quiet little man. He showed them in without saying a word. Rasul pulled back a trap door hidden beneath the foreman's table, revealing a tiny, windowless room lined with bales of yarn and unused cloth to muffle sound. It was ventilated by a shaft that opened at the back of the shop. Rasul flicked on a naked electric bulb to light the cramped space. With a sinking heart, Jonathan realized this room, with just enough space for two men to sleep, would be his and Sergei's sleeping quarters for the duration of their stay in Kabul.

He smiled politely at his host and made bowing motions to show his thanks for the accommodations. From the corner of his eye, he glanced at Sergei. The latter's previous suspicions seemed to have dissolved—along with those of the other mujahideen—back in Wright's Canyon.

Returning to the shop, Rasul invited them to sit on the floor. About ten minutes later, he and one of his young sons returned, carrying a gigantic bowl of rice, plus smaller bowls of lamb and fruit and big, flat pieces of *naan*. While the shopkeeper and his son looked on, the four men—Jonathan, Sergei, and the two guides—ate greedily.

By now, Jonathan had learned how to eat like an Afghan, which did not exactly mean the same standards of table manners he would have applied at one of Jennifer's dinner parties back home. Slurping, chewing with your mouth open, and eating with your hands were permissible, but talking during the meal or touching anything with your left hand was not.

Eventually they wiped the last traces of grease from the platters. Then, Rasul's son placed a bowl of water in front of them. They washed their hands, and then chatted for awhile, with Sergei interpreting for Jonathan. One of the guides smoked a cigarette, which Jonathan found extremely unpleasant in the poorly ventilated shop, but he didn't consider it prudent to express his opinion aloud.

When everyone except Jonathan and Sergei left, it was time to go to bed, but neither of them felt much like sleeping just yet. Sergei appeared no more excited than he about their cramped cubbyhole of a room. Sergei seemed to want to talk, which was fine with Jonathan. He had been waiting a long time for the chance to speak one-on-one with a former member of the Soviet Army in Afghanistan.

They sat in the dark shop and talked in whispers. Earlier, they had heard noises coming from the street, but now it was 9:00 P.M., and the city seemed to have gone to sleep. "So tell me, Sergei," Jonathan said in a whisper. "How is it you come to be here, in this war?" There were other, more important things he wanted to ask, but he had to lead up to those questions.

He figured Sergei to be in his early twenties, though the young man seemed much older, probably because his rough existence had matured him quickly. As he told the story of how he had been drafted and gone through officer training, Sergei smiled ruefully. "Only when I finished my training did it finally occur to me, 'Oh, so that is why they made it so easy for me to be an officer—they only wanted to send a Lithuanian boy to fight their war.' But it was worse than I even imagined. A lot of soldiers were defecting, not necessarily for ideological reasons like I did, but simply because they were being beaten by the officers. And the miserable conditions—I knew four men who were reported as dying in combat, but two of them actually succumbed to cholera, and two more died from drinking a bad batch of alcohol some corporal cooked up on base.

"And then I started noticing other things. I saw women and children being massacred by ground troops . . . the bombing raids . . . the mines on the mountainsides . . ." He shuddered. "I began to ask some questions, which is always dangerous for a military man. Why were we sent to this country? They claimed we were here to liberate the Afghan people, but why was it the Afghans didn't seem to want to be liberated? And what kind of liberation could be so terrible that people would accept it only at gunpoint, if then?"

For a long time, Jonathan didn't say anything. In the dark, he couldn't see Sergei's eyes; he could only hear his words.

"Eventually I got to know some Afghan officers," Sergei went on, "which was not easy, in spite of all that propaganda about 'fraternal socialist nations.' They didn't like us, and most of the guys I knew didn't like them. But I got to know some of these Afghans and, once they got over their suspicions of me, we became friends. One of them even gave me a Koran, and he taught me how to pray. Then, one day he was gone, and I heard a rumor that he had defected to the mujahideen. After that, it was just a matter of time for me. A few weeks later, after our unit had totally destroyed a village and all the people in it—small babies and women too—I sneaked out of camp late at night and walked over to the other side waving a white flag."

He let his voice trail off, and then he cleared his throat, seeming embarrassed that he had revealed so much emotion to a stranger. "So," he said, sounding more cheerful, "are you ready for tomorrow?"

"Why not?" Jonathan answered. "How's my Latvian accent?"

"Is that Latvian?" asked Sergei with a chuckle. "I thought maybe it was German."

"That bad, huh?" asked Jonathan. "I figured it would be better, if pressed, to pass myself off as coming from one of the smaller republics, like yours. Less likely to run into anybody who would know the difference."

"Well," said Sergei hesitantly, "your accent is rather . . . hmm, well nobody who really listened to you would think for a second that you were a native. You sound like a foreigner who's lived in the USSR for a good solid five years." He chuckled. "So just where *are* you from, really? England? Canada? Or the United States?"

"Let's just say," said Jonathan, "that I'm a long way from home. But I have another question for you," he went on. His heart beat faster.

"Oh, but Commander Wright!" Sergei whispered back. "Here I've told you all about myself, and you will not even tell me where you are from?"

Jonathan shook his head in the dark. "It's better that you don't know . . . just in case."

"In case what?"

"In case something happened to us here and we were—questioned." He shuddered at the words, knowing full well that the Soviets would never just *question* anyone. Khalid, and the experience of his brother at the hands of the Butcher of Kabul, had made that clear.

"I do not think that's going to happen," said Sergei with confidence. "I believe we're safe."

"I wish I had your assurance," said Jonathan. "Or some amount of faith, but . . ."

"But what was it you wanted to ask me?" Sergei inquired.

Jonathan drew a breath, and as he spoke he measured his words so as to sound nonchalant. "I was just wondering," he said, "if you'd ever heard of an officer named Drakoff."

"Drakoff?" asked Sergei. "You mean the Butcher of Kabul?"

"I beg your pardon?" asked Jonathan, stunned.

"The Butcher of Kabul," Sergei answered. "Oh, he is a fearful man, known for his cruelty to—"

"Yes, I've heard of him," said Jonathan. The name *Butcher of Kabul* had been ingrained in his consciousness ever since Khalid first said it to him. When he first heard about him, Jonathan had wondered if Drakoff and the Butcher could be the same man, but it had seemed too perfect, and he'd long ago dismissed the possibility.

"Colonel Grigori Simonovich Drakoff?" Sergei said. "He is about forty or forty-five, I would say. Is that the one?"

"I'm sure it's the same man," Jonathan answered slowly.

"So what of him?" asked Sergei.

"I'm just wondering if you've ever seen him."

"Sure," said Sergei. "We are likely to see him tomorrow."

"*What?*" This appeared to be working out more perfectly than Jonathan ever imagined.

"Well, sure," said Sergei, seeming surprised by the reaction his words had drawn. "We are here to listen around the market stalls, right? To hear what the officers are saying about transports?" That much Sergei knew, though Jonathan and Ali had agreed that only *they*—and Massoud—would know the full reason why Sergei and Jonathan were in Kabul. And only Jonathan knew about his secondary reason. "Well," Sergei went on, "one of the best listening spots is a market I know near the Nejat, where Party members go frequently. You can often see Drakoff there just after lunch, when the bigwigs go out to do their shopping." He chuckled. "He is no bigwig himself, of course, but he is a sycophant, and you will always find him hanging around important people."

"Hmm," said Jonathan, too excited for words but trying to sound as casual as he could. "Maybe we can stop by."

"Probably," said Sergei, not sounding so confident now. "Only . . . keep in mind that it's dangerous to spend too much time in places like that."

"I don't want to put you in danger," said Jonathan. *Here was a man who had defected from the Soviet Army,* he thought. He couldn't get so caught up in his quest—even this close to his goal—that he sacrificed the safety of a comrade.

"Oh, I am not worried about the danger to me," Sergei answered coolly. "I am a survivor. It is you I am worried about."

"I'll be all right," Jonathan replied. "I'm just curious to see him, after all I've heard—that's all."

"Sure, sure," Sergei said. "Just be careful how far you let your curiosity take you. Sometimes it can be a dangerous thing."

Jonathan spent much of the night lying awake and thinking about Drakoff. He couldn't wait for the day to dawn and, therefore, when he should have been sleeping, his mind was racing. Not until two in the morning did he finally drift off, and he got barely four hours' sleep before Sergei was shaking him awake.

Still they began the morning full of anticipation, Jonathan donning the uniform of a senior lieutenant and Sergei that of a junior lieutenant. Of course, Sergei was flirting with danger even more than Jonathan, but he didn't expect to see any men from his old unit, the 66th Motor Rifles, which was based far away in Jalalabad. Besides that, after weeks with the mujahideen, often spending days on end out in the open, his white skin was tanned a deep chestnut shade, and he'd taken the additional precaution of dying his dirty-blond hair with streaks of dark brown.

So out they went, looking like Russian soldiers, and they were soon swallowed in a sea of people dotted with many of the same. Military men, as a rule, stayed out of the tight aisles of the larger bazaars, where boys were known to run up and stab soldiers while merchants looked the other way. Instead, they walked up and down Kabul's main drag, the Jadi Maiwand, a wide street with stores on either side. There they found shops selling native-made items such as karakul hats and pieces of marble and lapis lazuli alongside Soviet underwear, rusty cans of juice from Bulgaria, and other exports from the fraternity of socialist nations. There were also shops for sophisticated tastes, more likely to attract senior officers—German cameras, Swiss watches, Japanese radios, Italian boots, French lingerie for the mistress back home in Leningrad.

Trying to be as unobtrusive as possible, Jonathan nosed around some of these shops, but he didn't pick up any useful information. He did, however, notice a Soviet infantryman behind a market stall surreptitiously giving a boy a handful of 7.62-mm Kalashnikov ammunition in exchange for a pack of Turkish cigarettes. Sergei told him he'd seen similar exchanges many times, though often the Afghan currency was not cigarettes but hashish or even stronger drugs.

After several fruitless hours, they stopped to buy a couple glasses of tea spiced with ground cardamom. Leaning against a mud wall and squinting in the sunlight, Jonathan turned to Sergei. "Is that it?" he asked. "If it is, we're out of luck, I think." He was frustrated by their inability to turn up any promising information about Soviet transports, but he was thinking about something else too. It was almost time to go look for Drakoff.

"Not necessarily," said Sergei. He looked upward, thinking. "We talked about the Nejat last night, and I suppose we should go on there." He laughed and, with a whisper, added, "Especially if we are going to see your friend. But it is a good place to go anyway for what we need. If I knew I was going home on leave and wanted something to take back to my family, I would go to the Nejat."

"Is it nearby?" Jonathan asked. Involuntarily, his eyes searched the soldiers around him, eager to find one that looked like his vision of Drakoff.

Sergei took a sip of tea. "Just up the street here. Good sheepskin coats in the market, I have heard." He thought for a moment. "If I were a general, I might go to one of the Turkomen merchants and buy a rug for my wife, maybe to go in my dacha. Besides that, there are probably lots of little knickknacks you could purchase for a few rubles and take back to your family and friends—or even barter for them, like the guy back there with the bullets."

"Then let's go," said Jonathan—a little too eagerly, he realized as soon as he'd said it.

"You *are* in a hurry to see him, aren't you?" asked Sergei with a grin. "Just let me finish my tea."

"No rush, no rush," said Jonathan as he gulped down his own and set down his glass.

A few minutes later, as they strolled toward it, Sergei pointed ahead to the marketplace and said, "Nejat. The name means *salvation*."

The place was crawling with young soldiers and officers buying trinkets, apparently to take home. Surely he and Sergei had struck pay dirt—and more importantly to Jonathan, somewhere here he would find Drakoff.

As they drew closer to the market, they heard some sort of commotion behind them. Suddenly two trucks screeched to a halt in the middle of the bazaar, sending dust flying everywhere. A dozen or more soldiers jumped out, brandishing AK-47s with their fingers ready on the triggers.

Jonathan's heart leapt into his mouth, but Sergei appeared perfectly calm. "Look," he said, indicating a line of five limousines that came in behind the trucks. "*Nomenklatura*." Sure enough, a number of well-dressed civilian men got out, along with their wives. "They live in Microrayon," Sergei explained in a whisper. "It is a group of mid-rise apartments in the nice part of town—all the top advisors from Moscow live there, plus all the top Afghan officials."

"How many people?"

"I don't know, maybe 10,000."

"Hmm," said Jonathan, turning around and walking away from the Microrayon delegation. "Why didn't you think of going there before?" he said in a hoarse whisper. "I'll bet we could find out what we want in no time."

"You must be joking," Sergei answered, sounding irritated. "All of Microrayon is surrounded by barbed wire, plus tanks and Soviet and Afghan units. It's better guarded than the Kremlin. You don't get anywhere near that place unless you're supposed to be there."

Stopping at a distance from the group, Sergei turned back around. "Look at them," he said, and Jonathan saw the anxious faces of the officials as they wandered about, always with an eye out for the Afghans in the vicinity. "Those people live in complete fear for their lives. A man can bring his wife to Kabul, but children are not allowed because there is too much chance of kidnapping. Curfew starts for everyone else at 10:30 and goes to 4:00 A.M., but you will not find a Party member outside after 4:00 or 5:00 in the afternoon, and they don't come back out again until long after daylight."

"They're like prisoners," Jonathan muttered.

Sergei nodded. "And they will not let anybody break into their prison." He watched them for a moment, and started at the sound of a vehicle coming from the other direction. "Speaking of prison," he muttered, "there is your man."

Slowly Jonathan turned around and looked in the direction of Sergei's gaze. A vehicle, a UAZ-469, or some similarly jeep-like contraption, headed toward the group of nomenklatura. A man stood in the back. Dressed in a khaki uniform, amid the dust of the market stalls, he almost seemed invisible. But as the vehicle drew closer, Jonathan got a better look at him, and he could see the slumped shoulders, the hawkish face, the black eyes darting back and forth like a vulture's. And there was something else—

"He looks so . . . " Jonathan didn't know any other way to put it. " . . . small."

Sergei chuckled humorlessly. "Yes, I would say he is about 1.5 meters, maybe 1.6—sixty kilograms or so."

About five-two, Jonathan thought as he watched the man hop down from his place at the back of the jeep and walk over to where the nomenklatura were disembarking from their vehicles. *Maybe 130 pounds.* In spite of the imaginary, movie-star likeness he had created in his mind, Jonathan realized now that he had expected the man at the very least to seem powerful, almost noble in his evil. What he saw instead was a slender, tiny creature who looked like he could snap in two. Yet when the man glanced at the Afghans, he looked so frightening—his mouth in a tight smile, his birdlike eyes sharp as razors—several men stared at their feet to avoid his gaze.

Suddenly, as he approached the gathering of party officials, the snarl turned into a warped smile, and his overly large head lowered in something like a bow. His manner transformed into one of unmistakable fawning. The metamorphosis proved a chilling thing to watch.

"Some say he doesn't exist," Sergei whispered softly, "but there he is."

"There he is," Jonathan repeated. He could think of nothing more to say, because he was busy studying the face of the man, who smiled like a jackal at the party officials and their wives around him. Ten feet away from Jonathan, with his back to him, stood a soldier with an AK-47 strapped to his back. He would have no trouble creeping over next to that soldier while everyone's eyes were on Drakoff and the nomenklatura, grabbing the rifle, and spraying Drakoff with a hail of bullets. In a split-second more, of course, they would grab Jonathan and beat him to death—if they didn't shoot him on the spot. But Drakoff would be dead too. *Dead and in hell,* Jonathan thought. *And then I could die too—satisfied . . .*

And then suddenly his own thoughts arrested him. *If Drakoff murdered Jennifer and Jon, and he ends up in hell, where do I end up if I murder him? Do I end up being a cellmate for eternity with the man whom I think of as my moral inferior? How am I superior to him if I become a murderer too?*

He suddenly realized Sergei was speaking to him.

"I'm sorry, what did you say?" he asked.

Sergei laughed. "You went somewhere for a minute there, didn't you?" He gestured to Drakoff, who had said his farewells to the officials and began walking back to his jeep. With terrifying swiftness, he had dropped his ghastly smile again, and once again was all snarls. He walked with a strange, strutting gait, which he may have intended to take the emphasis off of his physical frailty, but it only emphasized his imperfections. Sergei peered at Jonathan. "You look like you have seen a ghost."

Jonathan shook his head. "Just the ghost of Khalid's brother," he muttered. *And Jennifer and Jon.* And somehow, too, he thought he saw the ghosts of the good men who had died in this mission. Neeley, Khalid . . . Or maybe it was just that Drakoff carried a whiff of death with him wherever he went.

"Let's get back to business," he said, a bit abruptly, to Sergei.

"Sure, sure," Sergei replied, still seeming almost amused, which for some reason irritated Jonathan immensely.

After a few more hours of walking around, hoping for more news, they still had heard nothing about any transport planes of any size leaving in the next week. Jonathan was beginning to realize their quest was a foolish one. "What was I thinking?" he told Sergei. "That they'd just lay out the information for us?" He shook his head. "No, this is starting to seem like too much risk without enough chance of success."

"Maybe if you told me a little bit more about what we're looking for," Sergei said helpfully, "I could think of a better strategy."

Again Jonathan shook his head. "Like I've said before, it's better for you to only know so much."

They were headed back to Rasul's and passed an empty lot across from a leather shop. Three or four young uniformed Russian soldiers had a soccer game going with a handful of Afghan youths. The whoops and cries as they raced up and down the lot seemed very natural, and both the Afghans and the Russians looked like mere boys.

"Maybe we—" Sergei was saying, but Jonathan nodded toward the scene unfolding in the empty lot, like something out of a propaganda film—but it was real. He glanced around to see who was watching, sure that these two opposing groups of people couldn't possibly be having fun together. But there was no camera crew, no delegation of Soviet dignitaries.

He glanced at Sergei.

"What?" asked the young man.

"Nothing," said Jonathan. Somehow he hadn't expected anything like this. Nothing in Kabul, it seemed, was as he'd expected.

Jonathan and Sergei hoped, because Friday was the Muslim holy day, that most of the Afghans would be at the mosque, leaving the streets more open and the Soviets easier to identify. But in spite of this advantage, they didn't have any better luck than they'd had the day before. After lingering in various markets without learning anything, they made a last-ditch stop at *Amin's Samovar*, a popular teahouse with a pro-Soviet proprietor.

The room was full of Soviet military, sitting at tables drinking and talking and laughing. Jonathan felt an adrenaline rush just being there, knowing he was about to put himself in the jaws of danger. He glanced at Sergei. *If he can do it,* he thought, swallowing hard, *and he's a deserter, then I can do it.*

A dimly lit, dingy place, *Amin's Samovar* consisted of one large room with two doors off to the right side, one for the kitchen and one for the latrine, and, at the back, a verandah with a scenic view of the sewers along the street to the rear. What light there was came from a set of shuttered windows open to the elements—including buzzing flies—along the front and back, as well as from a few bare bulbs hanging from the cracked plaster ceiling.

The proprietor kept three large teapots, or samovars, brewing on a table along the front wall, but this was mainly for appearance's sake. In fact, from the looks of the crowd and the noise they generated, a lot more vodka than tea was being served.

Jonathan and Sergei took a seat on the verandah, near the door of the back room. They had a good view of the street behind the bar, and they saw people moving along the cobbled way, too narrow for two vehicles to pass at the same time.

A few cars crept past the pedestrians, edging precariously along the *juie,* whose stench the wind mercifully blew in the other direction.

An Afghan with a dirty towel slung over his arm walked up to them. "Please to ask drinks for the sirs?" he said in broken Russian.

"Two vodkas," Sergei ordered.

Jonathan raised his eyebrows at his devout Muslim companion, but Sergei said under his breath, "You think a real Russian soldier would be drinking tea?"

Suddenly, Jonathan looked up to see two men standing over their table. For an instant he thought something horrifying was about to happen. But, then, he realized that they were just a couple of drunk lieutenants.

"Hey," one of them said, "you don't mind if we sit down, do you? There's no more room."

Great, Jonathan thought, glancing up at the two surly-looking young officers.

"Sure," said Sergei.

"Don't mind if I do," answered the first one, a short, tough-looking fellow with blond hair, as he took a seat and motioned for his friend to join him. "I'm Karamashvili," he said, and gestured toward his comrade. "And this is Zhormanidze."

"Georgians," said Sergei, nodding his head. "I'm Paradidas, and this"—he indicated Jonathan—"is Sakta."

"A Lithuanian and a—?" The blond Georgian looked from Sergei to Jonathan.

"He is Latvian," Sergei put in.

Jonathan instantly wished that he'd been a bit more proactive about speaking when the short one said with amusement, "What is the matter with him—Sakta can't talk?" He looked at his companion, and both men laughed drunkenly.

Lighting a cigarette, the blond one turned back toward Jonathan. "So," he said, *"if* you can talk, we're from the 373rd. How about you?"

"Sixty-Sixth Motor Rifles," Jonathan answered hurriedly.

"Oh," said the blond one, exchanging glances with his partner, "so he *can* talk—interesting accent there, Comrade Senior Lieutenant."

This conversation was making Jonathan increasingly uncomfortable. He supposedly outranked these two, and they were making fun of him. But he was too flustered to become indignant with them. Just then, noises from the street out back commanded his attention.

Welcoming the distraction, Jonathan asked "What is all this?" He pointed toward the street, where a procession of motorcycles and jeeps was making their way. Everyone, including those in cars, pulled over and let them drive straight up to the back entrance of the café.

"You have never seen a general before?" asked the short one with a sneer.

Two guards jumped out of the first jeep and ran past where the four men sat, then hurried into the restaurant and looked around before coming back out. The guards motioned to the second vehicle, a closed car. Several more armed guards exited, followed by a major and a major general. Instantly everyone inside the establishment stood, many of them adjusting their collars and buttoning their shirts in order to be in uniform when the general walked by. Jonathan and Sergei stood up along with the rest.

Everyone seemed to recognize the stocky figure whose sharp black eyes under the high-peaked cap seemed to take in each soldier as he returned his or her salute. "Is that General Kharitonoff himself?" Sergei asked as soon as they sat back down.

"The only Kharitonoff I know," said the tall Georgian.

Jonathan committed the name to memory. *Huh-REE-tone-off*, it was pronounced. He suddenly became aware that the shorter man was speaking to him. "I beg your pardon?" he said.

"Comrade Lieutenant," the short man said, "I'll bet you know an old friend of mine in your unit, a Lieutenant Zmetania—do you?"

Jonathan didn't answer immediately. The name could be real, or it could be a setup. In either case, if the unit were small enough, it would be ridiculous if he didn't know about this Lieutenant Zmetania. *Feel free to jump in here any second, Sergei,* he thought.

"Uh . . . our unit—" Sergei began, but the short man cut him off.

"I was asking your friend here, do you mind?" Turning back to Jonathan, he said patiently, "Please go ahead, Comrade."

Jonathan just smiled and shook his head. "I have only been in this country for two days," he said slowly, "and I have yet to meet your friend, but I am sure he is in the same unit as we."

The man laughed and again glanced at his friend. "Two days, and you're already getting to leave post?" He smiled, glancing at Jonathan's rank, and looked at Jonathan conspiratorially. "You must be some kind of troublemaker, if you're nothing but a senior lieutenant. A man your age ought to be a major at least."

Here we go, Jonathan thought. The interrogation had started. "Well, I'm a lot younger than I look," he said, looking the short man in the eye. "And I suppose they think I just don't yet have the experience to promote me to captain." Now it was time to take the offensive, and get the focus off himself. "So," he said, "you fellows obviously have been here long enough to leave post. You been home lately?"

The taller Georgian said, "I'm going home next week."

Trying not to seem too interested, Jonathan asked, "When does that flight leave, Wednesday?"

The short one looked straight at him and said, "I would think you would know, as every Soviet officer who's set foot in this country since the year began, knows— the flights go out every Tuesday at noon."

"Oh, of course," Jonathan answered absentmindedly.

"There's something odd about you, Comrade Lieutenant," said the short one, who seemed to be the spokesman for the two Georgians. "Why don't you tell us what it is?"

"Me?" asked Jonathan with a laugh, his mind racing. He didn't dare look at Sergei. The seconds ticked by as both men watching him impatiently, and though Jonathan didn't know what to say, he opened his mouth to reply.

Just then he saw the shorter man open his mouth too, as though to ask yet another question, but the words hung midway without coming out. Then a red spot appeared on the Georgian's forehead. Instinctively Jonathan knew that the next sound he heard would be the report of a rifle fired from somewhere across the street, and then it came.

Now the blond head, its short spiky hair already turning crimson, fell forward, and Jonathan dove to the floor, yelling for Sergei to do the same. At that very instant the taller one stood up as though he could ward off the shooter, and from somewhere an AK-47 peppered his chest full of rounds until he fell limply on top of his companion.

Gunfire erupted from the rooftops across the way, on the street itself . . . all around them. Their waiter, just now returning with their drinks, dropped his tray of vodka glasses, screaming and rushing to get out of danger. Plates, food, tea, and chairs flew in every direction. Soviet officers who, only moments before sat peacefully sipping their drinks, now scrambled for cover, and those unable to move fast enough had their bodies torn open by bullets.

Jonathan and Sergei knocked the table over and crouched on the floor behind it, though the thin metal top didn't give them much protection from the rain of bullets. Looking around for an additional shield within reach, Jonathan spied the carcass of the dead Georgian, and motioned to Sergei to help him push it over against the table. Then the two of them crouched down, flat against the floor with the body and the metal table shielding them from the gunfire. The dead man's face, his eyes hollow and rolling back in his head, stared at Jonathan, blood trickling from the side of his open mouth.

A grenade lobbed from the rooftop across the street and exploded off to the left. If it hadn't fallen just outside of a low concrete wall separating the verandah from the street, they would have been killed.

"Sergei!" Jonathan shouted, "let's see if we can crawl out the front!" Sergei nodded and started off crawling in that direction while the attackers fired into the main room of *Amin's*.

Reaching the inner doorway, Jonathan noticed everyone had scattered to the perimeter. The center of the room was empty except for dead bodies, broken vodka glasses, and a litter of tables and chairs. The wooden shutters along the front wall remained open, as they'd been just before the attack, since no one had volunteered to stand up and close them. Bullets whizzed straight through the windows.

Behind the stone wall and below the table that held the samovars, a man pressed his body to the floor, trying to protect his life like all the rest—General Kharitonoff. He motioned for his guards to move forward and establish a line of defense. The squadron commander didn't look too excited about this, but he did as ordered. He and his men began the slow movement out to the street.

The point man had just cleared the door when a stray bullet from outside hit one of the samovars. All of a sudden, scalding tea came gushing out all over the man at the back, who screamed and went running forward, pushing his comrades out of the way in his panic.

In the midst of this confusion, the snipers outside picked off the guards while a couple more set off satchel charges in the vehicles of the general's entourage. In rapid succession, five blasts rocked the room, sending chunks of concrete falling from the ceiling. The dim electric bulb overhead shook and flickered.

Jonathan knew they had to get out of there without delay, and he pointed toward the kitchen. He began crawling in that direction with Sergei behind him.

Just as they got inside the swinging door, they found the teashop's owner, Amin, sprawled out on the floor with his throat cut. At the far end of the kitchen, Jonathan could see a door to the outside, which locked by means of a heavy wooden slide-bolt lying to the side. "Through there," he whispered, rising carefully to his feet. But when he looked around for Sergei, his companion was gone. What had happened to him? Jonathan glanced back and forth for a split-second, wondering what he should do—and then the gunfire started pouring into the kitchen. He realized the attackers themselves would soon follow. Now it was every man for himself. He had to find a place to hide.

He crawled to the side, looking for another window or exit. Just when he'd made it to the far wall, the men outside blew the door open and rushed in, charging straight through the kitchen and into the main dining room. Watching them run through the room, straight past the corpse of Amin with its gaping eyes, Jonathan realized something as chilling as it was obvious. Their attackers were mujahideen. In the panic of the moment, he'd completely forgotten he and Sergei were posing as *Shuravi* and that anyone shooting at them must be a mujahid.

The Afghans out front stepped up the fire. Then, he heard shots inside the restaurant. The intruders had taken out more of the Soviet guards.

In the distance, he could hear sirens and knew they were Soviets—the friendlies. Maybe if he could hold on through this mess, they'd blow out the rebels, and he could escape in the confusion.

As he inched his head up to look around, he saw a mujahid ducking back into the kitchen. Wild-eyed, the man looked around, uncertain of which direction to move. Miraculously, his eyes passed right over Jonathan, who tried to work his body through the doors of a cupboard. It was no use. The tiny space would not accommodate him. *Don't look down here. Look away!* Jonathan thought, trying to influence the mujahid's actions. At that instant someone shouted to the man from the main room, and he went running in that direction. *Thank you, God.*

Just as he ran through the door, the man fell backward, bleeding from a fatal head wound. Jonathan didn't have to wait long to find out why. Through the kitchen door crawled General Kharitonoff, holding a 9-mm revolver in one hand and an AK-47 in the other. He stood up and peeked out the door, then thrust the rifle in Jonathan's direction.

"Take this," the general ordered. Jonathan did as he was told, and Kharitonoff motioned for him to come look out the kitchen door. "I just dispatched that bunch who came through the kitchen," he said, sounding casual. "But I'm afraid it's just you and me left to defend against the ones outside. We've got to hold them off until reinforcements arrive."

Plenty of Soviet officers could be found out in the main room, but Kharitonoff was right. None of them were alive—only a bunch of uniformed corpses spread this way and that. Jonathan glanced sideways at the general, then down at the rifle in his hands. For a split second, he thought, *I could just do the job right now—I'm probably going to die anyway, so I might as well get one of their generals.*

He grasped the rifle, considering the thought for a moment. But he took a moment too long, and the general gave him a strange look. "Did you hear what I said, soldier?" he demanded.

Jonathan didn't answer, but only stared back at the general. Through the clearing smoke, he could see the mujahideen preparing to enter the front of the building.

The general looked at him for a split-second more, then jerked his thumb toward a table by the wall. "Set that on its side in front of the doorway," he ordered.

Jonathan did as told, putting it in front of the kitchen door. The table wasn't one of those cheap metal affairs like the one they had used out back. Used for cutting meat, this hardwood table wouldn't allow bullets to penetrate it.

Three more mujahideen rushed into the teashop. General Kharitonoff looked over the table and fired three quick shots from his Makarov 9-mm, killing the first one. Jonathan raised the AK-47 and fired on the charging men until he'd dropped the other two. Another one ran in behind the first three, barreling toward the table. The general stopped him with one shot.

The scream of the approaching sirens grew louder. If they could hold on for ninety more seconds, it would all be over. Jonathan didn't even allow himself to think about what he would do then.

The mujahideen turned up the pressure. They had obviously still not achieved their objective in this attack—the killing of General Kharitonoff. Again, three more of the mujahideen jumped through the front window and charged the table, but Jonathan ripped out a burst from the AK-47 and took out two of them while the general shot the third one in the face. *I'm glad I'm on his side,* he thought, stealing a glance at the rugged figure crouched beside him.

Kharitonoff pointed to the seven men they'd killed together. "Good job, soldier," he said. "Now let's get ourselves out of here."

The sirens were now no more than two blocks away. The mujahideen were running out of time. Jonathan could hear footsteps out front, then he saw a number of Afghans scurrying by outside the front window. *They must be pulling out!*

But at that very moment, he heard behind him the sound of something dropping like a fly ball hitting an outfielder's mitt. He'd forgotten about the open window . . .

Jonathan dove at the satchel charge six feet away, grabbed it, flipped it over his head back out the window, and rolled farther away to his right, back behind the cupboard where he'd tried to hide before.

The general had turned around and, realizing what had happened, crouched, and stared wide-eyed at the window.

For a split second, Jonathan wondered if the thing would blow up or not.

The blast rocked the foundations of the building, spewing a gigantic cloud of smoke and debris out into the streets and slamming General Kharitonoff against the hardwood table. Jonathan was thrown up against the wall behind the cabinet and blacked out.

AVENGED

CHAPTER TWENTY-ONE

Jonathan slowly opened his eyes to glimpse a radiant being standing before him, a figure framed in a light so bright, he could barely make out the face. An angel. It had to be an angel. The figure turned slightly, allowing the light to illuminate her features, and he saw she looked more like the Virgin Mary. Either way, it had to mean the same thing.

"I'm dead!" he gasped in English as he sat up.

"What was that?" a soothing female voice responded in Russian.

Jonathan didn't reply. The woman moved closer.

"What did you say?" she asked again. She had blue eyes with long eyelashes that fluttered when she blinked, and a wonderful angelic smile.

Jonathan looked around, his thoughts becoming clearer. The woman had long, silky blonde hair tucked under her cap—a nurse's cap—and she wore white stockings on her shapely legs.

"Where am I?" he asked, switching to Russian.

"You are in the *góspetal'*," she said soothingly, putting her warm, soft hand on his forehead.

Góspetal'? His brain churned slowly. *The Hospital?*

He stared at her. Her features were fine, her nose delicate, like a woman out of a painting instead of real life.

A hospital, yes, but where on earth am I?

Her voice broke through his concentration, and it took him a split-second to realize she was speaking to him in heavily accented English. "Do you understand me?" she asked.

He had just enough of his wits about him to shrug his shoulders and grin at her like an idiot.

"You don't speak English?" she said, in Russian again.

"No . . ." He answered slowly, meanwhile trying to think fast. "I don't know."

This seemed to satisfy her—for now. "Very well. How do you feel?"

"I don't feel anything." Actually, his head was pounding.

"Well," she said, adjusting a pillow behind his head, "you have been through quite an ordeal." She studied his face. "You have had a concussion."

"How long have I been here?" Without turning his head, he could see only rough white walls, and felt a source of light off to his right.

She looked at her watch. "You have been asleep for almost exactly sixty hours."

Jonathan sat up, wincing anew at the pain in his left shoulder. He could just barely see a white bandage extending below the edge of the hospital gown sleeve. Slowly he lifted his head toward the light—a window—and tried to look out through the gauzy curtains. "Where is this hospital?"

The nurse gently guided him to lie back down. "You are at the 122nd Motor Rifle Division Headquarters, seventy kilometers southwest of Kabul."

Her words hit him like an explosion. *Oh . . . my . . . God . . . he thought. How am I ever going to get out of this one?* Suddenly everything came back to him—the intial attack on the tea house, the gunbattle alongside the general, and Sergei—what had happened to Sergei? *Poor devil,* he thought. *He didn't make it.* But Jonathan didn't have time to mourn the dead. Fortunately, he was still alive—but without a clue as to how to get himself out of this mess. "Who are you?" he asked.

"I am Katerina Semyonovna Witonovich, your private nurse, assigned by General Kharitonoff." She smiled patiently. "Everyone here knows who I am, but we would all like to know who *you* are."

The silence seemed to last for an eternity. He looked around the small room. The window and a small bedside table and floor lamp lay to his right, to the left a small chair and what appeared to be a door to the outside. He could see a toilet through an open door in front of him and, beside it, an open closet nook where a uniform hung. *How am I going to talk my way out of this one?* Jonathan thought, letting his eyes rest on the three-paddle fan suspended from the center of the ceiling.

To fall asleep, something his head wanted desperately to do, seemed by far the most prudent thing at the moment. In this situation, the less said the better.

"Yes, Doctor," came Katerina's soft voice, "he finally woke up about two hours ago."

A man's voice replied, "Hmm, very good. It does not seem to be a serious injury other than the concussion and a few cuts and bruises. The shoulder wound looks ugly, but it is superficial. Did he ever say who he was?"

"No. He doesn't seem to remember. And . . ." She paused.

"And what?"

"And his speech—there is something wrong with it. I think it may be the effect of the concussion perhaps. He sounds like he is having to think about every word he says."

"Strange," said the doctor. "Oh, well. The general wants him given special treatment regardless, and if the general says special treatment, that is what he will get. Let me know when he wakes again."

As soon as the doctor left, Jonathan opened his eyes as though he were just waking up. He feigned difficulty focusing on the nurse, though he could see her perfectly well. "Uh . . . I'm sorry, what was your name?" he asked.

She moved toward him. "Katerina."

"Katerina," he said weakly, "may I have some water?"

"Yes, certainly." She poured some from a pitcher on the nightstand into a glass. "How do you feel?"

"Like my head's about to explode," he said, without much exaggeration.

"You have to understand. You had a very serious concussion," she said, holding the glass up to his lips.

When he finished drinking, he asked, "How long have I been here now?"

She looked at her watch. "It has only been two hours since you woke up the first time, so a total of sixty-two hours." Two and a half days. That would make today Monday, he calculated with a rising sense of anxiety. What did they know about him? How much had they discovered in sixty-two hours? He could only play it by ear.

"Can you tell me who I am?" he asked, trying to sit up.

"Now, now . . . stay on your back," she ordered softly. With a gentle touch, she grasped his right shoulder and fluffed the pillows under his head. From the look on her face, he could see she thought he was a little brain-damaged—which was exactly what he wanted her to think. She stood back and looked at him, her eyebrows knitting in bewilderment. "Do you know which unit you are in?"

"Unit?" He gingerly scratched his head.

"Military unit."

"I don't know any military unit," Jonathan stammered. He thought for a moment. "I am an engineer," he added. "I live in Riga." He had already fabricated a background story for himself as Senior Lieutenant Sakta in Kabul. Maybe he could use parts of it to keep them satisfied here while he figured out a plan.

This new information seemed to get her attention. "Riga, in the Latvian S.S.R.?" she asked.

Jonathan nodded his head. "Yes. I am a mechanical engineer. At least, I think I am."

"No," Katerina replied. "You are a senior lieutenant in the Soviet Army."

"Are you sure?"

Katerina smiled and pointed to the uniform hung up in the open nook. "Well, you would appear to be, though you do not seem to have any identification."

She pulled over a small cart from the doorway and turned back a cloth to reveal a collection of bandaging supplies. Jonathan helped her ease the hospital shirt off of him.

"Apparently in all the confusion after the attack, when they were laying the bodies out," Katerina explained as she clipped away the old dressing, revealing a large ugly patch of scraped skin, "the medics thought you were dead. While this was happening, the Afghan street urchins sneaked in and stripped the unattended bodies of valuable possessions, including IDs, wallets, shoes, and whatever. You are lucky you didn't lose your uniform—most of the men came to us naked. It was awful. These people here live like animals." She sighed, selected some kind of ointment and gauze from the cart, then resumed talking. "By the time they discovered that you were still alive, someone had apparently already taken your identification."

She taped the last edge of the bandage neatly in place, then stepped toward the bathroom to wash her hands. Realizing that she couldn't see him from the wash-basin, Jonathan quickly reached over to the cart, took one of the rolls of tape, slipped it under the sheet between his legs, and replaced the edge of the cover just as Katerina turned back to him.

"Now that you are awake," she said, "the doctor will want to examine you. I'll go get him."

While she was gone, Jonathan secured the roll of tape between the mattress and bed frame.

When the physician arrived with Katerina a minute later, he looked carefully in Jonathan's eyes and checked his reflexes. "Nurse Witonovich says you do not remember much of anything before you came here."

"That's right, sir," Jonathan slurred. He glanced at Katerina and noticed that she didn't wear any rank insignia.

The doctor took out a pad and began to write. "I am afraid you are suffering from a form of post-traumatic amnesia. This is not particularly common, but it is not entirely unusual either—not with such a serious head injury. And you certainly did have a very bad concussion." He glanced up at a calendar on the wall, the only decoration in the room. "But I expect your memory will return in the next two to three days."

"Are you sure?" Jonathan asked.

"Well, I expect so."

"Is that always the case?"

"Even in the most severe cases," the doctor replied, "it is impossible to destroy all personal history, and at most one may forget the early years of one's life, or the most recent years may seem sketchy in recollection. In fact, the memory loss is normally greatest with regard to the time period immediately preceding the event which precipitates the loss itself."

"So it's possible that I may never know who I am?" Jonathan asked, trying not to sound eager.

The doctor shook his head. "No, it is not possible, simply because someone will find out who you are by checking the records. Once they do that, we can reconstruct your past and bring those memories back into focus."

"Oh, I see," Jonathan said. "How long will that take?"

"Well, it should not take very long. But do not worry too much—we will not need to start looking unless you continue to have difficulty piecing it all back together yourself. Now just relax. Later this morning, General Kharitonoff wants to come and visit with you." The doctor looked at the nurse. "And," he added in an ominous tone, "I am afraid he is not the only one."

Jonathan looked as innocent as a lamb. "General who?"

"General Kharitonoff," the doctor replied with a clipped tone. "He is the unit commander here. He said you saved his life on Friday."

"I did?"

The doctor nodded his head. "That is what he says. You were one of just three who survived the attack at *Amin's* on Jadi Maiwand—just you and he and Captain Rostov. Because you saved the general's life, he put you up in a private hospital room." He paused. "You are quite privileged. In fact, no one else has even been in this bed. Now—yes?"

"Who is Captain Rostov?" Jonathan asked.

The doctor glanced at the nurse. "Another . . . soldier . . . who had the misfortune to be at the wrong place at the wrong time. He is in the next room. No special guest of the general's like you, but—"Again, he glanced at Katerina. "—He has friends in high places too."

Wonderful, Jonathan thought. The general himself was already enough of a variable to deal with. What if this other guy said something that made Jonathan appear more suspicious? One thing was certain, though. The patient couldn't be one of the two Georgians.

"All right then," the doctor said, reading from a paper in his hand, "I am going to test your memory about some other things, to see what you might have retained. First of all, what country are we presently in?"

"Oh, that's easy," Jonathan answered. "We're in Kazakhstan, of course."

"I see." The doctor wrote in his pad. "The General Secretary of the Communist Party of the Soviet Union—who is he?"

Jonathan shrugged. "I don't know—Andropov, maybe."

"Who was the founder of the Soviet State?"

"Lenin." He didn't want to seem like he'd forgotten *everything*—that would appear a bit too suspicious.

"Complete this sentence. *Schee i kasha*—"

"'—*Pischa nasha,*'" Jonathan announced triumphantly. It was a common peasant's rhyme, "Cabbage soup and buckwheat are our food," and he had learned it long before, when he was first studying Russian.

"Good," the doctor said. "What is your name?"

Jonathan shrugged. "I told you I don't know—all I can remember is that I'm an engineer from Riga. But Katerina says that I am a senior lieutenant in the Soviet Army, so I don't know. I wish someone would tell me who I am, so I could get back to my job."

"Very well," the doctor said, turning to Katerina, who had hovered in the background, watching the entire exchange. "See that he gets some rest, and I will examine him again tomorrow."

After the doctor left, Jonathan asked Katerina if he could get out of bed, and she said she didn't see any reason why not. She prepared him by first talking him through the motions. But when Jonathan put his weight on his feet, he partially fell back on the bed and grabbed her for support. The room seemed to shift. When things stopped spinning, he found his face just inches from hers.

"Maybe I should try that more often," he whispered. She had a lovely scent, like fresh lemons and eucalyptus leaves.

"You need to keep your mind on getting your memory back." She folded her arms and pursed her lips into a stern frown.

"Well said, Nurse Witonovich," said a man's voice from the door behind her. Katerina turned to see who it was. When she moved, Jonathan had a clear view of the doorway as well. What he saw made him wish he could pass out once more.

Standing in the doorway, appearing smaller than ever and, if possible, twice as sinister as he had in the marketplace, was Colonel Grigori Simonovich Drakoff, the Butcher of Kabul.

"So," he said, stepping into the room with his strange, jerky gait. He acknowledged Katerina for an instant, pausing to tip his hat, but it was quite clear what—or rather *who*—held his interest. He studied Jonathan carefully. "I understand you are some sort of hero, Lieutenant—"

Jonathan held up his hands in a gesture of helplessness. For the moment, at least, he truthfully couldn't seem to find a way to speak.

Drakoff turned toward Katerina. "I understand from the doctor that he has had a memory loss, but I was not aware he had lost the ability to speak as well." He looked back at Jonathan, and his lips curled in a terrifying smile. "You seem almost to recognize me, Comrade Lieutenant—perhaps we are making progress already."

"He is very tired," said Katerina, and in spite of his intense discomfort at this moment, Jonathan couldn't help but notice the defensive, almost maternal, tone she took on his behalf. "He has suffered terrible injuries to his head. I do not think he needs a lot of questions right now."

"Of course," Drakoff replied. "You and the doctor, you are the medical minds. I am nothing but a soldier." He looked at Jonathan, his gray eyes studying the patient with intensity. "A taker of life, not a preserver. But"—now he turned to Katerina again—"I am simply doing my job as you are doing yours. I was called from Kabul because I learned of Captain Rostov's involvement in the—well, shall we say, *unusual* events at Amin's Samovar. However, I have been unable to speak with him."

"Yes," said Katerina softly. "He does not show any sign of coming out of his coma any time soon."

Jonathan surreptitiously watched Drakoff, who now stood very close to the bed. The man's ridiculously small frame again astounded him. His wrists were as slender as a teenage girl's. It would take very little effort, almost no effort at all, to reach out and grab that wrist and crack it with a single hard application of pressure. Drakoff would cry out, but Jonathan would not let go. He would just keep squeezing, twisting the arm behind the screaming man. By the time the guards arrived, Jonathan would have his hands around Drakoff's puny throat—

"I am sorry, am I boring you?" Drakoff interrupted Jonathan's fantasy with unmasked sarcasm. "Perhaps you had better listen more closely. I said the man in the next room survived the shooting at *Amin's,* just like you and the general—only he is one of mine, and I have supreme confidence in his intelligence. Therefore I have hopes he will be able to identify you when he wakes up."

"But even if he's not able to," Katerina put in, looking at Jonathan as well, "that doesn't mean anything."

"I suppose not," said Drakoff, walking to the foot of the bed with his hands behind his back, inspecting the hospital room. Bending over beside the window, he looked out. "But I do hope he wakes soon. Captain Rostov is one of my finest men."

Jonathan nodded his understanding, but his thoughts were churning. Drakoff must be KGB. If one of his men had been on the premises at *Amin's,* he had quite possibly seen Jonathan and Sergei. A trained spook might have noticed something out of the ordinary, something he would remember upon awakening.

"Does he not speak?" Drakoff asked Katerina, pointing toward Jonathan.

"I can speak," Jonathan said. He swallowed. "And believe me, I'm more eager than anyone to discover my true identity."

"Of that I'm sure, Comrade Lieutenant." Drakoff's upper lip curled into an evil grin. "Say, that is quite a command of the Russian language you have there—where did you learn it?" Jonathan just stared at him. He followed Drakoff's line of vision as he turned to look at Katerina. She wore the same stony expression he had given Drakoff. "Oh, I did not intend to be unpleasant," the colonel sneered. "It is just that—well, your accent—"

"It's Latvian," said Jonathan.

"I beg your pardon?"

"I'm from Latvia," Jonathan said. "At least I know that much."

Drakoff brightened. "Well, we are making progress! We will have you back to your unit in no time."

And with that, he tipped his hat to Katerina again and excused himself. But he paused at the door. "By the way," he said, speaking to Jonathan and Katerina at the same time, "since the patient is such an outstanding hero, I saw fit to arrange for a twenty-four-hour guard." He smirked as though enjoying a private joke. "That way, you should feel perfectly safe here, Comrade Lieutenant. I am sure this will mean a great deal to you, after your recent traumatic experience."

Jonathan managed to walk around in slow, measured steps with Katerina's help. He still felt a bit wobbly from the concussion and the medication. To top it off, his entire body felt sore, and his ears still rang from the explosion. But some of his pain eased with the awareness of Katerina's loveliness and the way his heart raced at her touch.

There wasn't much space to move around in the small room, particularly while leaning on someone for support. More importantly, he needed to get his bearings so that he could begin plotting his escape. "Do you think I could try my legs in the hall?" he asked.

Once again, she assented. They left the room with her walking next to him, her arm in his to help stabilize him as he moved. Just outside the door sat Drakoff's man, and he jumped up from his chair when they walked out. The beefy, almost bloated-looking guard studied Jonathan with beady, jaundiced eyes, but he said nothing.

Katerina and Jonathan set off at a slow pace down the hall, which stretched in front of them for about one hundred feet. He counted eight doors on both sides and a door at the end. When they had gone ten slow paces down the hall, Jonathan looked back to see the guard walking behind them, staring ahead with set jaws and a grim expression.

"Do not pay any attention to the *shpeeoni*," Katerina whispered back.

"The *shpeeoni?*"

"You know, the *Geh Beh*."

Geh Beh. The KGB. So his suspicion about Drakoff was right, and of course it made sense. Only KGB, or an extremely high-ranking officer in the regular military, would have had the power to authorize the shootdown of the KAL jetliner. "Did I do something wrong that I don't remember?" Jonathan asked.

Katerina shook her head. "At least, I do not think so." She looked at Jonathan with gentle, sympathetic eyes. "You do not seem like a criminal to me," she said.

At this point, they reached the door at the end of the hall. It had a small glass window and seemed to lead to another corridor, as best he could tell. They turned and walked back toward his room, passing the guard.

As soon as they traveled far enough away on the other side, Katerina whispered, "Drakoff must think you are a deserter or something. Normally, of course, if a senior lieutenant were missing, there would be a report out by now." She shrugged. "But I overheard the general talking earlier, and he said that our communications in the field are not very good—they are two to three days off, so it could be a week before your unit misses you."

"Oh," Jonathan said. He looked at her, and he knew she didn't have to share this information. He thought again of the look she had given Drakoff. Maybe he had an ally after all.

"Of course, this is all in confidence," she warned.

"Who would I tell?"

She shrugged and smiled.

As they returned to the room, Jonathan glanced back at the guard. Sure enough, he was faithfully following just steps behind them. If he had any doubt the man belonged to Drakoff's team, the trademark sneer on his face proved it beyond a doubt. *If Rostov is anything like these guys, I hope he stays out permanently,* he thought, glancing with apprehension at the closed door of the room next to his.

Jonathan was no sooner situated back in his bed when he heard a commotion in the hallway, followed by a flurry of footsteps and someone barking commands. Within seconds, the door burst open, and a major entered the room. He stepped aside and stood at attention by the door, without looking at Jonathan and Katerina. Then, General Kharitonoff, his left arm in a sling, marched into the room.

Jonathan seized his first opportunity to get a good look at the man whose life he'd saved. Kharitonoff appeared to be in his mid-sixties and was square-jawed and burly, with a generous sprinkling of gray in his short black hair.

Jonathan tried to ease himself out of the bed in order to stand, but the general put out his free hand and said, "No, Comrade Lieutenant, do not get up—please. It was soldiers like you that drove back the Nazis from the very outskirts of Moscow and Leningrad in the Great Patriotic War," he said as he stepped back and looked at Jonathan. "I have few men who fight with such courage, as Friday's attack proved."

Suddenly the general came to attention and cleared his throat. "Lieutenant, my family and I are forever indebted to you. I hereby grant you a battlefield promotion to the rank of captain, and award you the Silver Medal of Valor in recognition of your bravery in combat." He signaled the major, who opened a small box and held it out for the general.

The general removed the medal—a silver disk attached to a gray ribbon—and held it up for Jonathan to see the inscription *Za Otvagoo,* "For Valor." Jonathan couldn't help but notice that the red enamel of the inscription had chipped away a bit, but without blinking he solemnly returned the general's salute. The general pinned the medal to Jonathan's chest and said, "If all our men fought with such bravery and nobility, we would conquer this miserable country within a fortnight."

Jonathan felt a twinge of guilt as he listened to these words. If this distinguished officer knew who he really was, he would have him shot on the spot. "Thank you, sir," Jonathan said quietly. "It's an honor to serve under your command."

A lieutenant entered the room carrying a camera. "Captain," the general said to Jonathan, "would you mind posing with me for a photo? Who knows, we may make the pages of *Krasnaya Zvezda*." When Jonathan returned an uncomprehending look, the general said, "Ah, you *have* forgotten everything, haven't you? *Krasnaya Zvezda*, the army newspaper—twice as great an honor as the front page of *Pravda*, if you ask me."

"Certainly, General," Jonathan replied. The two posed together shaking hands.

When they'd finished and the photographer left, General Kharitonoff looked at his watch and said, "I must go now, but would you do me the honor of joining me for dinner tomorrow evening?"

By now Jonathan realized he had been mistaken for a hero in Kharitonoff's eyes, if not Drakoff's. But the invitation to dine with the general seemed a bit excessive. *Could it be a setup?* Regardless, he didn't have any choice but to say, "It would be a great honor, sir."

"Good, then I will have my adjutant here to pick you up at 1930 hours tomorrow." Kharitonoff motioned for the major to write the engagement down in his calendar, then looked back at Jonathan. "And we need a name for you." He had a twinkle in his eyes. "I will think of one—until we learn your real one, of course." He laughed heartily as he stepped to the door.

Katerina followed him out into the hallway. The general said something Jonathan couldn't quite hear and kissed her on the cheek. Kharitonoff then looked back at Jonathan and said, a little louder this time, "Look after our friend here." Katerina face wore a melancholy smile as the general left.

Katerina stepped back into Jonathan's room and moved to the side of his bed. As she helped him remove the pin from his robe and put the medal and insignia back in the box, Jonathan noticed tears welling up in the corners of her eyes. As she gently pulled the blankets over him, he wondered what the general could have said that would bring her to tears. She was clearly not the general's wife, and yet they seemed to have some kind of relationship. *Well, she isn't wearing a wedding ring. Could she be his mistress, perhaps?* he wondered. *But how could that be possible? She seems so pure and innocent!* It was obvious that something existed between Katerina and the general, but Jonathan had more urgent questions to ponder at the moment.

~

Jonathan slept right through lunch, which, according to the custom in the Soviet Army, was served at 1600 hours. By 1800 hours, he was starving, but he knew they wouldn't serve him another meal for hours. He tried to ignore the rumbling in his stomach by focusing on his biggest concern: Drakoff. For months now, Jonathan had dreamed of the day when he would find the man. He had wanted nothing but to track him down and kill him. Finally, after surviving all kinds of perils and through an almost miraculous chain of circumstances, he now had Drakoff within his grasp.

Only *he* was the one in a vulnerable position, not Drakoff.

He felt like a turtle on its back, a trapped animal, and his misery and isolation in this hospital room proved to be almost more than he could bear. If he weren't still recovering from the shock of the blast, he probably would not have been able to fall asleep that afternoon. But as it was, he drifted off—into a familiar nightmare scene from his childhood. His father was beating his mother while Jonathan, strapped to a bed and unable to stop him, watched helplessly.

He awoke just before supper came at 2000 hours. Apparently, the doctor had deemed him incapable of digesting a regular meal for the moment, for he received a steaming bowl of *kasha*, or buckwheat, along with two pieces of toast and a cup of tea. Despite the bland fare, Jonathan was famished, and he would have enjoyed it thoroughly if the guard hadn't entered the room with his own supper. The man said nothing, but sat in the chair near the door and gave Jonathan a sinister grin that revealed several missing teeth.

Although he was grateful for the kasha, Jonathan couldn't help but notice that the guard had been given a much more appetizing meal—*borscht* with a big plate of beef stroganoff, and a bottle of vodka on the side. He ate as though from a trough, letting the soup drip off of his chin and onto his lap, chewing with his mouth wide open, swilling the vodka the way a donkey drinks from a pail.

Another Ivan the Terrible, Jonathan thought, recalling Tchinkov's driver at the International Trade Mart.

Just then Katerina entered the room and moved about gracefully, silently taking care of her nursing responsibilities. Jonathan smiled at her, and she smiled back. But she kept quiet, trying not to attract the attention of "Ivan." But her efforts proved useless. Raising his vodka glass as though in a toast, he winked at her and let his lecherous gaze run over her body.

She shot him a look of disgust, and then glanced around the room one more time to make sure everything was in order. Pausing at the door, she looked straight at Jonathan with a warm smile and silently mouthed the words *"Good night."*

Ivan gazed after her as she shut the door, pushed back his plate, and produced a pack of cigarettes from his shirt pocket. He sighed, settling back in his chair. Jonathan couldn't believe the man was actually going to smoke in the hospital room, but he watched him light a cigarette and begin expelling foul-smelling clouds of thick gray smoke. Ivan took long, luxurious drags and blew the smoke straight toward Jonathan, seeming to enjoy the added fact that his captive was still eating.

Jonathan watched him and suddenly had a bright idea. "Excuse me, Comrade," he said, wiping his mouth with a napkin and pushing back his plate, too. Ivan looked at him, startled that he had spoken. "I haven't had a good smoke in days, and you know how they are in these hospitals—could I have one of your cigarettes?" He inhaled deeply, trying not to cough. "That smoke smells *great!*"

Glaring defensively at Jonathan, the man clutched his cigarettes to his side. "Buy your own," he growled. "These are expensive." But clearly, the Brer Rabbit strategy worked. Jonathan had taken all the fun out of Ivan's harassment, and when he was finished with the cigarette, he put it out on his plate and left the room.

Soon afterward, an orderly came in to remove the trays, and Jonathan had more time to lie in bed and think.

So far, his movements had been so limited and so carefully watched, he hadn't been able to observe very much in the way of useful information about the layout of his surroundings. From his window he could see two buildings on the other side of a road that passed between. But he knew nothing about the hospital or its location on the base, and he could hardly begin asking questions without raising even more suspicion.

Abdul would undoubtedly have observed what had happened at *Amin's*. But given the fact that Jonathan would probably be presumed dead—as was most likely the case with Sergei as well—he had little hope that news of his survival had reached Massoud. And even if it had, the mujahideen couldn't do much to rescue him. He would have to rely on his own resources.

The next opportunity for more extensive observation would be when he was on his way to the general's house for dinner the following evening. Perhaps in the meantime, he could convince Katerina to let him walk the hallway again—maybe even outside.

He needed to think. But he also didn't want to, because thinking only made him aware of the impossibility of his situation. Even if he did manage to get away from the base safely, that didn't put him any closer to his objectives. Yet if he didn't act soon, he would become the victim of the same man who had killed his wife and child half a world away.

Jonathan's mind continued to race. With Ivan on guard—or at least his night-time replacement—he could do nothing at the moment except wait. And sleep. But he had already rested so much today, he wasn't sleepy anymore.

He reached over to the table by the window and picked up a copy of *Pravda*. Scanning the headlines, he saw plenty of "news" about events back in the States. The Russian propaganda was heavy. There was a trial in progress. Claus von Bulow, a wealthy scion of the privileged classes, had been charged with murder and would undoubtedly be acquitted. And the government in Washington was persecuting William Walker, a brave U.S. Naval officer, and conscientious lover of peace, because he had sold certain defense secrets to the Soviet Union.

There was more, but *Pravda* got old pretty quickly. He found a book at the back of the drawer in his nightstand, but his heart sank when he read the title, *Poems of Andrei Voznesensky*.

Jonathan opened the book and began reading. He was surprised to find himself drawn in—perhaps because the language and images helped him escape from his current circumstances—at least in his mind. One poem in particular caught his attention. The piece, called "Wedding," made him wonder anew at the nature of the relationship between Katerina and General Kharitonoff.

> *Oh how many of you, girls,*
> *Beautiful idiots and fools,*
> *Have perished for epaulets,*
> *An apartment and the furnishings!*

Once again, Jonathan couldn't bring himself to believe that a woman as beautiful and sweet as Katerina could fit such a description. His thoughts began to drift from escape plans to beautiful angels as he fell asleep with the book on his chest.

Some time around 11:00 P.M., he awoke with a start to see a man standing over him, a sour-looking Asiatic with a flat face and narrow eyes. Jonathan realized this must be Ivan's shift replacement—doing his best to intimidate the prisoner. The guard looked like something out of a nightmare, and Jonathan wished he would wake up to find himself back in Kabul—or better yet, New Orleans.

CHAPTER TWENTY-TWO

The next morning, Jonathan awoke once more to a vision. He stared at the beautiful face before the window, the radiant sunlight creating an aura around her. "You remind me of the Madonna in the painting by Leonardo," he said softly.

"What is that?" She looked up, startled.

Why can't I keep my mouth shut with her? he thought. *Remember, she's still the enemy.* But he continued, "I saw it in the Hermitage in Leningrad, I think. You remind me of that painting."

She smiled, embarrassed. "I have seen that painting, but I hear there is another one in the Louvre that is considered even more beautiful."

"Oh?" said Jonathan. He realized he had seen both of them, and the one in Paris was, in fact, better known. Maybe that was the one he was thinking of, and if so, he had just proved to himself why he should keep his mouth shut. Beautiful as she was, she was still a Soviet.

"Tell me," she said, assuming a businesslike manner, "how was your night?"

"Ah, it was fine," he said.

"You do not sound convinced."

He shrugged, and nodded toward the door. "My protector looked in on me pretty regularly during the night."

Katerina frowned. "Well, the *shpeeoni* must be up to their typical tricks. I am sorry about that." Holding her clipboard to her chest, she walked toward the bed. "Let me check your vital signs."

As she drew closer and put a cool hand on his arm, her beauty affected Jonathan even more than before. There was something gentle about her, something sensitive. He held up the volume of poetry. "Is this your book?" he asked.

Glancing at it, she shyly lowered her head, "Yes. I wondered where that was."

"So you like poetry?" he asked.

"Oh, yes," she said. "Mayakovsky, Yesenin, Akhmatova, Mandelshtam . . ." Then she stopped herself. "Of course, with some of those people, you cannot tell just anyone you read them." She glanced toward the door. "It could get you in trouble with people like our friend."

"I doubt he's ever heard of any of them," said Jonathan with a laugh. The truth was that he hadn't either.

"What do you read?" she asked.

"Not poetry," he answered. "Nothing really that I can remember, except maybe engineering publications and the like." He offered the safest answer he could give, since naming Robert Ludlum or Frederick Forsythe was out of the question.

"What a shame," she said with a trace of disappointment. "The way you appreciate art and the way you seemed to take interest in that book, I thought you would have a greater interest in literature."

Jonathan shrugged. He looked down at the volume of poetry. "What do you think of Voznesensky's 'Wedding'?"

"Oh, I don't know," she said with a wave of her hand. "It is certainly a very precise—almost cruel—portrait of a certain type of woman who sells away all that's dearest to her just so she can have some comforts of life."

"Do you know any women like that?"

"Of course, everybody does."

"Yes?"

"Why do you ask such a question," she said, laughing nervously. "Is that so hard to believe?"

"No reason," he answered, trying to think of some way to change the subject. "So," he went on, "tonight I visit General Kharitonoff."

"Yes," she answered, seeming a little puzzled by his manner. "I am sure you will enjoy the general's company. He has always been very kind—"

At that moment, the door suddenly flew open, and a guard—not Ivan but one of his alternates—stomped in. "Colonel Drakoff is on his way!" he announced. The guard stood stiffly beside the door and scowled at them for a full thirty seconds until the KGB colonel strode in.

Drakoff wore his khaki uniform as always, with gloves in hand and a military overcoat slung over his shoulders, which made him look very much like the stereotypical Nazi officer Jonathan had imagined he would be. But his small size seemed incongruous with the uniform, and if he resembled any Nazi it was Josef Goebbels, Hitler's scrawny, club-footed propaganda minister.

"Comrade Lieutenant," Drakoff began, a thin smile on his lips. "Or should I say Comrade Captain, since our general has seen fit to reward your valor?"

"Yes, sir," Jonathan answered, lapsing into his brain-damaged concussion victim role. "Is there something I can help you with?"

He had meant it to sound accommodating, but from the look on Drakoff's face, he could tell that the other man had taken it as sarcasm.

"Oh, no," Drakoff answered, "it is I who want to help *you*. And to do that," he said, "I need to know what you do know. I must learn more about your past."

"Well," said Jonathan, glancing up at Katerina, who watched the interrogation with thinly veiled hostility. Now that Drakoff was in the room, she seemed more distant, but that could be only because she didn't want the KGB man to think she was getting too close to her patient/prisoner. "I have some vague memory of being at university, then working as an engineer." He met the colonel's gaze as calmly and openly as possible, even though the sight of the man filled him with revulsion.

"Then why can you not remember how you came to be at *Amin's* last Friday?" Drakoff demanded.

Jonathan shrugged, the picture of innocent confusion. "I don't know, sir, it's not coming to me. It's as though everything is clear up to a certain point in my life, then it goes blank."

"No matter," Drakoff announced. "We're checking all the units and circulating your photograph among them." He looked significantly at Jonathan. "And more importantly, of course," he added, "there is Captain Rostov—I am sure he will be able to offer a great deal of insight, as soon as he wakes up from his coma." He glanced at Katerina. "That should be soon, yes?"

She nodded her head meekly, but said nothing. The fact that she had been tending to the other patient—a man who could very well provide Drakoff with information about Jonathan and Sergei that might blow his cover completely—made Jonathan feel somehow betrayed.

"I understand you are to have dinner with General Kharitonoff this evening. Do give the general my regards when you see him," Drakoff said to Jonathan. "But do not worry, *Captain,* I will return, and we will talk again." He looked once more at Katerina, then turned and marched out the door, followed by the guard.

As soon as they were gone, Katerina turned to Jonathan. "That man has a bad reputation, I should tell you," she said. "You must be careful."

Her comment, even though it didn't tell him anything he didn't already know, surprised Jonathan. He felt bad for thinking she was one of *them.* "So tell me," he said boldly, "what do you know about this Captain Rostov?"

She shook her head. "The doctor who came and examined you yesterday—he has also been in charge of Rostov." Looking a little embarrassed, she said, "Believe it or not, even though you are the general's guest, they have placed a higher priority on him than on you."

"Well, he *is* in a coma," said Jonathan helpfully.

"Yes . . ." she answered. "But it is more than that. He is one of Drakoff's men, you know." She held up a finger and lowered her voice to a whisper. "The rumor is that before the blast, he was to meet Drakoff at *Amin's* to give him some important information. But the attack happened before they could meet, and since then he has been in a coma."

"And Drakoff thinks I'm involved?" he asked in unfeigned naiveté.

She nodded her head.

The thought of Rostov made him squirm in discomfort. What if he really had been tailing Jonathan and Sergei in Kabul? What if he had seen them watching Drakoff in the marketplace that day and then followed them to *Amin's?*

Looking into his eyes, Katerina said, "I should not say this, because it goes against all my commitments as a nurse, but—" She looked away. "We should both pray that Rostov does not wake up for a long, long time."

His heart leapt. She really was on his side—there was no mistaking it. Cautiously he reached out to grasp her hand, but she pulled back. "I do not think you have anything to worry about right now," she added in a whisper, not looking at him, "but the first chance I get, I will ask the doctor how Rostov is coming along."

It was almost as though she had not noticed his attempt to touch her. But when she looked back at him, he could tell from her flustered expression that it hadn't escaped her attention. "Now," she said, again in a businesslike tone, "you need to focus your attention on getting better." With a significant look, she added, "You are going to need all of your energy. What you do not need are distractions."

Katerina left for part of the day, then returned in the afternoon, and they talked for almost two hours, with Jonathan trying very subtly to find out more from her about the base and its location. The only interruption was Ivan—now rested and more obnoxious than ever—who came in every hour or so and looked around, flagrantly defying the general's order to stay out of the patient's room.

At precisely 1930 hours, Kharitonoff's adjutant entered. "Comrade Captain," he said cordially, "the general is awaiting your arrival. I will escort you to his quarters now."

"Thank you, sir." Jonathan wore a dress uniform, which had been provided for him, complete with the gleaming insignia of his new rank. His shoulder felt stiff and sore, but the coarse uniform did not rub too badly, and he found he could move his arm fairly well. He hadn't really had enough time to plan for tonight, and now it was upon him. Drawing a deep breath, he said goodbye to Katerina and followed the major out past a glowering Ivan.

Walking through the hospital, Jonathan learned his room was on a wing situated at a right angle to the main entrance, where they exited to find a waiting automobile with the general's flag flying from its front antenna.

On the short five-minute drive to the general's quarters, Jonathan stole glances out the window while chatting with the major, but learned little of the base's layout. The car passed down a street with several low concrete buildings on either side before turning right onto an intersecting street with similar buildings. There was some open space here and there, but he had no sense of just where the compound's boundary or the main entrance was.

Once the vehicle arrived before an old two-story stucco building, Jonathan gingerly stepped out and followed the major up the steps, through the foyer, and into the general's office, a large square room with cracked white plaster, where Kharitonoff was apparently just completing a telephone conversation. Jonathan saluted, a courtesy that the general returned before motioning for him to sit down.

The red plush chair offered him was part of a matching set, probably antique, and the general's desk appeared to be made of mahogany. The old-fashioned elegance of the furniture contrasted sharply with the shabby walls.

"Well, my friend," said Kharitonoff when he had gotten off the phone, "how are you feeling today?" The general's smile seemed to extend from his dark eyes all the way across his rugged, square face.

"Doing much better, sir."

"Good. You certainly look much better—I see a little color is returning into your face. We have a table set here in my conference room. Shall we adjourn there?"

They entered to see a table set with white linen, china, silver, and crystal, and the general offered him a glass of vodka. Jonathan politely declined, claiming a fear of reaction with the medications he was receiving in the hospital. This situation was going to be tough enough even stone-cold sober.

Two enlisted men served them their first course, a traditional type of hors d'oeuvres called *zakuski*, which included *ikra*, or caviar. Of course the general had obtained the highest-grade beluga. In the U.S., it would cost $100 or more an ounce.

"Well, Captain," the general said, "I am certainly glad that you are dining with me tonight." He raised his glass toward Jonathan. "And if not for your quick thinking four days ago, perhaps neither of us would be here today. The Soviet Army—not to mention me personally—owes you a great debt. Can you imagine the propaganda coup the counter-revolutionaries would have had if they had me taken out?"

Jonathan had a mixed response to these words, yet there was nothing he could do but nod. Besides, everything had turned upside-down in the past week. Shot at by his allies, drinking with his enemy . . . nothing made much sense right now.

"Yes, sir," Jonathan answered. "I was just happy I could be there to do my duty."

The general gave him a funny look and said, "Yes, I am sure you were."

Next came the borscht, beet soup with sour cream to which the cook had added some Afghan herbs. They also opened a bottle of Russian white wine. Jonathan knew he couldn't continue to refuse the general's offers of alcohol, and he found the wine just as good as all but the best French Chablis.

"So," the general said after a toast *za mir*—to world peace, "I understand you are from Latvia. Tell me all about it. I was posted there once, and visited one other time on a holiday with my wife. I found it to be a beautiful region."

"Yes, sir, I agree," Jonathan said. This was truly a difficult situation, and his only hope would be to turn the discussion back to the general or onto some other topic. "I certainly think it's wonderful myself, particularly when you compare it to Afghanistan."

"Well, of course," said the general with a laugh. "When I retire, it is going to be to a dacha with a vegetable garden I can tend, and it has to be someplace with nice, rich soil like Latvia or the Caucasus, where I come from. No sand or rocks—I've had quite enough of that here."

"I don't think I have ever been to the Caucasus, sir," Jonathan said. "What is it like there?"

That got the general started, and from there, Jonathan kept encouraging him to talk. Soon he realized, to his extreme relief, he hardly had to say a word. He would introduce a topic by asking a question, and the older man would take it and expound on it with his considerable knowledge.

For the main course they had beef tenderloin, which was so tender he hardly needed the sharp steak knife that had been provided. Surreptitiously, Jonathan glanced at the blade. It could prove to be very useful, provided he had a chance to take it without being discovered.

"How do you find the wine?" the general asked. They had now switched over to a five-year-old Russian red.

"It's quite good," Jonathan answered. Actually, in spite of the fact he had plenty else on his mind tonight, his practiced palate told him the wine was a bit too young a grape to be drinking.

The general watched his face closely. "Do you not find the tannin a little heavy on this one?"

In fact Jonathan did, but a Latvian engineer—probably surviving on a couple hundred rubles a month—would know nothing about fine wines. He shook his head. "Tannin? What is that?"

The general smiled. "Oh, it just has to do with the age of the wine."

"I see," Jonathan answered. *Was that a trap, or was he just making conversation?*

The two enlisted men served the salad last, in the European tradition. As the meal ended Jonathan found himself, somewhat to his astonishment, conversing easily and comfortably with one of the highest-ranking Soviets in Afghanistan.

"Mikhail Filippovich!" the general said suddenly, startling his guest. "That is what I shall call you. I have been perplexed. You cannot remember your name, and I cannot very well sit here and call you nothing, and I grow tired of calling you only *Captain*."

"Yes, sir," said Jonathan. There wasn't much else he could say.

"Oh, you wonder how I choose a name like Mikhail Filippovich?" the general asked. "Mikhail was a very close friend of mine, someone I enjoyed and respected very much. So until we discover your identity, you will be Mikhail Filippovich—it is quite a compliment."

"Thank you, sir," Jonathan replied.

"Mikhail Filippovich," the general announced, "when we are here alone, please—I'm tired of being *sir* and *general*. You have saved my life, and because of that we are friends as well as fellow officers. So when you are in my home, call me by my first name, which is Andrei. Andrei Vassilyevich. No, I see you are shocked. Very well, then. I command you—when we are alone, you will call me Andrei Vassilyevich. Indulge an old man."

"Certainly, Si—, uh, Andrei Vassilyevich."

The general laughed. "Come." He rose, placing his napkin neatly on the table and lifting his wineglass. "Let us finish off this glass of wine in the parlor so the men can clear the table."

As his host rose and turned to the door, Jonathan looked down and saw that the general's steak knife had somehow not been removed after the main course. In an instant, he checked to see if anyone was watching, but one steward was working at the sideboard and the other had left the room. Jonathan deftly palmed the knife and slipped it up his sleeve.

"Are you coming, Mikhail Filippovich?" the general asked, turning around now.

"Oh, yes—"

The general held up a finger. "Is there something you wish to say?"

Way to go, idiot! Jonathan thought, his heart hammering in his chest. *What a stupid move—he must have seen me take the knife.* "Uh, what's that?" he managed to stammer.

"What is my name?" asked the general with an indulgent smile.

"Andrei . . . Vassilyevich?"

"Good," said the general, turning and leading the way into the parlor. "Now that you have remembered it, please use it."

Jonathan panted with relief as he followed the general down the hallway.

In the parlor, sturdy teak bookshelves stood on either side of a handsome fireplace with some sort of coat of arms on it, and the walls were a soft gray—much more pleasant than the rest of the house. A chessboard sat on a marble pedestal between two comfortable leather wing chairs drawn up before the fire.

As he paused behind one of the chairs, Jonathan slipped the knife into his pants pocket, where he hoped no bulge would show. "So, Mikhail Filippovich," the general asked, setting down his glass beside the chess board, "are you a chess player, or do you remember?"

Jonathan nodded slowly. "Yes, Andrei Vassilyevich. I believe I remember playing, but I think it must have been a long time ago." It had been. In high school, he had enjoyed playing chess to offset his "dumb jock" image and got to where he could beat all but the best of the nerds on the chess team.

"Oh, it is no matter," the general laughed, "I would beat you anyway."

Jonathan eased into the chair; the knife stayed put. Just then one of the aides brought in two brandy glasses, and the general inquired whether or not his guest would care for some Napoleon.

Jonathan accepted, and after that another aide brought in a box of cigars. Hesitant to refuse, though he detested tobacco, he inwardly grimaced as he took a fat cigar. At least he didn't have to inhale the repulsive thing.

Both men bit off the ends, and the aide flourished a cheap Russian lighter with which he lit the general's cigar. Puffing violently until a cloud of smoke erupted all around him, the general waved the lighter away, and it was Jonathan's turn. The heat and strong taste of the thing nearly knocked him over just getting it lit, but he endured it, and they sat back with their glasses of Napoleon brandy.

"You know," the general said, obviously enjoying his cigar so much that it made Jonathan wish he could as well, "Fidel Castro gave me a box of cigars once when I was in Cuba." The general had a faraway look in his eyes. "He promised me I would receive another supply every May Day."

"Oh yes?" Jonathan asked. "Very interesting. So you've spent some time in Cuba?"

"Yes, once. Long ago." Still with that misty-eyed expression, he went on. "Cuba—ah!—wonderful beaches. My wife loved them."

"I'm sure you miss your wife," said Jonathan, though he wasn't sure if he should get so personal with the general.

"I miss my wife, I miss my daughters, I even miss Cuba." The general took a sip of his brandy. "I miss a lot of things—many things I've had to give up in my zeal to defend the Motherland. But now, well, here I am—" He waved his hand around the room. "—In this vile place." Laughing, he said, "Of course, many would say a life that includes meals like the one we just enjoyed must not be all that bad, but they don't know."

Jonathan didn't quite understand the gist of that last sentence, because the general's phrasing was rather complex. But he comprehended well enough, especially when he saw the look in the general's eyes. He was finding it awfully hard not to like this man.

"Well, Mikhail Filippovich," Kharitonoff now said, sitting back with his cigar, "soon enough you will be telling me all about yourself as your memory returns, so before that I had better get in a little about myself." The general proceeded to tell him about his Cossack lineage—his grandfather who was a counter-revolutionary and perished in the Civil War in the early 1920s, his father who took part in the defense of Leningrad during the nine-hundred-day siege by the Nazis during World War II and then died in an Arctic labor camp.

"And then there is me," he said, and Jonathan thought Kharitonoff was about to fulfill his earlier promise and tell about himself. But instead he looked at the clock and stood up. "However," he said, "it is getting late, so I will have to let you get back to your room." He extended a hand. "I thoroughly enjoyed our conversation."

"Yes," said Jonathan, standing as well and returning the handshake. "So did I."

"And since I am indebted to you," the general said, putting a hand on Jonathan's shoulder and guiding him toward the front door, "I hope you will do me the honor of joining me for dinner as long as you are being cared for in the hospital. I expect the hospital food is not very enjoyable."

"Oh, sir, that is very kind," said Jonathan, a slight feeling of panic welling up, "but it is not necessary. I am sure you are much too busy to have me taking up your valuable time."

"Oh," Kharitonoff laughed, "you wouldn't want to refuse—and please remember, I asked you to call me Andrei Vassilyevich." He smiled. "Besides," he went on, "I very much enjoy stimulating conversation." They had reached the front door.

"I'm afraid I've done all the talking tonight—perhaps tomorrow I shall learn a little about you and your Republic of Latvia, hmm?"

"As you wish—Andrei," Jonathan replied. He had the sinking feeling that he was about to be sent to school to give an oral report on something he hadn't studied—but instead of being given an F, he would simply be tortured to death.

"Then it is settled," Kharitonoff said, clapping his hands for one of the enlisted men to scurry out and start the car. "I will have one of my aides pick you up tomorrow evening around 1900. Meanwhile, do you need anything?"

Jonathan seized the opening. "No, I am well cared for, but I would like to have permission to walk around outside to get my strength back if that is possible."

"Of course. Now go and sleep well."

On the ride back to the hospital, Jonathan reflected on the evening's events. Under different circumstances, he might have enjoyed his time. The general had been a gracious host, and he had enjoyed his company.

Still, all of this could be a trap. The feel of the cold steak knife pressing through the fabric of his pants pocket was comforting but, in actuality, was a pitifully inadequate weapon. And what if its loss was discovered?

The answer to all his problems would be to escape as quickly as he could. Perhaps freedom to walk outside would give him a better picture of the base and what it would take to get safely out. Of course, escape meant he would have to sacrifice his *other* goals—at least temporarily—but he had to think about survival now.

When he got back to the hospital, he saw that Ivan's replacement was on duty. Once inside his room, Jonathan took the knife from his pocket and taped it tightly under the lip of the washbasin in the bathroom, a spot where he had earlier hidden the roll of tape. He sat down on the toilet seat to make sure Ivan would not be able to see it if he came in to use the bathroom. When he felt satisfied that he had properly secured it, Jonathan prepared for bed.

He had just slipped under the covers when a gentle knock came at his door and Katerina entered.

"Katerina," he said. "What—"

"I am sorry to bother you," she said, addressing him in a formal tone. Even though it was long after the hours of her shift, she was dressed in her nurse's uniform. "But I have been instructed to come for you."

"For what?" asked Jonathan, fully on guard now. He wished he hadn't had so much wine and brandy at Kharitonoff's, but the general had insisted.

"Drakoff," she answered. "He demanded that you be brought in to see Captain Rostov. He wanted to do it himself personally tomorrow. However, I think I will escort you over there tonight."

"All right then," said Jonathan, relieved it wasn't anything worse. He was wearing his hospital gown, and she handed him a bathrobe hanging on a hook beside the bathroom door. Throwing off his covers and putting on the robe and a pair of slippers, he followed her into the hallway.

Ivan's replacement seemed to be gone. Katerina turned around and put a finger to her lips. "Quiet," she said gently, as she pushed open the door of the next room.

He followed her into the room. Several types of life-support equipment surrounded the bed. Another nurse sat beside an EKG machine, and she looked up briefly at Katerina and nodded. Jonathan stood behind Katerina, who now turned around and beckoned him to the bedside. "Come," she said.

The man lying in the bed had his face and body bandaged in several places, including his forehead. Machines registered his heartbeat and brain waves. Another machine controlled his breathing. Rostov's head lay back on the pillow, his chin raised, which made it hard to see what he looked like. Besides, his face was scarred, and his eyes were covered with bandages.

Katerina nodded to the nurse, who now carefully pulled back the eye bandages. "Come look," Katerina whispered to Jonathan, so he stepped closer to the bedside to get a better view. He was just going through the motions anyway. He wouldn't know Rostov, and he hoped Rostov wouldn't know him.

"Do you recognize him?" Katerina asked. She gestured to the man, and Jonathan let his eyes focus for a moment on the man's face. He studied the mouth, the nose, the chin, the cheeks—the *eyes*—and a growing sensation of horror overcame him.

He wanted to fall to his knees.

My God, he thought, barely able to contain his revulsion at what he saw. *It's Sergei.*

For a few seconds, no sound broke the quiet of the room except for the hum of the machines.

"You don't recognize him?" asked Katerina again.

"I have never seen him in my life," Jonathan managed to whisper.

CHAPTER TWENTY-THREE

The sight of Rostov—or rather, Sergei—was so unnerving, Jonathan didn't sleep much that night. But at least a reassuring sight greeted him when he awoke the next morning—Katerina's angelic figure, once again backlit by the sun filtering through the window. "Ah," he said softly, "my Madonna returns."

Katerina turned toward him with a troubled look. "Please don't call me that," she said in a soft voice.

"Why?" he asked, sitting up in bed.

She glanced at the door, although they appeared to be alone. "I am not worthy of such a name."

"What do you mean?"

She turned away. "It is nothing."

"No," said Jonathan. "I want to know."

Katerina was silent for several moments before finally saying, "My grandmother says she prays for me, but I have not found much hope or comfort in my family's religion." She looked at Jonathan. "I have been studying this a bit, and the old traditions feel so cold and empty. Often lately I have felt something is missing. I have wondered whether God is truly real, and whether He cares much for me. What do you believe?"

Suddenly Jonathan became wary again. Why was she so eager to discuss religion with him, when all he had done was make a reference to the Madonna? Was there a bug in the wall somewhere, and they had told her to obtain any incriminating evidence on him that she could?

But she seemed sincere when she sighed and said, "Sometimes I just feel so empty—" Her voice trembled, and she held out a hand in frustration. "I can't even say your name, because I don't know it, but . . . whoever you are . . . I do feel so empty sometimes, and I look for something bigger than myself."

"Well—" He hesitated, choosing his words cautiously. "I do believe there is something bigger than ourselves, and I have begun to hope that He can bring the peace I have been missing."

She seemed like a person who once had known peace but had lost it. *How strange*, Jonathan thought. *Maybe we've been brought together to help each other in different ways.*

"Peace," she said wistfully. "I have not known peace since the day my father died five years ago—he was inspecting a plant when the boiler blew up and killed him. I could not believe God would allow such a thing to happen. And then—" Katerina seemed unable to continue. After a few moments of silence, she went on. "It has been very hard to get over the pain of losing my father."

"But there is still hope," Jonathan said softly. "This isn't all there is. Tell me—what happened to your family's faith?"

Katerina shook her head sadly, "The Communists stole it from us. My great-grandparents, like many in Russia, were strong believers—Orthodox Christians—in the days of the czars. But when the state replaced religion after the revolution in 1917, my people were told the state would provide everything we needed—that God no longer served any purpose. Their goal was to make us so dependent on them and their five-year plans, we would never hope for anything beyond that. And most people no longer do. There is no hope in Russia any more because there is no God in Russia any more."

"But what about you, Katerina?" Jonathan probed. "The state can't control your heart. What do *you* believe?"

"I do not know," she replied softly. "No, I do believe there is a God—one greater than the government of my country. Faith is in my soul, in my heart, inherited from my father's fathers. But it is hard to be faithful in my country. I feel as if my faith is a seed, which lies dormant and only needs to be cultivated again so it can grow."

Again, Jonathan couldn't believe someone who was spying on him would say such things, even if she were just playing a role. "Katerina," he asked softly, "do you not have anything to look forward to in life?"

"I do not know. I just do not know if I can endure any more suffering." She looked at him, and a giant tear formed in her eye and rolled slowly down her soft cheek. "The kind of suffering that comes when you know and love someone too well, let them into your heart, and then they are gone."

Jonathan was just about to respond to her unintentional cue and tell her he knew exactly what she meant, that he too had suffered a loss more painful than he could describe. But a shadow filled the doorway to his room.

"Well," said a voice behind her. "I am indeed sorry to interrupt this tender scene." Drakoff had strutted in unannounced.

Despite his bravado, Drakoff seemed uncomfortable with Katerina's tears, so he ignored her and walked over to Jonathan's bedside. "So," he demanded. "Do we know who we are today?"

"No, sir," Jonathan replied, trying to sound cheery and upbeat.

Drakoff gave a tinny, humorless laugh. "Yes, well, I hardly expected you to." Like Ivan two nights before, he completely ignored the No Smoking signs and pulled a gold cigarette case from his jacket pocket, along with a gold lighter. Withdrawing a cigarette and lighting it, he waved the smoke away. "I would have imagined seeing Captain Rostov would enhance your memory," he went on, "but it seems it did not. Or perhaps," he looked at Katerina, "the patient was denied the proper viewing environment. If I had escorted you into Rostov's room, then we would have been able to see your reaction and might have put an end to this whole mystery." He shrugged. "Perhaps in measuring your reaction, we would have known for certain you had nothing to hide, and would have ceased to monitor your activities entirely. Instead, your friend the nurse here—"

"Pardon me, Comrade Colonel," said Katerina in a cold voice, "but he is a patient under my care—*and under the general's care.*" She added the last words with a significant look at the colonel. "Therefore it is my responsibility to provide as comfortable an environment as possible for his recovery." She hesitated, then smiled coyly. "Besides, what could you have possibly learned by observing our patient's facial expression?"

"Much," Drakoff answered, scrutinizing Jonathan with his hawk-like eyes. "I am sure I could have learned much."

"Perhaps you could tell me who this Captain Rostov is, Comrade Colonel," Jonathan said slowly. "It might help me to remember if I have ever met him— though, as you must know, I didn't recognize his face."

Drakoff chuckled, looking straight through Jonathan with his fierce gaze. "Of course you didn't. As to who he is, that is a state secret and none of your business." Then, seemingly on a whim, he relented. "Oh, very well. As I said, he was—*is*—one of my men. A very special man indeed. He has been under deep cover, infiltrating a unit of bandits." With an evil laugh, the colonel added, "He even adopted their ghastly religion, if you can imagine that, salaaming toward Mecca five times a day and forswearing alcohol, the whole bit. Anyway, after many months of silence, I received a communiqué from him, saying he was in Kabul and on the trail of a strange renegade."

He thought for a moment, and then seemed to come to himself. "But I am sorry—I am sure none of this is very helpful to you," he said with a note of sarcasm. He looked from Jonathan to Katerina and back to Jonathan again. "What I have told you are heavily guarded secrets." He stared intently at Jonathan. "But then, I am sure we are all loyal Soviets here, so there is no harm done."

Inside, Jonathan raged. He could have reached out and strangled Drakoff without even leaving his hospital bed. But, instead, he just lay there and endured Drakoff's presence. He had no choice.

Although gone for most of the day, Katerina returned that afternoon to take a walk with Jonathan. Of course they had to be chaperoned by Ivan. They walked along comfortably, Jonathan fabricating various details of a half-remembered past as an engineer in Latvia, Katerina asking questions now and then, and Ivan keeping a stony, disapproving silence as he walked five paces behind them.

As they toured the compound, Jonathan memorized as many details as possible about the physical environment. Unobtrusively, he tried to head in the direction where much of the traffic seemed to be going, and after fifteen or twenty minutes of walking, he was rewarded when the main gate came into view.

Rather than approach it directly, though, he pointed to a bench just a few yards away on a street that turned off to the left. From there, he could still see the gate. While he and Katerina chatted, he carefully noted the arrival and departure of the vehicles. As on all military bases, the guards primarily concerned themselves with trucks and cars coming in, which they thoroughly checked and identified before allowing them to pass. The vehicles leaving—especially those of officers—were normally waved through, or at most were given a cursory visual inspection and a review of papers.

The sight of this gave him hope and made him impatient to begin his escape. He wouldn't be able to stroll out, but if he planned it right, he should be able to get out somehow—if he could shake or subdue his guards without raising the alarm.

All this time, he had been talking to Katerina about whatever seemed benign, but he startled when something he said seemed to have an amazing effect on her. "What is it, Katerina?" he asked.

"The name you said the general gave you." She appeared to be on the verge of tears.

"Mikhail Filippovich? Why, that's just—"

Putting a hand over her mouth as though to stop herself from crying, she said, "Just stop it. Please do not say anything more. I do not want to hear it." She glanced over at Ivan. "Let us go," she said, standing up.

Kharitonoff seemed to be in good spirits when Jonathan arrived at his quarters that evening. "Mikhail Filippovich, my friend," he said with a big grin on his face. "I am delighted you could join me again." He looked at his watch. "It is early still—why don't you meet with me in the parlor for a Cuban cigar before dinner?"

"Certainly sir—I mean Andrei."

After the two men were settled in the parlor, the general offered Jonathan his choice of cigar and then passed him a lighter. "Mikhail Filippovich, do you feel up to the challenge of a chess match this evening?"

"Well, as I mentioned last night, I suspect it has been a very long time since I last played. But I would be happy to offer what competition I can," replied Jonathan.

"Good. It occurred to me that it might help you remember something about your past if you were to engage in an old pastime. Let us play."

The general had just executed his first move when a corporal suddenly interrupted and handed Kharitonoff a slip of paper. Reading quickly, the general grimaced and looked at Jonathan apologetically. I do regret this news, but I am afraid we will have to cancel our plans for dinner this evening. An emergency meeting has been called that I must prepare for. The corporal here will escort you back to your room."

"Yes, sir." replied Jonathan, switching to a less familiar tone now that they were in front of the enlisted man.

General Kharitonoff nodded thoughtfully. "Yes. It appears that some of the top-ranking Party members from Russia will be visiting us this Sunday, and I have been asked to prepare some of the local leadership on protocol."

Just my luck! Jonathan thought. This was the gold mine he had been searching for back in Kabul—he and Sergei. But all he said was, "I see, sir."

"You cannot imagine what it is like until you have experienced one of these visits," said the general absentmindedly. Then, he turned to the corporal and ordered him to bring the car around for the captain. After the man had gone, the general turned back to Jonathan and said, "At any rate, I will look forward to seeing you tomorrow evening. Oh, I was hoping to hear you speak of Latvia tonight. We must do that tomorrow."

"Yes, sir, but one thing—" Jonathan hesitated.

"What is it, son?"

So Jonathan told him about the strange incident with Katerina that morning. As with everything involving her, he knew he should keep his distance, but somehow he couldn't resist the temptation to learn more. Besides, after spending more time with Katerina, Jonathan had come to the conclusion that she was more like a daughter than a mistress to the general. He only hoped that he was right.

"I see," said the general gravely when he had heard the story. He glanced toward his study door. "The corporal can wait—come in and sit down with me for five minutes, but then I really must get ready for this meeting."

When they'd sat down, the general began, "Mikhail Filippovich was her husband."

"Was?" Jonathan repeated.

The general nodded. "He served as a major on my staff, and he was like a son to me. He would follow me anywhere and would probably have gone with me wherever I was posted next." Kharitonoff looked away, trying to control his emotion. "He was an outstanding staff officer, but he was not suited for battle. However, he wanted to see what combat was like, and that is one request I will not deny any officer under my command. He went out with one of our units, and then—" The general threw up his hands. "—An ambush. We did not know exactly what had happened for a long while, though, because no one survived. And so, since Katerina was a civilian nurse, she requested an assignment to my staff while she awaited news of his fate.

"Then, last month we discovered an outlaw stronghold. Among the things captured there were papers and other items that had belonged to Mikhail Filippovich. We also found his corpse, and the evidence made it clear that he had been tortured to death." He drummed his fingers on the desk, an expression of disgust on his face as he gazed out the window. "To be captured here as an officer is not good—before I would have let those animals catch me in the café last week, I would have put the last bullet in my head. Mikhail Filippovich must have suffered a great deal before he actually died."

He looked at Jonathan steadily. "Fortunately, Katerina had no idea how bad it was—we told her he had been shot, but of course we did not let her see the remains." He fell silent for a long time, and Jonathan, moved by the story, kept silent as well. "So you see," said the general with a gentle smile, "when I call you Mikhail Filippovich, it is quite an honor, because he was like a son to me. And Katerina is still like my daughter." He brightened suddenly. "You know, I have been trying for months now to convince her to go home and start her life over, but she insists she belongs here. Maybe you are the one who can convince her."

"Me?" said Jonathan.

"You," the general answered. "I gather from talking to Katerina that she likes you quite a bit. More than just a passing fancy." Suddenly, he laughed. Jonathan, who was staring down at his lap, glanced up at the general. "Why, you are blushing, Mikhail Filippovich! Have I embarrassed you?"

"No, sir."

The general held up a finger playfully.

"No—Andrei Vassilyevich," said Jonathan.

"Amazing," the general observed, looking Jonathan in the eye. "You strike me as a pretty tough one, and yet. . . . Ah well, perhaps an ignorant old man ought to stay out of the way and just leave the young people to their own devices." He stood up. "Well, then. Go back and see our lovely friend. It would perhaps be best if you visit a little earlier tomorrow, say 1600 hours? Be sure to come with your best chess game ready."

On his way back to his hospital room, confusing emotions surged within Jonathan. How could he want to kill someone like that? How could he hold onto the idea that Kharitonoff was "the enemy" when such couldn't possibly be true? And Katerina—so sensitive, so vulnerable. He didn't know what to think or feel anymore.

But there was no time for such thoughts. Not when Drakoff was on his tail and Rostov would wake up out of his coma any day. Late that night Jonathan took the first couple of preliminary steps in his escape plan. He eased out of bed, retrieved the steak knife from under the washbasin, slipped the top bed sheet out from under the blankets, took it into the bathroom with him, and set to work. Ivan was off-duty right now, but if his replacement barged in and demanded to know what Jonathan was doing, he would claim a bad case of constipation. The bathroom door was locked, and by the time the guard could force him to open it, he could have the sheet hidden inside the back of the toilet.

Jonathan finished what he was doing at a little after 3:00 in the morning, and to his great surprise, he dropped off into a deep, satisfying sleep.

After Katerina had taken his vital signs the next morning, she said, "Well, besides this amnesia and the remaining effects of the concussion, there is really no reason for you to be here. You are in almost perfect condition. I will leave this light dressing on your shoulder just so the wound is not chafed."

"Katerina," he said, taking her wrist in his hand and looking into her eyes, "the general explained everything to me. You have my deepest sympathy . . . beyond what you can ever know." He had no way of explaining to her about Jennifer, so he had to leave it at that.

She looked almost relieved to know that he knew. It seemed to make it easier for her to talk about it. Looking down at her hands, she said, "The loss has been very difficult for me to bear—such a waste."

"Yes," Jonathan said in a low voice.

She looked at him with anger in her eyes. "But none of it makes any sense. This stupid war. Our country loses some of its best men for something so utterly meaningless. None of it makes any sense."

He coughed and glanced around the room. "Katerina—?" he said, his eyes looking to the right and left.

"You are worried about listening devices?" she asked, still sounding angry. "This is the general's private room—there had better not be any listening devices in here. And if there are . . . " She raised her voice. " . . . If there are, I do not care what they hear. I speak only the truth."

She looked out the window at the drab, dusty buildings across the way. "We are not fighting here to protect these people. Such is obvious to anyone who spends two days in this place. None of them want us in their country. We are fools for even being here." Looking back at Jonathan, she said, "And I guess that is what makes this loss so difficult for me. To give one's life to defend the honor of one's family and country—now *that* has purpose—that is worthwhile! But to die in an unjust and imperialistic war . . ."

Biting her lip, she looked up at the ceiling. "He left home in such high spirits. Oh, he could not have been more proud if he were leading the army himself! He genuinely thought he was doing the right thing. But in the end, he realized just how wrong it was. To him this was not a war for self-determination and economic justice. It was an atrocity, and Mikhail Filippovich could not live with that."

Gently, Jonathan put a hand on her shoulder. "Believe me, Katerina, I really do understand how you feel."

She shook her head. "I don't think anybody could imagine such pain if they have never experienced it for themselves."

Jonathan winced. *If only I could tell her,* he thought. "So why do you stay here in Afghanistan?"

She shrugged. "Why go back?" Suddenly, she seemed to regain her composure and she turned to him. "So—are you ready for your walk?"

But Jonathan ignored the question. "Tell me, Katerina," he said, "does the general know how you feel about this war?"

She nodded her head.

"Doesn't that trouble him?"

"No, what troubles him is—" She stopped, and then spoke in a lower voice. "Well, I have to be careful what I say."

"I think we're able to be pretty honest with each other," he whispered back. He still held her wrist in his hand and he gripped it more tightly.

"Well," she said slowly, "again, I'd best not say too much. But he is an officer. And, as such, he has to do what his government demands, whether he agrees with it or not." She looked away. "Perhaps he will tell you himself the way he feels. I don't think that I can speak for him on this subject." Pulling away a strand of blonde hair that had fallen across one of her dark eyes, she studied him. "You understand that, don't you?"

"Of course," he answered, and he reached up to touch her hair.

She pulled away. "Now—about that walk?"

"Oh, yeah." Not knowing what to do with his extended hand, Jonathan brought it back and rubbed his chin. "Well, tell me—is there a library here on base?"

"Yes, the officer's library is just a block away from here. Why?"

He sat up. "Maybe there are some books about the Latvian S.S.R. there, and maybe it would help my memory if I saw them."

And maybe he could learn some more useful information about the compound, while brushing up for General Kharitonoff's quiz on his alleged homeland. He needed to act soon.

The library turned out to be a converted warehouse consisting of one gigantic room with rows of makeshift bookshelves and racks of periodicals along the wall. Aside from a lieutenant in a wheelchair—apparently the librarian—there appeared to be only three other people in the place when Jonathan, Katerina, and Ivan entered. Katerina knew her way around, and she guided Jonathan to the things he was looking for. To his surprise, he found the place had considerable literature on all the republics, including "his."

By the time he got ready to leave for the general's quarters shortly before 1600 hours, Jonathan believed he could pass an oral exam about Latvia—more or less.

He found the general waiting, with brandy and chess board ready. "Mikhail Filippovich, welcome!" he said. "Let us have that game of chess, and while we are playing, you can tell me all about your native republic. I hope you are prepared to lose to an old man."

Kharitonoff led off, and by the second move, he had two of his pawns in the center of the board. Jonathan, playing black, took one with his pawn. The general chuckled. "Now I know that you are an aggressive player," he said, "I shall conduct myself accordingly."

He mobilized his king's knight, then Jonathan moved his queen's pawn one rank forward from its starting position. This would indefinitely prevent the white knight from moving to a square from which he could launch an attack on Jonathan's queen and king.

"Ah," Kharitonoff said, obviously quite impressed. "So you lied to me, Mikhail Filippovich—you did study chess, particularly Bobby Fischer's work! Otherwise, how would you have known Fischer's variation on the Queen's Gambit—a most sophisticated move, although I must admit I would have expected it from a Westerner rather than a Soviet."

Jonathan, seeing the general staring him straight in the eye as though reading his thoughts, was intensely aware that everything he did was being scrutinized. That was one crafty character sitting across from him. "Oh, I didn't know that," he answered, forcing himself to breathe calmly. "I just play as I have always played." Of course he had never studied Bobby Fischer, and had learned to play simply by playing—but maybe there really was such a thing as a Western and an Eastern way of approaching the game. His world seemed full of little traps designed to betray him.

On the eighteenth move, Kharitonoff moved his queen into line with Jonathan's king, which was sandwiched between the black rook and pawn on the far-left file. Foolishly Jonathan moved his queen's bishop's pawn forward to shield the king; Kharitonoff took it with his queen and declared checkmate.

Jonathan smiled and threw up his hands in a gesture of defeat.

"You play quite well for an amateur," said the general. "I have got it down to about twelve moves with most of my staff. You lasted nearly twenty, and maybe you will do better next time. In any case, I am anxious to hear what you remember of your homeland."

Jonathan obliged the general, and as he listened to himself talking, he felt like he was doing a pretty good job. It was accurate information, without sounding *too* accurate, the way someone who had just crammed from a bunch of travel books would sound.

Midway through Jonathan's armchair travelogue of Riga, the general interrupted him. "Yes, yes—the Statue of General Cherniakovsky—is that not on the square at Cerniacovskio Aiksté?"

Jonathan had virtually memorized a map of Riga and all its landmarks, but this didn't ring a bell. "Andrei Vassilyevich," he said cautiously, "I don't know—perhaps my memory is bad, but I don't recall any such statue."

"How about the square, then?"

Jonathan shook his head. "Not to my recollection."

"Of course," said the general absentmindedly. "Forgive this old man his bad memory. I think it must be in the Lithuanian S.S.R.—in Vilnius, to be precise. Yes, I believe that is correct. My apologies, but I am always confusing the Baltic countries."

After that little test, Jonathan's "oral examination," as he thought of it, went pretty well. But then Kharitonoff dropped an even bigger bombshell. "Tell me, Mikhail Filippovich," the general asked, speaking slowly and gazing out the window, "what are your thoughts and opinions about this war?"

Jonathan, who had almost thought he was off the hook, sat up straight and prepared for another test. "Sir," he said, "that is not something it is my place to have an opinion about." He was really starting to sweat now, and he hoped Kharitonoff didn't see it.

"Talk to me that way when we're outside this building," Kharitonoff said firmly. "But when you are here, and I ask you a question, I want an answer. And don't call me *sir.*"

"Well," Jonathan said slowly, thinking of the way a Soviet soldier would answer, "wars are certainly not something I like. They are devastating, and one day when socialism is triumphant, perhaps then we will have no war. But for now I suppose we have to fight in order to preserve socialist freedoms."

"Hmm." The general chuckled. "A very correct, very clinical, even political answer, my friend. I do not think a computer in the Kremlin could have put it better. But now desist from this nonsense and answer my question. I want to know your real feelings. Do you think we should be here?"

"Honestly," Jonathan said, wishing this particular round of questioning would end, "I think we have to do what we are ordered to do. It's really not our choice to decide right or wrong, so we have to have confidence in our leaders."

"But do you have confidence in your leaders, my friend?"

"Well, I have confidence in *you,*" Jonathan answered carefully, "and I would like to think that you are exemplary of our leadership. So if you think that fighting this war is the right thing to do, then perhaps it is, and perhaps I should think the same."

Kharitonoff seemed amused by this answer. "So what you are saying is that you don't really think this is the right thing to do?" But mercifully, before Jonathan had to answer, he went on talking. "What you fail to see, Mikhail Filippovich," he said, folding his arms across his chest, "is that I am in much the same position. I am not the one making the decisions here. I am simply fulfilling the requirements of my profession and my position. I, too, am only following the leadership." He thought for a moment, and went on in a low voice. "I have proven my own inability to make the proper decisions—that is why I'm here."

Glancing at Jonathan, he smiled. "I am sure you wonder what I am talking about," he said. "You will likely never find out. In any case, the real leaders are coming here on Sunday. Top officials. I do not know exactly who yet. The final roster is not made. But it is rumored these are some of the future top leaders, men who have Gorbachev's ear. Men he has seen fit to send here to look in on this difficult situation in Afghanistan. Sort of a test of their leadership abilities." The general paused thoughtfully. "Really, it does not matter that you and I do not know their names. They are obscure now, but in their own minds—and in the view of political gossips whose job it is to follow such things—they are the future rulers. And they think they can fly in here on Sunday and leave on Tuesday, with all questions decided and problems solved in the meantime. In the end, it will be the same foolish, futile, endless war that it has been."

The general's words made Jonathan think, though not exactly about the subject at hand. If only he could get back to Massoud's camp in time—but he could see Kharitonoff was waiting for a response from him, so he said, "You sound like someone who does not believe in this war."

"Oh, now *you* are asking the questions?" asked the general pleasantly. "That is fine, we can do that. But let me just ask you one thing more."

"What is that, Andrei Vassilyevich?"

The general, who had been staring out the window, suddenly turned and stared straight at Jonathan. "How long have you been with the CIA?"

CHAPTER TWENTY-FOUR

Jonathan felt the blood drain from his face. The sly old fox had just been playing with him all along. "Sir," he said in a weak voice, "what was that?"

"You heard me," the general answered in Russian—then he switched to English. "Or maybe I should say it this way. How long have you been with the CIA?"

Jonathan shifted in his chair, his heart beating wildly. "Why would you think I'm working for the Americans?" he asked, still in Russian.

"Because you are *obviously* an American," Kharitonoff said. "How do I know? Well, let me see." He started to count things off. "First of all, there is your accent and your ability with the Russian language—which is good, I must say, but nothing like someone who has grown up speaking it." He returned to the more gentle tone in which he normally spoke to Jonathan and smiled at him across the desk. "Even in Latvia. *That* idea was a good one, but not good enough. A Latvian, even a stupid one, would still speak much better Russian than you do because he has been hearing it since the day he was born." The general chuckled. "It is only in movies that a spy from one country manages to pass himself off as being from somewhere else. In real life, it is much harder."

He looked up at the ceiling. "And there are many smaller things—for instance, your dental work. It is very clear, from the X-rays done by the doctor when you arrived at our *góspetal'*, that you had a superior dentist, the kind that would only be available to a Soviet if he were a major Party apparatchik or—" He laughed aloud, "—a general. Someone who could fly over to western Europe to get the best health care. And other aspects of your body noted by the doctor as well—an appendectomy scar sewed up so perfectly. On this side of the wall, only the best East Germans do such good work.

"Besides, your mannerisms are certainly Western—I saw how you had a tendency to hold your fork in your right hand when you ate, then you would notice what you were doing and switch. More significantly, even though you tried to hide it, I could tell from speaking with you that you have the kind of wide-ranging knowledge of the world, and of world events, that would be unlikely in a Latvian engineer. But the real proof was when we played chess." He pointed at Jonathan, but not maliciously. "You do not play like a Soviet. I should say that much like the

AVENGED

Russian language, chess comes *less* naturally to you Americans than to one of us." He stared at Jonathan. "I don't know what Drakoff thinks you are—I suppose you just mumble when you talk to him so that he cannot hear your accent. But he is no fool, and neither am I."

Jonathan tried to swallow the hard knot in his throat, and he sat there in silence for several seconds before he managed to say, "Then why haven't you arrested me, or is this some sort of game?"

Kharitonoff shook his head. "That is just further evidence of how little you really understand." He pointed toward his family coat of arms above the fireplace in the next room. "Do you see that? I know you can read Russian, so read me the motto there."

"It says," Jonathan read, squinting, "'*Vernost'. Chest'. Doblest'*—Loyalty. Honor. Valor."

"That is correct," Kharitonoff said. "And what about the first of these? Loyalty, yes? You see, as I told you on the first evening you came here, I am a Cossack by blood and lineage, and I am bound by the honor of a Cossack. Because I owe my life to you, loyalty and honor dictate that not only can I not betray you, I am bound to protect you as long as you are my guest."

The general looked down at his lap. "Besides," he went on in a lower voice, "I owe another debt, one much larger than the one I owe you. It is a debt to all mankind, for something so hideous that I . . ." He let his voice trail off, and shook his head. "That debt can never be repaid, I fear." Looking at Jonathan, he said, "But that does not concern you. Right now you have a problem, and because I am bound by my honor to help you, it is my problem too." He sighed. "But you and I both know this cannot go on indefinitely. Colonel Drakoff has been eager to interrogate you, and now that our guests are coming in from the Motherland, he has an excuse. To top it off, I have heard that his man in the room next to you—Rostov or whatever his name is—is about to come out of his coma. So Drakoff has seen fit to go over my head to Moscow, and received permission to begin the interrogation tomorrow morning."

"By 'interrogate' you mean torture, right?" Jonathan asked.

The general shook his head emphatically. "No, no. We are much more civilized than that. A few cc of truth serum and—*voila!*—your memory comes back." He studied Jonathan's face. "I can tell you are still wondering why I am revealing all this to you. Rest assured, my friend. When you leave here after having received this information, I will have repaid my debt."

Again, the general sighed. "There is a contradiction here. I am a man of honor, yet I am also duty-bound to serve my country, and it is painful when these two

30

priorities conflict with one another. Though I cannot think of you as my enemy, I must do what I must do. And tomorrow, Drakoff will have his way." He rubbed his forehead, then swiped his hand over his face. "So, my friend, these are our last moments together. In a few minutes, my aide will escort you back to your room. It has been a pleasure knowing you, and I shall always be grateful to you for saving my life."

"Thank you, Andrei Vassilyevich," Jonathan said quietly. "And just to set your mind at ease about one thing, I can honestly tell you that I'm not with the CIA or any part of the American government."

Kharitonoff chuckled. "Well good, then. Ha, ha! Those fools will be really confused when they receive that photo."

"Photo?"

"The one I had taken on Monday when I promoted you—a promotion which, I think you realize now, was not a legitimate one. That medal I gave you, it belongs to me. So, if you would, just leave it in your room when . . . if . . ." The general looked away. "You understand what I mean?"

"Yes."

"And the picture," the general went on hastily, "was never intended for *Krasnaya Zvezda*. I sent it special delivery through the diplomatic corps—that's the only way to send anything overseas quickly—to Mr. Casey at the CIA, with a personal note saying that it looked as though one of his agents had defected." He laughed again. "I knew I was operating outside normal channels to do so, but when you get as old as I am, you take a few liberties."

He stood up, and Jonathan did too. "Well, I am glad to know you are not one of them," said the general. As Jonathan opened his mouth to respond, the general suddenly put his hands up over his ears. "Do not even try to tell me who you really are. The less I know, the better."

Rather than shake Jonathan's hand, the general gave him a bear hug and kissed him on both cheeks. "I am sure you will understand when I say that you should get back to the hospital—and I regret that we will not be able to have dinner together tonight. Good luck to you, son." Then he turned away so that Jonathan could not see his face as he was leaving. But Jonathan could tell that the general was moved.

When Jonathan returned to his room, he found Katerina waiting for him. "Why are you here so late?" he asked her, hoping his face didn't betray anything. "Is something wrong?"

Looking over her shoulder at the closed door, Katerina whispered, "I must tell you, even though I know I shouldn't . . ."

"What?"

She frowned. "There has been a marked improvement in Captain Rostov's condition. He is expected to come out of his coma at any time." She looked at Jonathan with pleading eyes. "As a nurse, I am supposed to want that to happen, but I sense it will not be good for you when it does."

"I heard about Rostov," he began. "But that's not important to me now. What's important is . . ." He stopped, and then he thought, *What does it matter? The general has figured it out, and Drakoff is about to—what does it matter if she knows?*

"Yes?" she asked, waiting for him to go on.

"Would it surprise you if I were to tell you that I'm not a Latvian?" he whispered.

She smiled slightly. Sending a surreptitious glance once more over her shoulder, she whispered back, "Actually, it would surprise me more if you *were*." He must have looked disappointed at her appraisal of his Russian, because now she said more gently, "You put up a good act, but you gave yourself away even before you came out of your coma. I do speak English, you know. I had nine years of it in school." Switching to English, she said, apparently quoting some long-ago English lesson, "How far is it to New York? Do you have tickets to the baseball game?" She laughed. Still in English, she said, "Tell me—who is Jennifer?"

"Did I call her name out?"

She nodded.

"Hmm," he said. "Jennifer. Well . . . Uh, Jennifer is—or rather, she was—my wife. She died in a terrible accident."

"You must still love her, then, if she is the one you call out to when you are in pain." She bit her lip and thought for a moment. "So you do understand what I have gone through over Mikhail Filippovich." She still spoke in a whisper, her lips barely moving. "You must be an American. But then why are you here in Afghanistan?"

"I'm a journalist." He hated to lie to her, but the more he told her, the more he would endanger her. "I was in Afghanistan writing a story about the war for publication in the West, and I just happened to be at the wrong place at the wrong time." Knowing he must finish what he had to say, Jonathan prayed that Ivan would not come through that door. "Katerina," he said in an almost inaudible voice, "I'm going to have to tell you goodbye tonight. I have to go away, or they will kill me once the truth is known."

"Yes, I am sure you are right," she said, "but why are you telling me this? You are taking a great risk by telling me, aren't you?"

"Maybe," he said. "But I think I know you. And . . ." What did he have to lose now? If she didn't feel the same, he would never see her again anyway. "And I think I'm in love with you." He looked her in the eye without breaking his stride. But before she could answer, he said, "If I said I wanted to take you back to the West and show you what freedom is, that we would find our faith together, what would you say?"

She thought for a moment, and he could see many emotions crossing her lovely face at once. "But what *can* I say?" she asked finally. "I don't even know your name."

"It's Jonathan," he whispered.

She smiled. "Jonathan," she repeated. "Jonathan. Yes, I like that. Jonathan, I want more than anything in the world to spend more time with you. I wish there were some way that you could stay here with me, or we could disappear somewhere, but we both know that is not possible. I find myself—and I am afraid to say this— I find myself . . . Well, the last time—the *only* time, I must say—the last time I . . ." She sputtered, unable to get the words out.

"It only led to my being lonelier in the end than in the beginning. I couldn't bear it if you . . . But, I am being confusing. All I mean to say, Jonathan, is that I find myself in a very short time falling in love with you too."

"Well then, it's settled," he said with a smile.

"What is settled?" She seemed to be almost on the verge of tears. "Tomorrow Drakoff will question you, and even if you . . . Well, even if he doesn't have an opportunity to question you, how will we ever—"

"The general is your friend, right?" asked Jonathan confidently.

She nodded her head.

"And he's an influential man, correct?"

"You know he is."

"Then, could he get you an assignment to one of the countries in Eastern Europe—say, to work at the consulate in Prague?"

"I suppose so," she said, eyes gleaming. "What are you trying to say?"

"Today is June 14," he said. "Let's say we meet at noon three months from today, September 14, in front of the Soviet—no wait, make that the French consulate in Prague. Could you get transferred there that soon?"

"I could try," she said hesitantly.

"Katerina." He looked her in the eye. "Say you *will*."

"All right," she said. "I will."

"Then three months from today, I will be in Prague, and I'll sit outside the consulate every day until you arrive—even if it takes six months!"

"And then what?" she asked.

"Then," he said, "we will see. We'll see if it's meant to be. Czechoslovakia isn't paradise, but it's better than this place, and at least we will be able to talk freely. We'll have lunch in a café, listen to music, feed the birds in the park, go to the ballet—and talk about freedom, and faith. Then you can decide, and if you want to come with me and move to a different place, I will take you back with me to the West."

"You can do that?"

"I promise I can." How he would manage to do it, he didn't yet know. But he had accomplished many more difficult things, so when the time came, he felt confident he would find a way.

"I wish so much," she said, now starting to really cry, "that you were not in danger—that we could begin our lives together now."

They gazed into each other's eyes, and he tenderly reached down and put both his hands around her waist. Their lips met, and Jonathan did something he hadn't done in a long, long time. He surrendered to his feelings.

After several minutes of impassioned kisses and gentle words, Jonathan stepped back and held her hand in his. "It would be best if you leave now," he said, and when she started to protest he put a finger to her lips. "Three months—remember— just three months! But now I must go away."

"*Ya tebya lyooblyoo,*" she whispered.

In English, he replied, "I love you too."

She reached up and kissed him again, lingering for a moment more, and then she darted out the door.

At precisely 1900 hours, Ivan burst into Jonathan's room and announced, "Colonel Drakoff says to tell you to be prepared."

"I beg your pardon?" asked Jonathan from the bed. Except for their interchange regarding the cigarettes on his first night in the hospital, they had barely spoken to one another.

"Captain Rostov woke up about an hour ago," Ivan announced, "and the colonel is coming to debrief him—and you."

Great! Jonathan thought. *I'm not getting out of here a minute too soon.* "So he's coming here?" Jonathan asked stupidly.

"What did I just say?" Ivan demanded.

"No need to be harsh, Comrade," Jonathan replied. "You know I'm a little slow in the head after that blast."

Ivan grunted and went into Jonathan's bathroom, pushing the door almost closed. Lying in his bed, Jonathan could clearly see the guard's AK-47 propped against the doorframe. Listening carefully, he heard Ivan flipping pages—he must be reading on the toilet.

He waited a few moments and then crept cautiously from his bed, sliding without a sound along the wall until he reached the bathroom door. He could hear Ivan sniffle and crinkle his paper as he turned the page. Then, there was silence.

Suddenly Jonathan leapt through the opening, slammed his left hand into Ivan's forehead, and knocked the startled guard back against the wall. He brought the steak knife within two inches of the man's eyeballs. "Don't say one word, you pig," Jonathan hissed. "If you do, I'll gut you from top to bottom."

Wild-eyed and obviously terrified, Ivan tried to jerk his head forward, but Jonathan thrust him back and held the knife against his nose. Ivan did not move. Jonathan shifted the knife down to Ivan's jugular vein and held it there, the sharpened tip almost piercing the man's reddish skin, while he reached back and retrieved the AK-47 from its place against the doorframe. He brought it up to the Russian's ear with his right hand while sliding the knife into his pocket with his left. Ivan flinched as he heard the distinct click of the weapon's "safety" snapping into the fire position.

"Crawl off the commode," he ordered. "No, I didn't tell you to stand up! That's it. Move back into the other room. And remember—this weapon will be pointed at your brain every inch of the way. I said crawl, pig! On your hands and knees!"

"If you pull the trigger," the Russian muttered as he got down on all fours, his pants still down around his ankles, "there will be soldiers in here within minutes. They will blast you to pieces."

"Maybe so," Jonathan growled. "But you won't be around to see it, so what does it matter to you? Stop there. Okay, take off your shirt." Ivan was at the bedside, and Jonathan stood three feet away, well out of reach in case the Russian got stupid. "Now the pants," he said.

Ivan raised his eyebrows and looked at Jonathan with contempt.

"Come on," Jonathan whispered hoarsely. "Shoes and socks too."

While Ivan did as he was told, Jonathan pulled the small metal chair from its place beside the door and moved it to the center of the room, just under the three-blade paddle fan that hung from the ceiling. "Good. Now, I'm going to tape your mouth shut. Open wide—do it!" Jonathan stuffed a wad of cloth into his prisoner's mouth, then secured it with some of the adhesive tape he'd stolen on the first day.

"Now crawl over there next to that chair. Good . . . now stand up!" Next, he tied Ivan's hands behind his back with more tape. "All right, now get up on that chair," he ordered his prisoner. "There you go. Put your head in the noose—"

"Mmm-hmm-mmm!" grunted Ivan.

"Oh, I'm sorry . . . this noose." With that, Jonathan pulled the cord to turn on the fan, and immediately turned it off so that the blades spun quickly and then began to slow. As they did, they dropped a strand of rope with a hangman's knot tied at the end, which he had hidden up there earlier.

Ivan screamed against his gag, terrified.

"Oh shut up," Jonathan exclaimed. "If I planned to kill you, I would have done it by now, fool. Now put your head in the noose before I have to reach up there and do it for you." After Ivan did as he was told, Jonathan tightened the rope, leaving it just a bit too short for Ivan's height. The guard had to stand on his toes almost as far as he could reach.

Ivan stood there in his underwear, on his tiptoes with his head slightly to the side, the signs of strain evident in his face. "Good," Jonathan said aloud as he surveyed his work. "Now, while I finish what I'm doing, I'm going to lay this rifle down, but if you move or say one word, I will kick this chair out from under you so fast you won't know a thing. You understand? Hey, do you understand, soldier!?"

"Unnnggh," Ivan grunted. By now he was as humiliated as he was frightened.

The hangman's rope had taken Jonathan hours to make, and he hated to waste such a labor on a vile creature like Ivan. He had spent much of the preceding night cutting up one-inch-wide strips from his top sheet, which he knew would not be missed since his bed had been changed just that morning. He had braided the strips together into a thick cord, which, though it wasn't as strong as hemp, would be enough to support the weight of a 200-pound man.

After making sure Ivan's hands were bound securely, Jonathan used the remainder of the adhesive tape to increase the strength of the bindings on his makeshift rope. Then he quickly put on the guard's clothes. They were large on him, but they would do. Still, there was something revolting about wearing clothing that had rubbed against Ivan's skin.

He stashed the knife and tape in his pockets, then announced to Ivan, "I am sure someone will rescue you soon—whatever you do, don't move! If you step off this chair, it'll be the last step you ever take." Ivan tried to say something back through his gag, and from the look in his eyes it was clear he was furious. Jonathan stopped beside the bathroom door and turned back. "Oh, one more thing. Give Captain Rostov my best. I certainly regret that I will miss the opportunity to talk with him."

Jonathan felt the overwhelming hatred sparking from his prisoner's eyes, but Ivan could do nothing except stand there and try not to relax.

Easing open the door of his room with great care, Jonathan glanced outside. He saw no one in either direction up and down the corridor. He stepped out and walked in smart, quick steps up the tiled hallway to the back door, his AK-47 slung over his right shoulder. It was nighttime, and the place seemed to be practically deserted. He thought he was almost home free until he came to a nurse's station near the door. There he saw a heavyset nurse looking over a chart with a uniformed doctor. For a split-second, he thought it might be the same doctor who had examined him on the first day, and his heart skipped a beat. But the man looked up, and there was no sign of recognition in his eyes. Surely the other doctor would be in Rostov's room, tending to the newly awakened patient.

Jonathan emerged from the building and, keeping his head low, he walked swiftly around the side of the hospital building. He hurried to find a small area, enclosed by a slatted wall, which held mops and buckets and stacked drums of cleaning supplies. He wedged himself between a stack of drums and the front wall, and there he waited.

He had to force himself to stand still, knowing someone was bound to find Ivan at any moment. His body trembled and his palms were moist, but he kept waiting.

He stood minutes away from fulfilling his goal.

His hiding-place offered him an excellent view, and for several agonizing minutes, he watched two different vehicles pull up in front of the clinic and then leave. Neither of them carried the right passenger. Everything remained calm. No one who entered or left appeared frantic, and he didn't hear any siren. As far as he knew, no one had yet found out about his escape.

Then, twenty minutes after he'd taken up his position, he saw a Jeep-like vehicle, a UAZ-469 with a canvas top, pull up in front of the clinic. Behind the wheel sat the sullen-looking Asiatic night guard who ordinarily served as Ivan's replacement. Beside him sat Drakoff.

Jonathan darted from behind the stacks of barrels and around the wall. Just as Drakoff climbed from the vehicle, Jonathan stepped forward with his AK-47 at the ready.

"Ah, it's our Latvian," said Drakoff, seeming not the least bit startled—until he realized he had a rifle pointed at him.

"Stay seated," Jonathan ordered. He jerked his chin toward the driver. "Tell him not to move, or you die."

"Do as he says, Sergeant," Drakoff said, then he glanced up at Jonathan. "Now tell me what you—"

"Shut up!" Jonathan ordered. So as to appear less conspicuous, he slid into the seat behind Drakoff, holding the rifle on him. "Now, loosen your web belt and hand it to me."

Drakoff did as he was ordered, and Jonathan took the belt, which held a Tokarev in a holster.

"Tell your driver to do the same," Jonathan ordered.

Glancing at Drakoff, the driver started to undo his belt.

"Slowly," Jonathan ordered. "Drakoff's not worth dying for."

The sergeant dropped his pistol belt in between the two front seats, and Jonathan quickly scooped it up, pulling the weapon out of its holster. He did this with his left hand, using the right to keep the AK-47 in his lap trained on Drakoff. Now he lowered the rifle to the floorboard and edged the pistol in closer beside Drakoff.

"Colonel," he whispered as he pushed the pistol up against the seat and turned off the safety, "I have this automatic pistol pointed at your back, in line with your heart. Tell your driver to take us to the main gate."

"Who are you?" Drakoff demanded.

"You'll find out soon enough. Now tell him to drive!"

"Do it, Sergeant," said Drakoff, and they didn't leave a moment too soon, because just then, the front door of the clinic opened and a group of doctors stepped out.

"You are an infiltrator of some kind, are you not?" Drakoff asked. "That is why you are so afraid of Captain Rostov waking up. You know he will expose you."

Jonathan said nothing. His breath came hard and heavy from the adrenaline rush and, as the vehicle bounced along the bumpy road toward the front gate, he maintained his position with the pistol up against Drakoff's seat.

"I knew it," said Drakoff with a self-satisfied tone. "I am never wrong about these things." He glanced back at Jonathan. "You might be a little conspicuous the way you are sitting," he observed. "If you want to get safely through the gate, best to ease off a bit. Even if I were to make a false move, you could still shoot me, don't worry."

"Shut up," Jonathan ordered him, but he did ease back in his seat just enough so that he didn't seem to be sitting forward noticeably. He still sat plenty close enough to fire off a round and kill his captive before anybody could get to him.

They pulled up at the gate, and Jonathan could hear the blood rushing through his ears as the vehicle slowed down in a cloud of dust. A sentry looked in. "Oh, it is you, Colonel Drakoff," said the sentry. "Leaving us again so soon?"

"Yes," said Drakoff pleasantly, as though he were thoroughly relaxed. "I've been called away on another commitment."

"Nothing serious, I hope," the soldier answered, stepping back from the car.

"Thank you, Private," the colonel answered.

As they pulled onto the road, Jonathan studied the self-satisfied smile on Drakoff's thin lips. Unless there was some kind of hidden code in that interchange with the guard back there, it seemed as though his foe had gone to extraordinary lengths to get them off the base without incident. *Almost as though he wanted to help me,* Jonathan thought suspiciously.

Over the last several hours, General Kharitonoff had been periodically looking out his window to observe any individuals leaving the compound. After it had grown dark, he sat in his chair debating whether or not he should take any action before the next morning. Suddenly, a corporal entered and handed the general a message. It indicated that the general's Latvian guest had disappeared from the hospital. Unfortunately, the guard assigned to him had been nearly killed, and it was now believed that the patient was a spy.

He nodded his head and said under his breath, "You will have to be very careful, my friend," he muttered. "I hope you know what you are doing, but I have done all I can, and my obligation is now fulfilled. Now I will be the one in charge of searching for you, and I have a reputation for being zealous in my commitment to my job. Over-zealous." Kharitonoff shook his head, forcing away unpleasant memories.

The time had come to act. On his intercom, he ordered his adjutant, "Major Vronsky, please summon the officers on duty. We have a spy to catch."

"Where to, my friend?" Drakoff sounded too pleasant in light of the situation.

"Just keep driving the way we're going," said Jonathan, pointing in the direction of Kabul.

"Oh, to the city?" asked Drakoff. "So you can disappear again?"

Suddenly Jonathan understood Drakoff's motivation for helping him get off-post. *How arrogant can the man get? He thinks he's still in control, interrogating me now. And later his driver will overpower me and torture me till I tell him everything.*

"What do you want with us?" the driver asked. Jonathan could tell he was uneasy by looking at his eyes in the rearview mirror and quickly he realized why. "It is no good to be on this road after dark, not if you are a Soviet."

"Shut up!" Jonathan ordered. "Nobody told you to speak!"

"Stay calm, Sergeant," the colonel ordered coolly. "Can you not see that he is *not* a Soviet?" He glanced sideways at Jonathan. "Just what are you, anyway?"

"Your captor," Jonathan answered.

"I know that much," replied Drakoff. "And my guess is, I will soon know much more about you than our friend General Kharitonoff ever knew."

It was now exactly ten o'clock, and the sun had set long ago. If they wanted to live through the night, they had best make it to Kabul, and off of this road, as quickly as possible. The driver sped up to more than sixty kph, or about forty mph—top speed on this bumpy surface of pockmarked asphalt, gravel, and rocks.

"I have come to repay a debt," Jonathan said into Drakoff's ear.

"Oh?" asked Drakoff with apparent amusement. "What debt is that?"

"You'll know soon enough."

"Well, before we get to that, why don't you start by admitting you are not who you claim to be?"

By now, though, the vehicle was bouncing along the cratered roadway at much too high a speed. "Slow down!" Jonathan yelled as the driver entered a sharp curve.

But instead of slowing down, the driver cut the wheel sharply, slamming on the brakes as he did. The UAZ spun out, lifting off the ground with its two right wheels and nearly flipping over.

None of the three men in the vehicle were wearing a seat belt. The driver, at least, had the advantage of knowing what was about to happen, and he braced himself behind the wheel. He came out the least scathed.

Had Drakoff been a little larger and therefore higher in his seat, he might have been thrown through the windshield. Instead, the colonel slammed against the top of the dash, unconscious.

Jonathan hit the rear of Drakoff's seat hard. His injured left shoulder absorbed most of the impact, sending a shooting pain straight down to his hand. In agony, he let go of the Tokarev, but at the last second he grabbed the rear roof strut with his right hand, which nearly wrenched his arm out of its socket, but prevented him from flying into the dash or the center console.

Dazed, he came to himself just in time to see the driver turn around in his seat and lunge toward him with a knife he had produced from some hidden location. Jonathan instinctively rolled to the left as the man's right hand crashed down onto the seat back, ripping straight through the thin canvas cover and into the springs and foam. The driver, thrown off-balance, caught his weapon in a spring. Jonathan kicked the hand holding the knife.

The driver groaned in pain but didn't let go. Jonathan felt around for one of the firearms. Besides the pistol he'd dropped, there should be another, plus the rifle, but the latter seemed to have become lodged under the seat, and the pistols had gone flying with their sudden stop.

Instead of drawing back in agony, the driver managed to regain control of his knife, and now he lunged wildly at Jonathan. Then, suddenly, he changed his attack.

Backing out of his door, he swung around to the rear left door and threw it open, hoping to catch Jonathan from the side before he had a chance to roll toward him with another vicious kick.

And it might have worked. But as Jonathan moved to parry the renewed attack, his right hand fell on one of the pistols. He raised the firearm, and the sergeant opened his mouth in shock just as Jonathan pulled the trigger. The single shot burst through the soldier's forehead. As he fell backward onto the road, carried by his own momentum, the knife dropped harmlessly from his hand.

Suddenly Jonathan realized that he had completely forgotten about Drakoff all this time. He wheeled around to fend him off, but realized the action was unnecessary. The colonel's head rested on the dash, his nose dripping blood onto the khaki-colored surface. For an instant, Jonathan thought he had been cheated, until he felt Drakoff's carotid artery and realized he was only unconscious.

By the time Drakoff woke ten minutes later, Jonathan had used the bungee cord, which held the spare tire in place, to tie the colonel's hands together. He secured them to the roof support that ran between the front and rear seats after he removed Drakoff's and the dead sergeant's belts. Then, he bound the colonel's feet to the seat supports with the belts. Finally, he interlocked the two web belts and strapped his captive's chest against the seat with them.

They were bouncing along toward Kabul with Jonathan at the wheel when Drakoff's eyes opened, and he surveyed the scene. Even when he realized he was a captive, he did not seem frightened. "What do you want?" he demanded.

"To settle a score," Jonathan said in English.

"You are an American," replied Drakoff in English as well, narrowing his eyes.

"That's right," Jonathan answered. Keeping his left hand on the wheel, he held the Tokarev in his right, pointed at Drakoff's temple.

Still Drakoff maintained the offensive. "Did you think you fooled anyone with your atrocious Russian?" he demanded. "Hmm?" He laughed. "I doubt even your friend, the general, believed your nonsense. The fact that Captain Rostov requested to meet with me personally meant something serious was going on. I suspect you had something to do with it. I should have acted on my instincts and dealt with you sooner."

"Too bad," said Jonathan. He moved the pistol down from Drakoff's forehead to his spindly rib cage. "Now it's me dealing with you."

They continued speaking in English, with which Drakoff was clearly adept—much better than Jonathan was with Russian, in fact.

"Very well," said Drakoff, still sounding unimpressed. "But if you shoot me, what good does that do you? You are still stranded in Afghanistan, and the bandits won't know who you are. They will slaughter you just like they would any honest Soviet soldier." He shrugged. "On the other hand, you can get on the radio right now and call back to the base and begin arranging extradition—on my orders."

"Extradition?" said Jonathan. "What are you talking about?"

"We can trade you for one of our own assets currently incarcerated in your own country."

"So you think I'm CIA or something?" He found it funny how these Russians just assumed the connection.

"Aren't you?" asked Drakoff.

"No," barked Jonathan. "This is personal."

For the first time, Drakoff seemed to have been caught off-guard. "Personal?" he demanded. "How could you have something personal against me?"

"Oh, but I do," Jonathan said, still not raising his voice. "And so do 269 innocent people, but they're not here to speak for themselves. I can only speak for two of them—my wife and my son. The rest will just have to get their revenge from you in the afterlife." Keeping his eye on the road, he leaned toward Drakoff. "I'm going to be avenged here and now," he said. "You're going to pay for what you did on September 1, 1983. You are going to pay."

A light of recognition began to dawn on Drakoff's face. "You are talking about when I was stationed on Sakhalin Island? I was only fulfilling my duty as a Soviet officer. I don't feel any remorse for that."

Jonathan struggled to control his livid anger. "You don't feel any remorse? You're the Butcher of Kabul, and you don't feel any remorse? Two hundred sixty-nine people, including women and children, died that night, and yet you feel no guilt!"

Drakoff looked at him, as defiant as ever. "Whoever you are, you appear to be a soldier of some sort. Therefore you know that collateral casualties occur in any military action. In your own Vietnam War, your country—"

"How dare you compare those two?" Jonathan demanded in a fury, and he slapped Drakoff across the face with the hand holding the pistol, hitting him so hard that he burst the man's lower lip and sent a thin stream of blood seeping out of it. Drakoff sat forward in pain, but he did not cry out. He kept silent, his nose and lip bleeding. "How *dare* you?" Jonathan said again, his anger boiling even as images of napalmed villages flashed through his mind. *God, Oh God help me!* Jonathan still suffered tremendous guilt, but Drakoff couldn't possibly know what he'd done, and he wasn't going to let his enemy excuse himself so easily.

He slammed on the brakes and swerved off the road. He shut off the engine and sat in the silence, the only sound that of the two men breathing. Jonathan moved the pistol back up to Drakoff's temple, and his finger felt the trigger. The time had now come for him to complete his mission, to cleanse the world of this cancer called *Drakoff.*

"I can only assume," said Drakoff, blowing away a trickle of blood from his nose that had landed on his upper lip, "that you have already dealt with the other party to that unfortunate decision."

"What other party?" asked Jonathan. "The pilot? He was just a robot. You can't—"

"Who's talking about the pilot?" Drakoff sneered. He glanced at Jonathan. "You really don't know?" he taunted. "You mean you left the base without eliminating the man who actually sent the command to shoot down the jetliner?"

"What are you talking about?" Jonathan demanded.

"There were two authorities at work that night." Drakoff answered as though he were trying to upstage his opponent. "One government—that was me—and one military. That was him. We acted jointly. And later our grateful government repaid us by sending us to this vile place called Afghanistan. It is our punishment, our place of exile. I am like his demon, assigned to torment him for eternity. But he tortures himself even more, continually second-guessing the decision we had to make on a moment's notice in the middle of the night." He shrugged as best he could, tied as he was to the roof support. "I have refused to let my decision ruin my life, but he continually suffers pangs of conscience over what he calls the one black mark on his career." He looked at Jonathan, still as taunting as ever. "Surely he told you something about a secret shame of his? I am sure he would share that fact with anyone whom he invited to be his personal dinner guest."

In horror, Jonathan recalled Kharitonoff's unwillingness to talk about his own past combined with his veiled references to a vast debt he owed humanity. *So what? Drakoff's probably lying to try and save his own skin. Why don't I just end this the way I planned it?*

Drakoff saw the look of doubt in Jonathan's eyes, and he nodded his head with a vicious smile. "That's right," he said. "He was *Glozá*—The Eyes. We made the decision jointly, but he actually gave the order." He studied Jonathan's face. "Now," he went on, "if you are half the man you pretend to be, go ahead and shoot me."

Jonathan looked squarely at his enemy, the man he had dreamed of killing. "Go ahead," Drakoff taunted. "Or can't you?"

For a moment, Jonathan wavered between two choices and finally answered. "I can't."

"I didn't think so," Drakoff answered.

Jonathan got out of the driver's seat and walked around to the back of the vehicle, where he pulled out a fuel container. It had a couple of liters of gasoline, and he poured a generous portion of it onto the road and ground, but not too close to the UAZ. Then he slid next to Drakoff and reached into the latter's jacket pocket, where he had seen him stash his cigarette lighter the other day.

"What are you doing?" Drakoff asked.

"Inviting some guests," Jonathan answered with a wicked smile. He walked over to the puddle of gasoline and struck the lighter. "I heard what the guard said back there—these hills are crawling with mujahideen—bandits, as you people call them." Bending down, he applied the flame to the gasoline, and instantly a patch of ground at least as big as the UAZ ignited.

"You can't do this to me!" Drakoff exclaimed. For the first time, fear tinged his voice. As he walked back to the vehicle, Jonathan could see the taunting expression had left Drakoff's eyes. "Shoot me—go ahead! But don't leave me to those animals. You know what they'll do. Please. No decent person could do this to another human being!"

Jonathan laughed. "Could a decent person torture men and leave them to die in their own guts and waste? Could a decent commander order his soldiers to rape wives and daughters while the fathers watched?" Sitting in the driver's seat, he leaned toward Drakoff. "Could a decent man order the shootdown of a civilian jet-liner?" He shook his head. Now he stepped away from the vehicle, tucking both pistols into his belt—the second one had reappeared from under Drakoff's seat while he was driving. He slung the AK-47 over his shoulder.

"You know," he went on, standing in the road as the gasoline continued to burn a few feet away, "it took twelve minutes from the time the missile hit KAL 007 until the plane hit the water. *Twelve minutes!* Do you realize how long that is when you know you're about to die? And think about those twelve minutes multiplied by 269 people. Do you know how long that is? No? Probably never thought about it, have you?" He studied Drakoff's expression of hatred and terror. "Well, I have. It's two and a half days. Two and a half days!" Then he extended his hand toward Drakoff like a sorcerer making a curse. "I hope they keep you alive that long—and torture you slowly, like a pig roasting on a spit."

Drakoff screamed and cursed, his face a mask of horror, rage, and fear as Jonathan took off walking and didn't look back. After he crossed the next hill, he began to run, trying to put as much distance between himself and the vehicle as he could. After fifteen minutes, he stopped and dug in behind some scrappy bushes along the roadside.

He waited another half-hour until, through the darkness, he saw headlights over the hill and heard the engine coming down the deserted road. From what he could tell in the night shadows, eight or ten mujahideen had crowded into the vehicle. The Butcher of Kabul would soon endure the fate he routinely ordered for so many others.

Assured that Drakoff would be handled by his captors, Jonathan moved farther away from the road and began picking his way through the brush, trying to stay under cover. When he felt certain the road ahead lay deserted again, Jonathan began walking in the direction of Kabul.

A maelstrom of thoughts swirled through his mind during the hours Jonathan spent walking. The revelation that General Kharitonoff served as a second player in the KAL 007 shootdown nearly overwhelmed him. In light of the affection he had developed for the general, he had already experienced conflicting thoughts about him being a Russian—an enemy of the Afghans whom Jonathan aided. But not only was Kharitonoff a Russian whose life he had saved in combat, he was an honor-bound Cossack who had saved Jonathan's life by not revealing his identity as an American. And he was also as guilty as Drakoff for the death of Jennifer and Jon.

To further compound his misery, he had also discovered his own unwillingness to equal the brutality of Drakoff by killing him in cold blood. For more than a year, he had sought a way to put himself in the very place he now walked away from— face to face with the murderer of his family. When he found himself there, he could not do what he had set out to do. And it would not do to use as an excuse the fact that the mujahideen would find Drakoff and kill him. The truth is, Jonathan had proved, at least in this instance, he could not kill in cold blood. He was not the man he thought he was. But in a strange way, he found himself thankful he wasn't.

AVENGED

What to do about Kharitonoff? he wondered as he hiked toward Kubal. *What, indeed?*

Jonathan continued to make his way along the dusty road toward the city, which he judged to be about fifteen miles away. From observing the night sky out his hospital window over the last few evenings, he knew there would be a new moon tonight, so it would be pitch-black—which was both good and bad.

He traveled slowly, cautiously, careful where he stepped for fear he might put his foot down on a cobra, or a land mine, or the edge of a cliff. Several times, when he saw vague hints of life—sheep bones or discarded food tins—he quickly moved deeper into the sparse brush until he felt safe to go back out into the open again. Though he passed an occasional solitary, possibly abandoned house, for the most part, few people lived on or near the road—which made it all the more ideal for bandits to hide and wait for some unlucky traveler to happen by.

He stopped when he arrived at a small rocky outcropping at about two in the morning. He estimated that the city was no more than three miles away. With the rocks for shelter and concealment, he could rest until morning, when activity around the city's perimeter would provide crowd-cover necessary for him to make his entrance unseen.

He dozed fitfully for the next five hours, awakening at the slightest noise. At first light, he opened his eyes and looked down on Kabul, that cesspool of a city surrounded by swarming suburbs. The sight appeared more frightening now than when he had first seen it almost two weeks before. He wished he could avoid Kabul entirely, but trying to get back to Massoud's camp on his own would be out of the question. Rasul's tailor shop provided his only hope for help and safety.

In spite of his caution and his fears, he knew he had to move quickly—and not just because the Soviets would be looking for him now. If he didn't get word back to Massoud's people in time, the important Russian passengers on Tuesday's flight would be long gone, and his whole mission to Kabul would have been a waste.

Well, perhaps not a total waste. He had dealt with one of the men responsible for the deaths of his wife and son. But the other one still lived, back at the military base. And Jonathan had inadvertently made a friend of this enemy. Even if he found another chance to get Kharitonoff, he wasn't sure he could go through with the deed. He wasn't even sure he felt good about what he'd done, or allowed to happen, to Drakoff. Maybe, as the colonel said, he had just been doing his job when he ordered the jetliner shot down. *Just doing his job,* Jonathan thought. As he himself had done in the skies over Vietnam.

He shook his head. The entire business seemed all too confusing, and he couldn't think about any of it now. He felt certain about only two things. One, he wanted to survive, so he could live to meet Katerina in Prague. And two, he wanted to finish his mission here—and all that entailed.

He also knew he had better hurry up and find a suitable change of clothes. Not long after first light, he saw his new wardrobe coming toward him on the body of a solitary traveler. Scrambling behind the rocks adjacent to the trail, he watched as the rider drew closer. Jonathan could make out the features of an elderly Afghan on a worn-out nag.

He jumped out of his hiding place and brandished his AK-47, yelling in Russian. Scared half out of his wits, the man reined his horse and dismounted as quickly as his aged bones would allow. Jonathan indicated by sign language that he wanted both the horse and the clothes. He felt guilty for robbing the poor old fellow of his possessions, but really he had no choice . . . or did he?

In his pockets he had the steak knife, Ivan's lighter and cigarettes, which he'd almost thrown away in disgust—and Ivan's wallet. He looked in the wallet and, to his surprise, discovered a fat wad of rubles. Jonathan threw about half the money down in front of the man and motioned for him to take off his *tomban* and *peron,* the loose-fitting shirt and pants worn by most Afghan men. After the frightened Afghan complied, Jonathan tossed Ivan's emptied wallet off into the rocks. Even if the old man did retrieve it later, he'd have to be a fool to report Jonathan and return the wallet to the Soviets.

They exchanged clothing, the old man putting on the uniform, and Jonathan donning the old man's filthy, smelly garments. *Probably half the clothes he owns in the world,* Jonathan thought, or maybe all of them. When he put on the headpiece, he almost gagged at the combined odors of sweat, unwashed hair, and animals, and the *peron* felt scratchy on his body, like a feed sack.

The old man must have thought all of this pretty confusing—here this Russian soldier had started to rob him and then, instead, paid him a fabulous sum of money for his rags and his flea-bitten horse. He called after Jonathan as Jonathan rode away, probably shouting his thanks. Jonathan waved back.

With the old man's authentically filthy clothes, Jonathan could pass for a real Afghan. He rode at a deliberate pace, but not just because of caution. The old horse couldn't go much faster than he'd been able to on foot. "I'll bet your master calls you Lightning," Jonathan said to the animal as it loped along toward Kabul.

Early the next morning, Kharitonoff's adjutant, Major Vronsky, shook the general from a deep sleep by his shoulder.

"What news do you have?" asked Kharitonoff, his voice groggy. He sat up and pulled on his bathrobe.

"It is not good, Comrade General," Vronsky reported.

"Go on, tell me," the general ordered with a wave of his hand.

"We found the body of Colonel Drakoff's sergeant on the road to Kabul, but not Drakoff himself." From the dim light of Kharitonoff's bedside lamp, he couldn't see the expression on the major's face. "It appears bandits captured Drakoff and the vehicle."

"Ahh, Drakoff's worst nightmare has been realized," said the general. He felt a chill. "And the Latvian?"

"No sign whatsoever, Comrade General."

The general rubbed his tired eyes. "We cannot have this kind of nonsense with dignitaries coming." He thought for a moment. "Send word to Kabul to sweep the city for the Latvian. And hurry. If we do not capture him soon, we will not capture him at all."

Long after Vronsky left, the general sat at the edge of his bed, head in hands. He had pledged his loyalty to Mikhail Filippovich. And he despised Drakoff. But Drakoff was a fellow Soviet officer, and Mikhail Filippovich had crossed the line. *Now, I must be as dedicated to destroying my friend as I have been in preserving him,* the general thought. But this wasn't the first time in his life he'd been forced to make a difficult decision. "God help you, Mikhail Filippovich," he whispered to himself. "God help you."

After coming through several bustling settlements of temporary buildings, Jonathan arrived, near mid-morning, at the perimeter of Kabul proper. Security around the city had definitely tightened. Most of the streets had been closed, with no access allowed, and sentries stood guard.

He watched from a distance as long lines began to queue on Darulaman Boulevard near the Soviet embassy. The crowds of people in traditional dress, riding camels and donkeys, looked like a scene from a Cecil B. DeMille epic. He wondered if Kharitonoff had somehow sent out word to prevent him from entering the city. Regardless of the reason, he noted with alarm that the guards were checking everyone's identification. He hadn't counted on that, because he figured very few Afghans would have formal IDs.

To buy a little time, he guided Lightning into the midst of a group moving east, toward the old city wall. They appeared to be searching for an easy passage in, and the guards, overwhelmed by the magnitude of the crowds, completely ignored them as they passed by.

Up ahead, it looked like a group of travelers had found an unguarded gate, but by the time he got there, the guards had secured it. He realized he had better strike out alone if he intended to get any results, so he kept on riding along the streets outside the security perimeter. Lightning loped along, past open, rank-smelling sewers, past shacks built out of whatever objects the squatters could find, past roving gangs of little boys with makeshift toy rifles in their hands. No one paid any attention to a bent, stooped old man who rode a slow, old horse.

As the sun rose higher and higher and more time passed, he managed to locate a street, east of the Bala Hissar Fort, down which people streamed in, unimpeded. The two lone, weary-looking Soviet guards seemed to have given up on checking IDs. They paid no attention to Jonathan as he entered.

A crowd of some kind gathered in one open square, and he almost turned his horse in another direction, but he didn't want to look suspicious. Besides, he noted the place teemed with civilians—no Soviets and no Afghan troops. As he got closer, he realized a large group of men were celebrating something, cheering and laughing. He wondered what was going on, and if it had anything to do with the increased military presence, but he had no way of understanding what the men were saying.

After thirty minutes of traveling along anonymous streets, he arrived at the edge of the Shor Bazaar, a market he hadn't visited before on his forays with Sergei. He would have moved on quickly had he not seen several squads of Afghan troops moving in from alleyways on several sides, probably to search the market. *Were they searching for him?* He didn't know, and he couldn't take a chance.

Spying a group of six horses tied to a post, he dismounted and tied Lightning alongside them. The soldiers—barely a block away—were closing in from all directions. Looking around him, Jonathan could see no means of escape.

CHAPTER TWENTY-FIVE

A few yards off to his right, under a dull red canopy, Jonathan saw a vendor selling lengths of rope off of wooden spools about three feet in diameter. Casually he walked over and pointed to one of the spools, which had perhaps one-hundred feet of rope remaining. The salesman nodded his head and gave him a price in Farsi. Not understanding, Jonathan handed the man a twenty-ruble note, which seemed to complete the transaction.

Trudging back to Lightning's side with the spool in hand, Jonathan rapidly set to work. He unraveled about forty feet of rope and cut it with his steak knife. Sliding one end through the center of the spool and tying it so that the spool hung on the rope like a tire-swing, he took another piece and tied the AK-47 to the saddle, pointing forward and upward at a forty-five degree angle. He tugged on the weapon to make sure it was firmly attached, and then he tied the end of the long section of rope to the saddle and around the trigger. A couple of curious children gathered around to watch, but he shooed them away.

Next he untied the reins and ran them behind the trigger, pulling them tight, and switched the rate-of-fire control to semi-automatic. During this entire process, he kept his body between the rifle and any onlookers, so no one could see the weapon.

Up ahead, he could see the government troops, now no more than seventy-five yards away, slowly working their way toward him. To the north, they were even closer, moving into the market area and searching everyone as they passed. He untied Lightning from his hitching post and pointed him down an alley to the west. Taking the safety off his Kalashnikov, he whispered into the horse's ear, "I hate to do this to you, old buddy, but I need some help out of this mess."

The reins behind the trigger would create forward pressure from the horse's head. Backward pressure, the force pulling the trigger, would come from the weight of the spool dragging behind. The only thing this diversion needed was an "On" button. Jonathan reached back and slapped the horse's rump as hard as he could.

Lightning's ears went straight back, his eyes popped open, and he tried to kick Jonathan before rearing up and running due west down the narrow street. Lightning probably hadn't galloped so fast in his life. As he rushed down the street and people jumped out of the way in terror on either side, the rope began to unwind.

Just as the horse drew even with the patrolling troops, the rope reached the end of the uncoiled portion and tightened. The tightness pulled back the trigger, firing off several rounds of shots next to the group of men. They reacted immediately by jumping out of the way, into doorways, onto the ground—anywhere they could go to escape. As the spool bounced up and down with the forward motion of the horse's head, the trigger alternated between the tense backward position and the relaxed forward one, and the intermittent pressure kept the rifle shots coming. *Pa-chow! Pa-chow! Pa-chow-chow-chow!*

Pandemonium erupted full-scale among the troops on the street. They tried to shoot back, thinking there must be someone on the horse. By the time they saw the horse was rider-less, the creature had rounded the corner, out of their view. The spool bounced along behind the hack, knocking over one of the soldiers and catching his foot. The soldier screamed in terror as the horse dragged him for several feet—until he was able to work himself loose.

The troops now chased the nag down the street and, as they rounded the corner, they began firing after it. The shooting alerted an Afghan government squadron behind a barricade farther to the west. As the horse charged toward the barricade with a dozen or so Afghan troops in hot pursuit, the nervous soldiers at the western barricade opened fire. Immediately, four Afghan regulars hit the ground, wounded by the gunfire of their own allies.

The locals ran in every direction, thinking that a firefight must have broken out between government troops and mujahideen. As the panic spread, everyone surged away from the gunfire and toward the north and east. At the same time, the troops moving in from the north heard the shots and stopped their searches to run toward the sound of the action. Jonathan fell back into a doorway as the soldiers ran past him, then he moved into the surging crowd as it pushed northward through the narrow streets.

"I know what you are going to tell me," said the general to Major Vronsky as the latter entered his office. "The serial number of the AK from the horse matches that of the rifle belonging to Drakoff's sergeant."

"As always, you are correct, Comrade General," Vronsky responded stiffly.

"Stand at ease," Kharitonoff ordered, "and do not patronize me." He thought for a moment. "All right, here is what you will tell the Kabul detachment. Tonight we are going to move curfew up from 2200 to the time of sunset—1915 hours—and begin house-to-house sweeps."

"You want to search the entire city?" asked Vronsky.

"Yes," said the general, "and tell them not to worry about the source of the authorization. With all these dignitaries headed to my base, I am the most important member of the Soviet military in Afghanistan for now."

"Yes, sir," said Vronsky. "And if I may, Comrade General—"

"Go ahead."

"Well, sir, my recommendation would be that we at least cover the area around the market, and from there, north and east. It is not likely he went south, because that was the way he came in, and it is not likely he went west either, because that was the direction he sent the horse."

"Good reasoning," said the general. "Plot an axis from the market northward, and sweep every building in a ten-block-wide swath to the eastern side of that line, going north. Also, double all the guards on all the exits, and put an extra patrol around the perimeter of the city this evening. If they start right away, do you think they can complete the search by morning?"

"Yes, sir, I am sure they can."

"They had better," the general said. "Remember, those dignitaries are coming in on Sunday. There are all kinds of rumors as to who might be on the plane—could be our new foreign minister, Shevardnadze, and some Moscow boss named Yeltsin, maybe. It does not matter if we have never heard of him—he is big news at the capital, and it is our job to make sure everything goes well." The general rubbed his forehead. "How is it going to look if Kabul is shut down while we hunt for a fugitive? We must find him quickly."

Within an hour, Jonathan made his way to the tailor shop. He knocked according to a code Rasul had established when he and Sergei were staying there—three raps followed by two.

Instantly a small shutter slid back, and dark eyes peered out at him. Then, the door burst open and Rasul, chattering urgently in Farsi, pulled him inside. The tailor embraced him and quickly led him downstairs to the sewing factory.

"Where is Abdul?" Jonathan asked slowly in Russian, hoping Rasul would understand. Rasul just smiled at him. "Abdul? The giant?" He used his hands to indicate Abdul's size.

Rasul held up a hand, indicating that Jonathan should wait there, then returned a moment later with one of his sons.

The boy, who looked like he was about fourteen, spoke a little Russian. When Jonathan put the question to him, he answered and said, "Abdul not dead. He go now to get food, return . . . uh, afternoon?"

"Good—I'll wait here." Jonathan gestured at his filthy clothing. "I would like to wash off—do you have any clean clothes?"

"Yes, yes," the boy said. "We have *tomban* and *peron* that belong to the other Russian—he not come back with you?"

Jonathan shook his head. "No, and if he comes to this house, don't let him in. He is bad man. Spy."

"I bring you clothes and water for washing," the boy said. "Food later, yes?"

"Did you understand what I said?" Jonathan demanded. "Bad man. Spy."

The boy nodded his head. "Okay."

"Good," said Jonathan. He bowed his head slightly. "Yes, please—clothes and water for washing." He had not eaten for more than twenty-four hours, but he still wanted a bath more than he wanted a meal.

From out on the street, he heard sounds of shouting and cheering. Just as the boy started to leave, Jonathan stopped him. "What's going on?" he asked. "Is this some kind of holiday."

"No." The boy shook his head, and a smile stole across his face. "We hear good news. Butcher of Kabul has been captured. Mujahideen will repay him for great pain he has caused."

Jonathan nodded his head slowly. "That is good news," he agreed.

After Rasul's boy brought him the water and the clothes, Jonathan started to peel off his rotting rags. The boy and his father scurried out of the room—Afghans were very modest about nudity—but Jonathan hardly noticed. The water in the washbasin was cold, and there was no soap, but it felt wonderful just to splash a little on his face and under his arms.

Once he had washed and put on Sergei's clothes, he crawled into the hidden cubbyhole and fell fast asleep. He awoke to the sight of Abdul's bearded face as his Afghan friend shook him awake.

Abdul gave him a huge bear hug and fussed over him. Through the boy, Jonathan told him in very short order what had happened—including the news of Sergei's betrayal, which Abdul appeared to take very hard. Then, Jonathan added, "You and I are leaving tonight to go back to Massoud's."

When the boy explained this, Abdul looked very troubled, and the reply came back, "He say no, you cannot do that—too many soldiers here now. Must wait."

"Wait? How long?"

"He say three days."

Jonathan shook his head. "We can't wait—I'm leaving tonight whether you come with me or not." Of course the threat held no teeth. He had no way to get back to Massoud's. But he knew Abdul would comply because of the vow he had made to protect him.

Abdul frowned and said something, then the boy translated, "He say he will go with you, but you must stay here until tonight, because soldiers are passing by."

Jonathan, who needed the time to sleep anyway, said, "I can do that." He shook Abdul's hand and smiled.

Jonathan woke up thirsty, but he knew better than to crawl out of the cubbyhole unless he knew the coast was clear. He listened in the darkness, and he heard sounds of a commotion upstairs. Voices yelled in Farsi at one another, and there were boots stomping around in the room above him. He held his breath. A woman screamed. After more scuffling, the boots seemed to leave the building.

He remained motionless for what seemed like hours, although it was probably only a few minutes. Even so, he had plenty of time to think, and he had no shortage of thoughts to occupy his mind. He thought of Katerina, and of what he would say to her when they saw one another again. He thought about Sergei, the traitor, and reminded himself that he had better make sure Ali got the word about him as soon as possible. He thought, too, about Drakoff and the agony he must now be enduring—assuming the mujahideen had kept him alive.

Jonathan expected to feel elation, but he felt, instead, only numbness. Nothing was turning out quite as expected, it seemed. Not even the joy of victory over his enemy. Nor had the identity of his enemy turned out to be what he had foreseen. Yet, while it was true things hadn't turned out like he had thought they would, he was not sorry. In Katerina, he may have discovered something—someone—to give reason enough for it all. For the first time since he'd lost Jennifer, love seemed to be replacing hate as the dominant emotion in his life.

He pictured Kharitonoff, the smiling host, the gracious opponent, the compassionate father-figure, the honorable officer. He found it hard to get used to the idea that such a man could be his enemy. But if he had to get used to it, then he would. Already he could feel his attitude toward the general starting to change.

Suddenly, through the wall he heard three short raps followed by three long ones, a signal that the coast was clear. He lifted the bar securing the trap door in place from the inside and saw Abdul standing there waving for him to come out. The Afghan put his finger to his lips and motioned for Jonathan to follow him.

They crept in silence up the stairs to the main floor and out the back door. Somehow Jonathan expected it to be nighttime already, and his eyes had a hard time adjusting to the glow of the late afternoon sun.

They darted across a narrow alleyway, and into an adjacent building. They hurried through the back, Jonathan blindly following the huge man, then out the front door, across a one-lane street, and into another building.

Tiptoeing through the back door then down into another basement room lit only by a sputtering candle, they found an Afghan sitting there in military fatigues, a deep gash across his otherwise handsome face. When he saw Jonathan, he bristled to attention, then shook Jonathan's hand and said in flawless English, "Commander Wright, I am 'Zullah. It is my pleasure to meet you. You will be safe here, but we need to plan, and Abdul has asked that I translate for him."

Jonathan sat down while Abdul spoke rapidly to 'Zullah. The other man listened judiciously, then nodded his head, and turned to Jonathan. "The soldiers who searched Rasul's house were looking for you. Apparently, one of his neighbors told them he was sympathetic to the mujahideen. Rasul was able to convince them you were not hiding there, but they may be back."

"So all this searching going on in the city," Jonathan said, "is that all because of me?"

'Zullah nodded his head.

"Then, we have another reason why Abdul and I must get out of the city tonight," Jonathan replied. "I *must* return to Massoud's camp by tomorrow, if I must walk the entire way."

"But Commander Wright," said 'Zullah, "it is not possible to travel after dark, and they are searching houses even as we speak. This house belongs to one of our people, and it has already been searched. It would be best for you to hide here for two or three days until the curfew has been lifted."

Jonathan shook his head firmly. "No."

"What news is so important that it must not wait, Commander Wright?"

Jonathan looked the other man in the eye. "Ali's unit has been infiltrated by a traitor. I have to get the news to him."

'Zullah looked almost relieved. "Oh, that is news we can get to him through courier. I will arrange—"

Jonathan grabbed his arm. "There is something else," he said evenly, "and I can't tell you what it is because it would only mean death for you if you were captured.

I swear to you, though, it is news that can change the entire outcome of this war. There is an opportunity to strike a blow against the enemy, but that opportunity will soon be a memory if we don't act now."

While 'Zullah relayed all this to Abdul, Jonathan interrupted him. "Look," he said. "If we can't travel the city at night, then let's go now. How much longer to sunset?"

'Zullah looked at his watch and said, "Forty-five minutes, maybe an hour."

"That's plenty of time," Jonathan said. "What's the quickest way out of town?"

"To the northwest," 'Zullah answered hesitantly. "We have a passage there."

"How long would it take us if we were to go back through Shor Bazaar and south?"

'Zullah considered the problem. "We have a passageway there in the southeast quadrant, too, but it would take a bit longer—as much as an hour to reach. That would mean you would get there near or after the new curfew."

"Can you alert someone outside the city who will help Abdul and me get back to Massoud's camp?"

'Zullah nodded slowly. "I can send a messenger."

"Then we must go that way," Jonathan announced.

Abdul, looking confused, asked 'Zullah what they had been saying. They huddled for a moment, conferring in Farsi before the translator looked up and asked Jonathan, "Why must we go that way?"

"Because they would never expect us in that direction."

After another minute of discussion, 'Zullah turned back to Jonathan. "Okay," he said. "I will send a messenger to alert the guides outside the city, and then we will go."

Jonathan stood up, and 'Zullah held up a hand. "But you cannot go out there as you are. Every soldier in the city knows to be on the lookout for a Westerner, and the *tomban* and *peron* are not enough to hide you." He looked Jonathan up and down for a moment, then called out something in Farsi.

A boy ran in, and 'Zullah spoke to him, pointing at Jonathan several times. Abdul listened to this, and at first he looked troubled. Then slowly his face broke into a smile, and he chuckled.

"What's going on?" Jonathan asked.

"We are getting clothes for you," 'Zullah answered.

"Yeah?"

"Women's clothes—the *chadari*."

357

It was a humiliating way to make an escape in a country like Afghanistan—a man's world if there ever was one. But it also provided an effective decoy tactic. The soldiers would know better than to demand that a man lift his wife's veil for their inspection. "I'll do whatever I need to do if it will get me out of here," Jonathan said.

A few minutes later, they'd outfitted him in a *chadari,* a prison-like shawl that covered his entire body except for a few slits, which allowed him to see where he was going. The *chadari* served as the dress of a rich man's wife. Poorer women wore the *chadar,* a black scarf wrapped around the head, because they had to work. A woman wearing a *chadari,* which had no openings for the arms, advertised the fact that her husband was so wealthy, she didn't have to do anything with her hands.

Jonathan would have preferred to be dressed as a poor man's wife, since the absence of sleeves made the thing as claustrophobic as a coffin. For a moment he had a great sympathy for the plight of women in Afghanistan, especially when he noted, with envy, how comfortable the men's loose-fitting pants and shirts were by comparison. It didn't help matters that Abdul, who held up a little cracked glass mirror to show him how he looked, was grinning at him.

After a few more minutes, they set out, with 'Zullah playing the part of the "husband," Abdul walking alongside him, and Jonathan several paces behind—as befitted a proper Afghan woman. Farther back walked half a dozen young boys ranging in ages from eight to fourteen.

Out to the west, they could see the sun setting quickly, a gigantic orange ball in a field of red and gold. They proceeded without harassment, moving through the strangely quiet streets. When they reached the Shor Bazaar, they saw shop owners closing up their stalls for the approaching curfew.

From here on, they would have to adopt a strategic plan for getting Jonathan and Abdul to the point of departure. The young boys went ahead as scouts, spread out over several blocks, and, through hand signals, relayed back to the men the situation at the front. If the lead guide saw troops approaching around a corner, he would motion to the next boy, and so on down the line until the last one ran back with the information. That way, they could constantly adjust their route depending on the location of police, sentries, or other troops.

After about fifteen minutes of this zigzagging course, 'Zullah looked at his watch and whispered they had only fifteen minutes until curfew. They picked up the pace.

Now the last bit of sun dropped below the horizon. The streets had emptied, and the sound of their own footsteps seemed inordinately loud in the quiet of the street. Walking along, Abdul accidentally kicked an empty can, and it made the men jump.

Just then one of the boys ran back and hurriedly whispered something to 'Zullah, who turned around and said to Jonathan, "Bad news. There are sentries posted directly between us and our destination."

"How far is it?" Jonathan's voice sounded muffled through the hot, heavy veil.

"Around this corner and another block." 'Zullah looked at his watch again. "We must hurry—only one minute until they will arrest anyone still on the street, and maybe even shoot them."

They began rushing toward the corner, where they saw two government soldiers up ahead. All of them stopped except for two small boys, who ran straight ahead in the direction of the troops. Seeing this, Jonathan whispered, "No! Tell them to stop—they'll be killed."

"All will be fine," 'Zullah said. "Watch."

"You can't let them do that!"

"I promise it will be okay."

Laughing, the two boys ran past the sentries, who looked amused for a second until one of the kids shouted something at them. Then they looked back at the boys, who were now twenty yards past them. Suddenly one of the youths took out a rock and hurled it expertly at one of the soldiers, hitting him on the leg. Jonathan couldn't help but admire the kid's form as the soldier cried out in pain. Then, he and his companion yelled back at the boys and began chasing them.

"Come, we go now," 'Zullah whispered.

Abdul led the way, charging ahead as the two government sentries disappeared around the corner. He pointed to a door on the left, and the three men ran toward it. It opened just as Abdul came within two feet, and the instant 'Zullah and Jonathan were both inside, someone slammed it shut. The man who had shut the door, presumably the owner of the house, looked out through the shuttered window and then glanced back at Abdul with a thumbs-up sign.

"What about the boys?" Jonathan asked.

"Don't worry," 'Zullah replied. "It is a game to them. They outran those guards—by the time those fat soldiers could catch up with them, they were around the corner and two other corners, and now they are safe in a house two blocks from here."

"Are you sure?"

"Did you hear any gunshots?"

"No."

"Be glad we had such effective helpers conducting the decoy action," said 'Zullah, taking Jonathan by the arm and leading him to a set of stairs going down. "Now—we will hide in the basement here until it is very dark. When we get the signal that the street in front is clear, we will sneak out the back door of this building and dash across the street into another one. Then out the back of that one, down an alleyway, across another street, and we will be at the eastern perimeter."

"And then what?"

"Then," 'Zullah answered, "we will hope for mercy."

Jonathan would have liked something a little more concrete.

"I have your requested report of curfew violations, Comrade General," Major Vronsky announced as he entered his superior's office.

"Well, let's have it." The general sat back in his chair and drummed his fingers on the mahogany desk.

"Yes, Comrade General." The major glanced down his clipboard. "Uh, mostly routine violations. An old woman, wandering around disoriented in the center of town, escorted back to her home. A man, whose donkey had gotten away from a stable on the west side, was trying to retrieve it. Two boys throwing stones at government soldiers on Najib Street, near the southeast perimeter. A couple of teenagers who—"

"What was that?" asked Kharitonoff.

"—Teenagers who—"

"No, no, no—the one before that."

Vronsky glanced up at him. "Children throwing stones?"

"Yes," the general said. "Near the southeast perimeter. Were the children apprehended?"

"I don't believe so, sir. It appears they threw the stones and ran. Probably just some sort of childish prank, I would guess."

"That does not sound like a childish prank to me," Kharitonoff said. "Major, have that entire area swept at once—every house within a three-block radius. And concentrate on the ones nearest the perimeter—hurry!"

"But sir, with all due respect," Vronsky said, "if the intruder entered the city from the south, it seems highly unlikely he would return to that section for his escape."

Kharitonoff smiled thinly. "It is not what *you* would do, no. But it is the very thing *he* would do—and I know because I would too."

Abdul peered cautiously out into the black night sky. Then, he turned and nodded his head. "Let's go," said 'Zullah to Jonathan.

The three men ran from the house to the nearest doorway where they could hide. At least now, freed by nightfall from the burden of wearing the heavy *chadari*, Jonathan could move more easily. They spent the next several minutes moving slowly, from corner to corner and shadow to shadow. They took more than fifteen minutes to go just a few hundred yards.

Finally they arrived at their destination, a house just like the one they had left— except that the back of this one formed part of the city's ancient walled boundary. A man inside led them to a third-floor room with a narrow window through which they could faintly see the flat, barren wasteland of shanty villages beyond. The man lit a lantern, held it up to the window, took it away, then showed it again thirty seconds later, and repeated this once more before turning off the light and waiting with his three guests.

They crouched in the darkness, no sound but their breathing and the faint cry of a baby somewhere downstairs. The moon had not yet risen, so outside they could see nothing but pitch black. Why didn't the men out there signal back?

"This house is perfect for escape," 'Zullah whispered to Jonathan. "It is on a corner, and it juts out so far you cannot see this window from the surrounding houses. Long ago, the *Shuravi* came and sealed up the first and second floors for this very reason, but here"—he gestured toward the window—"is good. No one expects us to go out third-floor window, because it is so high."

Then suddenly the sound of vehicles some distance away startled all four of them. "It sounds like another search," 'Zullah whispered.

The roar of the jeep engines grew louder and louder, as though they were approaching the area, and Jonathan's heart began to beat faster.

Then, through the darkness, they saw it—a faint light flashing on and off. The owner of the house jumped up and brought over to the window a big bundle of cloth, which Jonathan saw was some kind of makeshift rope-and-sling assembly. Abdul nodded to 'Zullah, who said to Jonathan, "Abdul will go first. Watch how he does this."

Abdul strapped the sling under his buttocks, then climbed out the window, supported by the rope, which 'Zullah and the other man held. Like a rappeller, he stayed in this position with legs locked against the side of the house. He gave his helpers a nod to indicate he was ready. They eased him down until he disappeared into the darkness. A few moments later, the rope slackened when he reached the ground.

The sounds out front grew louder. Jonathan could hear the troops out on the street, banging on doors and shouting questions.

Now, the sling came back up. Gritting his teeth, Jonathan quickly climbed in. He lifted his body out the window, and he locked his legs. Then, he reached out and shook 'Zullah's hand. "I hope someday I can repay you for what you've done," he said.

"You already have," the Afghan said. "And I am sure you will again when you give Massoud your news—whatever it is."

The journey down the side of the building seemed to take forever, and he felt like a spider suspended on a thread. Finally, when he wasn't expecting it, his feet touched ground. He stumbled and fell. Just then, he heard more sirens. Abdul grabbed his arm and said something to him before jumping down on the ground and starting to crawl.

Jonathan followed suit, moving quickly behind Abdul in a cloud of dust so thick he had to squint to keep it out of his eyes and nose. After 200 yards—a long way to crawl at a high speed—Abdul got to his feet and motioned for Jonathan to do the same. As soon as he did, Abdul took off sprinting, and Jonathan ran after him, toward a cemetery a few hundred yards away.

Fifteen minutes later, they met up with their contacts, who guided them another three miles on foot. There on a dry riverbed, they met the same men who had taken them into the city a week and a half before, and they took off by truck for Massoud's camp.

For once, Wharton, Hollis, and McGinnis weren't wearing suits and ties. Nor were they dressed for undercover work. Today they were just three guys sitting on lawn chairs in suburban Virginia while somewhere down the street, some poor sucker pushed a lawn mower. In the yard in front of them, their three wives sat at a picnic table talking, and a group of young girls played.

"Nice of you to invite my girl to your daughter's party," said McGinnis, taking a sip of his drink as he observed the children. He was dressed in Bermuda shorts, and a flowered Hawaiian shirt covered his round stomach.

"Why of course, Mac," said Wharton, the host. "Why wouldn't we have invited her? Jenny and Marcie are good friends."

"Sure," said McGinnis, glancing over at his two subordinates. "But you know—it's still a nice gesture."

"What? You don't think we'd want to spend our down-time with our boss?" asked Hollis in an innocent voice.

"I know I don't," said McGinnis. "Speaking of which, I got a funny call from Casey the other day."

"Oh yeah?" asked both of the other men in unison, and Hollis said, "*Bill* Casey? The Great One called you?"

"I know, I know, it's hard to believe." McGinnis laughed. "But he had kind of a strange thing on his hands. He'd received a diplomatic pouch addressed to him from the Soviet embassy—no ID on it. But the Soviets did say it came from Afghanistan."

Hollis and Wharton looked at each other.

McGinnis took another sip of his drink. "Seems it contained a note, in English, signed 'General A.V. Kharitonoff.' Just a line or two, the note said something like, 'I see one of your agents has defected.'"

"*What?*" asked Hollis.

McGinnis held up a hand. "Casey had already had the general identified by the time he called me in. Turns out he's a big military leader down there in Afghanistan." He looked straight at Wharton. "And get this. Intelligence believes he and a KGB colonel named Drakoff jointly gave the order for the shootdown of KAL 007."

"He—"

"But wait," said McGinnis, "that's still not the best part. Guess who's in the picture with him—the defected CIA agent?" Before either of the other men could answer, he went on, "Casey wouldn't let me keep the picture, of course, but he did let me make a Xerox." He pulled something out of his pocket. "I brought this over because I thought you might like to see this, Rusty."

Wharton unfolded the paper, and Hollis looked at it over his shoulder. The scene appeared to be some kind of hospital. In the foreground was a Soviet general wearing a fat row of medals and a sling on his arm. Beside him, sitting up in bed and dressed in a hospital gown with a single medal attached to his chest, was a haggard and fatigued-looking man clearly identifiable as Jonathan Stuart.

Wharton looked at McGinnis. "He's like the cat with nine lives," he said slowly. "So he didn't crash in the desert like we thought."

"Apparently not," said McGinnis.

"But what do you suppose he's doing with the guy who ordered the shootdown that killed his family?" Hollis asked.

"You can figure it out," McGinnis answered. "What's his aim been all along—revenge, right? So . . ."

Wharton shook his head. "No," he said softly, his eyes gleaming as he spoke. "I think he's up to something more than that." He looked at the other two men, who were listening intently. "Put it all together. The shootdown back in '83, his apparent theft of a MiG, the fact that he's back in Afghanistan . . . All of that, combined with the fact that this guy is driven by a force greater than any of us can even imagine— he's determined to be avenged, and I think he's gonna take an eye for an eye."

"Meaning what, Rusty?" asked Hollis.

"Meaning he's going to replay the scene exactly, only in reverse. He's going to use that Libyan MiG to shoot down a Soviet jetliner."

"You think so?" asked McGinnis in a casual tone, taking back the picture and folding it up. But Wharton could see from his chief's eyes that McGinnis knew he was right.

"Mac, I'm sure of it," said Wharton. "We've got an American citizen about to commit an act that could start a world war." He spoke slowly and very carefully, staring hard at McGinnis as though *he* were the superior and not the subordinate. "We have got to get word to the Soviets before it's too late."

A scream from the yard startled all three of them, and they looked over at the girls, but it must have been only a squeal of delight because they were playing just as before.

"Rusty," McGinnis replied in a firm voice, "if we own up to this—to all we know and how far we've allowed this thing to go—then it will destroy the agency. Do you get what I'm saying?"

"No, do you get what *I'm* saying, Mac?" Wharton insisted.

Their wives had gotten up from the picnic table and were walking toward them. Wharton realized it was time for him to go fire up the charcoal and put on some hot dogs. But he didn't move. "Do you get what I'm saying?" he asked again.

"Are you boys talking shop over here?" asked Hollis's wife with a smile, but none of the men smiled back.

"I get what you're saying," said McGinnis.

"And?"

"And I'll consider it." From the look in McGinnis's eyes as he lifted his drink and took another sip, the decision would be an agonizing one.

CHAPTER TWENTY-SIX

"Katerina, my Dear," said General Kharitonoff, standing up and stepping over to greet her as she walked through the door. He kissed her on both cheeks, gave her a huge bear hug, then led her to a chair.

"I am just glad you had a little time for me," she said. "Things have been so . . . hectic for you lately, I know."

"Yes, well, our visiting dignitaries seem to be impressed with our facilities, much to my astonishment," said the general. He looked around. "Would you like something to drink?" he asked. "Tea? Coffee? Vodka?"

"No," she said, looking down at her lap. "Thank you, though."

"Katerina," he said, studying her face. "I know more than you think. And that is why I called you here."

She looked up. "Yes?"

He lowered his voice to a whisper. "I think you should know, I am pretty sure our friend got away."

"Oh?" Her eyes suddenly shone.

"Well, if I wondered before," he chuckled, "I know now."

"Know what?"

"There is no need to feel bad." He spoke, still at an almost inaudible whisper as he leaned toward her across his desk. "I know it was my job to catch him, and I discharged my duty as I should have, but"—he shrugged his shoulders—"I cannot say that not catching him is something I regret." He cleared his throat. "But, of course, that is something that need go no further . . . "

She nodded, and he could see her elation over the escape of the man he called "Mikhail Filippovich."

"You know," Kharitonoff went on, "this bunch that has come down from Moscow, they represent a real departure from the old leadership. They have taken a great interest in my input on the conduct of this war. In fact, they have even invited me to fly back with them and present my findings, firsthand, to the General Secretary himself."

"Oh, that is wonderful news," she said.

He chuckled. "Now, in the past, I would have been very suspicious of such an invitation, assuming it meant a one-way ticket, but this time . . . I may be wrong, but I feel like we can trust some of these new leaders. Perhaps we really will be able to pull out of this desolate country and leave it to the zealots and the mountain goats. Maybe then, we can get on to some of our own affairs."

Glancing at Katerina, he realized that, though she listened politely, she had long ago lost interest in his words. "I am sorry, my dear, I am sure you have no interest in any of this, but—"

"Oh, no," she protested.

He held up a hand. "Here is the point. I am returning to Russia for a week on that flight. And I was wondering if you would like to accompany me home for the week? My wife and I would love to have a young person in the house again."

Katerina's eyes lit up. "Oh, yes," she said. "Yes, I would like that very much."

He smiled. "Then start packing your bags. We leave Tuesday afternoon."

From the time he escaped from the 122nd HQ on Friday night, to the moment he arrived at the airstrip seventy-two hours later, Jonathan managed to get ten hours of low-quality sleep—three while hiding in the cubbyhole at Rasul's, and another seven while bouncing along in the truck, first to Massoud's camp, then to the airstrip. Therefore, when they arrived at the airstrip late Monday evening, he took advantage of the opportunity to get a good five hours of rest before daybreak. On Tuesday morning, he got up and ate a light breakfast before going over his plans with Ali and inspecting the runway and aircraft.

During the past two weeks, the mujahideen had stayed busy with the Foxbat. They had assembled a dozen or so deserters from the Afghan and Soviet air forces, who had done a thorough check on the aircraft. None of the men had ever worked on a MiG-25, but at least they had actual aircraft maintenance experience. Jonathan was pleased to discover they had sealed the intake and exhaust ducts to prevent dust and sand from entering the jet engine while they waited for him to return.

As the time for takeoff drew near, Ali and Jonathan conferred. Like Abdul, he had taken it hard when he learned Sergei had been spying on them all this time. But he was thrilled Jonathan had made it back to them alive. "Massoud has a request," Ali said to Jonathan as they stood on the runway. "Because you will fly so close to Kabul, he asks that you pass over the city, as a message to the people that the mujahideen are taking control of the skies."

"Hmm," said Jonathan, squinting into the late morning sun. "I appreciate the symbolism, but . . ." He was thinking this was a life-and-death mission, not an air show, but instead he heard himself saying, "If it means so much to him, then I'll do my best."

"Good," said Ali. "And I have given instructions to the men that all traces of this airstrip must be destroyed after you have left. It would not do for you to return here." He smiled a little sadly. "I understand now why there can only be one mission, and why we cannot have hope for an air force at this time. And Massoud understands too."

Jonathan nodded his head. "I'm glad."

Ali's voice held just the slightest tremble when he said, "So, will I see you again, my friend?"

Jonathan felt a little emotional at the moment, too, though whether it was because of parting or because he was about to come to the climax of his mission, he didn't know. He smiled and gave Ali a thumbs-up. "You can count on it."

"Good," said Ali firmly. "At any rate, it is time for you to go." He looked Jonathan in the eye. "I don't know who you are, and I don't understand why you risked so much to help my people, and frankly, I don't care. I only know what you have done and what you are about to do will make a difference in this world. On behalf of my people, I thank you."

The two men embraced, and then there was the inevitable bear hug from Abdul. Then, Jonathan got in the cockpit and waited for the signal to take off.

The camouflage netting lay draped over the MiG, and scrub brush littered the runway. A cordon of hundreds of mujahideen formed around the plane and stretched along both sides all the way to the end. As soon as the signal came that the Soviet transport was in the air, the closest ones stood prepared to pull the camouflage away while the others would clear the path of the runway.

A group of observers watched Kabul International Airport from several miles away. When the large transport began to taxi toward the runway, they would use a flashing light to send a signal to another group of observers down the line, who would do the same, until the message got back to the airstrip that it was time for Jonathan to take off. Finally at 12:20 P.M., after waiting nearly fifty minutes in the cockpit, the signal came.

Quickly the mujahideen stripped off the camouflage, and Jonathan watched in amazement as the runway took shape in front of him, with more than one hundred men moving across and clearing away the brush. Meanwhile he strapped himself in, flipped a sequence of switches—it was a lot easier this time than in Libya—then signaled the ground crew to start the engine.

Their external power cart, stolen from Bagram Air Base, began blowing compressed air into the engines. When it reached full RPMs, he idled until he'd gotten it up to the speed required for kicking in the main turbine. With the electrical generators functioning and the INS operative, he went through the flight check with the assistance of the men on the ground. One of these removed the chocks, Jonathan pushed his cockpit screen forward, and, after waving one last time to Ali, he prepared for takeoff.

He moved forward, gathering speed. Along the runway, he saw mujahideen on either side, waving and cheering. Gradually he took the throttle up to 100 percent, let off the brakes, and shot into the air, hitting the afterburner as he did.

He climbed slowly to altitude and set his course toward Kabul. In just a few minutes, it would all be over.

He had pre-set the aircraft's radio to the Soviets' frequency, and now he called in to the Kabul control center to identify himself. "Flight Control, Alpha 1. Difficulties with horizontal stabilizers. Request permission to return to base."

A radio operator working for Ali had spent all morning monitoring Soviet transmissions, therefore Jonathan knew a MiG-23 with the call-name Alpha 1 had gone out to conduct a reconnaissance mission in the northwest corner of the country. If the other plane were on station, it would be out of range of this transmission. The control tower would have no idea he wasn't Alpha 1, since their radar would simply show an incoming aircraft.

"Alpha 1, affirmative," came the reply. "Approach Kabul International, but maintain pattern until outgoing departs immediate area, over."

"Affirm Flight Control. Alpha 1 over."

Outgoing. From a distance of fifteen miles, he could now see the grayish-white Il-86 "Camber" as it lifted off the runway. The monster aircraft spanned sixty meters from nose to tail and fifty from wing tip to wing tip, with a payload capacity of 42,000 kilos. It was luxurious inside, too, with indirect lighting, extra-large windows, twelve recorded audio programs, and a bar-buffet on the lower deck— just the right sort of accommodations for dignitaries and generals.

The plane could hold 228 passengers.

At the end of the runway, a series of flares went off just as the Camber climbed to altitude. Jonathan smiled at the sight. Apparently, it was a precaution against surface-to-air missiles. Before Qudar Canyon, there had been no need for such a precaution.

Then, he saw four MiG-23s take off right after the Camber and pull up next to it, two in front and two in back. Escorts. He hadn't planned for that. Was it possible they somehow knew about his planned attack? But then he realized that the MiGs were flying *below* the passenger plane—another precaution against Stingers, not hostile aircraft.

Jonathan flew down and slowed as the passenger transport rose to about 1500 meters. Then, he came across as he had promised Ali, slowing to 450 kilometers per hour at a height of one-and-a half kilometers over the northeast quadrant of Kabul.

"Alpha 1!" the control tower barked at him. "Return to pattern at once and proceed with landing!"

"Affirmative, Flight Control," he replied. "Difficulty with control surface. Will attempt to regain control and circle around again."

"What's the problem, Alpha 1?"

"Nature of difficulty unclear at present, Flight Control. Will report shortly." With that, he began to head toward his target.

"Alpha 1!" Flight Control ordered. "Avoid path of outgoing flight! Correct course immediately and return to pattern."

But instead, he accelerated and came up less than a kilometer behind the two rear MiGs, whose pilots, for the moment, didn't even know he was there. They would soon enough.

Traveling at a speed of barely 450 kph, the MiGs made an easy target. And this time his missiles didn't malfunction. He looked down and saw the *Voroozhyonniy*—Armed—message on his heads-up display. Pointing the nose of his aircraft directly at the tail of the starboard MiG, he squeezed the button at the top of the flight control stick. He felt the missile drop loose and watched as it accelerated toward its prey.

The missile had barely passed the nose of his Foxbat when Jonathan steered to the left and brought the portside MiG into his crosshairs. Again he squeezed the trigger. And again he felt the missile drop loose from its pylon and accelerate toward the target.

All this happened within a few seconds, and, as soon as he had fired on the portside craft, he looked to the starboard again. At that moment, the aircraft exploded in a burst of flame. Then, the plane on the left blew into a million pieces. The remains of both aircraft seemed to hover in the air for several seconds before falling earthward. The sky filled with smoke.

"Alert! Alert!" he could hear flight control shouting over the radio. "Two aircraft down! Unknown intruder following formation!" A few seconds of silence followed, then he heard, "Watchdog Leader, be advised. Intruder on your tail. Repeat. Intruder on your tail. Alert!"

Jonathan had two Acrids left. He moved into position directly behind the Moscow shuttle. This was going to be much easier than dropping the two MiGs. Now he had the transport in his crosshairs, and he had only to push a button to send a missile flying right up one of the Camber's four turbofan engines.

But for some reason, he hesitated.

He stared at the plane for a few seconds, then suddenly one of the MiG-23s in front hit his afterburner, shooting straight forward and up. The other MiG did the opposite, decelerating and sliding back under the transport to move between it and Jonathan.

What a fool. Jonathan brought the Flogger into his crosshairs and again pushed the *Fire* button. The Acrid flew up into the tailpipe of the MiG. A few seconds later, it exploded into flames and tumbled earthward just like the other two. Something flew out and, a second later, Jonathan realized the pilot had ejected and was now floating downward under a canopy of silk.

Jonathan felt strangely relieved to see the Soviet fighter pilot had survived.

He accelerated. Just then, he sensed a motion off to his left. The last Flogger had zoomed off, only to loop around and get right behind his tail. *Adios, comrade.* Jonathan pointed his plane skyward, pushed the throttle to full power, and then counted the four seconds for the afterburner to kick in.

He could feel the g-forces pushing him back into his seat as he shot straight up. The speedometer crept past the Mach 2 point. There was no way the MiG-23 could match his speed, and it would have to fall off in a few seconds. The only danger now would be if the other guy had air-to-air missiles—but why would any Soviet aircraft be carrying air-to-air missiles on the Afghan front? They wouldn't have any reason to take on the extra payload.

And sure enough, the moment passed when the Flogger might have fired on him, and he looked back over his left shoulder to see the MiG falling back. If the other pilot had been smart, he would have continued upward even if he couldn't catch Jonathan. Instead he chickened out and dropped off. An unwise choice.

Jonathan nosed his own aircraft over and started a dive toward his adversary. Pushing forward on the stick, he could feel the g-forces pushing him back into his seat, and he knew he was passing far beyond the recommended five gs.

In a few seconds, he could hear the frame creaking under the excruciating stress of gravity, centrifugal force, and the wind itself. His head felt like it had a freight-train going through it at full speed, and even with the old "constipation" trick, he barely managed to stay conscious. He could only sustain this course for a couple more seconds. Then, with a huge amount of effort, he pulled the plane back up in one piece and found himself looking up the other pilot's tailpipe.

Without hesitation, he armed his fourth Acrid, brought the plane into his crosshairs, and fired. At that range, the missile couldn't miss. In seconds, the MiG-23 disappeared in a flash of light. This time, he didn't see anyone eject.

With all of the combat aircraft gone, now all he had left was his real quarry.

Flipping on the radar, he saw it fifteen kilometers away, headed back toward the airport. A huge, undefended aircraft filled with passengers.

An eye for an eye. Jonathan hit the afterburner and headed toward the target.

On the ground, mass confusion broke out. No one had prepared for an air assault, and the air-to-air missiles were locked away in a storage bunker. The smart move by the flight controller would have been to scramble half a dozen fighters to overwhelm the renegade aircraft with machine gun and cannon fire. But he was panicked and confused, so he ordered the ground crews to install the correct missiles.

The Soviet Air Defense Forces detachment at the airport had not done a drill for changing missile systems in a long time. Nobody could even find an officer with the keys to unlock the bunker. Finally, the officer in charge shot off the lock with his Makarov.

The planes on the ground were just being outfitted with missiles when Jonathan approached the Camber at 10,000 feet.

He didn't have any missiles remaining, but his GSh-23 gun would be adequate for the job. Yet, once again, he didn't fire at the optimal moment as he pulled up alongside the transport.

When he passed by, no more than fifty feet to the starboard, he could see frightened faces staring at him from the window—faces of people who knew they were going to die. He felt sure this was how the passengers on KAL 007 must have looked.

Just then, a voice crackled over his radio. "Attention, intruder!" it shouted. "This is Captain Scharakhov, pilot of the military transport. Request that you desist from attack. We are unarmed."

A few seconds later, another voice came on. "Attention, intruder," it said. "I am the ranking officer aboard this transport. What are your intentions?"

That voice—it sounded familiar. Could it be that *he* was on the flight as well, escorting the dignitaries back to Moscow? If it were so, then it had to be destiny.

"Intruder!" the voice repeated, and this time it left no doubt. "This is General Andrei Vassilyevich Kharitonoff. What are your intentions? This is an unarmed flight, and there are civilians on board."

That's right, thought Jonathan. *Just like Flight 007.*

"Intruder," Kharitonoff repeated. "There are women and children aboard this plane. What are your intentions?"

Jonathan began to slide back behind the aircraft, into firing position. "How dare you hide behind women and children who aren't even on board," he replied in disgust. "There aren't any women and children on your aircraft—but there were on Korean Air Lines 007 . . . *Glozá.*"

There was a long silence on the other end. Then Kharitonoff's voice, sounding shaken, returned. "Who are you?"

"I'm an avenging angel from the skies, general. And it's your life I want, you *murderer.*"

Did Kharitonoff recognize his voice? he wondered. It hardly mattered now. But wait—Who did he see in the window? He was surely starting to hallucinate. He could have sworn he saw Jennifer—with little Jon beside her. He shook his head as though to clear his thoughts.

He slid back, armed his cannon, and watched his heads-up display to confirm that everything was ready to go.

And then suddenly, seemingly out of nowhere he heard a woman's voice. *Where did that come from?!* He wasn't out of fuel—why was *she* coming on now? He looked at his control panel. No warning lights. And then he heard it again.

"Jonathan, no!" It was Katerina. No, Jennifer. Regardless of whose voice it was, he heard her as perfectly as though she were there in the cockpit with him.

Yet this was the moment he had waited for. He couldn't let it go now. He kept his crosshairs on the engine of the Camber. But his finger froze on the trigger.

Vengeance is mine saith the Lord. He heard the voice of Jennifer quote the long-forgotten scripture, and he yanked his finger off the trigger as if he had been shocked.

"General," he rasped into his microphone. "I could sentence you to death—" He swallowed hard against the knot of emotion rising in his throat. "—but instead I give you life."

He pulled his stick back and to the right, then slammed the throttle forward and prepared to hit the afterburner. But, before he sped away toward Pakistan, he whispered these three parting words, *"Vernost'. Chest'. Doblest.* Loyalty. Honor. Valor."

"Attention," said the general over the plane's P.A. system. He could see the frightened faces of the dignitaries and their wives in the first class section. Yes, he had lied about the children part, but not about the women. "Attention," he said again, his voice trembling a bit. "We have received word that a MiG squadron has scrambled from Bagram Air Base to chase down the intruder."

The passengers began to cheer.

"And," said Kharitonoff, speaking over them, "our pilot has received instructions to proceed to Moscow as originally planned, under escort of six MiG-23s armed with air-to-air missiles."

A few minutes later, after the general was seated next to Katerina, Major Vronsky came to him with a message from the cockpit. "Comrade General," the major whispered. "We have just received word that the intruder has been shot down."

Kharitonoff nodded. "Very well, Major," he said. "Now get back to your—"

"Begging your pardon, Comrade General," said the major, "but is it possible the intruder was the Latvian spy?"

"I said," the general replied with irritation, glancing sideways at Katerina, *"get . . . back . . . to . . . your . . . seat."*

As the major bowed his head and turned away, Katerina whispered to the general, "What was that he said? Could it be . . . ?"

Jonathan saw them coming up like bees from a hive, but he didn't have far to go to reach Pakistani airspace. He switched his radar back on to scan the horizon and saw another half-dozen MiGs approaching from the east.

He hadn't anticipated this. Apparently, they had scrambled them from another base. Not only did he have pursuers on his tail, but these other six now blocked his escape route from the front.

Looking up, he saw a heavy cumulus cloud about three thousand meters above him. He kicked in the full afterburner and nosed upward just as the planes from the rear and the front began to converge on him.

As he entered the cloud, he cut back on his speed, down to barely 450 kph. The plane shuddered as it decelerated. He pushed a button, throwing the canopy off the cockpit, then pulled the strap between his legs to activate the ejector seat. Just as he did, he remembered what Colonel LaVallee back at Luke AFB had said about the ejector seat.

Maybe he had just armed the plane to explode.

But nothing happened. The plane didn't blow up, and he didn't eject either. He slowed down still more, to just over 300 kph, scarcely above stall speed. In the middle of the cloud, he flipped the plane over and waited till it came about, then released his seat belt, and kicked himself out of the plane. By dropping out at such a slow speed, he avoided being thrown into the protruding rudder—but not by much.

Within fifteen seconds, the pursuers scored a direct hit with three Acrid radar-guided missiles from six miles off. In a flash, the plane exploded into bits of metal.

Meanwhile, Jonathan hurtled toward the earth. He delayed the deployment of his chute because he didn't want the Soviet pilots to see him. As his eardrums screamed from the rapid pressure increase of his descent, he held out his arms and legs to slow his speed. Counting, he estimated the amount of time left in his descent, but he kept his eyes on the horizon and willed himself not to think about how high up he was. At about five thousand feet, he popped his chute and prayed that it would open.

The drag chute popped out, yanking the main chute loose and, a split-second later, it flew open in a giant burst of silk. He slowed down to eighteen feet per second as he glided the last two thousand feet to the ground, unseen by the swarming MiGs. The explosion had occurred at some distance—six-and-a-half miles away and more than three miles up, well away from the path of his descent.

Falling gently now, he felt a vague sense of serenity as he watched little dime-sized bits of the Foxbat floating past him. He looked below and saw a treeless plain slowly rising up to meet him.

Countless thoughts raced through Jonathan's mind as he fell. About why he hadn't fired on the transport when he had it in his sights, and how he had heard Jennifer's voice from somewhere in his mind or his memories. About his mission, and how it had changed from a desire for revenge into something much bigger. About the general—the enemy that he couldn't kill. And Katerina. Would she be there to meet him in three months?

His reverie broke as he realized he was just three hundred feet above the ground, coming down within a quarter-mile of a small village. A group of people congregated below him, shouting to one another and waving pitchforks and shovels. As he fell, he realized they didn't look like a happy group. It occurred to him how this appeared from their perspective. Here was this *Shuravi* pilot coming toward them— a perfect opportunity to take revenge on all the infidels who'd spoiled their crops and desecrated their mosques and killed their loved ones.

It wouldn't matter to them that he had finally overcome his desire for revenge. They wouldn't even care when he claimed he wasn't a Russian—how would they know he was telling the truth? What else could he possibly be? Would they try to figure out what he was saying, or would they just go ahead and kill him?

Isn't this an ironic way for it all to end? he thought as his feet touched the ground and he fell to his side to absorb the impact. By then, the villagers swarmed around him.

CHAPTER TWENTY-SEVEN

"This was her favorite place, you know," Jonathan told Sonny as he looked around London's *Ritz Tearoom*. It was the fall of 1985, almost three months after Jonathan Stuart disappeared in Afghanistan.

"I know, Bubba," Sonny answered. "And I'm . . . well, touched that you'd invite me to come here with you on this day, of all days."

"September 1—the second anniversary," Jonathan said with a nod. His eyes glazed over for a moment, then he shook his head. He took a sip from his glass of Côte de Rhone and leaned toward Sonny. "You know, of course," he said, "I could never have done all this without you, Sonny."

"Well, I appreciate you sayin' so, but I—"

"Seriously," Jonathan went on. "I *really* couldn't have done it without you—from the beginning and up through what I thought was going to be the end."

"Yeah, well," said Sonny, leaning forward. "I for sure couldn't help you out of that last mess you got yourself into."

Jonathan looked up at the ceiling, recollecting the whole sequence of events. "When I thought I heard Jennifer in that plane, it was as though somebody spoke to me from beyond the grave. There I was, floating down through the air—couldn't have been more than ten miles from the Pakistani border—and these locals, of course, thought I was a Soviet pilot, so they came running at me with pitchforks, axes, and the like." He made a face. "I thought I was going to be skewered like a shish-kabob right there on the spot!"

He spoke in a hushed voice, but the tearoom suddenly seemed very quiet and very empty; so he lowered his voice even more. "Just as I landed, I fired my pistol in the air a couple of times to get their attention. Then, I started yelling, *'nanawatai,'* this phrase I learned from a friend who died on the trail coming in the first time. He told me they say it to guarantee safety and hospitality. But it's risky, and I wasn't sure if it would work. So, as soon as I'd shouted it out a couple of times, I laid the gun down and raised my hands in the air."

"Putting yourself at their mercy," said Sonny, nodding his head and taking a sip of wine.

"Precisely. It was a risk, but it was my only hope. They probably thought I was crazy. We just stared at each other for what seemed like five minutes. Then, finally one of the braver ones started edging toward me, and when he did, I said, 'Mujahid! Mujahid! Massoud, Massoud!'" Jonathan threw up his arms, demonstrating his gesture of surrender. "Then I looked at the guy who appeared to be the chief, and I showed him a document Massoud had given me. It had his seal, and it said that I was an officer under his command, and that I should be given safe passage."

He shrugged. "I was just lucky they were a pro-Massoud village, and not pro-Hekmatyar. They ended up taking me in a wagon back to Massoud's camp. Five days' ride." He laughed and took a sip of his wine. "What a bummer. There I was, right at the border, and I had to go all the way back into that awful country."

"Everything can't work out perfectly," said Sonny.

"True. Anyway, from Massoud's camp, Ali, Abdul, and I snuck back through Pakistan—they went with me all the way to Peshawar. Abdul probably would have come here if I hadn't insisted he didn't need to." He laughed. "So here I am after all that."

"So, was Massoud disappointed when you didn't shoot down the plane?" asked Sonny.

Jonathan shook his head. "I told him I ran out of missiles before I had a chance to finish the job, which was true, and by then the other planes had come to shoot me down. Besides, I think he got what he wanted out of the deal." In reply to a questioning look on Sonny's face, he explained. "Turns out they had distributed leaflets saying that Massoud's air force would be coming and a great victory would follow, but of course no one had believed them. Unbeknownst to me, they had painted the green flag of their army on the underbelly of the MiG. So I flew the plane over the city, and the people looked up and saw it. And then when they heard about it shooting Russian planes out of the sky, they went crazy. Apparently there were riots all over the city."

Sonny sat in silence for a long time, then finally said, "Well, what do you say to a story like that?" He looked Jonathan in the eye. "Except maybe this. I think you realize that it'll be a long time before you can ever go back home, if you ever do."

"I probably won't ever go home," said Jonathan, "under my own name, anyway. But I'm not so sure I'll miss it all that much. You know I had started moving my money out of the country a year ago, so I have what I need to live on. Besides, I feel like a new man—with a new identity now."

A look of confusion shadowed Sonny's face when he looked at him. "What do you mean by that?"

"Well, Sonny, I think I got something out of this adventure that I never set out to get. It was something Jennifer had. Katerina inspired me to look for it. I can't take responsibility for the way the Russians treat the Afghans, or the way the rival factions in Afghanistan treat one another. I've learned I don't have to be a prisoner of hate and revenge. If God is willing to forgive the things I've done wrong in my life, then I guess it's my responsibility to forgive others for their wrongs against me."

"Whew," Sonny whistled through his teeth. "So vengeance wasn't what this was all about in the end?"

"No," Jonathan answered. "Even though it turns out that Drakoff got his due—which I have to see as a service to humanity because of what he was doing to the Afghans—when it came down to it, I couldn't kill him in cold blood. That's why I let the bandits take care of him, instead of doing it myself."

"I'm sure he would have rather you'd done it than them," Sonny chuckled. "But what about the other one?"

"Kharitonoff?" Jonathan asked. "You can imagine, if I had second thoughts about Drakoff, a complete psychopath, how I would have felt if I'd killed Kharitonoff." He looked at Sonny. "I ultimately realized he already carried a great burden, one that he will bear for the remainder of his life. And, I learned it could just as easily have been myself in his place, forced to make a tough decision. War is war, whether it's a hot war or a cold war. And people are just people—whether they are Russians or Americans. This guy was just like you and me. I couldn't justify killing him."

"That's some change of attitude, Bubba. But you know, I can't say that I'm surprised to hear you say it. I have to admit that I'm probably a different person now than I was a year ago myself."

"How so?"

"Well, when we started this road show, I swore I was going to stay in the background and only watch your back. And I ended up doing a lot more than that, not all of which I'm proud of. I told you early on that I owed God a debt for the way He saved my skin during combat, and I realized I've just treated him like a life insurance policy. You know, something to keep me out of really big trouble—sort of living with the least amount of commitment I could, yet still hoping He'd bail me out of the big stuff, if you know what I mean."

"I do."

"But after everything that's happened, I've decided I want some things to be different," Sonny concluded, "and with God's help, they will be."

Jonathan was touched to see moisture in the corners of his stepfather's eyes, but he turned his attention to his glass in order to give Sonny a moment to catch up with his emotions.

"Thanks for everything, Sonny," Jonathan said a few moments later. "You've made a powerful difference in my life."

"Well, I guess we're all the better for having lived and learned." Sonny picked up a spoon and stirred his now cold tea. "So—now that it's over, you feelin' a little sense of letdown—no more worlds to conquer?"

Jonathan shook his head. "No. Now I'm off to Prague."

"Are you serious?" Sonny asked. "After all you've been through, you'd go smack into the Soviets' backyard?"

"Well," Jonathan drawled, with a twinkle in his eye, "they'd never think to look for me there."

"Why in the world would you want to do that?" Sonny loudly demanded, and a couple of old ladies at a nearby table looked up at him sharply.

"Why do you think?" Jonathan whispered back.

Sonny started to say something, but a look of understanding spread across his face as he smiled. "Whoa, son—this must be serious."

"I hope so. Two people who love each other and have a chance at a whole new way of life—seems pretty serious to me. And I can't wait to see where it leads," Jonathan said, feeling a contentment he hadn't felt since before Jennifer's death.

"Does she know who you really are?" Odom asked.

"Not exactly," Jonathan answered. "But if things go according to plan, she'll have plenty of time to find out."

EPILOGUE

Beginning in 1985, with authorization from Congress, the U. S. began supplying Stinger missiles to the mujahideen freedom fighters of Afghanistan. To most historians, that was to be the pivotal moment in the final determination of that war.

In September 1985, Katerina Witonovich traveled to Prague, Czechoslovakia, on a tourist visa; she was a no-show for her return flight to Moscow and categorized as a "missing person, presumed dead".

In March 1986, Joe McGinnis ordered the shredding and purging of all CIA records pertaining to Jonathan Stuart, his aliases and contacts. "It is done," he said. "Nothing good can come from knowledge of Stuart's existence by the Agency. Besides, we are sure he is dead." Within months, agents Wharton and Hollis "resigned" from the CIA and opened their own private security agency.

On February 15, 1989, after nearly ten years of bloody conflict, the Soviets withdrew from Afghanistan. Analogous to the U. S. withdrawal from Vietnam, it was considered the Soviet Union's only lost war; yet, some historians consider this event as the beginning ripple in the wave of events that would see the crumbling of the Soviet empire.

In April 1989, Poland held its first free election, and the Communists were ousted. Unlike its prior repression of such reform movement in 1956, a paralyzed Soviet regime could only observe the transition.

On November 9, 1989, the primary symbol of Communist oppression, the Berlin Wall, fell.

In August 1991, after a period of intense nationalistic and separatist movements within the constituent republics, there was an abortive coup attempt by hard-line Communists. Its failure led to a rapid rise in power by reformers, including Boris Yeltsin, and a new government without Communist control. On December 21, 1991, the Soviet Union collapsed and fifteen nations emerged.

In the summer of 1992, just outside Tbilisi, in the former Soviet Republic of Georgia, a small Christian orphanage was opened. With a seemingly large budget and energetic leadership, it flourished, attracting children from throughout the country. Although little was known of the origins of the founders, the two assimilated quickly into the community. Not only was the importance of their deeds recognized, but their message of the Gospel resonated purposefully throughout the countryside.

On August 31, 1995, the twelfth anniversary of the KAL 007 shootdown, a solitary figure entered the front door of the orphanage. A startled Katerina cried out to her husband and instantaneously Jonathan, sensing her trepidation, ran to her awaiting arms.

"General Kharitanoff", he cried out in disbelief. "You have found us!"

"Yes," replied the aged and weathered but still erect and powerful icon of the past, "but I have not come here to harm you, but rather to seek your forgiveness."

"Sir, forgiveness is not ours to give; it is only the Lord that forgives man of his transgressions," replied a calm but still shaken Jonathan Stuart. "However, I do choose to forgive you for your actions against my family, because I too have been freely forgiven for my own actions."

"But, what of your mission? I know now that you sought to avenge your family and the other 267 people, whom I mistakenly brought to their deaths."

"Andrei Vassilyevich," Jonathan's composure was quickly returning, "you and I have both suffered, but God works in strange and wonderful ways. Look about you. Katerina and I have three wonderful children: Jon, Mikhail, and Jennifer; so our previous families live on with us. But more importantly, the children we save, nurture and place into this world leave here as disciples to the Lord. Soon, there will be more than 270 such saints, but our mission here will not be complete until there are ten times that number!

"Is it possible that hope can come from disaster?"

"If you believe."

"Even for me?"

Jonathan embraced the sobbing old man, the person who had ordered the death of his wife and child, the person who previously bore the brunt of his immeasurable anger, and he felt nothing but love and compassion

"For everyone".

ABOUT THE AUTHOR

Eclectic is perhaps the best definition of the background of Russ Chandler. He worked his way through college (Georgia Tech—1967) and graduate school (Wharton—1970) and served as a captain in the U. S. Army Corps, and as an instructor of management at the University of New Orleans.

As an entrepreneur, he was instrumental in the development of two highly successful ventures. Interestingly, both ventures experienced significant initial agony. Ultimately, each was successful because of perseverance, the commitment to quality people and service and great timing which, in retrospect, Chandler concludes, "must have been God whispering in my ear."

In 1988, Russ accepted the challenge of conceptualizing an athletic village for the 1996 Olympic Games; and over the next eight years created, staffed, and managed that project as the only volunteer executive level manager in Atlanta's Olympic Games. As "mayor" of the village, with a staff of over 12,000, he had responsibility for the accommodation of 15,000 athletes and officials.

In the course of preparations for the Olympics, Chandler became acutely aware of the security issues surrounding the Olympics and conceived his first novel, *The Last Olympics*, which confronts terrorism within the Olympic Village.

Recognizing his own need for stewardship, Chandler has served on numerous non-profit boards, has endowed two university chairs, gifted a baseball stadium to Georgia Tech, sponsored various minority programs and has actively funded his church, as well as various ministerial and missionary programs.

Chandler is an avid outdoorsman and particularly enjoys time with his three daughters. His wife, Sammie, spends her time sponsoring children from third world countries for medical treatment in this country.

His objectives are to assist Christ-centered organizations, expand his own Christian knowledge and spirituality, and create interesting and exciting stories that have a moral basis. "I know, now, that whatever worldly success I have experienced," says Chandler, "is just the starting point of God's plan for me."